THE AUDACITY OF FAITH

THE AUDACITY OF FAITH
(The Diva Pack Transformation)

BY: W.T. BARLOW

XULON PRESS ELITE

Xulon Press
2301 Lucien Way #415
Maitland, FL 32751
407.339.4217
www.xulonpress.com

Printed in the United States of America

Paperback ISBN-13: 978-1-6628-1650-5
Ebook ISBN-13: 978-1-6628-1651-2

DEDICATION

MY FIRST NOVEL, *THE AUDACITY OF FAITH*, IS dedicated to my grandmother, Janelle (Jan) M. Rackard, who was the love in my life. Growing up, like many other people, I was the product of a dysfunctional family. So, like many other grandmothers during those days, she stepped in-raised me, and introduce me to the Word of God. She would drag my butt back and forth to church, despite my irritating, high-spirited, and playful disposition. Looking back, I now know that relentlessly keeping me involved in church was the greatest thing that was ever done for me. A belief in God created a solid foundation that would save me from an unsavory environment and help me realize my self-worth and true potential. Even though, at times, I have strayed from the path, I recognize that I am not perfect, and neither is anyone else. We are all sinners in need of a savior. However, during my failings, I would always hear Jan's (GrandMother's) voice singing hymns or praying the Word of God, correctively guiding me back on course. My grandMother is no longer with me, but the many lessons she taught through her enduring faith will always be with me. So, I dedicate this book in appreciation of my grandmother, Janelle, who loved and cared for me all her life (Father, I stretch my hands to Thee).

TABLE OF CONTENTS

PROLOGUE

I WROTE MY FIRST NOVEL AS AN EXPRESSION OF my thoughts and opinions on how I view the world and the predicament we find ourselves entangled. In this book, *The Audacity of Faith*, I offer my recommendation for a cure for all that ails us. Also, this book is in partial retort of President Obama's book, *The Audacity of Hope*. I believe that hope can only be found through faith in Jesus Christ. Because Jesus makes it clear that when we are mistreated, abandoned, or rejected, He will take us up; never leave us, nor forsake us. In my opinion, President Obama's book, although inspirational for some, did not name the author of our hope as it (he) should. The promise of our hope is in Christ Jesus, the author, and finisher of our faith. The Word of God says, "My people are destroyed for the lack of knowledge." It also says, "Train up a child in the way he should go, and when he is old, he will not depart from it." Sadly though, it seems these days, America has forgotten these words-never believed or understood them. I write this book as a testimony on how we should live within God's divine order and His boundaries; the only true way to finding a lasting peace. What I have discovered through the vicissitudes in my life is that the Word of God (faith) is sufficient for everything that this human experience can produce. A revelation of God's Word opens eyes to see that He knows the full range of our vulnerabilities, and has forgiven all our faults, failures, and disobedience. *The Audacity of Faith* is the story of five young and highly-educated professional women, who for the greater part of their lives, are miseducated under a system devolved to undermining the wisdom and knowledge of God, guided by an intersectionality-prone, politically-correct, post-truth cultural society, headed toward a decay in God-consciousness. These five women, while in college, will be the founders of a campus organization called the Diva Pack Sisterhood, which will engage in all forms of campus mischief for the sake of revenge and the bolstering of their own self-image. The Diva Pack Creed (among other things) will call for the Ascendancy of womanhood and the transference of power / wealth from men to women. However, these women, not having or knowing the wisdom and knowledge of God, will foolishly make a pact (covenant) and pledge to one another their lifelong support under an ideology crafted in the allegiance to a campus organization (Diva Pack Sisterhood) that aligns itself with organizations that have the character and nature of the feminist movement. The hearts of these women in the Diva Pack Sisterhood will be hardened against adhering to traditional roles for men and women in furtherance of a greater pursuit of power, extravagance, and dominance, attempting to change or diminish the cultural hegemony. Consequently, as a result of living within the Diva Pack Sisterhood Creed, the five founding members will suffer and endure many of life's painful lessons as they can find no peace or completeness within life, love, marriage, or the comfort of loved ones because of their ethics. Their misfortunes will not end until these women finally take a close examination of their lives and start searching and finding the truth, which is in Christ Jesus. This book focuses on the five founding members of the Diva Pack Sisterhood, and highlights the transformation of four of the founding members who will learn the true meaning of life through a revelation of God's Word; and then with an audacity of faith and armed with their newly found knowledge, will become committed to reversing the wrong they had done in creating the Diva Pack

Sisterhood; and amidst great controversy and resistance to its reform, these women will eventually succeed in transforming this ignoble campus culture they had created.

THE AUDACITY OF FAITH
(The Diva Pack Transformation)

INTRODUCTION

AS I REFLECT BACK, IT WAS A BEAUTIFUL SUNNY day, just like most days on the campus of the University of East Florida, located smack dab in the middle of North Lauderdale, and holding true to their daily routine, the students were gathered on the campus quad, ready for that artful game of persuasive conversation, not to mention giving their full attention and thankful appreciation for all the sexy bodies filling out the summer wear on display. You see, what was assembled on the quad that day was a small collection of the somewhat normal students; a large collection of the elite Alpha, Sigma, Kappa and Omega frat boy players; the wannabe frat boy players; the eternal bootie-watching bench-warming eternal geeks; the too-pretty-to-talk-to-you babes and almost-too-pretty-to-talk-to-you babes all gathered on the quad at the same time to once again feast on their own superficial BS. Now, as I recall, It was about 12:30 pm, and the sun appeared to be at the apex of fricken hot; it was so hot even the birds were hunting shade-it was like the desert man, Africa hot-no wind at all to move the palm trees surrounding the beautiful campus; it just felt like another scorching, muggy, and uneventful day. My name is Tyson, and yeah, I was out there, but I was just...you know, trying to be sociable; that was the only thing on my mind; and as I recall, I was just about to jet until, out of the corner of my eye, I spotted hanging out in the center of the quad, these very fine young honeys that, in the future, I would come to know as the Diva Pack. Yeah, you heard me right, the Diva Pack. In about a year from now, these young sisters would stake a claim to the quad like lioness roaming for prey. It was something to see; how they would look at people placed on their hit list, and how they would secretly size them up and stare them down. I can still see them now, scoping out people that would be the victims of a soon-to-come planned retribution. But on the quad, all they would do was pump themselves up with all sorts of loud domineering girl talk, trying to make themselves stand out as if nobody else mattered; and while in the act of flexing their self-importance, nobody ever dared challenge their sense of dominion. You see, at this time, I didn't know a whole lot about the Diva Pack, but I figured from looking at their aggressive nature and clannish behavior, the confidence of the girl was in the pack, and the confidence of the pact was in the girl. I will try to elucidate on that much later, but for right now, believe you this: these women were nothing Disney. I remembered that day as the crowd thinned a little bit and I could get a better look. I remember thinking, *Oh my! look-a-here, look-a-here, if my eyes have not deceived me, I've been blessed with a view of Raven and Sanaa*; two well-to-do, and well put-together ladies who would be members of the Diva Pack crew. Look at em, even now, acting as though their lot in life affords them privileges far above us mere mortal humans. They would stand in the center of the campus quad like they were a boss or something, acting like that piece of real estate belonged to them; I remember just thinking about their attitude; It was like they were trying to tell everybody, "Oh yeah, note to y'all little people, get ready-it's showtime; fifteen minutes of fame, starring us, is now on display. The reality show has just begun. Ladies and gentlemen, all eyes should be on us, and only us." These women thought they were the greatest thing since sliced bread, with bad attitudes and vainness to boot; but don't get it twisted, man, these sisters were fine, I mean fine to the function of X raised to the tenth power of fine; but regrettably, their conceitedness was only surpassed by their need to flaunt it; and you know what else? I noticed something really strange about these women; they always seemed to intentionally position themselves in social gatherings as if they actually were a lioness pack because once you saw one or two of them, people unaware didn't realize that there were others purposefully mingling throughout the crowd, keeping watch as if ready to pounce; at least that's the way it seemed to me. It sounds kind of primal, I know, but seeing was believing. I guess hence the name Diva Pack or Diva Pact, the rumor wasn't clear on whether it was pack or pact. But it was clear to me they were under the influence of both. Chrystal, Daedai, and Toni were the other three women that would unite this founding union of five, and judging by their looks and attitude, I guess the initial qualifications for membership in the pack extended to having an attitude, great looks, and a so-called pedigree. However, I can tell you that with the Diva Pack Sisterhood, good looks were mighty deceiving. So, let me get you acquainted with the founding members of this so-called Diva Pack Sisterhood. You've got Raven, Sanaa, and Chrystal; slender, long-legged, brightly skin-toned, bright-eyed girls who compel much attention. Raven is blasian, you know, mixed Asian / Black ancestry. Both Sanaa and Chrystal are from mixed Black / White ancestry. The other two girls, Toni and Daedai, are also drop-dead gorgeous women; however, they got that kind of ebony thick booty round-the-way-girl thang working for them. Toni is a Cuban / Puerto Rican / Jew, who brutalizes the Spanish language, and Daedai is an African American, of the foxy brown type, straight out of Chicago. On-campus, the guys were crazy about these ladies; some of them tried to spoil these women with lavish gifts and things, trying to spark some attention. Now, you know these girls took all them gifts, right, and they didn't feel shame about doing it either. Everybody knew these guys were just getting played. I mean, thinking these women would ever take them seriously...

please...give me a break. Look, these divas didn't play the numbers, man, and believe me, there wasn't any pity for hurt feelings; you can ask my boy Rick about that; he thought he was slick; yeah, slick Rick; he disappeared and we couldn't find his a**. My guys thought that was kind of funny, but I wasn't laughing. Because I understood the complexity behind the situation, and I was moved, silenced, and humbled by the immortal words of Mr. Michael McDonald, "What a fool believes, he sees, and no wise man has the power to reason it away." With these women, you had to be careful because if you were gonna try and bring it to them, and you were a lightweight or you were green, you got what my boy Rick got, which was absolutely nothing except maybe hurt feelings, a brown bag lunch, and a bus ticket back home, but that's another story. Anyway, everybody outside of the rumors who actually knew these five Diva Pack sisters and their other girlfriends knew they had real problems extending from their home life. They all came from highly dysfunctional families. Take, for instance, Chrystal and Sanaa; they came from that Connecticut / New York old money scene. Raven is from Silicon Valley, ye—ah, that part of California; need I say more? Their families had that new-generational, undisciplined view that everything revolved around them, and nobody else mattered except number one, and if it feels good, why not do it? Now, Daedai is from Chicago, and Toni is from Miami. However, they both come from middle-class bourgeois-bourgeois wannabes; the product of egg and sperm donors acting as real parents but devoid of the slightest maternal or paternal instincts, with their self-esteem solely based on keeping up with the Joneses; you know the type: the kind of people who put up multiple fronts while camouflaging the truth about their own fake family dynamic; happy only with the prospect of who and what they can control or dominate. Hey, I guess you could say like family-like daughters, you know, "birds of a feather," "the ties that bind." You get it. Toni and Daedai would be the most vocal and rowdy of the pack; they would act as though they were the enforcers of the group; by that I mean they were the type that whenever a situation would jump off, these two were the first ones to immediately get into somebody's face, ready for whatever-"b***h, bring it!" The vine held the rumor that these women belonging to the Diva Pack were only in pursuit of any advantage that they could get to expand their self-interests. I can tell you, also, that these women were devoid of any religious beliefs; they took on, instead, the ideology of feminism, supported by a misguided sisterhood aligned to the pursuit of an indulgent lifestyle with an eagerness to obtain money, power, and a desire to control all men; and as crazy as that seems, they even swore a pact or oath in blood, promising to protect each other's physical and financial wellbeing against all who would try to bring them down. Chrystal, Raven, Sanaa, Toni, and Daedai would be the founding members of what would be known as the infamous Diva Pack Sisterhood; and believe me, these women would be a force to be reckoned with. Now, you probably think I'm stretching the truth a little bit. Nope, I have experienced their resolve up close and personal. You see, I'm going to end up marrying one of these young women. Yep, and our relationship is going to be problematic right from the words, "I do," especially having to deal with the Diva Pack Sisterhood, her other girlfriends, professional alliances, and the expansive lifestyle to which they all thought they were supposed to have. My relationship with my wife was like the old country folk used to say, "It was a tough row to hoe." However, my wife and her associates would eventually come to understand that God is the only person worthy of their allegiance, and only through Him could they completely be made whole and forgiven. They would learn that He is a forgiving God and has forgiven all their sin, faults, failures, and disobedience before the foundation of the world. You ask, why? I'll tell you why! Because His mercy endures forever; that is why! As a result, I have witnessed my wife and her friends totally changed by the renewing of their minds to His Word. God is the only person who can profoundly change the hearts of men and women. He is the truth, the way, and the life. Believe that!

Diva, (Store 2019) "A person (female OR MALE) who ACTS like one—in short, a self-obsessed drama-queen! Also, The word DIVA (boazolaosebikan 2016) comes from the Latin word, "deus," meaning devil. The Italian word DIVA means goddess. The prefix DIVA is short for the word divination. A DIVA is a female goddess or a woman that is worshiped."

Diva is arrogant. Pride is a devil trait. It may work well in movies, but in real life, pride is guaranteed to destroy your relationship. The Bible says (Proverbs 16:18) pride goes before destruction and a haughty spirit before a fall. Words / names matter!

CHAPTER 1
(IN THE BEGINNING)

THE DIVA PACK STORY BEGINS THE SPRING OF 2008. It is sophomore year for the younger Raven, Daedai, and Toni; the first year and second semester of law school for Chrystal and Sanaa. At this point, they are just a normal group of friends, gifted academically, and maintaining excellent grade-point averages; hey, go figure-beauty and brains. Two semesters later, these women would cement their friendship by attending classes together or participating in a host of school functions, and since joining a sorority was totally out of the question, they would develop their relationships around, of course, men, and other similarly shared interest like music, books, current events, and, of course, politics. It is without a doubt that these women saw themselves as social revolutionaries, so they all got involved in the feminist movement, which would become the influential force behind their lifestyle, philosophical points of view, and the eventual creation of the Diva Pack Sisterhood. In the early stages of the Sisterhood, they would regularly meet on the quad to discuss the gossip of the day; you know, boyfriend-girlfriend stuff; and like usual, one or two sisters would call the others over to join the huddle, and you could see that even at this point, they were very clannish and biased for one another. I remember one day out on the quad, Raven and Sanaa called over to the other girls to

1

join in the conversation. As they congregated, Sanaa greets them affectionately, saying, "What's going on ladies?" They all answer in unison, "You got it, girl," and as the girls move close to the center of the quad, the girl talk seems to boost their camaraderie. It was all laughs and fun until, suddenly, Chrystal, breathless with concern, grabs Sanaa by the arm while pointing in the direction of a seemingly intimate couple getting it on at the other side of the quad; and then Chrystal shouts under her breath, "Sanaa, Sanaa, look who's trying to front your man." It was Sheila and Jordan appearing to be intimate. Sheila Morgan is this young girl that Saana knows as one of Jordan's friends. Sanaa doesn't like Sheila very much; I guess because it's two strong women that just don't mesh or it's the fact that irrespective of Jordan, saying that they're just friends. Sanaa knows that Sheila has a thing for her man. Jordan is Sanaa's on-and-off-again boyfriend; you know, the breakup-to-make-up kind of relationship; but it seems, at the Moment, Sheila is the one getting it on because Sheila is all up in Jordan's face. Sanaa calmly stares, and focuses in on the couple, and whispers under her voice, "Oh really," then she proceeds to walk toward the couple with a look on her face that's not angry, but seemingly very inquisitive about Sheila and Jordan having the unmitigated gall to be so intimately close in front of her face. When Sanaa is finally standing in front of them, they act surprised and concerned that Sanaa really gives a darn. Most particularly, Jordan is kind of perplexed at what Sanaa is doing because their relationship right now is supposed to be in the off position. In his mind, he is thinking, "What's the big deal, what do you care?" Irrespective of a presumed on or off status, right now, Sanaa could care less, and just stands there, staring at the couple, and not saying a word. This intensive stare down continues for about fifteen seconds, to the point that people watching could guess what's really in play here, and as Sanaa moves even closer, the whispering chatter comes to an abrupt hush- not a peep from anyone. Everybody just stares, waiting and assessing what Sanaa will do next. Sanaa maintains this weird stare for about four more seconds; her facial expression transitions from one of inquiry to a closed-mouth semi-smile, and as her eyes well up, she slowly turns to walk away. Sanaa passes through her friends that have gathered behind her. However, her girlfriends do not move until mouthing the words to Sheila, "We got you, b***h," Then her girls turn to leave while aiming a threatening stare at Jordan, and Daedai, holding true to form, lags behind the others, and tells Sheila, "I'll see you soon. I need to explain some things to you."

Sheila and Jordan remain silent, and after the verbal assault and stare down ends, Daedai and the girls leave the quad to catch up with Sanaa. Sanaa continues walking to her dorm with her head down, and appearing to be in extreme distress, now walking even faster so that her girls cannot easily catch up with her, until they shout, "Hold up, Sanaa." But Sanaa walks a few more steps, then abruptly stops. As she turns to face her friends, they see that her eyes are red and that she is emotionally stressed. Sanaa exclaims pridefully, "Yeah, what!" And with her arms crossed around her body and head tilted to the side, she asks, "What's up?" Daedai forcefully belts out in front of everybody, "Sanaa, why you didn't just jack that b***h? We had your back; all you had to do was just grab her a**, and we on both of them like white on rice." Sanaa then puts her hand over her face to hide any emotion, and Daedai, recognizing her emotional stress, softens her tone, and with empathy, says, "Sanaa, look, you are our sister, and what affects you, affects me, and I know affects us all. We just can't allow Sheila, Jordan, or anybody else, for that matter, to get away with dissing us like that. We got to stick together, right? Sanaa, if you let people cross you like that, they'll do it again." Interrupting, Toni says, "Hey, can't you see she isn't feeling us right now?" Sanaa then looks at her girls, and now being more composed, she pridefully asserts, "Hey, I need to go, and don't worry, I got this., I'll catch up with you guys later." Out of concern, Chrystal asks,

"Sanaa, are you sure you're alright?" "Yeah, I'm fine, I'll talk with you guys later." Daedai then agrees, "Ok, girl, see you later." Sanaa turns to walk away, and unnoticed by her girls, she dries her eyes with her fingers as she goes through the dorm door straightway up to her room. Daedai turns to the girls, "Y'all can tell she's still got a thing for Jordan, no matter how much she tries to dismiss the issue, and no matter how many times their relationship is on and off, they still have these lingering feelings for each other. Hell, they just been together too long. Wooh, since their first year." Toni, trying to act like the ultimate punisher of men, braggingly comments, "Let me tell y'all something, and hear me good, ladies, when I decide that a relationship is over, baby, it is over." Raven asserts quickly, "Hey! Everybody's not like you, Toni. Some people need to have a stable relationship in their lives, even though they may not be aware of it. I think that's where Sanaa is right now. She has this uncompromising pride that gets in her way sometimes." Chrystal, looking at Raven in amazement comments, "Wow, look at Ms. big-time psychiatrist; you got it all figured out, huh? But on this one, I must admit, you might be right because this is the first time I have ever seen Saana react this way. Well, alright then, Ms. psych lady, what do you think we should do about this situation?" Daedai interrupts, "I know what we need to do about this; we need to go kick that Sheila b***h's a**; that's what we need to do." Chrystal gently bites her lower lip, shaking her head in total disagreement, and meditates a minute, then looks at her sisters and says, "Sanaa told us that she could handle her own business. I think we need to back off and give the girl some space." Chrystal looks intently at Daedai to appeal to her understanding. "Daedai, you agree with that, right?" Daedai, evading eye contact with a bit of an eye roll, takes a deep breath, exhales, and replies, "I guess." Chrystal puts a crimp in the tension, and says, "Look, I'll check on her later; our study group is getting together to go over our notes for class, and after they leave, I'll talk with her.

4

You guys leave Sheila alone until we find out how Sanaa wants to handle things." Raven looks at Chrystal with a curt smile and suggests, "Alright, now look who's trying to utilize reverse psychology." Chrystal quickly squashes the comment. "Reverse psychology? Nah, never on my sisters. I don't play games like that. I just think it makes common sense to approach this from a distance; we need to find out for all concerned, what kind of support, if any, she needs. Realize, Jordan and Saana at one time were deeply into each other. Last semester, I remember how they used to be all over each other." Raven comments, "Yeah, I know you do, Chrystal, seeing as how you and Sanaa used to talk about the brother all the time." Chrystal, with a smile, nods her head in agreement, "Yeah, you right, but now it's so sad to see them like this." Raven then offers some words of wisdom, "Yeah, I feel for her, but what goes around, comes around. All in love is fair." Chrystal takes a deep breath, then exhales, "You are absolutely right," then she stares into a blank space, thinking back to their first year.

CHAPTER 2
(LOVE AT FIRST SIGHT)

IT WAS THE BEGINNING OF THE SCHOOL YEAR in August 2007. Chrystal, Jordan, and Saana, were all in Mr. Dulcie's contract law classroom. It was their first year in law school, and on the very first day, Mr. Dulcie asks Jordan to stand and recite a case study citing the rule of law, the holding of the court, significant decisive factors, policy justifications, and legislative intent behind the findings. Jordan was stumped; he did not know that the assignment was posted on the bulletin board outside of the classroom, and because of this mishap, he was immediately anointed with the lecture / scolding that most first-year law students usually hear. Mr. Dulcie looks up through his reading spectacles and inquires, "Mr. Davis, have you come into my classroom unprepared?" Jordan, unable to speak at this point, and feeling isolated and nervous, just stands there, enduring the enormous pressure from all the condescending, yet hypocritical smiles from his classmates, who at this point, are silently thanking God that it wasn't them being called on. All Jordan can do is stare into blank space, like a deer caught in the headlights. Finally, he is able to pull himself together and reluctantly comments, "Sir, I'm not prepared. I did not know the assignment was outside on the bulletin board. I just found out from this young lady sitting next to me." Mr. Dulcie's expression turns semi-serious

6

as he exclaims, "Mr. Davis, it is the responsibility of the attorney to always know his case and be prepared for each engagement. What are excuses, Mr. Davis?" Acting frustrated and being extra, Mr. Dulcie exclaims, "Oh! Never mind. Let me tell the whole class. Excuses are the tools of incompetence, which build monuments to nothing, and those who specialize in them seldom accomplish anything else. In this profession, Mr. Davis, ladies and gentlemen, there is never room for excuses. Now, I want everybody to look at your neighbor, to your right, and your left; take a good hard look, because that person sitting next to you, may not be here next year." Mr. Dulcie then forcefully, instructs, "Sit down, Mr. Davis. Son, I have extreme reservations as to whether you can become a lawyer, but we shall see. We shall see." Jordan takes his seat, feeling and looking confused as to how he was supposed to know that the assignment was on the bulletin board, seeing as how this was his first day in class. While listening to the rest of the lecture and briefly looking through his course packet, he notices right in front of his face on the syllabus where it states where the first assignment would be located. Inwardly angry with himself, he gasps, "Damn, I missed it." After class, Sanaa sees Jordan in the hallway feeling kind of embarrassed, and walks over to him, thinking in her mind, *he's kind of cute*, and having empathy for Jordan from what just happened in class, she says, "Hey, I was glad he didn't call on me. I wasn't prepared either." Smiling, Jordan responds, "Yeah, I got put on blast in front of the whole class this time, but you can bet, by everything great and holy, I'll be prepared next time." Sanaa smiles at Jordan through her glowing white teeth and supportively affirms, "Mr. Davis, I have no doubt that next time you'll be more than ready. I've heard that law school professors try to be extra with first-year law students to get in your head. They call themselves preparing students for the courtroom, and I must say, it is effective and instills a lasting impression. By the way, I'm Sanaa Howard, and you are?" For a Moment, Jordan seems to be at a loss for words, "I'm sorry, I'm Jordan Davis, and given what happened in class today, the very humbled Jordan Davis. Thank you, Ms. Howard, you really know how to make a brother feel better about himself, and after my run-in with Mr. Dulcie, I needed some words of encouragement, especially from such a gorgeous woman like yourself. Hey, Ms. Howard, you got another class right now?" Sanaa quickly answers, "You can call me Sanaa, and yes, I do have another class, and I'm almost late." Jordan now taken with her smile, style, and good looks, asks, "Sanaa, would it be a problem with us getting together after your class? Or maybe I can walk you to your dorm?" Jordan, with his feelings on the line, and Sanaa, understanding the gravity of the Moment, teasingly moves close into Jordan's body and comments, "I'll think about it, but right now, I'm late. I need to go." Nevertheless, Sanaa in a flirtatious gesture turns and walks toward her next class with a giddy expression on her face hidden from Jordan's view, and thinking to herself she kind of likes him, and knowing that he's watching her walk away, she decides to let him enjoy the full swing of her curvature as she walks toward her class. When Sanaa gets in front of her classroom, Jordan receives a generous look back and a smile as she goes inside. Jordan now sold out and physically attracted to Sanaa, walks zombie-like to her classroom door, and stops outside, where he can see her, but she can't see him from the angle at which he's standing. Jordan staring unashamedly at Sanaa and being taken with her extremely good looks and mannerisms, knows that Sanaa is the one. Jordan lives off-campus, and is aware that if he goes home, he won't be able to get back in time before her class ends, and wanting so badly to talk to her, Jordan makes up his mind that he needs to be within striking distance before some other guy can beat him to the punch. He turns his back against the wall outside of her classroom, slides down on the floor, pulls out one of his law books, and begins to study. At this point, he could care less about students in the hallway walking back and forth around him. Jordan, being tired from studying all last night and early into the morning, loses his focus for studying, and it causes sleepy eyes, as he forgets where he is, and even his mission. Jordan lowers his head restfully to take a Moment, and while in a semi-state of sleep, he loses all sense of time, and while in deep sleep, he experiences a correcting voice from the player side of his brain, forcefully commenting, "Hey player, what's wrong with you? Why aren't you studying? And why are you sitting out here on this cold floor? You're waiting for what? Waiting on who? Man, you don't even know if this girl likes you." Before Jordan can make sense of the voice in his head, Sanaa's class ends, and as Sanaa and students exit the classroom, the voice in Jordan's head yells, "Wake up, fool! Wake your butt up!" Half asleep, with eyes trying to focus, Jordan hears a sweet voice, "Oh! You were waiting on me? How sweet." As Jordan jumps to his feet, he advises, "Oh, ah, well, I was just a little tired and wanted to sit down and study for a minute or two, that's all." Sanaa replies, "Oh, I see," Knowing he's lying, she looks at Jordan and says, "You just happened to get tired right here next to my classroom?" "Alright, I'll come clean," Jordan confesses and comments, "I just didn't want to miss out on getting a chance to talk to you, that's all, and I couldn't wait till class tomorrow to see you. I enjoyed our conversation earlier, and I dug your style, and I wanted to take my shot at you right now while everything was fresh because I think we might have a lot in common. So, Ms. Howard, are you free right now?" Sanaa, acting very guarded, pauses, takes a deep breath, and says, "Again, just call me Sanaa. I'm finished with my classes for today, so I guess I'm free." Jordan suggests, "In that case, maybe we could take a walk down to the Lakeside?" Sanaa thinks about it a Moment, and realizing she is attracted to Jordan, agrees conditionally, "Ok, I'll go with you, but first, we got to get something to eat. I'm starved." "What do you want to eat?" Jordan asks. Sanaa says, "Right now, I could make do with just a plain old hamburger and fries." Jordan agrees, "Ok, let's do that." Jordan takes Sanaa's backpack and carries it as they go downstairs to the student's lounge for food. Jordan and Sanaa put in their order, and stand waiting for almost an eternity. After finally getting their food, it's tough finding a place to sit down. The law school cafeteria is uncommonly crowded due to the first days of school. Jordan leans over to Sanaa and whispers, "How about we pack up this food and head on out to the Lakeside? We can eat on the way or have a picnic when we get there." Sanaa agrees, "Yeah, that sounds like a plan." The Lakeside is the nickname for a spot located at the edge of campus, where students can go to relax or have outings. The Lakeside is set up for students to have a nice beach-like scenic view, with lush green palm trees and comfortable benches to make for an amazingly comfortable outing. As Sanaa and Jordan venture toward the Lakeside while shouting out to all their friends, they notice that many of the public areas and buildings are now shaded from the approaching twilight of the day, and as the couple walk and enjoy each other's company, the sun is slowly setting, changing the sky and the atmosphere to a cool violet blue, bringing with it a much-needed relief from an unrelenting heat. Sanaa and Jordan feel a cool breeze blow across their faces, and the feeling is so invigorating that they stop for a Moment to satisfy themselves in the coolness of the drift as they thankfully invite the change in the temperature. As Sanaa and Jordan continue walking, it seems as though the colorful change in atmosphere has been purposely orchestrated for a bourgeoning romance. Finally, after being delayed by several stops along the way during this quarter-mile stroll through campus, they finally arrive at Lakeside and immediately begin looking for that perfect spot. Jordan and Sanaa eventually come across a beautifully landscaped benched area close to the lake, veiled by the many plants and palm trees surrounding the zone. They know immediately it's their spot. Jordan acting all the gentleman, takes napkins out of the food containers and wipes down the bench, making it clean for Sanaa to sit. Sanaa, taking note of his care and unashamed chivalry, inquires, "This is what you do normally?" Jordan immediately replies, "Yes, this is what a real man does for his woman." Surprised by what Jordan has called her, and inquisitive whether Jordan misspoke, Sanaa smartly comments, "Oh, I'm your woman now?" Jordan replies confidently, "Whether you're my woman now, eventually, or never, this is what I do. What you see is what you will get." Sanaa nods her head, "Ok, fair enough." As they sit down, Saana, being inquisitive about Jordan as a person, requests, "Tell me things about yourself I don't know, Mr. Davis." Jordan contemplates for a minute, "Sanaa, I'm just me. I don't have any hidden agendas. I know I have this aggressive edge about me, but what person trying to become a lawyer doesn't have that edge? Certainly, you do Saana; I've sensed it, and I can see it in you. I will admit that I am a little forward-speaking and politically incorrect sometimes because I just say what's on my mind, but believe me, there's nothing asymmetrical about me that screams, "buyer, beware." I'm just like any other person; needing love and wanting to be loved. I come from a meager background growing up in Over-town Miami, and knowing the area, you can surmise that there were some economic dys-functions. What family, living in that type of environment, does not exhibit some form of dysfunction? I think, through it all, I turned out pretty ok. If I seem secure and confident, I must attribute that to my grandMother. Her name was Janelle. She tried to teach me the correct things about life and helped me develop a foundational belief in something greater than myself. That was the knowledge of God and His Word. I have my faults, but overall, I think I'm a well-grounded young man. I live by a positive philosophy, and I can rise to meet all occasions." Jordan then stares at Sanaa eye-to-eye, and says, "I see what I want, and I go after it. What about you Saana? What's your story?" Bowing her head and thinking about how to answer, Sanaa looks at Jordan and replies, "Well, my greatest attribute is that I'm loyal-loyal to my friends, my lover, whomever that might eventually be, and my social causes. I am not into the religious thing, and neither were my parents; we didn't do church. It's kind of hard for me to believe in something I cannot see. How can I believe in absolute truth coming from flawed men who they say wrote the Bible? I figure if there is a God, He loves me because I try to treat everyone like I want to be treated. That must count for something, right? I guess I'll figure it out one day. But on another tip, you are absolutely right; I do have an edge. I come from a family that loves to compete, and everything is a competition. I think I get that from both my parents. I never had to want for anything because my family has money, and they take good care of me. I guess you could say that makes me a little spoiled. So, sue me! I like having my way, and I like having nice things. That does not make me a bad person, and if people can't get with that, screw them. So, Mr. Davis, why law? Why the legal profession? I mean, what is your thing? Criminal law, politics, becoming a judge, what?" Jordan looks down in deep thought, then looks up and explains, "I didn't come to law school to practice law, well, not in the traditional sense. What I really want to do is entertainment and sports law; that is where my head is. Everything else seems boring to me." Sanaa, being surprised, comments, "Oh, you like music, huh?" Jordan affirms, "Yeah, very much. I'm partial to jazz though. I love jazz; it's my first love." Sanaa comments, "Oh really, well, then, who do you listen to?" Jordan perks up, excited to talk music and replies, "The greatest band ever is Earth, Wind, and Fire. Maurice White is the man. My second group of artists are the Rippingtons, Kirk Whalum, Lailah Hathaway, Ramsey Lewis, George Duke, David Sanborn, Oscar Peterson, Coltrane, and Jazz Funk Soul. When it comes to composers / producers, I like Hans Zimmer, John Williams, David Foster, Thom Bell-Linda Creed, Charles Stephney, and Baby Face Edmonds, to name a few. My boys make jokes about my musical taste because they think that the music I listen to is sleeping music. They say it's music to go to sleep by, and they make fun of jazz; they don't get the intelligence of it. I don't mind their criticism though; it's cool. I can't slam my boys for that because, like them, I grew up under similar conditions, lacking exposure to a lot of things, and I used to think the same way. However, through study and musical exposure to the art form, I gained great respect for jazz, the artist, and his or her genius. However, I do realize that jazz, most often, is an acquired taste and not meant for the uninitiated." Sanaa's eyes fill with surprise being familiar with what Jordan is expressing, and nods her head in agreement, "I know exactly what you are talking about because my favorite up-and-coming artist is Esperanza Spalding, and my girls can't get with her style. To them, it is like she's playing in Chinese. They love her voice and are amazed at how this small woman can handle and play this enormous bass instrument, but they can't get into her music. I think you hit the nail on the head though. The esthetic constraint on most people to appreciating jazz is that jazz is an acquired taste, not meant for the uninitiated; you are right." Both Sanaa and Jordan are excited to hear about their shared revelations. "Sanaa, I like Esperanza Spalding too. This girl is going to be a special talent. She's the type of talent I would love to manage. She has a beautiful silky-smooth voice, unlimited range, and the agility to perform in various genres. I love her music. I've always had an ear for good music, and a sixth sense for recognizing talented people. That is mainly the reason I wanted to do entertainment law; I love music. Hell, that was my undergraduate major." Sanaa, bewildered at this point, looks at Jordan and inquires, "Why didn't you perform or do something in music?" Jordan then begins brooding inwardly, thinking about the success, failure, and heartbreak of the industry, and not wanting to go into all the minutiae, replies, "I did, Sanaa, but that's another long and time-consuming story. Right now, I've got the most beautiful, interesting, and exciting young woman I have ever met sitting beside me, and I don't want to waste time revisiting a music career that might have been. I'd rather talk about us, and what we can be." Jordan then leans over to be face-to-face with Sanaa, and first testing if she is willing, he then moves in and kisses her passionately. Sanaa, fully enjoying all the romance, takes control of her emotions while masking her true feelings, and says, "Hmm. That is a thought.? What can we be?" Sanaa turns serious and says to Jordan, "Listen up and hear me well; trust is not an easy thing for me. You seem to be a real smooth operator; I mean, you got all the right moves, and the words just seem to flow right out of your mouth. Now your kiss, it's ok, but you seem sort of practiced, my brother. I wonder how many other women you've brought up here and told them the same thing you're telling me?" Sanaa, now genuinely curious, stares straight into Jordan's eyes and asks, "Do you have a steady girlfriend? Are you interested in a girlfriend? And if not, what is your idea of a relationship? I need to know." Jordan calmly leans back on the bench while tilting his head to make eye contact with Sanaa, and confesses his truth, "From the very first Moment I laid eyes on you, I knew I had to have you. So, to answer your question, yes, I do have a girlfriend. Her name is Sanaa. I really do hope she feels the same way." Sanaa looks at Jordan and lightheartedly acknowledges, "See, there you go again with those smooth words. I'll have to think about being your girlfriend though." Jordan, with a smile responds, "Oh! You'll think about it? Think about it? Jordan, being surprised at Sanaa's response, says, "Ok." Jordan then trying to get a more favorable response, playfully takes her in his arms, and passionately tickles her with kisses, repeatedly. Sanaa, now flushed from the barrage of kisses, manages to catch her breath, sobers in her thoughts, and jokingly affirms, "Well, after giving the matter due consideration, I think we can hang." They both smile and laugh at the comment, and continue to enjoy the sparring back and forth, like two high school teenagers competing in some sort of verbal gymnastics, until suddenly and unexpectedly, something more serious takes hold of them both. It is a magnetic and magical Moment compelling something deeper. As they stare into each other's eyes, it is like, exhaling on the heels of an exhaustive search for the perfect soul mate. After coming down from their emotional high, Jordan, staring at Sanaa, comments, "Damn, can this be? I mean, we just met. But I know what I want." Sanaa looking up at Jordan, and emotionally drained, affirms, "I don't understand this myself. I know I like what I'm feeling, but I think this is just too fast." Sanaa gently lays her head on Jordan's shoulder, and thinking about what she's feeling, a smile comes across her face as she sits up and teasingly conveys to Jordan, "Look, boy, no matter what or how I feel right now, you still not getting any tonight, especially not on the first date; and even in the future, I'm still not sure." Jordan, with a smile on his face, calmly responds, "Whoa, Nelly, hold up. Wait a minute; ain't no pressure for that. I think we need to spend time getting to know each other before all that. But I have no doubt that when you ready, you will eventually make love to me. But Sanaa, don't get it twisted, I want you so badly right now I can taste it, and it's such a sweet taste." Smiling girlishly from his unashamed honesty, Sanaa looks up at Jordan and passionately kisses him, and then again acknowledges, "See, there you go again with all that smooth talk." Then looking across at Jordan's watch, she exclaims, "Oh! The time! We need to go; we got constitutional law in the morning, and you need to get in the books too." Jordan reluctantly agrees, "Alright." And while preparing to leave, Jordan enfolds his arm around Sanaa and whispers, "I never expected what happened today, but I feel so good." Sanaa looks up at Jordan and softly admits, "Me too, Jordan; maybe we just need each other." As they leave Lakeside, they walk like a couple six years in, holding hands on their stroll, headed toward Saana's dorm. When they finally arrive out front, Jordan kisses Sanaa and says, "Good night, Ms. Howard." Sanaa throws a kiss as she walks away, "See you tomorrow." Jordan waits and watches her go through the dorm door, then goes to his car to make the seven-mile trip home. After about an eight to ten-minute drive, Jordan arrives at his apartment complex. He and his roommate share an apartment in Pembroke Harbor; a nice complex, catering particularly to college students, with affordable rent, and it looks good too. The complex is newly renovated and comes with amenities, such as two pool areas, a clubhouse, and three tennis courts. What more could a bachelor ask for? Jordan parks his car, walks to his apartment, and as he puts his key into the door-knob, he can hear voices through the door, and as he comes in, he sees his roommate Tyson, and their friends Michael and Jalen clowning around. Jordan, still reeling from being with Sanaa, flashes a big smile as he comes through the door, and in a rapper-like gesture, greets his boys, "Yo, what's going on, yo?" Michael comments, "Ain't nothing but you and that fine honey; ain't that right, player? You struck gold, playa; beauty and brains, huh? I saw you and your girl walking earlier; you hitt'n that, man?" Because Jordan has a reputation for pulling the ladies, normally, Michael's inquiry would be of no conse-quence; however, Michael was now inquiring about Ms. Howard, and Jordan wasn't having it, "Yo, man, that's my girl, and right now, this discussion is way off limits, dog." Michael, caught off-guard, replies, "Damn! Man, you in love with this girl, or something?" Michael stares at Jordan, waiting for a response, and Jordon, trying to hide his true feelings, quickly asserts, "Nah, man, that's just my girl." Michael, recognizing Jordan's sensitive attitude towards Sanaa, backs off, "That's fine, player; it's all good, and it's ok if you are in love; you don't need my permission bay-bruh; all I want to know is if the girl has a friend as fine as she is. I could use some of that lovie dovie stuff myself." Having an ulterior motive, Tyson interjects quickly, "Oh, really? What about that honey you were all up into over at Biscayne Hall? What happened to that, huh!?" Michael, attempting to evade the question, knowing that he dumped the girl, changes the discussion and exclaims, "Hey! Later for these ladies' man; what time is the game coming on?" Letting Michael off the hook about the girl from Biscayne Hall, Jordan quickly answers, "I think it comes on about seven or eight o'clock, but I can't watch the game with y'all tonight. I got a lot of cases I need to study." Jalen comments, "Alright, Perry Mason, go ahead and get that law stuff working, baby! Me and Michael gonna run out here and get some brew; we'll be right back." Being down for a brew himself, Tyson suggests, "You guys hurry back, man, the game is starting in a little bit. Oh! and bring some chips too!" Jordan then turns and goes to his room to study. Back on campus, Chrystal is hanging out with Sanaa in their room, trying to study, but they keep falling back into talking girl stuff, and, of course, the headline features Jordan Davis, currently the sparkle in Saana's eyes. Chrystal and Sanaa were supposed to go with their girlfriends to a feminist rally, but that was low on the priority list of things they wanted to do. They advised the girls that they couldn't go because they needed to study. However, that did not stop Raven, Daedai, and Toni as they are in line at the campus amphitheater right now. Nothing was going to stop these girls from participating in this rally. Raven, Toni, and Daedai will be the first to closely bond. I guess Daedai, Raven, and Toni had an immediate connection to one another; they are sort of like-minded in things. From outside in the lobby, Raven, Daedai, and Toni can hear the women inside the amphitheater getting fired up from the preshow. When the girls finally get seated, they are surprised at the substantial number of women in attendance. After about thirty minutes of pep stuff, finally, the lady hosting the rally introduces the quest speaker; she's one of the regional directors for the feminist movement. Daedai, Toni, and Raven are all pumped with anticipation as to what she is going to say. The speaker lectures about equal treatment for women, social and economic justice, the fight against sexual harassment, and how the traditional image of women has changed from the stand-behind-your-man housewife, to the board room executive. The speaker is defining women as socially equal too, or above men, in all things, and that women should never see themselves as limited and devoid of possessing all of life's chances irrespective of their traditional maternal and or conjugal instincts. The idea conveyed in this rally is that the instinct of women working toward a strong nuclear family in the traditional sense is degrading to the progress of all women. Raven, Daedai, and Toni eat this stuff up, and since the girls are already strong women, the speaker just confirms in their being how they must comport themselves in furtherance of the expectations this movement dictates. The girls are beguiled because of a lack of knowledge; they fall prey to feminism by not having the mature life experiences to fully understand the consequences that manifest with this type of ideology or way of life. The girls are captured; hook, line and sinker. This is the beginning of their indoctrination. Like they say, "Teach one, reach one." After the program, Raven, Toni, and Daedai leave the amphitheater, all pumped up from the rally, and Daedai comments, "Hey, guys, we got to go tell Chrystal and Sanaa about what went down here tonight; they really need to hear this message." "That's a good idea; we do need to do that," Toni agrees, "But right now, I got to go pee." Daedai squinches, "Ooh, me too, girl." Raven laughingly comments, "Y'all really need to have those bladders checked out because y'all always got to go to the bathroom whenever we go somewhere. So, while y'all in the bathroom, I'm gonna get me something to eat." Daedai responds explosively, "You got nerve to talk about us? "B***h, you need to check out your stomach; it's got to be a little tape worm up in there somewhere cause that's all you do is eat; you the only person I know that can eat like a sumo wrestler and not gain one inch." Raven, with eyes wide open in astonishment, replies, "Y'all need to stop hate'n; it's not my fault that this finely-tuned, body of a goddess is a miracle of womanhood." To further mess with their heads, Raven continues, "Y'all just jealous; you're jealous because I look good, really good, exactly the way you wish you could. So stop all the hate'n; go do what y'all always do, and I'll see you people back at the dorm." One hour later, Chrystal and Sanaa are finally getting focused on their cases for the next day's class. Then, like gangbusters, in burst Toni, Daedai, and Raven, excited about the rally they've just attended, and Toni breathlessly, asserts, "Hey, ladies, you guys study hard, because we're going to need women like you on the front lines. The time has come and is now because there's a new revolution permeating throughout the world. Women are finally flexing their muscles and serving notice to all men, that the sisters are taking over. Raven jumps in, trying to talk while swallowing the food in her mouth, "That's right; it's a well-known fact that for a long time, men have been institutionally biased against our progress, irrespective of the fact, that we outthink them two to one. Ladies, we are a force to be reckoned with. We plan, organize, and get things done quickly, tactfully, and without conflict. So why shouldn't we take the lead in everything? It all comes down to this: men can get with the program and step aboard, or they can step off. This train is leaving the station." "Sure, you right, girl." Toni and Daedai exclaim, acting as Raven's amen choir. Chrystal then thinks to herself, *I can't buy in to this stuff*, and comments, "You guys are actually sold on this feminism stuff, huh? I personally never gave it much thought till now. But can you honestly take this stuff seriously after this woman tells you that men are not the dominant gender, and that they are not to be respected in their role as men?" Toni responds arrogantly, "What the lady was trying to get across, my sister, was that the old stereotype of the male as the dominant gender won't work in this society anymore. We have evolved to understand that women can no longer be viewed as subservient or the helpmeet to the man. Women must realize that they are equal to men in all aspects; we hold the power." Sanaa's facial expression reflecting concern, comments, "Toni, I don't know if I agree with that. I think the different genders have roles to play. I like the role I'm assigned; how about you, Chrystal?" Chrystal says, "Sanaa, I feel the same way. I like guys putting me first and doing nice things for me." Raven quickly interrupts, "Y'all just don't get it; we're talking about the same thing but with a different strategy. You see, what we possess as women should not be limited to just insignificant vanity but rather be harnessed and utilized to our advantage, deploying the power of our femininity in taking control over those same men that would seek to denigrate, exploit, and belittle us. This power has always belonged to the woman. You must know that the controlling influence behind any seat of power has always resided within the woman. Even the most powerful piece on the chessboard is the queen. When she falls, so does the kingdom. So I ask you, why shouldn't we rule in the first place? Crown us, damn it! With what we possess as women, we will no longer be the ones having the power assigned to settling for second-class status, submitting, and cleaving unto any man. Oh, and by the way, my body is my own, and I make the decisions concerning it. I tell you this, the only thing I'll be submitting unto is the almighty greenback. Excuse the pun, but you can take that to the bank. I like being a liberated woman; it suits everything about me. Look, ladies, Toni, Daedai, and I will be joining the movement as loud vocal advocates, and we want you to step up and join in with us. Are you in with us?" Sanaa stares at Raven with raised eyebrows and lips tightly folded, and correctively exclaims, "Raven! This is not like you; I know you. Well, at least I thought I knew you. You are the smartest of us all, yet you buy into this kind of thinking. Ladies, y'all need to stop, take a deep breath, and get a grip on reality. It is now and will always continue to be a man's world; that is the order of things. It needs to be that way; it makes sense." Daedai interrupts assertively, "Sanaa, who in the hell do you think made those rules? Man made those rules. As a liberated woman, equal to any man, why do I have to abide by them? What we are saying is that those rules can and will be changed. It starts now, and it begins with us and the millions of women across the world who are feeling disenfranchised by this male-dominated society." Sanaa, now amazed with all the rhetoric, responds, "Wow, at this point, I'm kind of glad I didn't go to the rally. This lady, whoever she is, did a number on you guys. This stuff is crazy. No disrespect, but I am not feeling it! I'm sorry, my sisters, I can't join this." Chrystal agrees with Sanaa, but trying not to completely blow off her friends, she tactfully compromises. "Ladies, you know what, we can revisit this at another time, but right now, Sanaa and I got to get back to studying." Raven rolls her eyes with an expression of disappointment and calmly responds, "Alright, ladies, we'll leave and let you guys study, but keep in mind what we discussed. The truth is always liberating." Raven, Toni, and Daedai leave the room, and as soon as the door closes, Sanaa and Chrystal look at each other in utter amazement. Chrystal questions, "Did we just hear what I think we heard, or is my mind playing tricks on me?" Sanaa nodding in the affirmative, sayings, "Nope, your mind is not playing tricks on you, because I heard the exact same thing you heard, and it was crazy." Sanaa then jokingly comments, "Can you imagine, in your mind, Raven, Toni, and Daedai as the three feminist revolutionaries boldly going where no women have gone before." With that visualization, the girls slowly begin to laugh, harder and louder, until tears start rolling out their eyes. Chrystal comments, "It seems that what we have here, is the willing suspension of disbelief, mixed with a heavy dose of the audacity of tenacity." Now laughing hard, trying to catch her breath, Sanaa utters, "Girl, I'm about to throw up; please stop!" Chrystal continues with her hardcore chuckling, but soon she sobers and says, "Wait a minute, wait a minute. I don't like making fun of them, but this was some of the most off-the-chain funny stuff I have ever heard, girl. Whoo! We needed a good laugh, right? Especially with all this doggone studying we got to do. So now, ok, fun times over; let's get back to work." Still thinking about the girls, Chrystal suggests, "Maybe we can start with the holdings and policy justifications in the supreme court cases of Phillips vs. Martin Marietta Corp. (1971), Griswold vs. Connecticut (1965) or maybe Loving vs. Virginia (1967). Sanaa nods her head and says, "Now that's the kind of women's rights I can get behind."

CHAPTER 3
(SIX HATED THINGS, YEA, SEVEN AN ABOMINATION)

AS TONI, RAVEN, AND DAEDAI LEAVE THE graduate dorm and head for their dorm, Toni shares with them that she has a date tonight and she'll catch up with them later. Jokingly, Daedai inquires, "Well, who is this most unfortunate guy?" Toni, staring at Daedai, replies, "Hey, I think you got me mixed up with some of your other friends because if a guy has a date with me, he should consider himself fortunate to be in my presence, thank you!" Raven quickly warns, "Be careful, Toni; remember, you are in control, right?" Toni says, "Hey, that's the only way I fly." As they break off toward their dorm, Daedai and Raven say, "See you later." Toni goes in the direction toward the quad; she's going to meet up with Carlton, a frat boy player with a rep; however, Toni has recently opened herself to him, and feels he might be someone she can trust and hang with. After meeting Carlton on the quad, Toni agrees to go to a frat party with him, but cautions Carlton to remember that she had been in a relationship with Walter, his frat brother. Toni worriedly says, "I don't want there to be any problems at the party, Carlton, because the breakup with Walter and I was not a mutual agreement; it was hard for him, and I know he got hurt. You sure this is ok?" Carlton confidently says, "It's not a problem, and from what I understand, Walt's been over that situation for a long time. I'm not even sure if he's in town. Walter is a grad student now, and hardly ever comes to fraternity events anymore." Toni contemplates the situation for a minute and then hesitantly, agrees, "Ok, I'll go, but let's go to my dorm first. I want to freshen up and put on something else." When they arrive at the dorm, Toni says, "Wait here in the lobby. I'll be right down, ok?" Carlton agrees, "No problem. It's still early; take your time., I'll be here when you come down." Toni walks away and gives Carlton a look back with a smile as she goes up to her room. Carlton pulls out his phone and makes a call to his frat brothers, letting them know that he and Toni will be coming soon. Carlton then puts in his earphones and listens to music as he patiently waits for Toni. Raven and Daedai come down from their rooms, passing through the lobby, headed to the Rock Bottom Lounge (a student-type alcohol-free night club on campus), and notice Carlton sporting his fraternity's hoodie, rocking and bopping to the music on his Beats headphones. Raven and Daedai know unquestionably he's waiting for some girl in the dorm to come down. As Raven and Daedai walk pass Carlton, they give him that you-ain't-all-that kind of look, and Raven judgmentally comments, "Look at him, just prowling for anything that got legs and looks like a woman. Girl, let me tell you, when those frat boys get to drinking, they turn into animals; octopus hands everywhere, and they ain't taking no for an answer either. So, all I can say is b***h, beware. I hope whoever this poor girl he's fooled into going out with him got her mace ready." Daedai and Raven laugh girlishly as they exit through the dorm doors. Raven then suddenly stops and thinks out loud, "Wait a minute... you think? Nah!" Daedai asks, "Girl, what are you thinking about?" Raven comments, "You don't think that boy was waiting for Toni, do you?" Daedai quickly squashes the thought, "Hell no, Toni didn't even come back to the dorm, remember?" Raven thinking about it, says, "Yeah, you're right, but I don't understand why she didn't give us the full story on this mystery date."

Daedai interjects quickly, "I know why." Raven then stares at Daedai as if thirsty for an explanation, "Why?" Daedai sarcastically asserts, "Because maybe she didn't want your know-it-all, hypocritical a** all up in her business." Raven, expressing a look of insult, comes back, "My, hypocritical a**? Well, if I'm hypocritical, then that makes you a super-hypocritical know-it-all a**." Daedai concedes and responds, "Well, in that case, it's probably best we don't know who he is. Anyway, I hope she's carrying her pepper spray." Raven and Daedai laugh and joke as they continue on to their destination. Meanwhile, Carlton, now deep off into his music, does not notice that Toni has come down and is standing behind him. Toni taps him on the shoulder, and being surprised, he snatches off his headphones and turns to see who dares interrupt Flo-rida. When he turns around, his eyes bulge and his jaw drops, responding to how beautiful Toni looks. All he can say is, "Damn, Toni, you look good." Toni blushes a little before answering, "Thank you," and Carlton, still bedazzled by Toni, puts away his headphones, and asks, "You ready to go?" Tony says, "Let's go." Carlton and Toni leave the dorm and go to Carlton's car. On the way to the frat house, Toni and Carlton stop at Burger King for some burgers, fries, and milk shakes. While preparing to eat, Carlton advises Toni, "It's not good to drink on an empty stomach, right?" Toni responds, "I don't know. I only drink a little bit sociably; drinking is not my thing. I don't like things that distort my thinking." Carlton, attempting to be sensual, suggests, "Well, in that case, you can get intoxicated on me. How about that?" Toni replies, "That's a thought, but as I said, I don't like things to distort my thinking. So, in your case, I will probably enjoy just a little bit of you, but I won't get intoxicated; now, could you please hand me my burger and fries?" Carlton, thinking about what Toni just said, smiles as he reaches to give Toni her food. He thinks to himself, *This girl is something else... class and style, just my speed*, and then he teasingly says, "Here's your non-alcoholic shake, Ms. Lady. Toni answers in a proper tone, "Thank you, dear heart," and she continues, "Now, Carlton, you are going to have to excuse me because I'm about to pig-out, ok?" Toni smiles and informs Carlton, "This is something else about me you are about to find out; I love me some Burger King." Carlton smiles and comments, "Go for it, baby; dig in." After they finish eating, they clean everything up, and then get on their way toward the frat house. Thinking about the social environment she's about to go into at the frat house, Toni asks, "Who's going to be at the party, Carlton?" He says, "I don't know. I know that our ladies' auxiliary group will be there. They don't miss a party for anything. Maybe some of the football players will be there, and whomever my brothers invited. Why?" Toni conceals her true reason for inquiring, but rather confides in Carlton, "I feel bad because if I would have known about the party in advance, I could have invited my girls." Carlton says, "I'm sorry, but they can come to the next one, alright?" Toni, secretly feeling insecure about going to the frat house without her girls, asks, "You think it's too late to invite my girls now?" Carlton says, "No, I don't think so if they got a ride to the frat house." Toni responds quickly, "Yeah, they do. They have a car; let me call Raven." Carlton agrees, "Ok, make your call, and while you're doing that, I'll turn into this gas station and get some gas because I don't want to have to do this after the party. It won't take long, Toni; the house is only a couple of blocks away." Toni comments, "I know where the house is, Carlton; take your time." After Carlton gets out to pump the gas, Toni hits Raven's digits. The phone rings and rings, but no one answers. Back on campus at the Rock Bottom Lounge, Raven and Daedai are on the floor dancing and partying to the max. The music is so loud that Raven, pre-occupied with dancing, does not hear the phone or feel its vibration. Toni then tries Daedai's number, but she gets the same results. Looking confused, Toni thinks out loud, "They don't ever miss calls. I guess they must be asleep. Let me try Sanaa." Sanaa answers her phone, and Toni asks, "Sanaa,

Chrystal with you?" Sanaa answers, "Yeah, we're still studying." Toni inquires, "Sanaa, I hate to ask at this late hour, but is there any way possible you guys can come to the beta's house party?" Sanaa states, "I wish we could, but we got cases we have to study." Sanaa asks, "Toni, you at a frat party by yourself?" Toni replies, "No, I'm not there yet. I'm headed there with a friend, but I would feel much better if you guys were coming." Sad to let her girl down, Sanaa apologizes, "Toni, we hate not being there for you, but we got to be prepared for class on Monday; you know how that is. Did you try calling Daedai and Raven?"' Toni exhaled\s exhaustively, "Yeah, I did, but I can't reach them at all." Toni pauses silently as she hears Carlton hanging up the gas pump. She then whispers, "Hey, girl, that's alright; everything is good." Sanaa, expressing concern, comments, "Toni, you be careful at that frat house. If you get into a situation, call us and we will get you help. Now, what is the name of this friend you're with?" Toni whispers, "His name is Carlton." Sanaa asks, "You trust him?" Toni says, "Yeah, I think so; so far, so good. You guys go on back and study, I'll be ok. If I run into a problem, I'll call you." Sanaa says, "Alright, girl, be careful. I'll see you later." Toni quickly whispers, "Later, I got to go now." And she hangs up. Carlton, is now at the car door; he gets in with a smile, and asks, "You contact your girls?" Toni affirms, "Yeah." Carlton looks at Toni, "Well, are they coming?" Toni says, "I think so." Carlton nods his head, "Well, then, you ready to roll?" Toni agrees, "Let's roll." Toni and Carlton make their way for a couple of blocks, and when they turn the corner, they can see the frat house down the street. They pull up to the house and can hear the music thumping from outside. Carlton exclaims in excitement, "Damn, they getting down in there, Toni; let's go party." Toni, now feeling a little more relaxed, and walking with her head swaying and moving to the thump of the music, says, "Let's do this." As the couple approach the door, they see several people hanging around outside. When Carlton opens the door, his frat brother Johnny is trying to push him the donation cup. Carlton pushes past the cup, grabs his brother, gives him the fraternity shake, and says, "I already paid my dues, bruh." Johnny laughs it off. "What's up man? Took you long enough to get here." Carlton says, "I had to make a few stops, man, but we're here now. Me and my girl are ready to party." Toni looks at Johnny and recognizes him from when she dated Walter, and in a nervous voice, she comments, "What's going on, Johnny?" Although semi-buzzed, Johnny recognizes Toni, and while trying to keep his balance, mutters, "Ain't nothing but a party, Toni; come on in." Carlton grabs Toni's hand and moves through the crowd toward the booze set-up. "You want something to drink, baby?" Toni says, "I'll have a Sprite." Carlton nods to affirm her request, "No problem." He pours himself a scotch and ginger ale, and makes Toni a cup of Sprite and ice. However, before Toni can take a good sip, Carlton grabs her drink and places both drinks on a nearby table. Carlton takes her hand, pulling her toward the dance floor because the DJ has just slammed his favorite jam. As they move to the dance floor, the beta's girl auxiliary have broken into their step moves, and the brothers on the other side of the floor, not to be outdone, break off into their step moves, but Carlton remains oblivious to all the Greek traditions going on and keeps his eyes and his mind steadfast on Toni. Toni, with prior experience dating Walter, understands all the Greek stuff happening around her, and is very aware that Carlton has chosen to stay with her over his brothers. She knows, at this point, that Carlton sees her as special, and that he respects their newly-formed relationship. Carlton's frat brothers start calling him to join in the step line, but Carlton tries to ignore them. But Toni, understanding the Greek way, insists, "Carlton, go and get with your brothers., I want to see what you can do." Carlton stops dancing, looks at Toni, and says, "You want to see what I can do, huh? Hold it down right here and watch this." As Carlton goes to join his brothers, Toni smiles proudly to see him do his thing. She also finds out that Carlton can really step.

She smiles and cheers him on as he does his thing with his brothers. Toni gets totally caught up into the powerful rhythmic chants from the step. After Carlton finishes stepping with his brothers, they start fraternizing and reminiscing about the times they pledged, and all the hijinks their big brothers put them through. At the same time, Toni feels the vibration from her phone and walks to a location where she can hear, and says, "Hello, hello," and Raven exclaims, "What's up, girl? I see you been trying to reach me." Happy to hear her voice, Toni says, "Dang, girl, I've been trying to reach you all night; were you asleep?" Raven comes back, "Girl, please. Daedai and I have been dancing our butts off at the Rock Bottom Lounge. We found a couple of cute guys and have been intriguingly preoccupied. What's up with you?" Toni conveys, "I was calling to invite you and Daedai to a frat party, but now that I see you guys are preoccupied, my effort was in vain." Raven excitedly asks, "Are you still at the party?" Toni affirms, "Yes, I'm with a friend." Raven comments, "Oh, with a friend, huh?" Toni says, "Yes, with a friend." Raven inquires, "Well, does this friend have a name?" Toni answers, "If you must know, his name is Carlton." Raven responds, "Alright, ok! Is this the party at the beta's house?" Toni says, "Yes, how did you know?" Raven replies, "Just a guess. Daedai and I may drop by; it's still going strong, right?" Toni quickly answers, "Yes." Then in an apprehensive tone, Raven inquires, "They're not acting crazy, are they?" Toni says, "Not as far as I can see; are you coming or what?" "Yeah, Daedai and I are gonna come by," Raven confirms and then asks, "Oh, um, Toni," Raven, reflecting back on something she noticed earlier, inquires, "Did Carlton pick you up from the dorm?" Toni says, "Yeah, why?" Raven replies, "No reason. I just asked. Daedai and I will see you in a little bit, ok?" Toni, somewhat puzzled by the question, responds, "Ok, see you later." And they end the call. Raven goes immediately to tell Daedai about the party. Raven looking for and finally finding Daedai, asks, "Where are those guys we were with?" Daedai says, "I don't know. I think I scared them away." Raven, looking disappointed, exclaims, "You scared them away? How? Why?" Daedai confesses, "I told them we are virgins saving ourselves, waiting for the right guy; and that we won't have sex until we get married." Raven laughingly shouts, "What? Oh, you b***h, you lying b***h." Daedai says, "I only said that because when they thought I was still in the ladies' room, I overheard them scheming to get us drunk so they could take advantage of us." Raven quickly replies, "Well, -damn Daedai, wasn't that our plan for them?" Daedai smacks her lips arrogantly, and answers, "Yeah, but hearing them trying to plot and scheme on us made me mad. So, I blew up their damn plans." Raven stares at Daedai, shakes her head, exhales, and declares, "Daedai, you... you need help, girl; you need some serious counseling." Daedai replies, "Wait a minute, woman, you know you just as crazy as I am. It's like the pot trying to call the kettle black." Raven states, "That may be true, but Daedai, you are really touched. Anyway, forget them guys, I just talked to Toni, and she has invited us to a frat party." Daedai, looking astonished and per-plexed, says, "A frat party? I thought you didn't go to those type of parties." Raven ignores Daedai and responds, "Well, our friend is there, and she has invited us, so we got to go. By the way, I got my mace and I know you do too, so let's go party." Raven pauses and says, "Oh, I almost forgot, remember that frat boy that was in the lobby when we passed through?" Daedai thinks back, "Yeah, why?" Raven smartly affirms, "Well, that frat boy was waiting for Toni; he was taking her to the party." Daedai exclaims, "Oh, snap, and all that stuff we were talking about that boy, and he was there waiting for Toni. I hope she got her mace." Raven confidently responds, "She doesn't have to worry about that anymore-her back up is on the way; let's go." Raven and Daedai head back to their dorm to freshen up and change their clothes. After which, they head to the parking lot. Before they leave, Daedai tells Raven, "You do know you're chipping in on gas, right?" Raven looks at

Daedai in shock, "Child, please; don't play that with me, after I spotted you drinks at the Rock Bottom. Consider that my chipping in, chic!" Daedai, offering a word of warning, replies, "Ok, Ms. Thang! If we run out of gas and have to make out like the Flintstones, it's on you." They both start laughing and continue digging at each other as Daedai drives out of the parking lot. While driving, Daedai starts thinking about Toni at the frat party, and suddenly remembers something and blurts out aloud, "Oh, snap! Raven, Isn't Toni's ex-boyfriend, Walter, a member of this fraternity?" Raven says, "Yep." Daedai inquires further, "That doesn't bother you? Raven, you know, that Toni's break-up with Walter was bad. You think he's going to be there?" Raven thinks about it a minute, "I don't know, but that could make for a very uncomfortable situation. So, if you can step on it, maybe we can get there and see." Daedai puts the pedal to the metal and they soon arrive in a neighborhood not too far away from the frat house. Daedai slows down because of the area and because they are coming up to a red light. When Daedai stops, across to their left, they can see inside a church located on the corner. What draws their attention is the steady beat of a bass drum that causes them to keep staring into this corner church. They hear this bass drum thumping and tambourine flittering, which sounds so musically alluring it keeps them deeply entranced. The banging is so strong, and the cadence so rhythmically pulsating, they can't help but be curiously engaged. Then, they hear a piano and a choir sort of chant-singing. Raven and Daedai, sitting at the stoplight, feel the powerful spirit of whatever is coming out of this church; and not knowing what has come over them, they start mocking the people inside. They start throwing arms and hands, mocking the people praising and worshiping, and Daedai starts shouting and acting like she is being moved by the Holy Spirit. However, Raven, who has sobered in her antics, is now captured and fully engaged with everything she is seeing. Raven has become fixed on the praising of the people inside, and as the pulsating sounds from this little street corner church becomes more powerful, Raven, not understanding what she is feeling, comments, "Daedai, I feel something on me." Daedai looks at Raven in agreement and says, "I think I'm feeling something weird too." As they continue to watch the people shouting and running back and forth, a silent curiosity falls on Daedai and Raven; these two girls are not mocking or playing around anymore. Something has overtaken them, and they know it. What is happening is so powerful that Daedai and Raven forget they are sitting in the middle of the road. They have not noticed that the stoplight has turned green, until, suddenly, they hear from behind, the honking of cars ready to move. After realizing that the light has turned green, they slowly move away, thinking about what they have experienced. Attempting to camouflage the strangeness of what is happening, Raven mockingly says, "Wooh, hallelujah! Hallelujah! I know those people in that church got to be tired, girl. I'm tired just sitting here acting like church." Still under a supernatural sensation, Daedai comments, "Ye-ah, I'm tired too, I think? I mean, I wonder with all that stuff they're doing, what is it all about? Do they know something we do not know, Raven? Because right now, I feel kinda good, for no reason at all, and I can't explain it." Not willing to admit what she's feeling, Raven immediately looks at Daedai with a kind of hollow stare and says absolutely nothing; she holds her head down and remains silent. Daedai and Raven both realize they are experiencing something neither one of them has ever experienced before. So, rather than talk, they focus straight ahead. However, not being able to hold inside what she is experiencing, Daedai intently stares at Raven and questions, "We're not going to talk about this?" With a serious expression on her face, Raven stares back at Daedai, who is now thirsty for an answer, and says, "Talk about what?" Acting as if she's not feeling anything, Raven leans over to her window and turns her head slightly to evade eye contact and remains silent.

A few minutes / miles later, they finally arrive in the area of the frat house, but the street in front of the house is packed with cars, so they park about three houses away. As they walk and get closer toward the house, they see a crowd of people hanging outside and can hear and feel the music from the side-walk. The music is so overwhelming that Daedai and Raven forget all about their prior unresolved experiences, and straight-away start walking to the beat as they head toward the frat house. When they get to the door, Johnny is still there as the donation host, mumbling, "Oh yeah, more fine ladies; just what this party needs. Y'all bring y'all fine selves on in here, this party is off the chain." Raven and Daedai take a peek inside, and liking what they see, with her head bopping to the music, Daedai tells Johnny, "Oh yeah, we can work with this!" As they walk through the door, for some reason, they immediately start to feel uncomfortable and can't explain the sensation. They can actually see the uneasy expressions on each other's faces, but they dismiss it and immediately start scanning the room for Toni. Raven sees Toni over at the corner of the frat house, and they start moving toward her. Before they can reach Toni, Carlton leaves the frat line to come back to his date. Raven and Daedai walk over to Toni, "Hey, lady, your friends have landed." They start high-fiving each other, and Daedai politely comments, "Toni, are you going to introduce us to your friend?" Toni immediately apologizes and says, "Raven, Daedai, this is my friend, Carlton." They both echo, "Hey, Carlton." Carlton responds, "Hey ladies, y'all doing ok?" Raven replies, "We're fine, just a little thirsty. You guys got something to drink in here?" Carlton affirms, "Yes we do; would you like me to get you something?" Daedai, acting very proper, says, "We would certainly appreciate that, Carlton, thank you." Embarrassed by the limited variety of alcohol, Carlton says, "Ladies, there's not a great selection of drinks to choose from, but we do have the teddy bear punch, which has been rumored to raise the dead; can you handle some of that?" Raven insists, "Bring it on; we'll try it." Carlton says, "Alright, ladies, I'll be right back." Knowing the ingredients in the teddy bear, Toni shouts, "What the hell? Are you crazy!? Y'all not gonna drink the teddy bear, are you? Raven inquires, "Toni, aren't you drinking it?" Toni quickly answers, "No, I'm just drinking Sprite. Raven comes back, "Ok, good, because we all can't drink tonight. Somebody needs to be sober to get us home after the party. I guess that's got to be you, Toni." Not wanting to play chaperone, Toni replies, "Hey, I invited you guys to watch over me, not the other way around." Daedai calmly responds, "Well, think of it this way, you already got your man. Raven and I have to work the room to get ours. So that calls for us to get a little bit loose; you understand, right?" Thinking about what Daedai is saying, Toni pleads, "Y'all please don't embarrass me up in here tonight." Daedai softly replies, "We aren't going to embarrass you, Toni. We just want to have a little fun. Now, you go run along to your man, and let us do our thang, ok?" Daedai and Raven hit the floor with the eye of the tigress, walking like models on a runway straight to the middle of the dance floor. The frat boys are on them like flies on you-know-what. They dance their butts off for about an hour continuously. Then they grab the brother they want to be with and get intimately close as the DJ plays a slow jam. Toni and Carlton are busy conversating and really enjoying each other, and everything is good until about 1:30 am when, suddenly, the unexpected happens; Walter comes through the door. It appears that wherever Walter has come from, he has had a little bit too much to drink, and he's acting frat boy rowdy, loud and out of control. Toni spots Walter as he enters the room, and she quickly grabs Carlton's arm. "I thought you said he wouldn't be here." Carlton, surprised to see Walter, says, "Believe me, Toni, if I knew Walter was going to be here, I would have never brought you here." Toni asks, "Well, what are we going to do now? I think we need to leave before he notices that I'm here." Carlton exclaims, "Oh, snap! that fool Johnny just pointed us out to

Walter. Let's move around and try and head towards the door so we can get out of here. I don't want to fight with my frat." Walter is now laser-focused on Toni and Carlton as they move toward the door. Walter intentionally maneuvers his way into their path, cutting them off. He stands in front of Carlton and Toni, visibly intoxicated, staggering and trying to stand up straight. With his six-foot-five-inch football player frame, Walter is now looking down at Toni, "How about a dance for old times' sake?" Toni politely declines, "No, Walter., I'm about to leave." Walter then stares at Carlton holding Toni's hand, "You and Carlton leaving? Oh! It's you and Carlton now?" Walter stares at Carlton up and down, and in an intoxicated voice, mumbles, "Thanks, frat, thanks for holding it down for me, but your services are no longer required." Walter then arrogantly winks at Carlton and comments, "You can leave now. I got this." Trying not to be combative, Carlton says, "Walter, you're drunk, man; leave us alone, please. We don't want to make a scene in here, right?" Walter then mutters arrogantly, "It ain't gonna be a scene, Carlton, because you're leaving, and Toni's staying right here with me." Carlton steps ahead, pulling Toni behind him to protect her because he feels that in a minute, he's going to be forced to make a move, and doesn't want Toni to get hurt. Standing behind Carlton, Toni makes a plea, "Walter, please stop this. I'm sorry about what happened between us, but we are not together anymore; please don't do this." However, her pleas fall on deaf ears. It is like trying to reason with a wounded animal out for blood. Carlton is not as big as Walter in stature, but Carlton knows nothing about the back-down. So, when Walter tries to push him aside to get to Toni, Carlton immediately goes into action and goes low on Walter, grabbing both of his legs and slamming him to the floor. The impact is so great that they break a table in the process, spilling drinks all over the place. Afraid that somebody is going to get hurt, Toni screams again, "Walter, please stop it." Carlton is now on top of Walter, pounding him with all his might. But Walter then lands a solid blow to Carlton's ribs, and Carlton grimaces in pain from the impact. The effects of the blow causes Carlton to eventually fall to the side and relinquish his advantage. Walter then tries to get on top of Carlton, but he's too drunk, and Carlton moves so quickly that Walter can't maneuver fast enough. So when Walter tries to get on top, Carlton quickly maneuvers his way behind Walter and gets him in a chokehold. Wrapping both legs around Walter's body puts him in a position where he can't move, and Carlton continues to apply pressure to Walter's neck, almost causing him to pass out until, suddenly, the frat brothers seeing Walter going limp, move in and grab Carlton to keep him from possibly killing Walter. Out of breath, and breathing hard, Carlton looks down at Walter, and the brothers shout, "Don't worry about Walter, man; just take Toni and go." With his adrenaline pumping and shirt torn in several places, Carlton looks around for Toni, then goes to her and says in an exhausted tone, "Toni, I'm sorry about all this." Not caring about an apology, Toni asks, "Baby, are you alright?" She embraces his face with her hands, and as the brothers help Walter to his feet, he sees Toni's affection toward Carlton, and can't stand it. Walter quickly breaks away from his brothers, pulls up his pants leg, pulls out a gun from a leg holster, and points it directly at Carlton and Toni, who are now heading toward the door. Daedai screams in terror., "He's got a gun, he's got a gun!" Walter manages to get off a round before his frat brothers standing nearby take him down. Surprised by the stinging sensation in his body, Carlton slowly turns toward Toni, and with a concerned expression on his face, indicates that something is wrong as he collapses into Toni's arms, forcing them both to the floor. Toni screams as she sees blood coming from Carlton's torn shirt. Daedai and Raven anxiously shout at the top of their lungs, "Call 911! Hurry, please! Call 911. Hurry! He's been shot!" The frat brothers, after wrestling the gun away from Walter, keep him pinned to the floor while calling and waiting for the police. Toni screams, and cries,

"Carlton, stay with me. Please, baby; stay with me." As Carlton slowly starts to lose consciousness, Toni cries and screams as she holds Carlton's unconscious body on her lap. Daedai and Raven quickly rush to her side and yell at the brothers, "Did y'all call 911?" And again, Ravens screams louder, with tears in her eyes, "Did y'all call 911?" The brothers immediately confirm the call, "Yeah, they're on their way; we told them to hurry; someone has been shot." As the girls huddle around Carlton's blood-soaked body, some of the brothers try to stop the bleeding as best as they can by applying pressure to the wound. Then, hearing the blast from the booming sirens headed their way, Daedai gets up and runs outside, screaming, "Over here, over here; hurry." Upon arrival, the paramedics grab their bags, pull out the gurney, and let the police rush in first. Then the paramedics follow, and immediately start rendering medical attention to Carlton. The police take control of Walter, secure his gun, and move everyone back so the paramedics can have room to work. The police gather information from the brothers about the incident, and immediately handcuff and arrest Walter for attempted murder. The paramedics place Carlton on the gurney and prepare to take him outside to the ambulance. Crying her eyes out, Toni asks the paramedics over and over again, "How is he? Is he gonna make it? Is he gonna make it?" One of the paramedics stops for a Moment and says, "Ma'am, I don't know. His pulse is very weak, but know that we are doing all that we can." The paramedics place Carlton inside the ambulance, and when they go to close the door, Toni, wiping the tears from her eyes, screams, "I'm his girlfriend! I have to go with him." They let Toni inside, and as she sits down next to Carlton. Daedai and Raven shout to Toni, "We'll be following close behind, and we'll meet you at the hospital." They find out from the paramedics where they will be taking Carlton, and the girls immediately sprint to the car, and Daedai floors it, trying to keep up with the ambulance.

CHAPTER 4
(THE MIRACLE)

A SHORT TIME AFTER CHASING THE AMBULANCE, Daedai and Raven finally arrive at the hospital. They find that parking is a problem; however, they get lucky, finding a space in the upper deck of the parking garage. They get out and immediately make their way toward the trauma center. Coming into the center, they stop Momentarily at the admissions desk to find out where Carlton has been taken. Upon learning that he is back in the surgical area, they make their way quickly down the hallway where they see Toni in tears. Traumatized, overwhelmed with grief, and about to pass out, the attending doctor is holding Toni up. Raven and Daedai run to assist the doctor with Toni to keep her from falling. They find out that Carlton died Moments ago. Hearing the bad news, the girls give out a surprised type of gasp and scream, "Oh no!" They take the news of his death very hard, while at the same time, they try to console Toni, who seems to be in shock, crying and murmuring, "He's gone, Raven, Daedai, he's gone. Oh my God, it hurts so bad, and it's all my fault." Daedai tilts her head back, takes a deep breath to control her emotions, and says, "No Toni, it is not your fault; it's Walter's fault. He was out of his mind with jealousy. Out of rage, anger, and stupidity, he shot Carlton. Walter pulled that trigger; not you." Toni can only hang her head and continue to cry. Daedai and Raven embrace

Toni tightly to help calm her down while at the same time con-tinually reassuring her that she had nothing to do with what happened at the party. Later, after all the crying, Toni tempo-rarily sobers in her emotions so she can think, but as she stares at Daedai and Raven through eyes seeking absolution, the tears start flowing again. The girls reach out for Toni again and hear a women's voice asking, "Which one of you girls is Toni?" Toni looks up with tears in her eyes, "I am." Toni tries to focus through her swollen eyes, and sees this older woman walking towards her, Bible in hand, saying, "I'm Carlton's grandMother, and he's waiting to see you." After hearing this, Toni's legs almost give way. She turns to see if Daedai heard what she heard. Toni then turns back around and slowly walks toward the grandMother, "Ma'am, I'm so sorry to tell you this, but Carlton passed away a few minutes ago. Carlton's grand-Mother's expression doesn't change; she just stares at Toni with this unconcerned attitude as she clutches her Bible to her chest and comments, "That may have been his condition min-utes ago, but right now, truth assures me that he shall not die, but live and declare the works of the Lord. So, Father, I thank You on behalf of my grandson that You have healed his body and have severed all ties with the spirit of death. Toni, I said, Carlton is waiting to see you." Carlton's grandMother then starts murmuring something that the girls cannot comprehend, and slowly walks over to an empty seat in the lobby and sits down. Toni and the girls look at each other and start discussing among themselves that maybe Carlton's grandMother is in shock or something, and as they start walking toward the grandMother, suddenly, they hear the faint sound of footsteps running and a voice yelling loudly, "Toni, Toni, he's breathing, he's breathing." As Carlton's nurse gets closer, Toni asks, "What did you say? What-did-you-just-say?" The nurse says again, "He's up and breathing." Toni murmurs, "Huh-huh, no, I saw him die." The nurse says, "Well, he's got a pulse and a heart-beat now." Raven and Daedai jump up and down for joy, but

Toni looks bewildered and in total disbelief as she turns to look at Carlton's grandMother, but the grandMother is doing this trans-like murmuring thing, and Toni can't figure out what's going on. Her facial expression now resembles a person trying to hold on to reality, and being a scientific-minded person, Toni cannot comprehend in her mind what is happening. Toni starts walking slowly, then moves quickly down the hallway, not sure of what to expect. She turns the corner to enter the room and immediately stops, and then being overwhelmed with surprise, she puts both hands over her mouth to filter out her screams as she sees Carlton lying in bed fully awake, motioning with his hand for her to come to him. Toni stares at Carlton somewhat in shock, and as she sobers back to reality, she then runs quickly to Carlton's bedside and plants a big fat kiss on his lips, and Carlton says in a weak voice, "Wow, for kisses like this, I don't mind getting shot." Toni smiles and gently lays down beside Carlton, holding and kissing him. Carlton jokes again, "Hey, this is pretty good for a second date, huh?" Toni smiles, then says with tears in her eyes, "Carlton, I am so sorry about this." Carlton says, "Toni, none of this is your fault, baby. It's mine. I wanted so badly to show you off as my girl. I used poor judgment and put you in harm's way. Can you ever forgive me?" Toni exclaims, "Forgive you? Carlton, I care for you now more than you could ever imagine; you own my heart." Hearing Toni's words, Carlton smiles and while still in a guarded state, he drifts slowly back to sleep. The nurse immediately steps forward and advises everyone, "We must let him get some rest now; you can come back later." Toni says, "Ok, but I'll be right outside." They leave the room, walking back to the lobby, and Daedai being curious, asks, "Toni, what does it feel like to be in love? I mean, I've dated a lot of guys, but I can't really say I was ever in love with them." Toni looks at Daedai and says, "I don't know. I guess it's a feeling of completeness, happiness. This experience is new for me too, Daedai. I never cared for anyone like this, and my feelings for him are so unexpected.

Remember, I didn't even trust him earlier. These feelings could come from the mix of all the things that have happened tonight, or maybe there was always something special about him that I felt inside. I mean, to even go to a frat party where I knew Walter might be-means craziness, or just a deep-seeded desire to be with Carlton; you pick. It is, what it is. I know at this Moment, I have serious feelings for him." Daedai and Toni continue talking as they head back toward the nurse's station, and then they see Chrystal and Sanaa moving through a crowd of fraternity brothers and police officers, who are still talking about Carlton's miraculous recovery, and when the girls see Toni and Daedai, they run to them. Concerned about her friend, Sanaa asks, "You ok?" and before she can answer, Chrystal excitedly comments, "Toni, we heard that your friend was the one that was shot at the party. We got here as quickly as we could. How is he?" Toni pauses a minute before answering, stares at Carlton's grandMother, then back at Chrystal, takes a deep breath, and declares, "Thanks be to God, he's in stable condition." Sanaa looks around, "Where is Raven?" Daedai says, "Tapeworm woman went to check out the vending machines." Chrystal remarks, "As usual, eating, huh?" and they laugh as Raven comes down the hall, munching on vending machine food. Raven sarcastically rebukes her friends, "Oh, you guys laughing at me, huh; after I come bearing gifts of food?" Daedai exclaims, "Oh, yeah, Kit Kat bars." Raven speaks to Sanaa and Chrystal, and after saying their hellos, they also reach for some of the candy bars. Sanaa says, "Toni, they had it out on campus that Carlton had died. Why did they say that?" Toni hangs her head, looks up, and says, "Sanaa, not too long ago he was pronounced dead. I saw Carlton take what I thought was his last breath. I guess he just had a lot of fight in him, or maybe his grandMother. No, never mind, he was just really lucky." Being concerned and angry over the shooting, Chrystal inquires, "Toni, did they arrest Walter?" Toni affirms, "Yes, the police arrested that drunk fool and took him to jail for attempted murder. I feel bad for Walter, though, knowing how our relationship ended. I think I caused problems for everybody tonight. I went to this party against my better judgment, but I never would have imagined that Walter would do something this crazy." The girls continue to comfort and console Toni and assure her that what happened was not her fault. The next morning, after being up all night with Toni, Sanaa, and Chrystal struggle to get up for class. Sanaa looks at the messages on her phone and sees that Jordan has been trying to reach her all morning. Sanaa calls Jordan back, and when he answers, she greets him, "Hey, baby." Jordan inquires, "Hey, where have you been? I've been calling you all morning, girl." Sanaa apologizes, "I'm sorry Jordan, I was sleeping so hard. Did you hear about the shooting at the beta's frat house last night?" Jordan says, "Yeah, but what does that have to do with you?" Sanaa replies, "Nothing directly, but the guy who got shot last night is my girlfriend's boyfriend," Jordan, in surprise, exclaims, "What!" Sanaa says, "Yes, Chrystal and I went to the hospital last night to be with her." Understanding the situation, Jordan comments, "Wow, is the guy alright?" Sanaa, in a soft voice affirms, "Yeah, he made it, but from what everybody was saying, he was very lucky." Jordan inquires, "Where is your girlfriend now?" Sanaa says, "Toni is still at the hospital with Carlton and his parents." Taking a deep breath and exhaling, Jordan comments, "Man, it's getting bad, right?" Sanaa says, "Yeah, everybody's got to stop man; stop this crazy violence." Jordan replies, "I agree one hundred percent, baby. I just called to say good morning." Sanaa responds in kind. "Well, good morning to you too, sweetheart." Loving to hear Sanaa's voice and the way she talks, Jordan remarks, "God, I love hearing the way you say that, but, uh, go ahead and get ready. I'll see you at the Law building; I got something to ask you later." Sanaa exclaims, "What? What do you have to ask me?" Jordan says, "I'll tell you later; now go get ready for class." Sanaa, not liking the hold-out rebukes, "Oh no, you're not going to leave me hanging like this." Jordan pleads, "Sanaa, it's nothing to do with us. I'm just trying to help out a friend. I'll tell you what it is later, ok?" Sanaa relents, "Ok, but don't ever tell me you got something to ask me and then say, but I'll have to ask you later; that drives me crazy." Jordan apologizes, "Ok, baby, I won't handle it like that ever again, but right now, I got a long drive to get to class, ok?" Sanaa reluctantly gives in, "Alright, Jordan, see you there." On the way out of the door, Tyson asks his friend, "Jordan, did you talk to Sanaa for me yet?" Jordan advises, "Don't worry, I'll ask her later at school." Tyson pleads, "Yo, man, don't forget now." Jordan reassures him, "Tyson, I got you, man." Jordan leaves the apartment and heads for the parking lot. He starts his car and makes his way to campus. Tyson stays at home because his classes are on Tuesdays and Thursdays. When Jordan gets to campus, he sees Sanaa and Chrystal walking swiftly toward the Law building, Jordan calls out to Sanaa from behind, "Baby, hold up." Sanaa shouts, "Hurry up, boy, we're almost late." Jordan catches up and says, "Hey, Chrystal, how are you doing?" Chrystal replies, "I'm doing fine. I'll see you guys in a minute, I got to run in here." Chrystal breaks off to go to the girl's room, and Jordan and Sanaa go into class. Sanaa takes her seat, and Jordan sits behind her, which is his seat on the seating chart. Sanaa turns around and whispers, "What is it you wanted to ask me?" and just before Jordan can answer, he sees Chrystal coming into the classroom, and Jordan whispers, "You're asking me this now? Wait till after class." Sanaa exclaims, "Oh, my God!" And whispers to Jordan, "This better be worth all this drama boy." Professor Dulcie then interrupts the chatter with a double fake cough and acknowledges everyone, "Good morning class." Then he starts in with his ritual of calling the attendance from his color-coded, laminated, seating chart. Jordan sits back and thinks to himself, "Damn, I'll be so glad when I get out of this class," then that little voice in his head rebukes his attitude, "Sit up, fool, we need an A in this class." Jordan then looks at his beautiful Sanaa and somehow finds the motivation to adjust his attitude and pay strict attention to whatever Professor Dulcie has to say. Meanwhile, on the other side of campus, Raven and Daedai are on their way to class, and while walking down the sidewalk, they see some of the brothers they met at the party. They see that the brothers are watching them and start walking with a little swing in their hips. The brother that likes Raven follows them inside the building and up to their classroom. However, Raven and Daedai go inside the room before the brother can attempt to make his move. The brother notices another student heading into the classroom and asks her to do him a favor. He writes out a note for Raven, asking her to meet him tonight about 6:00 pm down by the infirmary. Then he waits to see the student give Raven the note. Raven reads the note, then stares at the guy standing in the doorway. Raven then acts like she's surprised and dumbfounded by the contents on the note; knowing all the time that she was all up in this brother's face at the party. The brother pleads and gives Raven that sympathetic look, placing his hand over his heart in a begging gesture, and Raven gasps with mouth open and eyes squinted as if to say, "I don't know you like that," and the brother knowing that she's full of it; knows she knows what happened between them at the party. So, he again does a pleading gesture with his hands, and Raven inhales and pauses to think for a minute, and looks at him, this time, with a some-what welcoming expression, blushing and thinking that he's cute and funny. Smiling at the brother, Raven nods her head and mouths the word *yes*. All the while, Daedai, watching what she considers to be sick character acting, thinks that the whole thing between Raven and this guy is comical until she sees Raven agree to meet the guy. Then Daedai stares at Raven like she just grew a furry tail. Surprised that Raven said yes to this boy, she whispers, "Raven, I hope you know what you're doing," and then Daedai whispers again, "Raven, why can't he come to the dorm and pick you up?" Raven whispers back, "I don't know. Maybe he's got an old girlfriend in our dorm and doesn't want to cause any drama." Reacting negatively to what Raven is saying, Daedai replies, "Raven, girl, that ain't saying much about you, or don't you remember the conversation we had critiquing Carlton. Raven admits, "Yeah, I know. I remember, Daedai, but last night, Toby and I were starting to get so involved, then the fight broke out, and everything just stopped. I just want to reacquaint myself with him and see where things can go." Daedai comments, "Oh, ok, so his name is Toby, huh?" Raven says, "Yes, his name is Toby." Daedai takes a deep breath, exhales with a kind of "I give up" attitude, realizing she's going do it anyway, and gives in. "Alright, then. Go for it."

CHAPTER 5
(WHAT TO BELIEVE)

OVER AT THE LAW SCHOOL BUILDING, JORDAN, Chrystal, and Sanaa are finished with class and heading toward the exit. Jordan interrupts, "Chrystal, excuse us for a minute, I need to holla something at Sanaa, please. I'll only be a minute, ok?" Chrystal says, "Ok, be it far from me to breach the confidentiality of this most private Moment. So, I'll just go over here to the little girl's room, but you guys hurry up. Sanaa, we got class." Sanaa turns to Jordan, "Now, what's so important that it took all day for you to tell me what's on your mind." Jordan swallows in his throat and says, "You know my roommate, Tyson, right?" Sanaa, with a suspicious expression on her face, answers, "Yeah, and?" Jordan continues, "Well, he's kinda sweet on Chrystal." Sanaa exclaims, "What!? That's what this is all about?" Looking like a scolded puppy, Jordan confirms, "Yeah, can you talk to her for him, please? He likes the girl; he likes her a lot." Sanaa then asks with an inquiring yet mocking tone, "Why doesn't he talk to her himself?" Jordan replies, "You know how it is; it's hard for him to find the right opportunity or situation to break the ice, and he figures, what can be better than an introduction from her friend to get things rolling?" Sanaa comments, "So what am I now? What does that make me, Jordan? Ms. Handy Howard, matchmaker extraordinaire?" Jordan jumps in quickly, "No, baby, it's not like that. Tyson is just trying to get recognized; you know, a good introduction." Realizing that Jordan is just trying help his roommate, Sanaa capitulates, "Jordan, I will talk to her, but I am not promising anything." Jordan responds quickly, "Ok, baby, that's fine. Just tell her to come with you to the apartment Saturday to watch some movies and chill. Tell her that some of my friends are coming over and we're just going to have fun. This is the plan, if things do not work out between the two of them, you can make an excuse to get back to campus; how about that?" Sanaa looks at Jordan in astonishment, and makes it clear, "Jordan, I am not going to lie to Chrystal. I am going to come clean with her about how Tyson feels and the purpose of our visit Saturday. If she is willing to meet Tyson, then we will come. I am not going to lie, and I am not promising anything, ok?" Jordan exhales and says, "Alright, baby, that's fair. Just let me know what she says." At this point, Chrystal comes out of the restroom looking at Sanaa and Jordan, "Are you guys finished with your little private conversation?" Jordan looks at Sanaa, then looks at Chrystal and apologizes, "Sorry about that, Chrystal. Sanaa, I'll see you later, baby, I'm going to the house." Sanaa says, "Ok, babe." Sanaa then turns to Chrystal, smiling with an endearing and questioning eye, "Chrystal, I got something I need to ask you." Being skeptical as to Sanaa's petitioning smile, Chrystal cautiously inquires, "What is it?" Sanaa quickly and nervously responds, "I'll ask you later; we got class right now." Chrystal exclaims, "Oh no you didn't. You're trying to do me like that? Girl, you know that ain't right." Understanding how she feels, Sanaa insists, "I'll tell you what it is after class because I need time to explain information that has recently come to my attention, ok?" With a confused look on her face, Chrystal gives in, "Oh, alright, I don't know if I like this Sanaa, but ok." Later that evening, over on the other side of campus, Toni is back from the hospital and on campus. She goes to Raven and Daedai's room and finds Raven getting ready to rendezvous for a date. Raven comments, "Hey, Toni, how is Carlton doing?" Toni affirms, "He's doing much better, thank God. But I've been thinking about something that's pressing on my mind. You guys may think I'm crazy, but I think Carlton's grandMother had something to do with Carlton's recovery. I can't explain it, but I just feel that her chanting or whatever the hell she was doing last night had something to do with that boy surviving." Raven laughingly raises both hands while twiddling her fingers, "Oh, creepy voodoo stuff, huh?" Peeved off by her antics, Daedai comments, "Raven, it's not like that; his grandMother was just praying." Raven replies, "Daedai, don't tell me you believe in all that stuff, like God, demons, ghosts, spirits, and all that crazy stuff." Toni stares at Raven and answers in a sort-of nervous voice, "Raven, I tell you the truth, a lot happened that night that I can't explain. I major in chemistry. I'm a science person, but I know enough biological stuff to know that what happened last night is unexplainable. I am only saying that maybe there is something to this religious stuff. Look, I saw Carlton die. I felt his pulse slip away, and just like that; he comes back? Uh-uh, no, and check this out, there's something else you need to know. The doctor told me and his parents that the first x-ray showed damage to his organs when he first came to the hospital. After this mysterious and miraculous whatever you call it, they quickly did another x-ray, and things had changed." Looking at Toni confused, Daedai inquires, "What things changed?" Toni takes a breath, exhales, and explains, "I don't know all the medical terminology they were talking, but the doctor looked perplexed as hell trying to explain how his previously damaged organs now look normal. He said the organs looked like they just healed. Yes, he said healed. Now you tell me what's up with that?" In sort-of-a dismissive-like manner, Raven remarks, "Toni, they make mistakes in hospitals all the time; maybe the damage wasn't as bad as they originally thought." Toni asserts, "If that's possible, then riddle me this, joker woman, what happened to him internally that caused his death in the first place? If the first x-ray wasn't accurate, even though it revealed damage, why wasn't there a trace of damage found in the second x-ray, huh? Or are you saying Carlton being shot was all in our imagination? Lost in the complexity of Toni's logical questions, Raven gives in, "Toni, I don't know, but you need to stop spinning your head around and around trying to figure this thing out. You just need to be happy that Carlton is alive and well, right?" Still contemplating everything that happened, Toni looks at Raven and relents, "Maybe you're right; maybe you're right." Quickly changing the subject, Toni inquires, "Now, who is this guy you're supposed to be meeting?" Raven excitedly replies, "His name is Toby," Toni, surprised at hearing the guy's name, stares at Raven like she just grew horns on top of her head and exclaims, "Toby? Raven, Toby? I remember him from when I was dating Walter, he was a wild brother back then. Are you sure you want to go out with this guy?" Raven softly clarifies, "Toni, he was so nice to me at the party, and it seems like he likes me. I think he's cute. I just want to see how he really feels about me." With a frown on her face, Toni relents and says, "Ok, then, when you ready to go, Daedai and I will walk you downstairs." Putting a halt to that thought, Raven says, "No thank you, ma'am; you guys just want to be nosey. Hey, I'm a big girl, I'll be ok." Daedai stares at Raven like a concerned parent, and says, "Ok, but if you need us, we there." Thankful for the support, Raven replies, "I know, Daedai. See y'all later." Still skeptical about her date, Toni comments, "Alright, girl, have a good time." As Raven leaves and pulls the door closed, Toni looks at Daedai and states, "I hope she knows what she is doing. I never really liked Toby, I always thought he was an a**hole. But how could I tell Raven that, especially after her talking about how nice he had been to her? Then again, maybe the boy has changed, I don't know. However, there is one thing I do know, girl, I got to get some sleep. Daedai, I'll see you in the morning. I'm going to my room and lie down." Daedai begins yawning, "Girl, I'm about to turn in too. I'll catch you later." After Toni leaves, worrying about her homework, Daedai puts off going to sleep and starts completing her assignment, but she soon realizes that the persistent yawning and sleepy eyes won't allow her to continue studying. So, she turns off the lights and goes fast to sleep. Over at the graduate dorm, Chrystal and Sanaa are busy studying, and Chrystal looks over at Sanaa and asks, "Sanaa, what is it you wanted to ask me?" Sanaa says, "Hold on Chrystal, let me finish this sentence." After she is finished, Sanaa begins to explain, "Ok," she takes a deep breath, exhales, and continues, "Jordan's roommate Tyson-you know him, right?" Chrystal, giving a curious look, replies, "I've seen him around. I think he's cute." Sanaa responds, "Oh, really! Well, Mr. "cute" has a crush on you, and he wants to get to know you." Chrystal softly replies, "What?" Sanaa affirms, "Yes, Jordan has been pushing me to ask that we come to his apaerment on Saturday to watch movies so Tyson can get acquainted with you. I told him I can't make any promises, but I would ask you. What do you think?" Chrystal thinks for a minute and asks, "You're coming with me, right?" Sanaa assures her friend, "Girl, I got your back all the way. I didn't even think you would consider going." Chrystal wittingly responds, "I've seen Tyson around campus; he's ok. I think he can have the pleasure of my company. But Sanaa, make sure Jordan and Tyson understand that we are just coming to watch movies, ok?" Sanaa says, "Ok, I'll tell him. Now let's get back to work." Sanaa and Chrystal start to focus on their case studies and work late into the night. A few minutes later, they give up on studying and both girls turn in for the night. About 2:14 am, over at the undergraduate dorm, Daedai is awakened by the continued ringing and vibration of her phone. Coming out of a deep sleep and hating being interrupted, Daedai is Momentarily not able to focus until she finally manages to see the many calls that are on her phone. She immediately clicks to answer, and a man's voice comes over the cell phone asking, "Is this Daedai Charles?" She answers, "Yes, who is this?" The man says, "I'm Sergeant Douglas Johnson, campus police. Are you a friend of Raven Chung?" Daedai nervously answers, "Yes, what's wrong?" Sergeant Johnson advises, "Raven has been admitted to Holy Cross Hospital; can you come to the hospital?" Daedai exclaims, "Oh Lord, oh Lord, is she alright?" Sergeant Johnson says, "Yes, she's stable." Daedai shouts, "Stable! Stable! what happened?" Officer Johnson says, "Calm down, Ms. Charles, calm down. Come to the hospital and we'll fill you in on what happened." In a scared and trembling voice, Daedai cries out, "I'm on my way, I'm on the way, Mr. Officer." Daedai throws on clothes and quickly runs down the hall, taking the stairway down to Toni's room. Daedai begins banging on Toni's door as if she's a crazy woman. Daedai then screams at the door, "Toni, wake up! Toni, wake up! Raven's in the hospital," Toni comes to the door, along with ten other girls coming out of their rooms, trying to find out what's going on. Standing in the doorway, rubbing the sleep out of her eyes, Toni says, "Daedai, what's wrong?" Daedai excitedly shouts, "Toni, Raven's in the hospital; we got to go, we got to go right now." Toni responds excitedly, "Ok, let me put on some clothes and we out of here." The two girls rush out into the parking lot, get into Daedai's car, and rush to the hospital. Toni, now crying, yells at Daedai, "What happened?" Daedai answers in a trembling voice, "I don't know; the police officer wouldn't tell me over the phone." Daedai starts driving as fast as she can, running two stop signs and a yellow light about to turn red. Four or five minutes later, they enter the emergency center of the hospital. They get out of the car and both start running toward the emergency center's front desk. Daedai explains to the nurse, "Ma'am, we're looking for our friend Raven Chung. Can you tell us where she is?" The nurse at the desk says, "Give me a minute; let me look at admissions." The desk nurse eventually finds Raven in the computer, and she says, "Oh, I see her; she's here in the back. I remember the campus police and paramedics bringing her in."

Toni asks nervously, "Can you tell us what happened to her?" The nurse advises them to go back and talk to her doctor and police. "They will answer all questions." Toni and Daedai thank the nurse and rush toward the back. They finally see Raven lying on a hospital bed, bruised and battered as the police are finishing up their questioning. Daedai and Toni rushed to Raven's side, trying to be careful not to hurt her. Daedai anxiously asks, "What happened, Raven?" Raven looks up at Daedai with inflamed and puffed eyes and starts crying, and in a stressed voice, exclaims, "Daedai, they hit me, forced me down, and raped me." Daedai angrily asks, "Who, Toby?" Raven insists, "No, it wasn't Toby, but it had to be somebody already in the frat house." Toni shouts, "Frat house? What were you doing at the frat house?" Raven shamefully looks at Daedai and Toni, explaining, "I was in Toby's room, and we were-I was in Toby's room, ok?" Toni, understanding the situation and trying to be non-judgmental, states, "Raven, no more explanations needed, but where was Toby in all this?" Daedai interrupts angrily, "That's what I want to know. Where was Toby while those animals did this to you?" Raven says, "Daedai, we drank a whole lot. I got plastered and was in the bed, basically naked and passed out. Toby said he woke up hammered and stumbled his way to the bathroom down the hall. He said he felt like he was about to throw up, and in rushing, he might have inadvertently left the room door open. Toby said while he was in the bathroom, it turned into one of those love affairs with the commode, hugging it, and holding on for dear life, offering that old promise to God: 'Lord, if you get me out of this one...' Then throwing up everything and everywhere, he thinks he eventually passed out. He said the next time he opened his eyes, he was lying on the cold bathroom floor, looking up at a spot on the ceiling. While trying to get to his feet, he said he could hear me moaning and screaming, and he ran wobbling back down to the room. There he saw me in the condition you see me right now. Toby then locked me in his room and immediately called the police. He went throughout the house, trying to find the people that hurt me, or at least find out who was in the house. He found no one out of place. He said there was one frat who was in his room. Toby questioned him, but the brother said he drank too much and was out cold. He said he did not hear anything at all. Toby came back to the room and was stressed as if he felt I was going to blame him for what happened. Toby kept repeating, 'Baby, I'm sorry. I don't know how this happened; nothing like this has ever happened in the frat house.' He just kept on saying that. I was trying to speak to calm him down, but I was too weak and hurting too bad to deal with him. Then there was a knock on the door, and it was the police. Toby went downstairs to let the police in. The police told Toby this might be the last straw for the frat house. The police officer stated that bad things keep happening here. Then the campus police showed up, and since we were students at the school, I guess we became their case to handle. When they came upstairs to the room, I was lying on the bed, not able to move very much. I think Toby was trying to explain to the police the situation as much as he could. I was out of it. I mean, out of it. I could not respond to anything or anybody. All I could hear was that searing and penetrating sound of that damn ambulance siren getting closer and closer to the house. In my half-dazed and bruised condition, I remember crazily thinking to myself, 'I know people get used to hearing sirens and never pay them much attention; but right now, I hear its sound, and it's a dark and frightening sound, and I know it's coming for me.' After they put me in the ambulance, I don't remember much after that; everything was so surreal. I guess the stress and shock was too much for me. I guess I passed out. However, I do remember them rolling me into the emergency center, and the police waiting to interview me. After about an hour, or what-ever amount of time passed, they came in to talk to me. I guess they had to wait until I was fully cognizant and stable. They questioned me as to what happened. But all I know is that I was beaten and raped. The guys who raped me made sure I couldn't see their faces or even tell how many there were in the room. They had something over my face, and I was so intoxicated that my struggling was in vain. All I could do was surrender under the weight of the bodies on top of me. I had no choice but to let go and hope for the nightmare to end." Crying, Toni exclaims, "Damn, Raven, that's horrible." Sitting up and trying to pull herself together, Raven tells her friends, "Just as you guys were coming to my bed, the police finished their questioning and were leaving." Daedai, all in a rage, angrily asks, "Raven, did they find out who did this to you?" Raven says, "They told me they would know more after they get the results from the lab tests." Back at the frat house, the police are busy performing a thorough investigation, questioning the fraternity members, one by one. They have even secured the right to take DNA samples from all the brothers, whether they lived at the frat house or not. Later in the afternoon, after walking out of the hospital without permission, Raven, Toni, and Daedai are now back in Daedai and Raven's room. Raven suggests, "I think the police suspect Toby of doing this. They don't believe his story about what happened. Daedai, they think he set me up to be raped. I don't believe that. Toby would not do that to me. I know he wouldn't do that." With their heads down, looking at the floor, Daedai and Toni evade eye contact with Raven, trying not to let on how they truly feel about Toby's involvement. Raven is stunned at their silent expression of disbelief, and shouts, "What!? He wouldn't do that to me." Raven screams again, "He wouldn't do that to me." Toni comments, "Raven, I know you like Toby, and you feel in your heart that he's a good guy, but right now, you can't rule out the possibility that he might have been involved in this. For your sake, I pray that the police are wrong to suspect him." Raven continues shaking her head right to left in a non-affirming manner, "Nope. I will not believe that Toby would do that to me." Then Raven's cell phone rings and she answers, "Hello." Chrystal asks, "Girl, you ok?" Raven says, "Yeah, I'm fine, just a little sore." Chrystal states, "Girl, before Sanaa and I could get to the hospital, we heard you had been released and were gone. How did you get released so quickly?" Raven explains, "I just told them I wasn't staying; they were going to release me soon anyway, so I just left." Chrystal, in surprise, exclaims, "Raven, oh my God, you're in your room?" Raven says, "Yeah, Daedai and Toni are here with me." Chrystal anxiously says, "Alright, Sanaa and I are on our way over there." Ravens comments, "Take your time; we'll be here." The cell phone rings again, and Raven answers, "Hello." Toby says, "Raven, it's me," and in a trembling voice, he pleads, "Raven, I want you to know that I would never do anything to hurt you. You must believe that, baby. I'm at a loss on how this could have happened." Raven reassures Toby, "I know you wouldn't hurt me. I believe you. Are the police finished interrogating you?" Toby replies, "Yeah, but they're saying they may have to talk to me later, and they asked me not to leave town like I'm a criminal or something. Baby, I am sorry for all this mess. I'm going to find out what happened, and they are going pay for hurting you." Raven quickly asks, "Toby, do you care for me?" Toby answers, "Yes! Of course, I do." Raven continues, "Well then, I want you to let this go. Leave it to the police, please." Toby, not believing what she asks, hesitates to say what's really on his mind, but concedes, "Ok, I'll try. I got to go now. I'll catch up with you later." Raven says, "Ok, I'll be here." As Raven ends the call and checks her phone for messages, there's a knock on the door. Daedai yells, "Who is it?" A voice shouts. "It's Chrystal." Raven opens the door, and Sanaa and Chrystal rush in and hug Raven tightly and question if she's alright. "We heard what happened. Have the police made arrests; are there any suspects?" Sanaa anxiously inquires, and as Raven hunts for words, Toni interjects quickly with a double fake cough and motions with her head not to mention Toby as a suspect, then quickly comments, "No, they're still questioning people that have a relationship to the frat house. However, the police haven't come up with anything as of yet." Chrystal assertively complains, "That's so like the cops; they're so slow unless trying to give you a ticket. Oh yeah, they can get it right then." Raven states, "I think they're doing the best they can do, Chrystal. I believe I'm partially culpable though. I shouldn't have gotten out of my mind drunk that night." Sanaa quickly exclaims, "What!? Whoa-wait a minute, girl. What happened to you is not your fault; it's the fault of those animals that raped you. I hope to God, when the police find out who did it, they take them son of a b***hes for a ride out to the Everglades and kick the living sh*t out of their dog-beat asses before taking them to jail. I am so angry about this I don't know what to do. I'm sorry, but I want somebody to hurt bad for this." Daedai nods her head, agreeing, "That's exactly how I'm feeling, Sanaa; men think they can treat us any kinda way, do what they want, try to get away with it, and they think we're supposed to lay down and take it? Not this sister. You can take that to the bank or any other secure place you might want to stick it. Raven, the people who did this to you will not get away with it, even if I have to make calls to the lady from the feminist movement to bring an army down here to get you justice. I'll do what I have to do. Like they say: no justice, no damn peace. The police can have a few more days to get themselves together and make an arrest. If not, I'm going to start making my calls. Right about now, I'm developing a serious dislike for all men. I know it ain't fair, but that's the way I feel." Chrystal comments, "I feel you, girl. I feel you. However, we do need to start becoming aware of our environment and the people we deal with because there are a lot of jerks lurking around, trying to take advantage of us. Raven, keep us informed on what happens, ok? We are always here for you. Sanaa and I need to leave because we've been invited over to Jordan's place to watch movies, but we'll check in on you." Raven says, "Y'all go ahead. I'll be ok. As they leave, Raven hollers out, "Say hello to your new beau for me." Sanaa says, "I will; see you guys in a little bit."

CHAPTER 6
(PLAYING HARD TO GET)

CHRYSTAL AND SANAA RETURN BACK TO THEIR dorm and take about twenty minutes to freshen up. Sanaa, who is dressed and ready to go, waits in the hallway talking to a student. Chrystal then comes to the door, looking sexy as ever, and Sanaa, feeling the vibe, remarks, "Oh! It's like that, huh?" Chrystal, looking down at herself, admiring what she has on, says, "Well, you know, I don't want to disappoint." Sanaa says, "Let's go, then." On the way to Jordan and Tyson's apartment, Sanaa asks, "You are ok with this, right?" Chrystal looks at Sanaa and assures her friend, "Don't worry, Sanaa, I know what I'm dealing with." Sanaa sarcastically replies, "Ok, Ms. Thang!" After a few minutes driving against the backdrop of a beautiful sunset, Sanaa and Chrystal reach the apartment complex and pull into the parking lot. Tyson and Jordan are still doing some last-minute cleaning, preparing for their dates. Jordan looks at Tyson and remarks, "Man, look-a-here, don't you blow this; what you do reflects on me, you got that?" Tyson says, "Don't worry, man. I like Chrystal. I plan to be the perfect gentleman until she needs me to be something different." Jordan then rolls his eyes, "Yo, man, I don't even want to know what that means." Chrystal and Sanaa knock on the door, and Tyson tells Jordan, "I got it, man." Tyson opens the door, and immediately is captured on how beautiful and fine

Chrystal looks; he's at a loss for words, and Sanaa, seeing Tyson looking like a deer caught in the headlights, says, "Hi, Tyson," and walks past him as she gently lays her hand on his chest, then turning to acknowledge her friend, "You know Chrystal, right?" Still gazing at Chrystal, Tyson then sobers in his thoughts, "Come on in, ladies, and have a seat." The girls enter and take a seat on the couch, and Jordan brings out two cold drinks and says, "Hey, Ms. Howard." Sanaa responds, "Hi, Mr. Davis." Jordan hands the girls their drinks, then bends over and kisses Sanaa, and everybody in the room can feel the electricity. Tyson, attempting to break the ice with Chrystal, inquires, "What type of movies you like, Chrystal?" Chrystal thinks and then answers, "I guess I'm like most women when it comes to movies. I like romantic comedies." Trying to relate and show his sensitive side, Tyson agrees and comments, "Hey, I like romantic comedies too." Knowing what he's trying to do, Chrystal then makes him real, and comments, "Oh, really! Well, name a few romantic comedies that you like." Knowing he has put his foot in his mouth, Tyson mutters, "Uh, well, I can't think of any offhand, but I know I like them." At this point, Sanaa has turned her head to the side, trying to keep everybody from seeing her silently laughing. Coming to Tyson's rescue, Chrystal asks, "Hey, can I suggest something that all of us will probably like?" With a smile on his face, Tyson quickly responds, "Sure, tell us." Chrystal thinks for a minute, and suggests, "How about, *The Holiday*? Sanaa agrees, "Yeah, I like that movie." Sanaa asks Jordan, "Baby, you cool with that movie?" Jordan says, "Yeah, that's a really funny movie." Tyson replies, "Hey, great selection Chrystal, now let me see if I can find it on the dish." Jordan brings out some chicken wings, dip and chips, and they all settle in and have a good time watching movies. Since all four of them are sitting so close on the sofa, Tyson figures he'll do the old yarn bit so he can put his arm around Chrystal's shoulders, but he almost has a heart attack when his arm accidently brushes gently against Chrystal's hair during his maneuver. However, Chrystal does something unexpected. She moves in closer under Tyson's arm, and keeps looking forward as if nothing happened. At this point, Chrystal can sense Tyson staring at her and can see that his confidence and everything else is rising. After the movie, Jordan comments, I'm going to clean up the kitchen." Sanaa, trying to let Chrystal and Tyson have some privacy, says, "Let me help you with that, baby," Sanaa gets up and goes to help Jordan in the kitchen, leaving Tyson and Chrystal, still hugged up on the couch. Later, after Tyson notices that Jordan and Sanaa have slipped quietly into Jordan's room, Tyson then takes his arm from around Chrystal and looks straight into her eyes, and says, "Chrystal, I'm really glad you came tonight. You don't know how many times I wanted to talk to you, but the timing never really seemed right. I would just look at you, trying to figure out how to approach you. I guess I just didn't want to be rejected by you. Looking at Tyson, smiling, Chrystal, jokingly teases, "Oh really, well you do know that that can still happen if you don't handle me right." Completely caught off guard, surprised, and confused by her response, Tyson mumbles, "Oh, ok." Laughing at Tyson's reaction, Chrystal grabs his arm and says, "Tyson, I'm just playing with you. I know you used to watch me; you watched me a lot, boy." Tyson says, "You did? I mean, you knew?" "Yes, women notice these kinds of things," Chrystal admits. "But most times, you won't know she knows. Tyson, you think I blindly came to your apartment, not knowing you were interested in me. I came because I was interested in you too." Tyson looks at Chrystal, thinking back, "I never saw you looking at me." Chrystal responds, "I know, because you were so business trying to get my attention, and I was so exceedingly good at not paying you any mind. Tyson, when I first felt you staring at me, it was like you were trying to undress me." Tyson interjects quickly "Nah, nah, you got that all wrong, girl." Not letting Tyson off the hook, Chrystal continues, "Tyson, I'm a woman, I know that look. Baby, that day, you had the eye of the tiger.

Your eyes were saying you wanted something, right then and right there. That made me kind of nervous. But, after a while, you started looking at me differently. I liked that. You seemed to be very sincere. I knew all the time you were on the hunt for my attention. I was ok with that. I kind of liked the idea that you wanted me. Although, I thought you would have made your move a lot sooner." Tyson says, "Chrystal, I didn't even think you had a clue I existed." Chrystal wittingly replies, "Like I said, Tyson, women always notice this type of thing. It is up to the hunter to know the prey, and it's up to the prey to know the hunter. Tyson smiles as he absorbs Chrystal's hunter parable; then thinks about it for a minute, sits back in his seat, and comments, "Chrystal, the way you push that parable, I'm confused right now which one of us is actually the prey." Loving what he said, Chrystal smiles and states, "Don't worry about it, baby. You got what you went after, didn't you?" And with an agreeing expression on his face, Tyson says, "I think I did." And he continues, "Chrystal, you cannot imagine the times I thought about you sitting here next to me. I guess what I have for you is a healthy infatuation, and please tell me that didn't turn you off?" Chrystal smiles, looks into Tyson's eyes, and comments, "No, no it didn't. I like your honesty; it's refreshing, and no, I don't consider that a weakness. As far as I'm concerned, you got what you wanted. Now it's up to you to keep it real." Tyson asks, "Chrystal, can I kiss you?" Without saying a word, Chrystal leans forward, and Tyson receives her passionately with a kiss. When their lips part and eyes slowly open, Tyson, tasting the sweet residue from her lips, takes a deep breath and smiles. Chrystal, in turn, smiles back, knowing that it felt good to her too. As she sensually places her hand to Tyson's chest, she suddenly gets excited in noticing the lateness in hour from her watch. Chrystal quickly comments, "Tyson, Sanaa and I have to leave now, but we'll get together again soon." Not wanting Chrystal to leave, Tyson implores, "You have to leave right now?" Chrystal says, "Yes, Sanaa and

I have law schoolwork to do, and it takes a lot of studying, Tyson. We need to get back to the books. If you hand me your phone, I'll put my number in your contacts and we can talk later," Tyson gives her his phone. Chrystal puts her number in his contacts, and hands it back. "Here's my number," she smiles and comments, "I do expect you to use it, ok?" Tyson says, "Believe me, I will call." Then, embarrassed to ask, Tyson inquires, "Um, Chrystal, I'm sorry, but I don't know your last name." Now with a look of surprise and astonishment, Chrystal exclaims, "What? You mean to tell me, after all this time, looking at me, and supposedly wanting me, you didn't even care to find out my last name?" Tyson swallows deeply in his throat, and nervously says, "Well, at the time, just knowing the name Chrystal was plenty enough for me." Chrystal, being totally disarmed, looks at Tyson with a sobering expression and comments, "I got to give it to you, bruh, you came up with that one quick, huh? That was really quick thinking." Tyson replies "Chrystal, I'm not trying to play games. Look, my full name is Tyson Devin James, and I'm glad to finally get with you." Chrystal gawks at Tyson and exclaims, "Boy! I already know your full name," Chrystal pauses, looks at Tyson, and lightheartedly asserts, "Ok, alright, look, if you make fun of my last name, I'm gonna hurt you." Tyson pleads, "I promise I won't do anything like that." With a squinch in her eyes, Chrystal says, "My full name is Chrystal Denise Cleary." Chrystal stares at Tyson, waiting for his response. Tyson smiles and says, "Wow, that's the most beautiful name I've ever heard, and it's Chrystal Cleary that I like you." Chrystal smiles and gives Tyson a flat-handed love tap on his chest, and remarks playfully, "You promised not to poke fun at my name." Tyson leans over and kisses her cheek, and says passionately, "I got what I wanted, and I like every single thing about you. 'You had me at hello.'" Suddenly, Sanaa and Jordan emerge from Jordan's room, and Sanaa suggests, "It's that time, girl; you ready to go?" Looking at Tyson, Chrystal says, "No, but I know we got to study. Tyson,

I'm really feeling you. Thanks for the best first date ever." Tyson responds in kind, "Chrystal, I'm feeling you too, girl. I will be calling you later." With eyebrows raised in amazement, Sanaa stares at Chrystal and exclaims, "Oh? What's going on here?" Chrystal quickly responds, "Let's go, girl; we can talk in the car. Good night, guys." Chrystal is the first out of the door, and Sanaa kisses Jordan before she walks out. Tyson follows the girls to the parking lot and makes sure they're safe, and when Chrystal gets inside the car, she motions, "Come here." Tyson walks to her window, Chrystal leans out, and with her hands cradling his face, she gives Tyson a long French kiss for him to remember the evening. Tyson takes a deep breath, licks his lips, and says, "Y'all be good; see you later." Both girls wave and say bye. Standing in the doorway, Jordan throws Sanaa a kiss, and she responds in kind. Sanaa and Chrystal leave the parking lot and head back to campus. Tyson walks back to the apartment a happy man, and when he gets inside, Jordan inquires, "Well, how did it go?" Tyson gratefully says, "Thanks Jordan. I owe you one, man." Trying to act serious, Jordan comments, "Hell no, my brother, you owe me more than just one; you owe me a lot for putting this thing together." Jordan smiles, "So, I guess you and Chrystal hit it off well?" Tyson responds, "All I can say is that I don't know what tomorrow may bring, but right now, I got what I went after." Jordan says, "Ok," as he nods his head in the affirmative while giving Tyson a high-five. Meanwhile, Sanaa and Chrystal are steadily making their way back to campus. The traffic is exceptionally light, and feeling extraordinarily good, Chrystal decides to just cruise. She appears as if her mind is somewhere else, seemingly satisfied with everything and everyone. Taking note of her intriguingly relaxed roommate, Sanaa asks, "Chrystal, aren't you going to tell me what happened between you and Tyson; inquiring minds want to know." Still looking forward, Chrystal smiles within her thoughts and comments, "That boy didn't even know my last name, then she looks intently at Sanaa, and says,

"But then he more than made up for it by being so honest about how he felt about me; I told him I really liked that. He really had good conversations for me, Sanaa. He was a little shy, but I thought it was so cute to see him all intimidated like that. I realize he was acting that way because he likes me and was trying to impress me." With a look of surprise on her face, Sanaa inquires, "Chrystal, are we talking about the same person? My boyfriend's roommate, Tyson? Shy? I don't think so." Chrystal comes clean and says, "Sanaa, to tell you the truth, I already knew about Tyson. I just never said anything to you about it. I was checking him out at the same time he was checking me out." Sanaa says, "Oh, I see. That explains everything." Chrystal says, "So, you see, tonight was not really a blind date for me. I just saw it as a chance for him to make his long-awaited move. Tonight, we just talked about how good it was being together, and when he kissed me, girl... it felt so good I couldn't stop blushing, until, unfortunately, I looked down at my watch and saw the time. Sanaa, I was not trying to keep you in the dark about anything, I just wanted this to flow innocently, and believe me, it did. I had a great time. Tyson has a little player in him, I realize that, but he's really a nice guy; well, at least that's the way he seemed to me." Sanaa smiles and comments laughingly, "Well, knowing Mr. Nice Guy, I'll bet he'll be calling you before you can get back to the dorm; watch." Chrystal replies, "Alright, Sanaa, leave him alone. My man handled his business tonight." Sanaa smiles, then looks at Chrystal and jokingly suggests, "If you can just drive a little bit faster, maybe you and 'your man' can get to handle a little more business before we get into the law books." After about six minutes driving, Chrystal playfully looks at her watch and sarcastically remarks, "Well, look-a-here, we have arrived, and no call from Tyson yet; how about that? So, tell me, should I be worried? I think not." Conceding the Moment, Sanaa says, "Ok, I hear you. I'll leave your man alone, for now. Over the next two weeks, Sanaa and Chrystal grow closer in their relationships with Tyson and Jordan, double dating quite often.

CHAPTER 7
(LOVE IS NOT FOREVER?)

TWO WEEKS INTO HAVING FUN AND ENJOYING each other's company double dating; Chrystal and Tyson versus Sanaa and Jordan are presently engaged in a grueling tennis match in which they play to a tired and sweaty mess. After which, when the girls head back to the dorm, and Sanaa finally gets to the room, she rushes to use the bathroom, sits down on the commode to finally get some relief, and then her cell phone begins to ring. She thinks to herself, "Now who is this?" She answers the phone, and before she can say the "h", in hello out of her mouth, she hears her Mother, Mrs. Rachel Howard, crying her eyes out, yelling, "Baby, it's over, baby it's over; after all these years, it's over." Sanaa starts crying from hearing her Momma crying, and says, "Momma, calm down. Tell me what's wrong. Momma, tell me what's wrong." Sanaa's Mother exclaims, "Baby, I hate to put this on you like this. I know you're busy with your studies, but I'm so hurt; I need you right now. Sanaa's Mother continues in a trembling voice, "That bastard, your Father, left me for another woman, and I'm so hurt right now, I don't know what to do." Surprised by her Mother's claims, Sanaa shouts, "What? Daddy did what? Momma, this can't be true. Maybe you're overreacting to something that can easily be explained." Her Mother states, "Baby, with all that is within me, I wish that were true. I wish I could wake up from this nightmare and see that it has all been a bad dream. Your Father was caught in the act, Sanaa. I asked hurtful questions about this woman, then I asked him if he loved her. He said he did, and from that point on, everything seemed to move in slow motion. I stood there with a sharp pain in my stomach, feeling like I wanted to throw up. I don't know what enabled me to keep standing because I felt like passing out." Still finding it hard to believe, Sanaa states emphatically, "Momma, there ain't no way Daddy would ever leave you." Her Mother says, "Sanaa, I'm telling you the truth. Your Father would have never come clean if I hadn't cornered him with the truth. I had no clue that he was cheating, but in all relationships, you get this awareness, this feeling that something is wrong. You do your best to try and work through your problems. Lord knows I did what I could. I tried to talk to him about our situation because I wanted to know what was happening to us. He just acted as if what I was perceiving was all in my head and dismissed my instincts as being paranoid. Sanaa, I was not being paranoid, and suspicion got the best of me. So, I tried following him around." Feeling her Mother's pain, Sanaa says, "No, Momma, no." But her Mother continues, "Sanaa, you know me. I'm not that type of woman, but I was driven to do it; but I soon discovered that I wasn't cut out to do that sort of thing. So I went to the extreme and hired a private investigator." Sanaa exclaims, "Momma, you did what?" Her Mom says, "Yes, I got me an investigator, but to his credit, during the consultation, he didn't pull any punches with me. The investigator said that I may not like what he uncovers about my husband. Boy was he ever right. Come to find out, this affair was not recent at all like I had thought. This affair had been going on for months." Painfully crying, Sanaa interrupts, "Momma, please tell me this is not true." "Sanaa, sadly, it is all absolutely true," Rachel answers her daughter. Sanaa's Mother, now incredibly angry, continues, "Baby, on top of all the other things, this man got this woman an apartment, a little hideaway. Sanaa, the investigator found out that the money that was paid for the apartment was being funneled through our businesses, with the help of that frick'n CPA Mark Greenburg, that son of a b***h! Girl, when I finish with both of their a**es, they are going to wish they never met me." Shaking her head in disbelief, Sanaa responds, "Momma I just can't believe this." Her Mom further confides, "Oh, but wait a minute-it gets deeper. The investigator shared with me that the woman your Daddy is seeing is from New Orleans, and he said that the woman's Mother is one of those persons who practices putting roots on people. He said a lot of people don't believe in this kind of stuff, but he says he's seen it before; he says he has actually seen husbands under a spell of witchcraft do the same things my husband is doing. He told me about these powerful evil water spirits in the spiritual world known as marine spirits. Incubus is the male demonic spirit, and Succubus is the female demonic spirit. He said that when a person dreams and he or she has sexual intercourse with one of these evil spirits, wittingly or unwittingly, the demonic spirit establishes a covenant (agreement) with that person, which gives that evil deity permission to attach itself as a soul tie to the person, enabling them to manifest evil into the person's life, causing all sorts of problems in his or her life and relationships, particularly, marriages. The investigator said that I might want to look into that as a possibility for his behavior. So, I looked at that investigator intently. I stared straight into his face, and I asked him, "Do you really expect me to believe in that BS?" Then the investigator stares back at me, and calmly asks, if I believed in God. I said, 'Yeah, I believe there's a God,' Then the investigator says, 'Well, Mrs. Howard, if you believe there's a God, then you must believe there's a devil,' and the investigator just left it at that. Sanaa, you know I don't believe in that hoo-doo mess, but I would rather that be true so I can figure out how to fight, rather than just feeling helpless and angry." Sanaa's Mom pauses for a minute, then shouts, "Nah.

No, to hell with all that voodoo-hoodoo crap; my husband is just a damn-idiot fool." Feeling her Mother's anger, Sanaa pleads, "Momma, calm down. Momma, please calm down!" Her Mother screams back, "Calm down! Sanaa, this fool, your Father, was fronting this b***h, using my money! Using my money! Sanaa, baby, you know me; nobody messes with my money. Now he can have that low life wh**e, but he won't ever have another chance to get his hands on my money." With tears streaming down her face and concerned about what her Mother is plotting to do, Sanaa inquires with a voice of concern, "Momma, what are you planning to do?" Rachel goes silent over the phone a Moment, then pulls herself together and apologizes, "Sanaa, I'm sorry to lay all this at your feet, but I had to talk to somebody. I know you love your Father, but you need to understand, he has to pay for this. I was a good wife. I took good care of my family, and after all these years, don't you think I deserve better than this? Baby, I am not going to do anything crazy, but I got to get me. I'm going to come at his a** with all I got. I'm going to be armed with dates, times, places, pictures, phone records, and even finances. Sanaa, sweetheart, do not stand in my way because it is about to get ugly between me and your Daddy. I'm asking you to stand down because your feelings for your Father may hinder what I need to do. Sanaa, I got to go now, but I will call you back later, ok?" Sanaa then does exactly what Mother had just foreseen; Sanaa tries to mediate the situation, commenting, "Momma, remember what you always used to tell me; you told me, 'don't make important decisions while you're angry.'" Her Mother thinks for a minute, then responds in a tone and manner not to be dismissive, "Sanaa, I'm really hurt and disappointed with your Father, but right now, I'm not out for blood, baby, I'm just coming into the realization that I got to become a real b***h and handle business for me. Now, do not worry about me. I'm ok. I'll call you later tonight." Sanaa, trying to keep her Mother on the phone, loudly pleads, "Momma! Momma! Wait." Then she notices that her Mother has hung up. Now appearing lost in her thoughts, Sanaa starts crying and thinking out loud, "Oh man, oh man, oh man." As Sanaa wipes the tears from her eyes, she hears the phone ring and answers anticipating that it's her Mother; she exclaims, "Momma?" "Nope! not in this lifetime," Jordan replies, "What's going on, baby?" Sanaa is silent over the phone, and not knowing what has just transpired, Jordan eagerly continues in his thinking, "Hey, Sanaa, what did Chrystal say about my boy Tyson?" Sanaa answers with an attitude, "Nothing," followed by an abrupt silence. Jordan now being perplexed, inquires, "She said nothing, nothing at all?" Still harboring an attitude, Sanaa answers sternly, "No, nothing." Jordan's attitude now changes to a concern that something has happened, "Sanaa, what's going on? You ok?" Still reeling from what her Mother just told her, Sanaa does not answer immediately, but then with total emptiness of feeling, she responds, "Nothing, baby." Noticing that something's not right, Jordan asks again, "Sanaa, what's wrong? I can hear it in your voice that something is wrong." Sanaa arrogantly exclaims, "Well, I don't want to bore you, since you're only concerned about Tyson and Chrystal. But my Mother just got off the phone crying, telling me that she caught my Father cheating on her. She is really upset, and I don't know what she's going to do. I'm scared she's going to do something crazy." Trying to think from the outside looking in, Jordan makes a big mistake, commenting, "Sanaa, don't worry, sweetheart; these are grown and intelligent people. I'm sure they can find a way to work through this problem." Sanaa, with a grimace of irritation, screams, "What? What did you say? Did you not hear me? Jordan, did you not hear what the hell I just said? My Father just got caught cheating on my Mother; he has abandoned her, and you're trying to tell me they can work through it?" Jordan is now fairly sure that he probably said the wrong thing, and quickly responds, "Sanaa, I'm sorry. I didn't mean it like that-I mean, the way it came out." Sanaa's attitude turns even nastier,

"Yeah right. Men, you're all dogs, and you probably understand my Father, don't you? All you men do is run to anything that opens their legs for you." In shock from Sanaa's tirade, Jordan exclaims, "Sanaa! You think of me that way? Is that how you see me?" Sanaa responds arrogantly, "You're a man, aren't you?" Trying to calm the situation down, Jordan says, "Sanaa, baby, I can see you're upset." Sanaa quickly shouts, "Oh you damn right I'm upset." Jordan then silently thinks about what to say and do next, and calmly gives in, "Sanaa, I'm sorry if I said something to upset you; maybe we can talk about it later, ok?" Sanaa replies, "Suit yourself. I'll see you when I see you." Jordan, being confused, comments, "Wow, Sanaa, it's like that now? You for real?" Sanaa arrogantly responds, "Jordan, there's one thing that you can always be sure of, I'm always for real." Jordan pauses for a minute, and there's complete silence on both ends of the phone. Jordan then breaks the silence, and concedes, "Alright, baby, I'll talk to you later." Saying nothing in response, Sanaa hangs up and immediately starts crying. Jordan hearing her hang up, looks at his phone, thinking, *What the hell just happened? I don't understand this.* Coming into the living room, Tyson sees Jordan hurtfully brooding and staring vacuously into space, and inquires, "Hey man, everything alright? you look like you just lost your best friend." Trying to hide the hurt he's feeling, Jordan comments, "Nah, man, it ain't nothing like that. It's just I don't understand these females. One minute, they're one way, and another minute, they're the complete opposite." Tyson looks at Jordan, thinking this could be serious, and asks, "Yo, man, what did you do to Sanaa?" Jordan quickly looks up at Tyson, "Why is it that I must have done something to her?" With a skeptical look on his face, Tyson comes back, "Well, you know what they say, once a player, always a player." Jordan shouts, "What? Tyson, you way out in left field on this one, man; you got this all wrong. I didn't do anything to Sanaa, I was just trying to be her boyfriend. I can't share with you our conversation, but Sanaa seriously misinterpreted what I was trying to tell her, and she went off on me." Trying to come up with a reason for the situation, Tyson comments, "Look, man, it could be that time of the month or something like that. I don't know, but I'm about to call Chrystal; you want me to say something or find out what's wrong with Sanaa?" Jordan quickly interjects, "No, no Tyson. Leave it alone, man. I got this." Feeling that Jordan wants to figure things out on his own, Tyson agrees, "Alright player, talk to you later." Tyson walks away, aware of what his friend is going through, but at the same time, he's thinking about his new relationship with Chrystal as he heads toward his room and takes out his phone to call her. Back over at the graduate dorm, Chrystal is coming back into the room from the showers and hears the phone ringing; she picks up and says, "Hello." Tyson answers, "It's just me, baby." Not completely dried off, Chrystal says, "Boy, I just got out the shower, and I'm a little wet." Tyson quickly responds in a sexy manner, "Hey, I can work with that." Chrystal sarcastically replies, "Oh, I bet you could, but let me call you back when I get myself comfortable, ok?" Tyson agrees and comments, "Alright, but I'm going to head out for a minute, I'll be back in a few." Chrystal goes silent over the phone as her mind starts speculating and calculating; she asks, "You do have your phone with you, right?" Tyson comically answers, "Yeah, I'm talking to you, aren't I?" Chrystal sarcastically responds, "Well, be that as it may, I will call you shortly because I don't want you to get too preoccupied." Tyson then inquires, "What do you mean by that, girl?" Being hip to all kinds of game, Chrystal exclaims, "What I mean? What I mean is that I'll be calling you shortly." With a smirk expression on his face, Tyson responds, "Ok, baby, no problem." With her instructions made clear, Chrystal says, "Alright then, bye." Tyson thinks to himself, *Damn, I see what my boy Jordan was talking about. We haven't even been dating for a whole year yet, and already she thinks I'm messing around.* Tyson then thinks introspectively, "Shoot, maybe it's a good thing that she thinks that I'm cheating." After stupidly reasoning his relationship strategy, Tyson packs his gear and heads off to the basketball court to shoot hoops with his boys. About thirty minutes later, just like she said, Chrystal is on the phone calling, but the phone just rings and goes to the answer service. Chrystal calls Tyson's number two more times, with the same results. Tyson has left the phone in his gear bag and could not hear it ring. He is so into the game, talking all kinds of trash, that he forgets that Chrystal reminded him she would be calling. When the game is over, Tyson, trying to catch his breath talking with the fellas and walking slowly toward his bag, abruptly remembers Chrystal, and yells, "Oh, snap! Chrystal." He rushes to his bag to check the phone. Chrystal has called him three times over two hours. All he can do now is just look at his phone and think about what he's going to tell her. He thinks to himself, *I'll just tell her the truth. I don't want to lie to her.* Tyson speed dials Chrystal's number. It rings about three times, and Chrystal is sitting on her bed, looking at the phone, knowing that it's Tyson calling, and she just stares at the phone, letting it ring, thinking to herself, *Should I answer this man?* She answers, "Hello." Tyson says, "Chrystal?" Chrystal answers like a parent ready to chastise a child, "This is she." Tyson takes a deep breath, "Baby, look, I'm sorry, I can see by my phone you called me. Look, I apologize for missing your call; the phone was in my gear bag while I was on the court playing ball, and I lost all sense of time." Tyson goes silent and listens to see if she is still on the line, "Baby? Baby? You there?" Sounding none too happy, Chrystal responds, "Yeah, I'm here." Sensing Chrystal is upset, Tyson says, "Baby, you do believe me, right?" Chrystal sarcastically replies, "Hey, you grown. I don't own you." Tyson comes back, "Chrystal, don't be like that now. I told you the truth. We haven't been together a minute yet, and you think I'm out here cheating on you?" Chrystal immediately becomes shrewdly reserved, "I never mentioned you were cheating on me, so Tyson, are you saying that you haven't known me long enough to cheat on me? Is that what you're saying?" Tyson quickly exclaims, "Nah, girl, look, that came out all wrong. What I meant was, you and I are hitting it off really well, and to me, what we have is real. Well, it's real for me. So, if we both feel the same thing, we don't need anybody else in our lives, right?" Once again, surprised and disarmed by Tyson's blatant honesty, Chrystal remains silent. Tyson, seeking a response, inquires, "Baby, you there?" Not willing to let him off the hook so easily, Chrystal comments, "I'm here. I'm just getting a feel for the person that I'm giving all my time and attention to. Tyson, you know that I do not like being disrespected. I will treat you well, and I give you a piece of me that a lot of guys wish they could have, but only you can have, so don't disrespect me." Feeling a little usurped and disrespected himself, Tyson puts on his big boy pants and says, "Chrystal, what I told you was the truth; are you going trust me or what?" Chrystal shouts, "Hey! trust is earned, Tyson. Right now, though, everything between us is good; we cool. I hope you don't disappoint. Look, Tyson, Sanaa is coming into the room. Call me, and we'll talk later." Glad to get out of this situation, Tyson quickly agrees, "Alright, baby." He waits to let her hang up first. "Wooh," he breathes out, exhaustively relieved. Tyson then takes a towel from his bag, wipes the sweat off his face, and then packs his gear to leave. While driving home, he critically examines his conversation with Chrystal. He thinks to himself that he might have appeared weak to Chrystal. Now grumbling about the situation, the old testosterone starts to rage; he starts talking to himself, mumbling and rambling on, signifying fiercely, "I'm the one wearing the pants in this here relationship, and I don't need to apologize for every damn thing I do. She ain't running nothing here. She must not know who the hell she mess'n with, boyie! Baby girl must have me confused with somebody else, and I'm gonna let her know about this too; you damn right I am!"

CHAPTER 8
(THE TRIP)

THE NEXT DAY, IT LOOKS CLOUDY OUTSIDE, BUT it feels cool. Still feeling bewildered and overwhelmed by his phone call with Sanaa, Jordan has waited a day before calling her, thinking he would let her cool off a little. When Jordan finally calls, Sanaa does not answer the phone. He gets in his car and drives to campus, and then goes to her dorm, but he soon discovers that she has gone home early for the weekend. Jordan feels robbed of a chance to explain to Sanaa that he was just trying to comfort her. But then he reasons that her going home is no reason for her not answering her phone. Jordan thinks to himself, *she knows it's me calling*. He continues thinking, *maybe she does not want anything to do with me anymore. I cannot believe this is happening, but if that's what it is, that's what it is. Law school chicks-I should have known.* Over in Raven and Daedai's room, Raven is hanging up her phone and says, "Daedai, I'm going out for a little while." Daedai says, "You want me to come with you?" Raven replies, "No, I'm meeting up with a friend." Daedai comments, "Ok, I don't have to tell you to be careful, right?" Raven calms Daedai's apprehension, "Daedai, it's not like that. I'm just chillin. I'll see you later." About fifteen minutes after Raven has gone, Daedai's phone rings, "Hello." A man's voice says, "Daedai, it's me, Toby. I've been trying to call Raven all day, but she isn't answering; is she there?" Daedai says, "Toby, she's not here right now. You want me to tell her you called?" Toby answers, "Would you, please? Thank you, Daedai." Daedai replies, "I'll make sure she knows you called. Take care, bye." After they hang up, Daedai thinks to herself, *I wonder who Raven is with? She must have kicked my boy Toby to the curb. I wonder what is up with that.* The following day, its late Friday afternoon, and Jordan and Tyson are in Jordan's car, making their way to see what's happening on campus. Tyson has plans to go see Chrystal and probably take her to the movies. Jordan, on the other hand, plans to just hang out on campus, checking out what's on the quad. When they get to campus, Tyson goes his way, and Jordan walks to the quad; he takes a seat, and to his surprise, nothing is going on. Seeing that nobody is doing anything on campus, he reminisces about all the good times he used to have at his undergraduate school; he thinks about the fun, sun, sultry blue water, and the pure white sand on the world's most famous beach in Daytona. So he has a thought; he figures it's a good time for a road trip to his alma mater. He thinks to himself, *yeah, it's time to visit that sacred land known as Bethune-Cookman University. I can check out the band, my frat brothers, and the campus scene.* Thinking about all the good times he had in undergrad, he's now more motivated to go. So he thinks out loud, *I'm going, even if I have to go by myself.* So, Jordan starts briskly walking toward his car so he can go to his apartment and pack for the trip, and as he's walking, Jordan hears a voice from behind calling out his name. He turns around and sees Sheila Morgan, a young lady who has been trying to get with him for a long time. Sheila is this fine-looking girl from Atlanta, Georgia, who has the most beautiful butterscotch skin you have ever seen, but to Jordan, she's not Sanaa. But, feeling that Sanaa has all but dumped him, he stops and talks to Sheila. Sheila is a free-spirited, on the wild side kind-of young lady. But right now, Jordan could care less about that. Sheila says, "Hey Jordan, what are you up to? And where's that girl I always see you with?" Jordan, now thinking like a man with no boundaries, answers, "She's not happening right now." Jordan inquires, "Where you off to, Sheila?" "Nowhere," she says. "I just came from the student union to see what was happening on the yard, but there's nobody doing anything. I noticed you walking like you were in deep thought about something, so I called out." Jordan nods his head, "Yeah, I was just in thought about going up to BCU since there's nothing happening around here." Sheila gets all excited, "Oh yeah, you're going up to BCU? I have a cousin that graduated from Bethune." Jordan says, "Bethune is my undergraduate school. I'm taking a little trip up there to change the pace." Jordan thinks for a minute and daringly inquires, "You wanna roll with me?" Sheila looks at Jordan for a minute, "What about your girl?" Jordan answers in a guarded yet self-assured tone, "Sheila, that ain't happening right now. Do you want to go?" Sheila smiles at Jordan, and after taking a deep breath, agrees, "Yeah, I'll go, but I need to pack a few things and let my room-mate know where I'm going, ok?" Jordan nods his head, "That's cool. I got to go to my apartment and pick up a few things myself and I'll come back to pick you up. Better yet, in about half an hour, meet me in the dorm parking lot." Sheila moves toward Jordan and places her hand on his chest in a flirtatious manner, and says, "I'll be waiting when you get here." Jordan nods his head, "Ok, I'll be right back." On his way to the apartment, Jordan hears his phone ring. He picks up, and it's Tyson. "Hey man where you at?" Jordan says, "I'm on the way to the apartment." Tyson curiously inquires, "I thought you were gonna hold it down on campus." Jordan replies, "Nah, man, change of plans." Jordan hears laughter in the background on Tyson's phone, "Where you at, man?" Tyson says, "I am at the movies with Chrystal, getting spoiled, dude." Jordan says, "Hey, have a good time, man. Oh, hey look, Tyson, Chrystal's gotta bring you home because I'm heading out. I'm riding up to BCU." Tyson hears this, gets upset, and exclaims, "What? Damn, man, you're going up to Daytona Beach, and you didn't tell me?" Jordan, on the defensive, explains, "Tyson, it was a last-minute thing, man." Somewhat disappointed, Tyson replies, "Nah man, you wrong for that, but that's ok. I got my hands full right here, and I can think of a few things to keep me occupied." Jordan says, "Yeah, I hear you thinking man; you're thinking you and Chrystal can have the apartment all to yourselves for a couple of days, right?" Tyson flashes a big smile, "Yo, man, this will give me and Chrystal some quality time together." Jordan laughs, "Quality time, huh? Well, be nice, man; my match-making reputation is still on the line. See you later." Jordan hangs up, collects his things for the trip, and heads out to meet Sheila. Meanwhile, back in New York, After having major problems with her flight, Sanaa has finally arrived home, but forgot and left her key at school, and is knocking on her Mother's door. When her Mom opens the door, Sanaa drops her bags and rushes to hug her Mother. They embrace for about thirty seconds, all the while her Mother is holding back tears, attempting to mask the pain and reassure her daughter, "Sanaa, it's okay, baby; your Momma's okay." After they finish embracing, Sanaa's Mother looks at her, giving that once-over parent inspection, then gently wipes the tears from her daughter's eyes, "Baby, let me help you with those bags." Her Mother reaches down and takes her bags, then heads into the house. Sanaa walks behind her Mom, immediately remembering all the good memories she had in the room. Looking around, she is overwhelmed with mixed emotions. Caught between the memory of a happy unified family and that of a selfish Father's act of adultery threatening to destroy it. Just thinking about it brings tears to Sanaa's eyes, and angrily asks, "Momma, what is Daddy doing? Why is he treating us like this?" With a comforting calmness, her Mother clarifies, "Sanaa, this isn't about you. It may be of concern to you, but it's about your Father and I. Do not misunderstand, even with all this craziness; your Father loves you very much. Baby, sometimes people just drift apart." With a perplexed and agitated expression, Sanaa asks, "Momma, when in the hell did this drift happen?" After a deep breath, Sanaa's Mother explains, "It hasn't been great between your Father and I for quite some time, but I had no idea it would push him to find someone else. I always thought that your Dad and I could always at least talk things out." Sanaa's Mother pauses in silence and says, "Right now, I have gotten over the initial shock and awe of everything, and I think I've moved on. It's not an easy thing to get someone you love out of your system, and I guess what they say is true: time does heal all wounds; it's just that it doesn't take that long for me to heal. I think, for me, it's a matter of self-preservation. Like I told you over the phone, it's time for me to be and act free, and right now, I think I like that feeling." Sanaa stares at her Mother, bewildered at what she is saying, and marvels at how quickly her Mom has gotten over her Father. She says, "Momma, I'm glad you're not hurting as much anymore, but Momma, I still have some choice words for my Daddy. I'm extremely upset with his cheating white a**. He broke up our family. My family is my strength and support. My foundation, Momma; I feel empty inside, really empty. This break-up is affecting me deeply, Momma. I even jumped all over my boyfriend the other day because he got caught up in his words trying to encourage me. So, what do I do now, Momma?" Sanaa's Mother calmly replies, "Sanaa, as I told you, your Father's and my mess does not concern you, even though it affects you. What you need to do is continue in your studies and be the best lawyer you can be. Now you apologize to that young man at your school whose feelings you hurt; he was just trying to help you. Sanaa, do good things with your life, and do not worry about me. I'm going to be alright. I think you should talk to your Father and hear his side. You only get one Momma and one Daddy, girl, so you have to take us as we are, and love us in spite of our imperfections." Sanaa looks at her Mother and says, "I love you, Momma." Her Mother responds in kind, "I love you too, baby." Relieved that her Mother is not grieving, Sanaa says, "Momma, I'm going to try and talk to Daddy, but what he did to us was wrong; it was wrong, and it's hard for me to get past that. I'm going to call him later and see if he can meet me somewhere to do lunch because if I go over there where he lives and that b***h is there, it's going to be trouble." Sanaa's Mother quickly interjects, "Sanaa, come on now, remember what I told you. This is my problem, not yours, ok?" With her head down and eyes evading contact, Sanaa half-heartedly agrees, "I got it, Momma. I got it."

Back in Florida, Jordan is heading toward campus with nothing on his mind but the road trip; he's all into the idea of heading out of town, and for right now, he's forgotten all about his situation with Sanaa. After a few minutes of driving, Jordan turns into the dorm's parking lot, and sees Sheila waiting. Sheila has on her low-cut jeans, revealing every curve on her body, and added to that, she has on this pink half-shirt to show off her fit abs and stomach. Jordan drives up and can't help but stare, and comments, "Damn, Sheila, you fine as hell, girl; you ready to go?" All hyped up for the trip, Sheila says, "Let's go." Jordan opens the door for Sheila to get in, then grabs her bags and puts them on the back seat along with his. They ride out of the parking lot to US-95, and Sheila looks at Jordan and asks, "Where are we going to stay when we get to Daytona?" Jordan looks over at Sheila, "I got this. I'm gonna get us a hotel room on the beach." Looking down at her newly polished toes, Sheila nods her head with a smile and says, "Let's go do this." As they ride, Sheila immediately starts thumbing through Jordan's CDs and asks, what kind of music are you gonna jam for us?" Jordan says, "Check this out." Jordan puts on some of his funky jazz soul music, and to his surprise, Sheila loves it. Sheila starts dancing in her seat, and they both have a good time jamming to the music. Sheila then looks at Jordan, "You made this CD?" Jordan says, "Yeah, I made it for when I go on road trips." Bouncing and dancing to the music, Sheila comments, "I love this music." After a few minutes of intense jamming, the playlist breaks down to a slow and sultry jazz fusion. Listening and loving the change in the mood, Sheila relaxes back in her seat and stares at Jordan with that kind of look, and he notices her staring and says, "What?" And then smiling with a sort of serenity in her expression, Sheila whispers softly, "Nothing, baby. I'm just enjoying myself." Sheila then puts her hand on the back of Jordan's head and briefly massages the back of his neck, and states, "I needed this, Jordan. I really needed this." Sheila then leans over toward her door, resting her arms over the open window, and with her head slightly outside, she enjoys the cool breeze of the evening gently stroking her hair and face, as they ride US-95. Three hours later, back in New York, with phone in hand, Sanaa is debating what to say to her Father; practicing in the mirror how she's going to give him a piece of her mind, but then changes her intentions after remembering what her Mother told her earlier. Sanaa finally sobers in her thoughts and calls her Father's number, and when he answers, she hesitates to speak, and she immediately feels uncomfortable speaking with her own Father-the man who has loved and cared for her and been at the center of her well-being her entire life, but now, she feels as if she doesn't even know him. After her Father repeats hello for the third time, he then pleads, "Sanaa! Sanaa! Speak to me. I know it's you." Sanaa hangs up the phone, confronting all that she is feeling inside, and thinks to herself, *how do I do this? I better not talk to him while I'm angry. I'll call him tomorrow.* Back on Highway I-95, after hours of driving, Jordan and Sheila need a break. They drive into a rest area and make a quick pit stop, grab a bite to eat, and are back on the road. Feeling well-rested, Sheila asks, "Jordan, you want me to drive the rest of the way?" Jordan replies, "No, baby. I got this. I've traveled this road plenty of times during my undergrad days. Just relax. I'm wide awake. We'll be there soon." Sheila comments, "Alright, captain, you got it." After another hour or two, Jordan and Sheila reach Daytona Beach. They cannot help but stare at the massive Daytona 500 International Speedway, and Jordan starts telling Sheila about the time when he was a band member at Bethune, and the band did a half-time show inside the racing facility. He shares with her how the race-track area was so steep that it is was hard to walk down to the middle part of the field where they were to perform. Jordan remembers, "It was like going down a very steep hill; we had to lean backward to keep from falling forward until we got to midfield, where it flattened out, but the people really liked our show. It was surprising that they loved our show, seeing as how our music was so culturally different from our audience. We jammed though, danced our butts off, and they liked it." Jordan says, "Marching in the band was like a generational thing for me. My Father marched in the band when they were called the Marching Men of Cookman. If you think the Marching Wildcats are great, you should have seen the Marching Men under the direction of Mr. Samuel C. Berry; they set the foundational standard for the Marching Wildcats that you see today. The Marching Men of Cookman had to compete extremely hard in those days because they were small in number. They would come to band camp and work out like they were in the military. My pops says in those days, they had to even pledge the band, and they practiced whole notes constantly to develop their sound and tone so that when they took to the field against a power house band, such as a Florida A & M University, they could produce a bigger sound to compete. And Pops said the Marching Men brought it hard every game. The method behind their greatness was the same as it is now: paying strict attention to detail. My pops used to say that Red Dog, that was Mr. Berry's nickname because he was red in complexion and was an Omega Psi Phi man. Pops said that Mr. Berry was such a strict perfectionist that in explaining to the band how precise he wanted them to perform, he would often say to them, "When one person spits in a spot, he wants everybody to spit in that same spot," meaning that their movements with their hands, arms, instruments, and hats all had to be synchronized to do the same thing at the same time. That is what made the Marching Men so unique: the detail. Pops says they would practice with just their hats and gloves sometimes just so Mr. Berry could see their head and hand positions / movements. Everybody had to do every routine exactly the same way, and Pops says that the band was so physically fit they could march a whole parade pointing and driving, making nineties all the way and not break a sweat, and at the end of the parades, looking at the high school bands that participated, he said they would be dripping sweat and exhausted. The Marching Men, in Pop's days, did what you call the fast march. It was something like the scramble that the Florida A & M band does, but it was technically more precise and pretty.

"To perform at such a high energy level as fast marching, you had to be in great shape, which called for many days of running laps, 100-yard point and drive drills, calisthenics, push-ups, and stomach crunches, or else you could pass out in rehearsal. After the Marching Men's physical conditioning at band camp, they could literally march five consecutive parades and still be able to perform a perfect half-time show. Also, Pops used to brag all the time about how great the tuba section used to perform, and would reminisce about all the acrobatic things the guys used to do with those white tubas." Sheila curiously asks, "Did your Father play the tuba?" Jordan says, "Nah, my pops was trombone section leader of the great dirty dozen." Sheila smiles, "The dirty dozen." Jordan explains, "Yeah, all I can say from what Pops told me is that the guys in the band during those days were really hard characters, real hard guys. As a matter of fact, the whole band was made up of hard men. You worked hard, pledged hard, marched hard, and you 'played' hard. Red Dog didn't want women in the band because the pace was so intense; he felt that they couldn't keep up with the demands of the performance. Also, there was that problem once a month for which Red dog did not have any patience. The Marching Men of Cookman was just that, marching men. However, in the years to come, and during my years, the girls coming into the marching band, including the Arista-cats and the Fourteen Karat Gold dancers, would tear down those stereotypes. Pops used to say back then the Marching Men were really something to behold when they took the field. People just don't know that back in those days, Kaboobi and his guys in the tuba section were the inventors of all this show-dogging you see nowadays with tuba sections. They would do acrobatic things like twirls, flips, and splits with those tubas that had never been done before. You would have to have seen it to believe it." Listening to Jordan very intently, Sheila comments, "Wow, I can hear from the way you talk you loved the band." Jordan nods his head, "Yeah, Bethune-Cookman is very special to me and my pops." Sheila points, saying, "Well, judging by the marque and the buildings outside, you are now back home, my friend." Looking around at everything, Jordan takes a deep breath, "Yep, we're now entering sacred ground. We'll come back later and walk around. Let's head to the beach, get a room, and then come back, if that's alright with you?" Liking the idea of getting settled, Sheila comments, "That works for me. I'm anxious to get to the room and take a shower, change clothes, then go out for something to eat." Jordan agrees, "That sounds like a plan," and Jordan and Sheila head to the beach.

CHAPTER 9
(SURPRISE, SURPRISE, SURPRISE)

BACK ON CAMPUS IN FORT LAUDERDALE, DAEDAI and Raven are talking, and Daedai asks, "Raven, what's going on with you and Toby?" Raven nonchalantly replies, "Nothing. I'm just into someone else right now." Being surprised about this new person Raven is seeing, Daedai inquires, "Do I know him?" Raven stares at Daedai, not saying a word. Waiting for a response, Daedai looks at Raven with wrinkled brows and asks again, "Raven, do I know him?" Raven bends her head down in deep thought, trying to figure what to say, and confesses, "Know her. No, I don't think you know her." Daedai's facial expression turns to one of shock and disbelief as she stares intently at Raven and comments sadly, "I didn't know you went out like that." Raven admits in a soft tone, "I didn't either; it just happened." Frustrated, angry, and upset, Daedai comes back, "Raven, who the hell you think you talking to? Boo-boo the mo**er f***ing fool? This thing ain't just happened. When did you discover you were a fr**k'n lesbian?" Raven struggles to clarify, "Daedai, it was something that just happened, and right now, I just enjoy her company; we just clicked. I'm not sure if I'm fully a lesbian. I guess I'm bi. I still like guys. I guess what I am doing is experimenting. I even feel uncomfortable talking about this Daedai." Still angry, but highly curious, Daedai sarcastically inquires, "Ok then, does your new friend have a name?" Raven says, "Her name is Courtney, Daedai." Daedai inquires further, "Well, what did you tell Toby? Does he know?" Raven says, "No, he doesn't know about Courtney; all he knows is that I'm seeing someone else, and he didn't take that too well either, but that's where I am, Daedai. I hope this doesn't change anything between us." With a tortured expression on her face, Daedai replies, "No, Raven, that doesn't change our friendship, but you're a lesbian now, what the f**k do we have in common?" Afraid of losing her friend, Raven pleads, "Daedai, don't be like that. I'm just experimenting; it ain't nothing serious. I just need a break from men." Daedai shouts, "A break from men? Yeah right." Daedai hangs her head and goes silent, then she lays back on her bed and stares up at the ceiling, trying to digest this new revelation in Raven's sexual orientation. Tears begin to roll down both corners of Daedai's eyes because she feels she's lost her best friend. Suddenly, Daedai sits up and looks into Raven's eyes with an overwhelming expression of hurt, and being too embarrassed to make eye contact, Raven hangs her head in distress as Daedai rushes out of the room. Knowing that her friend is upset, Raven curls up into a fetal position, hugging her pillow with various issues clouding her thoughts, and being inundated with emotions, she eventually falls asleep. Two and a half hours later, there is a sudden and loud knocking on the door. Surprised and shaken by the loud knocking, Raven awakens, hearing someone calling, "Raven, Raven. Open up. Come to the door." Raven quickly gets out of bed and rushes to the door, and sees it's her neighbor, Teri. Raven worriedly asks, "What's wrong, Teri?" As Teri quickly steps inside the room, she shouts, "Raven, Daedai is plastered drunk, sitting on the grass outside of the Rock Bottom Lounge, crying and talking to herself. I think I heard somebody say she got into a fight and beat a girl bad. Come on, Raven, let's hurry up and get her to the room before campus security finds out what's going on and reports her." Deeply concerned, Raven comments, "Let me put on my shoes; go ahead, I'm coming." Raven catches up with Teri, and they both streak through the hall and down the stairs, headed to the Rock Bottom Lounge. They start out walking fast, and then fully running, trying to get to Daedai before the campus police. When they finally reach the Rock Bottom Lounge, they go around back and see Daedai on the ground, drunk, crying, shaking her head, and repeating over and over again, "I beat that b***h's ass. I beat that b***h's ass." Out of breath from running, Raven screams, "Daedai! What's wrong with you?" Daedai looks up at Raven through diluted and swollen eyes and comments, "What the f**k you care, lesbo? All I know is I kicked that b***h's ass. Sheeee won't... she won't put her hands on me no more." Teri looks around to see who's watching, and forcefully instructs, "Daedai! Get up; let's go before you get in trouble." Teri's voice is so forceful it shocks Daedai. Daedai stops talking for a minute, looks up at Teri, squinching to focus her eyes, and says in a drunken stupor, "You want some of this girl, I'll bust you up too," and Daedai starts crying." Before Daedai can pass out, Raven and Teri grab her arms and lift her up. Daedai's appearance is that of someone who has been in a serious fight. A student standing nearby says, "The girl she was fighting was put in a car and taken to the hospital by her friends; she had cuts, bruises, and hurt feelings, but nothing really serious. But make no mistake about it, Daedai kicked her butt." As Raven and Teri walk with a staggering Daedai back to the dorm, Raven notices a mouse starting to form under Daedai's right eye. Raven says, "Teri, when we get to the room, go to the ice machine and get ice so I can treat the swelling on this woman's face." However, before they can get to the back entrance of the dorm, Daedai starts throwing up on the grass. Teri and Raven watch until she finishes, and again they grab and hold her steady as they pro-ceed slowly to the dorm's back entrance. When they finally get Daedai up the stairs and into the room, they lightly place her on the bed. Raven removes Daedai's puked-on clothing, and

Teri rushes to the ice machine to get ice. When Teri gets back to the room, Raven comments, "She's out for the count, girl. I'll have to deal with her swelling tomorrow." Teri agrees and then curiously asks, "What was this lesbo shade Daedai was throwing at you?" Caught off guard by the question, Raven evades looking at Teri, but replies, "Child, Daedai is just drunk, talking nonsense." Still confused by what Daedai said, Teri shrugs her shoulders and accepts Raven's explanation, "Alright, then, I'll just leave the ice over here. I'm going back to my room; see you in the morning." Raven says, "Thanks Teri, good looking out; see you tomorrow." Teri leaves, and Raven is now feeling bad, thinking that Daedai acting out is partly her fault. Raven turns and looks at Daedai, who is knocked out on the bed, and shakes her head with disappointment as to Daedai's lack of understanding, then covers her with a blanket and goes back to bed.

CHAPTER 10
(DECISIONS, DECISIONS)

BACK IN DAYTONA BEACH, JORDAN AND SHEILA
are traveling down the beachside strip, and when they stop for
a red light, Jordan notices across the street to his left a hotel
where he and his frat brothers use to party, and he points it
out to Sheila, "Hey, let's get a room over there." Sheila looks
at the hotel, "Yeah, that looks nice." Jordan and Sheila drive
into the hotel, bypassing the bellhop, and immediately goes
in and get a double bedroom. Wanting to get up to the room
right away, Sheila takes the stairs rather than waiting for the
elevator. Jordan gets all their stuff out of the car and struggles
with everything to the hotel lobby. Jordan takes an exhausted
breath and then takes the elevator up to the room. When he
opens the door, he hears water running in the bathroom. The
bathroom door is left ajar, and looking through the bathroom
mirror, he can see the silhouette of Sheila's naked body in the
shower. Jordan pauses a minute and thinks to himself. *Is this
what I really want to do?* He reasons with himself that he is
still in love with Sanaa. But also thinking at the same time, *she
did kick me to the curb, and Sheila is fine as all outdoors*. Jordan
whispers under his voice, "This is going to be difficult. I can see
that now." Then Sheila comes out of the bathroom with a
towel wrapped around her body, exposing just enough to playfully tease Jordan, and he cannot help but look. Sheila then

takes the towel from around her body to dry her hair, intentionally exposing herself, which makes Jordan go crazy. Jordan swallows deeply in his throat and gets up, acting like he's not affected by Sheila's gorgeous physique, and he mutters, "Oh, boy, uh, yeah, let me go take a shower myself." Jordan quickly goes into the bathroom and closes the door. Thoroughly excited, he starts breathing hard, undresses, turns on the shower, and then steps under the cold water to calm himself down. Jordan thinks to himself, *Oh, my God, she is so fine. I must really love Sanaa a whole lot. This is definitely not like me because right about now I should have been bouncing up and down all up in Sheila. Sheila wants to be with me. I know this, but I am not sure if I can do this. Sanaa must have something working on me. I don't know what this is. I guess I'll just take Sheila to dinner, go visit the campus, and see what happens after that.* After taking his shower and calming himself down, Jordan comes out of the bathroom and has a towel wrapped around his waist. Sheila immediately sits up on the bed, and seeing Jordan's well-defined physique, gives Jordan that look, but he does not respond or make eye contact. Jordan then turns his back to Sheila and puts on his underwear underneath the towel, quickly throwing off the towel to put on his pants. Sheila, with an awkward look, stares at Jordan, feeling somewhat rejected, and questions in her mind whether anything is happening between him and her. Speaking in a calm tone, Sheila asks, "Jordan, is everything ok? You feel funny being with me? Is this about Sanaa?" Jordan looks at Sheila in a most humbling manner, and explains, "Sheila, I don't know what's wrong with me; maybe it is Sanaa. I don't know. I think I got a lot of unresolved issues with that situation. Can you understand?" Sheila nods her head and says, "I respect you being honest with me. Hey, ain't no pressure. Let's go get something to eat, visit the campus, and have a good time; that's what we're here for, right?" Somewhat relieved by Sheila's response, Jordan stares at Sheila, and seeing the sincerity in her eyes, smiles and agrees, "Let's do this." Sheila and Jordan get them-selves together and head out to eat. They find a nice seafood restaurant on the strip and pig out. With a full stomach, they head to the campus. When they arrive on campus, Jordan notices that a lot has changed in such a short time as he admires the growth of the school. Jordan says, "Campus life is so good for students these days. My pops would often com-ment that when he went to school here, the football team, baseball team, basketball team, and the band all lived in one dorm: Cookman Hall. Some of the living arrangements would have three or four guys in a small room. But he said they would have a ball, and there was always something going on at Cookman Hall. One day, the old man had me rolling on the floor laughing when he was telling me about the time his roommate and frat brother Fredrick Reed and Reed's Jacksonville home-boy Herman would get into craziness. He says, as homeboys from the same high school, these two were always pulling pranks on each other, and Reed was the ulti-mate comic. He could come up with stuff that was totally unique and off the wall funny as hell. Pops, in reminiscing an old incident, says he was just sitting in the room one day, minding his own business, when Reed and Herman came in the room arguing about something, and from the look on Herman's face, and knowing how Reed can tear a person down, something was said that was insulting to Herman. Reed went to his bed and sat down; his bed was about two beds down from my pops' bed, and Herman, still standing, is brooding and upset about what was said, so he calmly walks over to the tiny room closet, grabs a big box of detergent, comes back, stands in front of Reed, and dumps the entire box of detergent over his head. Reed just sits there, surprised and draped in blue detergent. Reed then stares at Herman and nods his head with an expression on his face, as if to say, "ok, ok, I can top that." Then in a kind of slow motion, Reed turns as he's clearing the detergent out of his eyes and looks at my pops with the blue detergent draped all over him. Pops says he has now fallen off his bed and is on the floor laughing his butt off and can't stand up. Herman, meanwhile, is now casually sitting on his bed near the door, staring at Reed, as if saying, "your move." Reed then calmly stands up with the detergent streaming off his body like blue snow rolling down a mountain top and walks decisively over to his trunk. He opens it and pulls out this big-ass, gigantic plastic tube of Johnson & Johnson baby powder. He then surgically opens the container and walks over to Herman, who is still sitting on his bed. Reed then ever so calmly and ceremoniously pours and empties the entire tube of baby powder on top of Herman's head. Herman is now looking like the vaudeville singer Al Jolson, but in the white face, about to perform the music from my dear old "Mammy." Then Herman takes a repulsed deep breath and just sits there as if also saying to himself, "alright, ok; I can top that." Pops says what they were doing was so surreal, the way that it was happening, and at this point, my pop is still on the floor cramping in pain and about to throw up from laughing so hard. Pops says this went on back and forth for about twenty minutes, and it even spilled out into the hallways, and now everybody on Cookman Hall's first floor, mostly band members, were cheering and laughing. Pops says he saw band members rushing past the room door laughing as they were watching Herman and Reed act up. My pops said he was cramped up in his stomach so hard that he couldn't stand up and had to crawl to the doorway to see what everybody was laughing at. After a while, Herman did eventually give up, and they stopped without anybody fighting. They brought their butts back to the room, soaking wet, with every piece of trash or debris that was in Cookman Hall hanging off of their bodies. Pops says he was through; he could not stop laughing, and these two sick individuals in need of some serious counseling coming back in the room, had the nerve and unmitigated gall to look at him sideways like he was crazy. My pops would smile thinking back on those days, commenting,

"We did some crazy things, and this was just one of a million crazy things that happened in the notorious and infamous Cookman Hall." Pops told me that the band members had some of the greatest times. "My greatest memories" Jordan says, "was when a lot of us, after drinking or whatever, would get together in somebody's room, and attempt to get philosophical about religion / politics and things of that nature; we didn't have a clue in hell what we were talking about. We knew absolutely nothing about anything of substance, but I guess hearing ourselves talk and expressing an opinion was therapeutic because, for some reason, we enjoyed it." As Jordan looks around and takes note of all the new buildings on campus, he remarks, "This school has grown so much, which can only be attributed to the blessings of a higher power." As Jordan and Sheila continue walking through campus, they walk past several fraternity and sorority plots. Jordan then tells Sheila about his fraternity, Alpha Phi Alpha. He tells her how the brothers in the fraternity and William J. Briggs, a soon to be frat brother and roommate of his Fathers, would change his pops' thinking about himself, making him aware that he was somebody special and that he was in the company of a group of young men going somewhere. Jordan states further, "I also had that same experience because from the time I became an Alpha, man, I knew I was in the company of brothers who, by their very attitude, academics, and belief in God, would transcend the norm." Jordan, now with a tortured expression on his face, turns and looks at Sheila and says, "There is one thing nowadays I don't understand, though. My Father is no longer active in the fraternity, nor does he get excited about it as he used to. I asked him why, and he looked at me intently, and instructed, 'Son, always put God first; never make covenants, agreements, pledges, or bow ritualistically at any altar to worship anything except at the altar of God. Never give life or light to the spirit of anything except to worship the light and life of the Spirit of God within you; or to give animation to any graven image, symbol, or idol; for God is a jealous God, and you shall not wittingly or unwittingly put anyone or anything before Him. Everything you will ever need is in the Word of God. Always put God first; you understand me, son?'" Jordan looks at Sheila and says, "I didn't know what the hell he was talking about, but he said to me, 'Just keep reading the statutes of God, and pray that God will open your spiritual eyes.' I just say, 'Ok, Pops. I'll do that.'" As Sheila and Jordan continue walking toward the band area, Jordan feels an even greater sense of pride, knowing that he was once a member of the greatest band ever. Jordan smiles and reminisces again about his pops, who was a member of the Marching Men of Cookman, along with some of his other band brothers, like: Dr. James Poitier, Dr. Hiram Powell, Dr. Carl Sims, Fred Reed, Wm. Zachary, Sam, Kabobi, Popa Joe, Herman, Larry Handfield, Willie Barber, Fortune Bell, Bryant, Philly Dog, Frasier, Jimmy "Coyote Fart" Murry, "Puny Demon," Andre, Sweet Pete, Clyde, Dr. Ronald Carter, Jay-rue, Skin Daddy, James Brooks, OB, Clarence, Mike, Florida Flute, Frig, and the rest of the dirty dozen trombones, and all others; each one a part of the history and fabric that makes the band so great today. Jordan states proudly, "Dr. Donovan Wells, Dr. Poitier, and the other assistants have kept up the tradition, and have made the band even greater than ever. However, there is one man, Samuel C. Berry, Red Dog, the band's director back in the day, that created the band's character and laid the foundation." Jordan recalls, "Mr. Berry was before my time, but I can remember seeing the respect in my pops' eyes when he talked about the band and Mr. Berry. My pops gives Mr. Berry credit for growing him up and changing his perspective on life. The wisdom imparted was not only for my pops, but for all the guys in the band. He was like our Father figure away from home, along with school presidents such as Dr. Richard V. Moore and Dr. Oswald P. Bronson. Pops used to say that the secret to the band's success was that Mr. Berry was always meticulously detailed about everything, on and off the field.

Mr. Berry would always tell them as young men, they must have discipline, and they need to learn to listen; practice listening. He would often say, 'Even the wine-o on the streets can sometimes tell you something useful.' In other words, never judge a book by its cover. Every time Mr. Berry came to the podium, you could always count on either a good tongue lashing or some needed words of wisdom to live by. Mr. Berry and his assistant Mr. Vincent L. Smith III consistently made them aware of the importance of having a professional attitude and appearance. It was always about being competitively prepared. My pops admired Mr. Berry." With an expression of reverence, Jordan admits, "I miss being in the band; we had so much fun. Interjecting to break up all the nostalgia, Shelia says, "I remember passing through Bethune's campus with my cousin many times on the way to the football stadium, but this is the first time I've had a guided tour; thank you, Jordan. I enjoyed hearing about the genesis of the Marching Wildcats, and I think, for sure, Ms. Bethune had to be an extraordinarily awesome and audacious lady." Jordan agrees and states, "She started this school with a little bit of nothing; but with prayer, some pocket change, and an audacious faith, look at this University now. I guess her prayers and the little bit of money she had, mixed with head, heart, and hand was enough seed to consecrate what is known as our sacred land. Shelia smiles, looks at Jordan, and inquires, "What do you mean 'sacred land'?" Jokingly, Sheila suggests, "It's just a school; what's so sacred about it?" Jordan then looks at Sheila intently and replies cynically, "I can understand you don't get it, and I really can't explain it; you would have to have gone to school here to understand, and even with that, you won't get it until you've graduated and reminisced back in the day. For me, this was the greatest time of my life, with the greatest people I could ever know. It's strange because Pops used to say the same thing. He told me that his graduating class, after the ceremony of lights, went out into the middle of the yard, and for about two hours, sang "Jesus the light of the world." He said that evening as they held hands singing, something spiritual came over each and every one of the graduates. It was so powerful; they could not stop singing. Pops said that it was something he will never forget. At the time, I did not understand what he was talking about until I went to school here. Bethune-Cookman is something special, something blessed. I hope these students and administrators understand the sacrifice it took to make this school what it is, and continue in the heritage and character, which is distinctively Bethune-Cookman. Jordan catches himself rambling on and says, "Hey, enough reminiscing; let's go to the beach, get a few drinks, hang out, and enjoy the day." Shelia responds playfully, "Now that's the second-best plan of the day." Sheila smiles and says, "Let's go, Wildcat."

Back in New York, Sanaa tells her Mother that she made the call to her Father but could not speak and hung up. Her Mother advises, "While you are here, Sanaa, you might as well try to talk to your Father face to face and clear the air, no matter what your Dad's and my problems are; he's still your Father, and you only get one, so make the best of it; meet with him to talk it out." Sanaa calmly looks at her Mother and accepts her wisdom, "Momma, I'll try." A few minutes later, Sanaa notices her phone ringing and notices that it's Chrystal. Sanaa answers the phone, and Chrystal says, "Hey, girl, you alright? Give me all the details; come on with it." Sanaa says, "I'm hurting, Chrystal. I guess more than my Mother; she's taking the situation a lot better than I thought." Chrystal asks, "Sanaa, did you talk to your Dad?" Sanaa admits, "I called him, but I could not bring myself to hold a conversation with him. It felt like I had called a stranger. It was like everything that I believed growing up just went away. I mean, the idea of a whole family, with a Mom and Dad forever, just vanished. Until now, I never considered the fact that my Mom and Dad are not physically related. I have both their blood, but the reality is, they are not bound by relatedness. This is the reality that I face, and I cannot come to terms with that. My parents are only bound by a license, a piece of paper." Understanding Sanaa's feelings, Chrystal replies, "Sanaa, you will eventually need to put on your big-girl pants and talk with your Father like the mature woman that you are. I think, for the wellbeing of your family, you must talk to him. You are his daughter, and you will always be Daddy's little girl. You are all he's got. I don't think he ever intended to break ties with you. It's just one of those grown folk situations; it happens, it hurts, but you have to move on. Be like your Mom; she will never let a person see her sweat. Like you always tell me: 'It's not about getting revenge; it's about always getting better.'" Sanaa breaths deeply and says, "Alright, I'll talk to him later. Hey, forget about what I'm dealing with here. What are you and that Tyson boy up to?" Chrystal playfully asserts, "You mean, my man, Tyson." Sanaa replies, "What-ever. What's up with you guys?" Chrystal responds, "Well, my dear, we've had the crib all to ourselves, and I'm loving every minute of it. However, I had to put mister man in check on how he's supposed to treat the person he's dating. I think he got the message." Sanaa curiously inquires, "You guys are alone? At Tyson and Jordan's apartment?" Chrystal answers, "Yeah." Sanaa further inquiries, "Ok, well, then, where is Jordan?" Chrystal comments, "Hey, Tyson said he was going on a road trip." Not too happy to hear that Jordan's not in place, Sanaa questions, "A road trip?" Chrystal says, "Yeah, he said Jordan went on a road trip. I think he mentioned he was going to visit his undergrad school in Daytona Beach." Surprised at hearing this development, Sanaa asks, "He went to Bethune?" Chrystal responds, "Yeah, that's what I think Tyson was babbling about. I'm surprised you didn't know that." Sanaa pauses for a Moment and asks, "Who did he go with?" Chrystal says, "I think by himself. That's the understanding I got. You cool with that?" Trying to disguise her feelings, Sanaa responds dispassionately, "Well, he's grown. I ain't got no chains on him." Understanding the situation with Jordan, Chrystal encourages her, commenting, "Sanaa, you got to stop this attitude with Jordan, you know he misspoke concerning your parents. Stop faking like you don't care; you know you love Jordan." Sanaa comes clean, "Yeah, I know, but this thing with my Dad makes me kind-a angry with everybody, and I let my situation with him spill over into my relationship with Jordan." Chrystal replies, "Well, then, you might want to call him and explain." Not yet sober in her thinking, Sanaa agrees, "I'll call him, but I need to be thinking straight when I do. I don't want to make things worse than they already are." Chrystal shrewdly warns and replies, "Hey, girl, word to the wise; don't wait too long. Sanaa, I hear Tyson calling me. I got to go. Call me back and let me know how you're doing, ok?" Sanaa says, "Ok, girl, I'll talk to ya later." Chrystal whispers, "Bye now."

Later in the evening, back in Daytona Beach, after walking up and down the strip and playing in the water for hours, and then taking it to the hotel's pool for a swim, Jordan and Sheila are now tired and a little lightheaded from the consumption of all the beer and mixed drinks they've ingested. They go upstairs, sit on the floor by their beds across from each other, and just start insanely laughing; neither of them knowing why. It was just a Moment of comic release to culminate all the fun they had together. However, As the laughter slowly subsides, they stare at each other intimately. Sheila crawls over to Jordan and passionately kisses him on the lips, and as she moves back, she looks into Jordan's eyes, saying, "Jordan, I know you're conflicted, and I don't want to pressure you, but I do want to be with you; however, for right now, I think it's best we just remain platonic friends. Is that alright with you?" Jordan, with his head down, looks up at Sheila, "I like you very much too, but for right now, I think you are right. I don't know what the future holds with my other situation, but things could change. I don't know, but Sheila, you have definitely moved the needle with me." As Sheila stands, looking down at Jordan, she smiles compassionately, taking in everything Jordan is saying, then she nods her head in hesitant agreement and softly says, "Baby, I'm going to take a shower and go to bed. We got to get up early in the morning and hit the road back to school, ok?" As Sheila moves toward the bathroom door, Jordan gently grabs her hand and just holds her there for a minute, and staring into Sheila's eyes, he says nothing until, eventually, letting her go. Sheila slowly enters the bathroom, looking back at Jordan, all the while communicating silently through teary eyes that she feels the same. As Sheila goes through the bathroom door, Jordan leans back against the bed, placing both hands behind his head, looking up at the ceiling in deep thought; he knows he feels something deeply for Sheila, but all he can see is Sanaa's face. Jordan takes a deep breath and exhales, only to fall back into deep thought. After bedding down for the night, in separate beds, they fight the urge to lie down next to each other. Staring at each other, receiving only Momentary stretches of sleep throughout the night, then finally falling into a deep sleep. Suddenly, they hear the ring of Jordan's alarm clock, and slowly wake up, smiling at each other, "Good morning," Sheila whispers softly. Jordan looks at Sheila in awe, "Damn, girl, even when you're just waking up, you're beautiful. You ready to get some breakfast and hit the road?" Sheila says, "I'm ready when you are." After about an hour or two getting ready, checking out, and getting breakfast, Jordan and Sheila hit the road back to Fort Lauderdale.

Back at her home in New York, Sanaa's Mother has made breakfast. Mother and daughter sit down to eat as they look at each other, and not a word is spoken. Sanaa's Mother breaks the silence, "Baby, do you blame me for the breakup with your Father?" Sanaa quickly responds, "No, Momma, why would you say something like that?" Sanaa's Mother replies, "Because of all the times we've had breakfast together, we've always had a lot to talk about." Sanaa thinks about what her Mother is saying and says, "I'm sorry, Momma, my silent brooding has nothing to do with you or Dad. Right now, I have a lot on my mind centered around my own relationship." Out of concern, Sanaa's Mother inquiries, "Baby, what's happening with you and that Jordan boy?" Sanaa says, "Momma, sometimes I let my temper and pride overshadow me. I jumped all over Jordan when he was just trying to give me a sympathetic shoulder to lean on. Being all caught up into you and Dad's drama, I couldn't understand his way of helping me cope with the situation. Right now, I don't even know if I can repair things. But first, I know I need to deal with my Dad." After Sanaa and her Mother finish eating, Sanaa goes to her room, then contemplates for a minute on how she's going to approach a phone call to her Father. Somehow, after considering her options, she musters up the strength and calls her Dad to make a lunch date. Surprised, and at the same time happy to hear from Sanaa after she hung up on him, he says in a nervous voice, "Sanaa, there's something important I need to tell you when we meet." Sanaa says, "Let's meet around 6:00 at Jojo's." Her Dad agrees, "Ok, it's a date." Sanaa says, "I'll see you later this evening," and they hang up. Sanaa thinks to herself; *I wonder what it is he needs to tell me. I hope he isn't sick or anything. Damn, I should have asked him while he was on the phone.* Sanaa then immediately seeks her Mother's wisdom and information on the subject, "Momma, is there something wrong with Daddy?" Her Mother responds, "Sanaa, now you know I'm the wrong person to ask that question." Sanaa explains, "No, Momma. I mean, is Daddy sick or something like that?" Sanaa's Mother quickly exclaims, "No, baby, ain't nothing wrong with that fool except he has lost his damn mind; why do you ask?" Sanaa says, "When I was talking to him on the phone, he said he had something important to tell me, and his voice sounded kind of nervous." Having an idea what her Father is not saying over the phone, Sanaa's Mother states, "Sanaa, whatever he tells you, good or bad, just remember to control yourself; things are never as good or bad as they seem, ok?" Sanaa looks at her Mother, suspiciously searching her eyes for any hidden concerns, but concedes, "Alright, Momma, alright." Later that evening at the restaurant, Sanaa sees her Father and walks over toward him. He reaches out and takes her hand, "Hey, baby, how's Daddy's little girl?" Sanaa stares into her Father's smiling face and sarcastically replies, "Not so little anymore, Daddy." Sanaa's Father hears her words but does not react to the tone of her comment. He says, "Sanaa, I've been waiting for a chance to see you because I need to do some explaining. Sanaa's Father then moves in close and kisses her on the cheek. Sanaa receives the kiss, but can't help but feel she's being conned or something, so she gives him a half-hearted smile as they walk to their table to be seated by their waiter. Her Father apologizes, "Sanaa, I'm sorry for everything that's happened with your Mom and me. Somehow, we just fell apart." Sanaa quickly interjects, "Daddy, I don't think she sees it that way. She sees you as someone she gave her whole life too, and you just dumped her. Daddy, for the life of me, I don't see how you could do that; not you, not my Daddy, not the man that raised me. That man would never do anything like that." With a tortured expression on his face, Sanaa's Father listens intently and just hangs his head. After minutes of listening to Sanaa's rebuke, he confesses, "Sanaa, I messed up. I formed a relationship outside my marriage because I was unhappy at home. That does not mean that I do not love you or care about your Mother. My affair started as nothing serious, just a mid-life lustful one of those things, and before I knew it, there were emotions involved. I am so sorry for the embarrassment and pain I have caused you and your Mom. Since I'm confessing and coming clean with everything, Sanaa, there's something else you need to know, and this is hard for me to tell you. So I'll just say it. Julia and I, the woman I'm involved with, we have a son, your half-brother. He's now close to one year old, and I'd like for you to meet him." Sanaa's face contorts as she looks at her Father in total rage and anger, and shouts, "What?!"

And screams again, "What?!" Sanaa becomes irate and loud, yelling, "Does Momma know about this?" She screams again, "Does Momma know about this?" Mindful of the environment, Her Father tries to discreetly quiet things down and whispers, "Sanaa, calm down, please. I think your Mother knows." Sanaa stares at her Father through swollen teary eyes, then angrily and frantically stands up and slams the table with both her hands, and with stunned patrons looking on, she then snatches the tablecloth off the table, pulling the entire spread to the ground, and loudly screams, "Why, Daddy? Why?" And before he can answer, Sanaa grabs her chair and throws it against the table as she turns and walks away. But as she's walking out, she turns and screams across the restaurant at the top of her voice, "I don't ever want to see or talk to you again; so you, your bas***d a** son, and your whore of a mistress, ya'll have a nice f**king life." Emotionally spent, Sanaa races out of the restaurant, finds her Mother's car, and after getting in, she cries while violently hitting the steering wheel, cursing her Father with everything she can think of until she manages to bruise her hands. When she finally arrives at home, Sanaa enters and rushes past her Mother without saying a word. Sanaa slams the door to her room, after which there is nothing but complete silence. Sanaa's Mother stands in the middle of the room, silently contemplating what she thinks her Father might have told her. Feeling every part of her daughter's pain, Sanaa's Mother goes back to her seat on the sofa, picks up a glass, and completely gulps down a tardy she had fixed as a nightcap. Sanaa's Mother then leans back into the soft sofa, takes a deep breath, exhales, and cries herself to sleep.

CHAPTER 11
(LADIES SHOULD NOT FIGHT)

BACK ON CAMPUS, DAEDAI FINALLY WAKES UP and has an extremely painful migraine coursing through her head. Raven asks, "Are you alright?" Daedai squinches to see Raven, and says, "Yeah, I'm fine. I just got this really bad headache." As Teri from down the hall comes into the room, Raven is admonishing Daedai, "That's what you get when you drink to the extreme." Teri adds her two cents, "Yeah, Muhammad Ali, you were torn up last night." Somewhat embarrassed by her actions, Daedai states, "I didn't go there to do that much drinking. I went to meet up with this boy named Jevon, who I thought liked me. I guess I was wrong with that idea. When I got to the Rock Bottom Lounge, I went in and walked around. I saw Jevon out on the floor dancing when he was supposed to be waiting for me. So, I stood by myself, watching him flirting with this girl, and yeah, I had had a few drinks from the bottle I stashed away in my bag. I had planned to share some of my drink with him. I waited for Jevon to turn around and look for me. When he continued to dance with this chick, through two songs, mind you, I guess the alcohol influenced my better judgment to go stand on the dance floor right next to him." Teri briefly interrupts, "Daedai, did you say, Jevon? Jevon Moore?" Daedai says, "I didn't know his last name. We met the day before, and he gave me the impression that he and I had something going on." With an expression on her face as if Daedai should have known better, Teri informs her, "Daedai, Jevon Moore is one of the biggest wh**es on campus." Raven adds on to that, "Damn, girl, you know how to pick 'em, huh?" Daedai comes back quickly, "Oh, and you got room to talk; As far as that goes, you don't have such a great track record your damn self, Raven." Ravens answers, "Well at least I'm not beating people up over a boy." Daedai, getting frustrated comments, "Look, Ms. Thang, this girl started it. I just finished it." Teri says, "Daedai, her friends had to take her to the hospital." Daedai gives Teri the once up and down and replies, "Hey, it's better she go to the hospital rather than me, don't you think?" Raven curiously inquires, "Tell me this, why did y'all start fighting in the first place?" Daedai takes a deep breath, "I admit, I had a few drinks while watching them on the dance floor, but I didn't try to start a fight. Being just a little jealous, I guess I wanted to interfere with whatever was going-on between him and that girl. I wanted him to see me. So, I stood next to them, calling his name, and he just rolled his eyes around the room like I wasn't even there. As I was turning around, about to walk away, the girl he was dancing with said, 'Hey b***h, can't you see I'm with my man.' I said to her with a smile, 'He didn't seem like your man yesterday while he was kissing me on my neck.' Surprised and upset by what I said, she immediately turned to face Jevon. He just rolled his eyes away from her as he had done to me and said nothing. I kind-of gave a smirk laugh, as if to imply, 'damn, this fool ain't about nothing.' So, when I was about to leave, this girl lunged at me and took her sweaty hand and gripped my face like it was a basketball or something and tried to push me down. That was her first, and last mistake. I drifted to the right, and at the same time, pushed her hand away, then I got up into that b***h's grill with a full clip, locked and loaded. I dotted that eye, drop kicked her a**, and went straight for the weave. Then I gave her about eight or nine solid reasons to never put her hands on me again." Not condoning what Daedai did, Raven warns, "Damn, Daedai, you got to learn to control your temper." Daedai arrogantly suggests, "Hey, don't start no stuff, won't be no stuff. But you are right. I'm too much of a lady to even think about fighting over some boy." Teri, adding her two cents, "Sure you right, Daedai. It is beneath real women to be seen fighting over these fools. We got to demand respect in all things, and if he can't get with that, then he got to go, enough said." Daedai shouts, "Girl, preach!" After Teri offers her comments, she says, "Ladies, I got to run. Talk to you later." Teri leaves the room, and Raven looks at Daedai with a seriousness, "We need to talk." Daedai says, "Talk about what?" Raven's expression becomes more intense and confronting, "Daedai, stop playing games, ok? I know that you're upset about this thing I'm doing." Daedai quickly responds, "Nah, nah, Raven. Call it what it is-not something you are doing; it's a lesbian relationship." Raven concedes, "Ok, a lesbian relationship. I told you it wasn't serious. I'm just experimenting." Daedai then stares at her friend and says, "Raven, there's no such thing as experimenting. Either you are, or you are not. Personally, I don't think it's normal." Getting highly argumentative at this point, Raven exclaims, "What do you care, Daedai? It's not like you're religious or something like that; you don't even believe in God." Daedai forcefully comes back, "Look, woman, you don't know what or who I believe in. But there is one thing I believe for sure, that it ain't normal for a woman to put her face in another woman's crotch and slurp at the unthinkable, and it definitely ain't normal for a man to put his penis in another man's big intestine. But you go ahead and do your thing; it's your life. I don't want to talk about it anymore." Daedai pauses a minute, stares at Raven, and then capitulates, "Raven, I don't like it, and I can't understand why you are doing it. Lord knows I will never agree with it. But you will always be my friend; that will never change." Raven looks at Daedai, thankful not to lose her friendship, and says, "Thanks, Daedai.

I needed to hear that from you. One other thing, Daedai, while I'm going through this phase, Toni doesn't need to know about this, ok?" Daedai stares at Raven and says, "As I said, it's your life. I'm not going to talk about this anymore." Understanding her feelings, Raven replies, "Thanks, Daedai," and both girls grab their books to study.

The next day, it's morning back in New York, and Sanaa's Mother has once again made her breakfast. However, after being called, Sanaa has not come to the table. Sanaa's Mother goes and knocks on her door. She yells, "Sanaa, come to breakfast, honey." Sanaa answers through the door, "Momma, I'm not hungry" Sanaa's Mother says, "Sanaa, we need to talk. Please come to breakfast." Sanaa's Mother stands at the door and listens, and there is no response, so she turns and walks back to the dining room table and starts eating breakfast by herself. About five minutes later, Sanaa comes out of her room and comes to the table, sits down, and inquires, "Momma, you knew that Daddy had a child with this woman, didn't you?" Her Mother stops eating, and slowly looks up from her plate, and staring at Sanaa, she comments, "I wasn't sure about it until now. The investigator told me that the lady your Father was seeing had a little boy. Putting two and two together, I reasoned in my mind that this boy might be your Father's child. After all the information I had been given by the investigator, I couldn't dismiss the possibility this little boy was your Father's child." Sanaa looks at her Mother with an expression of empathy, but asks, "Momma, why didn't you tell me?" Sanaa's Mother explains, "Like I said, Sanaa, I wasn't absolutely sure. I admit that there may have been a refusal on my part to believe it, but I could not tell you something like that. What if I would had been wrong?" Sanaa now looks at her Mother in complete awe, knowing that her Mother had been carrying around this burden. Sanaa says, "My Father is a complete fool. To think that he traded a great woman like you for a woman that is not even worthy to drink your bath water. It causes me to view my Father in a totally different light. Momma, if I can mature to be just half the woman you are, I would be so immensely proud and grateful for just having that half." Sanaa's Mother, surprised by her daughter's comments, wells up into tears and says, "Thank you, baby. You made my day. I love you so much." Sanaa responds likewise, "I love you too, Momma." Sanaa's Mother inquires, "Sanaa, don't you think you should get in contact with Jordan and try to straighten things out before you leave today?" Sanaa answers, "Ok, Momma. I was going to do that, but I heard he went to visit his undergrad school for the weekend. I will talk to him when he gets back to campus." It is mid-morning back on campus, and Jordan and Sheila have arrived after an hour layover in a small town, trying to extend the trip. When they arrive on campus, Jordan helps Sheila bring her bags to the dorm, and while walking up the sidewalk, Toni happens to be exiting through the dorm door and passes by Sheila, and then seeing Jordan carrying Sheila's bags, she greets him, "Hey Jordan, what's going on?" Jordan, caught off guard running into Toni, awkwardly nods his head as he passes. Toni, being very curious about what she is seeing, peers back to connect the dots of something she is contemplating about Jordan and Sheila. Sheila is so eager to get upstairs to shower she does not notice Toni passing as she rushes toward her dorm with Jordan following. Figuring that something is going on between Jordan and Sheila, Toni turns around and purposely yells out, "Jordan, you know Sanaa will be back later this evening, and she asked about you." Jordan does not turn around, but raises his arm, indicating that he heard Toni, and keeps moving forward. He suddenly realizes that, eventually, he will need to do some explaining, but right now, he is with someone that he has come to like a whole lot, and knows he needs to square things up with her. When Sheila and Jordan reach the dorm lobby, Jordan does not go upstairs; instead, he asks Sheila to go with him to a private room next to the lobby so they can talk. Sheila looks at Jordan, not expecting anything, inquires, "What's wrong, Jordan?" As they sit down, Jordan reveals his feelings, "Sheila, I am so confused right now." Jordan smiles and says, "You give great friendship, girl, and I'm totally feeling you. There is something inside me that's extremely attracted to you. I did not expect this to happen. I didn't realize how much of a mature woman you are, and I'm really digging on that." Sheila interrupts, "Jordan, stop; you're hurting my heart. Look, I know you're conflicted in your relationship with Sanaa. I get that, and I don't want you to feel like I'm pressuring you to do anything. I'll be here. I'm not going anywhere. We had a good time, and we will always be the best of friends, and let's leave it at that, ok?" Jordan looks at Sheila in amazement, then he leans over and kisses her with a passion that was held back throughout the trip. When their lips part, Jordan stares into Sheila's eyes and reluctantly says, "I gotta go. We'll talk, ok?" Knowing this may be the last time they will be together, Sheila responds softly, "Take care Jordan; see you around," And before Jordan leaves through the door, he looks back with an expression of regret that he has to leave, and he says nothing, but his body language lets Sheila know, without a doubt, there's something in his heart for her. Jordan turns and walks through the dorm's lobby now more confused and conflicted than ever as he goes to his car. The main issues in Jordan's thoughts right now are what Sanaa is going to say after hearing from Toni. However, he settles in his mind and heart that he is not going to call her. She will have to call him. He starts his car, leaves campus, and makes his way to his apartment. Sanaa arrives on campus late in the evening, and after getting a heads up from Toni, she calls Jordan right away. As his phone rings, Jordan is watching television and sees it's Sanaa. He looks at his phone and listens to it ring, and in his mind, he thinks of Sheila, juxtaposed to his confrontation with Sanaa. However, he decides to answer the phone. Jordan answers, "Hello." Using the sweet voice tone that Jordan is used to hearing, Sanaa says, "Hey, baby." Jordan, surprised at the change in Sanaa's tone, pauses briefly and thinks cautiously before saying anything, and says, "Hey." Now displaying a sober attitude, and in complete sincerity, Sanaa says, "Jordan, I want to apologize for being such a b***h. I realize now that you were only trying to be there for me. I was so angry at my Dad that I lost all control and reasoning. While I was home, I had a chance to get things off my chest. I come to realize how great a man you are, and that I love you so much. I am sorry, Jordan, for being so caught up into my parents' mess that I took your feelings for me, and my feelings for you, for granted. Baby, can you forgive me?" At this point, there's total silence over the phone. Continually running through Jordan's mind is the thought of Sanaa's attitude in contrast to Sheila's maturity. Feeling insecure and concerned, Sanaa asks again, "Jordan, baby, do you forgive me?" Realizing that he is still in love with Sanaa, Jordan eventually responds, "Baby, it's alright; everything's good." Not satisfied with Jordan's response, and in need of a definitive answer, Sanaa replies, "Jordan, I need to hear you say, you forgive me, baby, please." After a slight pause, Jordan says, "I forgive you, Sanaa, but I hope you realize, from now on, I'm always for you, not against you." Sanaa quickly interjects, "Jordan, please believe me. I know that now, ok?" Jordan, in his manner of speaking, says, "Ok, then, we good." Jordan then asks, "Sanaa, let me call you back later, I got some things I got to finish doing around here." Not fully connecting all the dots from the "tea" dropped by Toni, Sanaa hesitantly agrees, "Alright, baby, then maybe later you can tell me all about your trip to BCU?" Caught off guard by Sanaa's inquiring statement, images of Sheila immediately pop into Jordan's head, and he nervously swallows in his throat and says, "Oh, okay, baby, bye." Knowing that she has Jordan wondering how much she knows about his trip, Sanaa whispers, "Bye, now." Later, after unpacking the rest of his clothes and putting them in the hamper to be washed, Jordan sits on the couch in front of the television again, thinking about what Toni may have told

Sanaa. He is worried about the inferences that can be drawn from what Toni saw. He reasons to himself that it's quite reasonable for Toni to conclude that he and Sheila went together on his road trip. Even though nothing happened, he knows he will have a hard time explaining things to Sanaa. So, he sits thinking, what if Sanaa brings the matter up, how will he explain it? Coming into the room, Tyson interrupts Jordan's train of thought and asks, "What are you thinking so hard about, man? Let's go play some basketball." Jordan slowly looks up at Tyson and says, "Ok, that might work right about now. Hold on a minute, let me go get my gear." Jordan and Tyson go to Jordan's car and make their way to their favorite basketball court, where there's always a full-court game and quality competition. On the way to the court, Jordan is constantly thinking about Sanaa, and almost runs past a stop sign, but stops in time. Tyson curiously looks at Jordan and asks, "What's wrong, man? Ever since you came back from that road trip, you've been acting like your head is in the clouds. What's up with you, man?" Jordan slowly looks at Tyson and reveals, "Tyson, Toni saw me carrying Sheila's bags into the dorm after coming back from the trip." Tyson thinks a minute, then exclaims, "Oh, snap! You were with Sheila? Hey, playa, you struck gold again. Sheila is so fine." Jordan quickly says, "Yeah, but nothing happened, man." Tyson looks at Jordan intently with a smile, "Yo, dog, this is Tyson. I know you, and you trying to tell me that you had that fine honey up there in Daytona Beach all by yourself and you ain't hit nothing, please!" Jordan pleads his case, "Nah, we didn't do anything. I wanted to, but I kept thinking about Sanaa. I told her I was conflicted in my relationship with Sanaa, and she understood, and she wasn't mad or felt cheated. Sheila was great, man. I could talk to her about anything, and to my surprise, she turned out to be a good friend. To be perfectly honest, man, I developed feelings for the girl, but I realized I still love Sanaa. The reason I've been in deep thought around the crib is because I don't know what

Toni told Sanaa, so I'm a little bit on edge. Tyson, now I told you this in confidence; don't let Chrystal try to pick information out of you, man." Tyson quickly responds, "Yo, man, I got your back. Everything we discussed is already forgotten, bruh." Jordan pleads, "Tyson, don't let me down, man." Tyson answers, "I got you, man. You figured out what you're going to tell Sanaa?" Jordan looks at Tyson, "I don't know; that's why I'm thinking so hard." Tyson then comes up with an idea, "Look, man, check this out. You tell Sanaa that Sheila and her boyfriend went on the road trip with you to Daytona, and on the way back, the boyfriend found out he had to go into work right away; you dropped him off at his house and volunteered to help Sheila take her stuff to the dorm." Jordan looks at Tyson with raised eyebrows, "Damn, Tyson, where did all that come from?" Tyson says, "Man, when you got to be inventive, you got to be inventive, you know." Jordan looks at Tyson, "I feel bad lying to her, man." Tyson quickly interjects, "What's the alternative, Jordan? If you tell the truth, knowing how Sanaa is, you gonna be in the doghouse, bruh. If you do what I suggest you do, no one will be the wiser. Look, Jordan, you don't even have to say anything unless she asks. Now that's the best solution. But if Sanaa pushes you for information, and I believe she will, you got a canned answer about the entire trip, man, and with that, you debunk anything Toni could have said. You feel me." Not liking the situation, he is in, and particularly not wanting to lie to Sanaa, Jordan reluctantly agrees, "Yeah, I feel you, man. But I'm gonna think on that, ok?" Tyson looks at his roommate, and understanding his dilemma, caringly relents, "Alright, Jordan, you think on it, man. Hey, we almost to the park. I think a little basketball might take your mind off everything." Jordan breathes in deeply, exhales, and says, "I hope so, man. I hope so." After a couple of hours of ball'n, Tyson and Jordan are now exhausted and soaking wet from playing multiple full-court games. They decide to call it a night and head back to the apartment. When they reach the home front,

Tyson, concerned about his boy's mental state, looks over at Jordan as he parks the car, and asks, "Where is your head at now, man?" Jordan slumps back in his seat, looks at Tyson, smiles, and blurts out, "Damn, man, I had forgotten about everything till you brought it up again, damn!" Tyson laughs as they leave the car, "Well at least I got it off your mind for a little while, right?" Jordan smiles at Tyson, "Yeah you did man, thanks." Jordan and Tyson give high-fives and both head into the apartment. After a shower, getting some food, and rehydrating, Jordan sits on the couch and thinks to himself, *it's time to make that call*; however, before he can reach his phone, it starts ringing. As he picks up, he sees it's Sanaa. He hesitates for a minute, and then answers, "Hey, baby." With a sexy voice that just drives Jordan crazy, Sanaa whispers, "Hey, baby, how are you doing?" Jordan answers, "I'm good." Tyson and I just got back from playing ball, so I'm icing myself down." Sanaa, teasing with Jordan, murmurs, "Ahh, poor baby. Does it hurt?" Jordan, dismissing the playful teasing, responds, "Come on, now." He pauses for a minute and inquires, "Sanaa, I didn't want to ask you earlier, but is everything alright back home?" Sanaa nervously answers, "Nope, but I'm alright." Sensing that she's still hurting, Jordan says, "Baby, you want to talk about it?" However, after asking the question, Jordan thinks to himself, *damn, I cannot believe I asked that. I hope I don't say the wrong thing and set this girl off.* Sanaa takes a deep breath, exhales, and comments, "Sometimes I wonder why men can't understand when they got a good thing. They just lie, cheat, and hurt the person that loves them the most." Jordan silently swallows in his throat, thinking she is hinting at him. He continues to listen, but then interjects, "Sanaa, that goes both ways; not only for men, but for women as well." Sanaa is noticeably silent over the phone, then agrees, "Baby, I see where you're coming from, and you are right; it does go both ways. But I feel so inflexible on men because my Father took advantage of my Mother, who is a great wife and Mother. I came to find out that there was a lot more in this saga of betrayal. I had lunch with my Dad one day, and to add salt to the wound, he told me that he had a son with this woman he is with." After Sanaa said this, the silence over the phone was such that you could hear a pin drop. Trapped in his own dilemma and not knowing what to say, Jordan is afraid to speak. Sanaa finally comments, "That's the reason why I feel the way I do about you guys right now. Jordan, when he told me this, I went slap-off. I showed out, babe. I could not control the rage that came over me, and I said things I should not have said. I feel bad in my soul, but I can't change my situation or my attitude about it. I hope I can get over this somehow." Sanaa takes a deep breath, exhales, and continues, "Ok, enough about my painful trip home. What about your trip to BCU, and what did you do while in Daytona Beach?" This was the question Jordan did not want her to ask. Jordan thinks a minute about what he is going to say and blurts out. "Oh, nothing. I was just a little pissed off about how you showed out on me, so I decided to take a road trip to my undergraduate school for a few days, just to clear my head; it was nothing special." Sanaa again apologizes, "I am so sorry for my attitude. Did the trip help things?" Jordan replies, "I think so, and on top of that, you've said your piece and calmed down. I just want things to get back to normal." Sanaa agrees and says, "Ok then, we'll leave it at that. Are you coming over later?" Jordan explains, "Can't tonight, babe. I got to catch up on the books." Sanaa says, "You are so right, I need to get in the books myself. Well, I guess I will see you tomorrow. Love you." Jordan responds in kind, "I love you too, baby. Bye." Jordan waits until Sanaa is off the phone, then he takes a deep breath and exhales to release all the stress of his conversation. Jordan immediately grabs his law books and begins to study. However, he is suddenly interrupted by Tyson being nosey, trying to find out what Jordan told Sanaa concerning the road trip. Tyson excitedly inquires, "Did you say what I told you to say?" Jordan answers, "Nah, man. The conversation didn't even go there, but I thank you for the advice, bruh. I hope all this is behind me now." Tyson, with a perplexed expression on his face, looks at Jordan with all seriousness and exclaims, "Jordan! Are you out of your mind? You better stay prepared and alert, man. Remember, Toni saw you. Sanaa is still connecting dots, man." Jordan briefly looks at Tyson and realizes that he's right. It may not be over. Jordan stares into blank space, thinking that Tyson is definitely on point, but not being able to do anything about it, he shrugs it off and focuses on his books.

CHAPTER 12
(THE PROBLEM WITH FORNICATION)

BACK ON CAMPUS, AS RAVEN IS COMING OUT of her dorm, she is confronted by her estranged boyfriend Toby, who approaches her terribly upset. Toby stops her and inquires, "Raven, is it true what my frat brothers are telling me, that you are in a lesbian relationship with Courtney Brinson? I can understand you being mad about what happened at the frat house, but under no circumstances did I ever think it would drive you to become a lesbian; or were you a lesbian all the while you were dating me?" Raven listens intently with her head down, staring vacuously at the ground, saying nothing. Toby continues, "I thought you cared for me. You didn't even have the common decensigh to say you didn't want to be with me anymore. What is wrong with you, Raven? The person I cared for wouldn't do that. My frat is laughing at me now, talking all kinds of smack behind my back about this thing with you and Courtney. Can you please tell me what's going on with you?" Raven looks up at Toby with eyes expressing sympathy for a person she still has feeling for, and explains, "Toby, I'm sorry. I don't know what's come over me. Ever since that night I was raped at the frat house, the thought of a man on me or touching me makes me sick. That is why I was avoiding you. What I am experiencing has nothing to do with you, baby. I know what happened to me was not your fault. I do not blame you. It's something screwed up in my head. To be truthful, I don't even believe I am a lesbian at heart. I just find comfort and friendship in Courtney right now. Please understand, I didn't mean to hurt you; it's something screwed up in my emotions right now." Trying to grasp Raven's explanation, Toby keenly listens while searching her eyes to find some measure of closure, and holding his peace, he stands looking at Raven until, with a sobering expression on his face, he finally surrenders to the fact that he has lost her forever. Toby then slowly and silently turns from Raven, expressing through his eyes the hurt he feels inside as he walks away. Raven gasps in tears, knowing that she has hurt Toby badly. With everything in her being, Raven wants to call out to him, but realizes it's best not to obscure her many unresolved issues and continue on in confusion, so in tears, she lets Toby go. Raven was initially headed to meet up with Courtney, but after her talk with Toby and being emotionally drained, she decides to go back to her dorm, not knowing that Courtney was watching the entire conversation with Toby, standing out of view inside the science building. Coming back from Toni's room and entering her room, Daedai sees Raven on her bed crying her eyes out. Daedai quickly rushes to sit beside her friend, "Raven, what's wrong? Why are you crying? Who messed with you!? Just tell me. I'll handle everything. Raven, talk to me." Raven turns on her bed, sits up, wipes her eyes, and says in a teary voice, "I just talked with Toby. I had to explain about being with Courtney. I know he didn't understand, and Daedai, he was so hurt. I looked into his eyes, and I could sense the hurt and disappointment he felt. I'm crying because I still feel something for Toby, and I didn't realize how much until he was walking away from me. Daedai, I am so confused; my emotions are all over the place. What's wrong with me?" All Daedai can do is just shake her head. Then there is a knock on the door. Daedai yells, "Who is it?" A voice answers, "It's Courtney." Daedai says, "Come on in, Courtney." As Courtney comes through the door, she speaks,

"Hey, Daedai." Daedai responds, "Hi, Courtney." Courtney looks at Raven sitting on the bed, "Can I talk to you privately for a minute?" Daedai instructs, "Y'all go ahead and talk. I'm going down to Toni's room." Raven says, "Thank you, Daedai." Daedai replies, "Not a problem." As Daedai leaves the room, Courtney walks over to the bed and sits next to Raven. Courtney says to Raven, "While waiting for you at the Science building, I saw you and Toby talking, and I saw you start crying. Do you want to talk about it?" Looking at Courtney with tearful eyes, Raven explains, "He knew that you and I were seeing each other. His frat brothers told him, and because I didn't handle this the right way, I hurt him." Surprised and a little bit confused, Courtney replies, "Are you telling me you still have feelings for Toby?" Raven answers, trying not to upset her new friend, "Courtney, I would be lying if I said I did not have feelings for Toby. Like I told him, right now my emotions are all over the place. I am not sure about my sexuality. I said to him, 'Courtney is my friend and my comfort, particularly after what happened to me.'" Somewhat surprised again at what Raven is saying, Courtney replies, "Oh, you just using me? Is that what our relationship is about? That's all I mean to you?" Raven becomes resolute in her position, "Courtney, I told you I'm confused. I don't know if I can be committed to a lesbian relationship; it still feels strange to me." Courtney calmly comments, "Raven, I'm not here to pressure you, but I've been with you intimately. I know you, and from how we interacted, there's no doubt, at least in my mind, about your sexual orientation." Pleading for understanding, Raven replies, "Courtney, I'm messed up emotionally; please believe me. I don't want to lead you on. I'm trying to be truthful with you." Courtney stares at Raven, then stands up from the bed and says, "Go ahead, Raven, find out who you are. I'll be around, but don't take too long." Raven tearfully looks up at Courtney and whispers, "Ok." Courtney bends over and kisses Raven on the cheek, then leaves the room. As the door closes, Raven lays back down on her bed staring up at the ceiling, thinking continuously about Courtney and Toby. A half-hour later, Daedai comes through the door holding two big boxes of doughnuts: Krispy Kreme and Dunkin Doughnuts. Daedai has a smile on her face, knowing that the only thing that will cheer Raven up is food, and the doughnuts worked its magic exceptionally well. Daedai knows immediately that she has been successful in lifting Raven out of her sadness when seeing Raven's eyes light up after smelling the aroma of fresh doughnuts. Daedai comments, "Damn, girl, you are so easy. All somebody has to do is bring you some food and you forget about everything." Raven just smiles and reaches for the doughnut box and says, "Girl, you know how to change my mood quickly. Thank you, Daedai. I needed this." While Raven ravenously chomps down on the doughnuts, all Daedai can do is just look at Raven, shake her head with envy, and comment, "You won't gain one damn inch, will you?" As Daedai continues watching Raven eat, she starts licking and smacking her lips, tasting the flavor of those doughnuts in her mind, and food envy starts messing with her head because she's trapped by diet restraints and can't pig out like Raven. Daedai is tempted, but refuses, thinking to herself, *I have worked too hard for this body, and I am not going to let Raven mess that up, uh-uh. Nah, can't do it.* Then to make things worse, Toni enters the room, and as soon as she sees the boxes of doughnuts, she yells, "Oh, doughnuts! Y'all got doughnuts." She runs to pick out her favorite doughnuts and begins pigging out with Raven. Rolling her eyes to the ceiling with both hands clasped on her hips and with agitated feet tapping the floor, Daedai is trying hard to maintain a modicum of willpower as she watches Toni and Raven going to town eating doughnuts that she can't have. Not being able to stand it anymore, Daedai quickly turns and leaves the room. With a mouthful of doughnuts, Toni looks at Raven and says, "What's wrong with her?" Raven says nothing and just pensively stares at the closed door.

The next day, sitting in his room, Tyson gets a call from his Mom informing him he has an important letter from the court. He says, "For what, Momma?" His Mother replies, "I don't know." Tyson says, "Momma, open it and read it to me." Tyson's Mother opens the letter, reads in silence for a minute, then explains in summary, "Baby, this is an order for you to appear in court. It alleges two women are claiming that you are the Father of their babies and are claiming child support from you." Tyson yells, "What!? Momma this has got to be a mistake; look at the name on the letter again." Tyson's Mother looks down at the letter, "It's your name, baby. They're talking about you." Tyson says, "Momma, no girl ever told me she was pregnant." Tyson's Mother replies, "Even though that may be true, Tyson, you need to plan time to come home so we can work on legal representation." Tyson concedes and says, "Damn, ok, Momma, I'll let you know when I'm coming home, ok?" Expressing the seriousness of the situation, Tyson's Mother exclaims, "Boy, this is nothing to play with. This is serious, so prepare to bring your butt home right away. You hear me?" Tyson says, "Yeah, Momma. I'm coming. I'll be home in a little bit. Bye, now." Tyson's Mother says, "Bye," and hangs up. Now in shock, Tyson quickly looks around the room, searching his thoughts, imagining those not-so-distant sexual encounters, and thinking to himself, *this can't be happening; this can't be real. I couldn't have gotten these girls pregnant. I used protection.* Then it dawns on him that there were instances where he did not use protection, but he thinks to himself, *this was a long time ago though.* Now thinking things through, he finally admits to himself that that he could possibly be the Father. Tyson then bends over with elbows resting on his knees and his hands cradling his face, and he starts repeating over and over, "Damn, damn. I done messed up, messed up bad. Oh boy, what I am I going to tell Chrystal?" Tyson hears the door open and can hear Jordan coming through the apartment, yelling, "Tyson!" And then knocking on his room door. Tyson takes a deep breath and walks to open the door. Jordan walks in, "What's up, roomie?" But suddenly, Jordan's expression and attitude quickly change as he becomes aware of Tyson's unusually serious demeanor. Jordan inquires, "Roomie, you ok?" Sitting on his bed, Tyson looks up at Jordan and says, "Nah, bruh. I got some problems." Tyson then goes silent and slumps back on his bed. Staring at Tyson, anticipating an explanation, Jordan asks "Well, are you going to tell me what's wrong? Or do I have to guess?" Tyson sits up, with his head bent down, and staring off into blank space, "Man, I just found out I may have gotten some girls pregnant. Jordan exclaims, "Pregnant?" Tyson replies, "Yeah, man. My Mother called me and said she got a certified letter addressed to me. It said I have to go to court because these girls are alleging that I am the Father of their babies. So I got to go home and sort this mess out, man." Jordan inquires, "You think these babies might be yours?" Tyson just shakes his head and looks up at Jordan, "Man, I'm not sure. I don't know." Thinking about Tyson's relationship with his girl, Jordan asks, "What are you going to tell Chrystal?" Searching for words, Tyson mutters, "I...I don't know, man." Jordan comments, "Just call her and tell her you have to go home for a couple of days," Tyson states, "Man, you know these law school chicks; they don't let nothing go without a complete explanation. You know this!" Jordan says, "Well, Tyson, just tell her as little as you can. You don't want to defend against this right now until you find out the truth." Tyson responds hopelessly, "Jordan, I know my lady, man; she's going to push me to find out everything. She harbors suspicions about me already, man, and believe me, I've been doing everything I can to build trust with her because I'm crazy about the girl. I don't want to mess up this one, man." Jordan asserts, "Now is the time to see if she's ever going to trust you; appeal to her on that level." Holding his head down in thought, Tyson finally surrenders to Jordan's way of thinking, "You're right, man, I have to convince this girl to trust me. After all, it's not like I'm playing around behind her back. I just can't tell her everything right now. I just need a little time to work through this problem without her thinking something negative. I'm going to think about how to frame what I can say and then call her." Jordan looks at his roomie with empathy, "Hey, if Sanaa tries to pump me for information, don't worry, I got your back. I don't know anything, man." Tyson looks up at his friend, "Thanks, Jordan." Later that evening, Tyson eventually calls Chrystal, and she's a little pissed at him. She says, "I thought you had forgotten all about me. You finally found time to put me on your busy schedule, huh?! What's up with you, Tyson?" Tyson quickly responds, "Chrystal, you know it's not like that. Look, I got something to tell you." As Tyson takes a deep breath to share, Chrystal replies, "Tell me, baby, what is it?" Tyson pauses for a Moment in his thoughts, "Chrystal, I got to go home for a couple of days. My Mother is a little under the weather, and I want to make sure she's ok. Chrystal exclaims, "Oh my God, is she ok? What's wrong with her?" Tyson replies, "She didn't say; she tried to convince me that it was nothing serious, but that's my Mom. I need to make sure she's ok." Chrystal inquires, "Your Mom lives in Atlanta, doesn't she?" Tyson says, "Yeah, my Father lives in Miami, and Mom lives in Atlanta after they divorced," Chrystal asks, "You know how long you'll be in Atlanta?" Tyson quickly responds, "Just a few days, baby. I'll be right back, ok?" Chrystal questions further, "When are you leaving, Tyson?" Tyson says, "I'm going to catch a train leaving out sometime tonight." Wanting to be helpful, Chrystal asks, "Tyson, do you need my help you with anything?" Grateful for her caring attitude, Tyson says, "Baby, you've already done it by showing me your level of concern. Believe me, I need that right now, and I love you for it. Right now, I need to go finish packing. I'll call you before I go to the train station." Chrystal then asks, "Tyson, do you need me to take you to the train station?" Tyson answers, "No, baby, Jordan is going to drop me off." Chrystal says, "Ok, then, have a good trip." Sensing Chrystal's anxiety, Tyson says, "Baby, I'll call you before I leave, and call you when I get home, ok?" Chrystal comments, "Ok, I'll be here if you need me. I hope your Mom gets better soon. Bye, now. Tyson vocalizes a kiss through the phone, "Bye, baby. I'll call you soon," and he waits for her to hang up first.

Over on campus, Toby's frat brothers are hanging out around the quad, shooting the breeze, and horsing around, and one of the brother's spots Courtney walking across the yard and points in her direction, and exclaims, "Hey, there's that girl who's trying to turn Raven out. We need to talk to her." The brothers follow Courtney until she is slightly away from campus, and after seeing no one around, they quickly move in and surround her. Startled and fearful, Courtney asks, "What do you guys want?" She knows they are from campus because she's seen some of them before. One of the brothers steps forward, "Why are you trying to mess up our frat brother with Raven?" Courtney responds in surprise, "Mess up your frat brother with Raven? Raven and I are close friends, and anything else is none of your damn business." One of the brothers aggressively approaches Courtney, saying, "We've been checking out Raven ever since she got to this school, and she ain't gay. So why are you trying to turn her out. There's a lot of gay girls around here; you can have your pick of the litter. But you need to stay away from Raven. She has a boyfriend." The brothers step closer toward Courtney's face, grimacing and sneering, pointing their finger at her and threatening, "Don't let us see you with Raven anymore, you understand? Are we clear?" Fearful that the brothers might hit her, Courtney starts backing up; however, in a trembling voice, Courtney attempts to stand her ground, "I understand what you're saying, but Raven wants to be with me. She wants me." The brothers silently and contemptuously stare at Courtney up and down, then walk toward her, leaning in and intentionally bumping into her body as they pass, and one brother, as he passes, looks back and states, "You've been warned, girl. Leave Raven alone. She already has a boyfriend; we aren't going to tell you this again, lesbo." Fearful from this close encounter with these five massive brothers, Courtney starts breathing extremely hard, then turns around and nervously makes her way back to campus. After she is back on the yard, she heads toward the middle area of the quad. Out of breath and still frightened, Courtney sees a lot of familiar faces on the yard, and she now feels more at ease. Courtney sees a steel bench and immediately goes and sits down to catch her breath. While trying to recover from this ordeal, Courtney pulls out her cell phone and calls Raven. Raven picks up, "Hello." Courtney nervously answers, "Raven, I need to see you right away. I've been attacked by Toby's frat brothers, and they threatened me." Surprised at hearing about this incident, Raven exclaims, "What!? They did what!?" Overdramatizing the incident to the bone, Courtney magnifies the incident purposely, stating, "Raven, Toby's brothers attacked me while I was on the way to the corner store. They said you already had a boyfriend and threatened me if I talk to you again." Raven asks, "Where are you now. I'll come and get you." Courtney says, "That's ok. I'm on my way to you right now." Thoroughly upset at what has happened, Raven starts pacing the floor thinking about what they had done to her, and thinking, *why did they do that? My life does not concern them. Toby and his frat brothers cannot control who I see or what I do.* Becoming increasingly angry, Raven anxiously continues to pace the floor, then there's a knock at the door. Raven yells angrily, "Who is it?" In a trembling voice, Courtney says, "Raven, it's me." Hearing Courtney's voice, Raven rushes to open the door, and seeing Courtney, Raven grabs her and kisses her as her lover. Raven brings Courtney into the room, and they both sit on the bed and Raven states, "Tell me, word for word, what happened. I'm going to file a police report against Toby and his frat brothers. I have unresolved issues with them also. Courtney quickly interrupts, "No, Raven, don't. They can't stop what we have. In time, they'll come to accept it." Raven comments, "Courtney, that may be, but those guys can't go around threatening people. I feel that I should call the police, but I won't, only because you asked me not to. But I am going to give Toby a piece of my mind. Who does he think he is?" Seeing that Raven is upset, Courtney embraces her face and gently kisses her on the lips, and as their lips part, Raven can hear Daedai's key going into the door. Raven and Courtney hastily release from each other's embrace when Daedai comes through the door. Daedai is surprised to see Raven and Courtney sitting so close and pretending like they were not about to get it on. Daedai apologizes sarcastically, "Oh! I'm sorry. I'll come back later." Courtney quickly interrupts, "No, no, Daedai. I was just about to leave." Courtney says, "Raven, I'll call you, ok?" Looking at Courtney's demeanor and realizing she has calmed down, Raven says, "Ok, talk to you later." As Courtney leaves the room, she speaks to Daedai as she passes, and Daedai falsely contrite, says, "Sorry I interrupted whatever you guys were about to do." With an expression on her face of being insulted, Raven sarcastically comments, "We were not about to do any-thing Daedai. The girl just got threatened by Toby's frat brothers, and I was just trying to comfort her. Furthermore, if I were going to do something, I wouldn't do it here." Searching for an explanation on why everybody's just sitting around, Daedai exclaims, "Later for that; you're telling me this girl just got jumped and all you're doing is sitting here? Uh-uh, no, Lord. Talk is over; it's time to call the police." Raven quickly attempts to calm Daedai's outburst, "Daedai, Courtney and I don't want to call the police. We know that those guys are nothing but talk. They can't stop anything we want to do. So, let it go. However, I will be calling Toby about this." Daedai suggests vigorously, "Well, if you need back up, I got your back." Raven looks fondly at her friend and says, "I know, Daedai, I know. But I'm going to handle this one myself." Daedai relents,

"Alright, go ahead. I'm out of it." Looking at the time, Raven says, "I got to go. I'll see you later." Daedai looks at Raven, "Alright, see you." Feeling bad about what happened, Raven goes straight to Courtney's apartment and spends the rest of the evening at her place. About 10:30 pm, Chrystal's phone rings and she sees it's Tyson, and she quickly picks it up, "Hey, baby." Tyson says, "Hey, I'm about to catch this train, and I wanted to let you know that I made it here, and I'm ok." Glad that Tyson has called, Chrystal says, "Baby, have a safe trip, and tell your Mother I'm hoping for her to have a swift recovery, and you take care of yourself, ok?" Missing Chrystal already, Tyson says, "I'll call you when I get home, baby. I love you." Chrystal responds in kind and then hangs up. The next day, Jordan and Sanaa are leaving class, and Jordan has noticed that Sanaa is looking at him awfully funny, and he inquires as they walk, "Baby, is everything alright?" Sanaa looks at Jordan with a penetrating stare, and says, "Let's go somewhere we can talk in private. I don't want all these people in my business. Being familiar with Sanaa's negative body language, Jordan knows that the jig is up. Anticipating an argument, Jordan nervously swallows into a dry throat, knowing that the Sheila's dots have been connected, so he takes a deep breath, exhales, and says, "Ok, baby, let's go around here." When they round the corner of the building, they find that there are no students standing nearby. Sanaa stops suddenly, stares at Jordan, and asks, "What is this I hear about your road trip, Jordan?" Trying to play it off, Jordan asks, "What do you mean, baby?" Sanaa immediately reacts to Jordan's BS and responds forcefully, "Oh, you trying to play me like that?" Jordan, now knowing that Toni is the culprit behind all the drama, holds true to the game, "Sanaa, just tell me what's wrong, baby; what did I do?" Visibly upset with her eyes welling up as she moves closer into Jordan's face, Sanaa states, "I heard you took a girl with you to Daytona. Is that true?" With that question, Jordan can feel every muscle in his body tense up, knowing that he can't ask who told her about Sheila. So, as he stares out into blank space, he thinks about what Tyson told him to say, but in the absence of a better explanation, he figures it's just better to come clean with the truth. So with Sanaa all up in his face, Jordan finally surrenders under the weight of Sanaa's questioning, "Sanaa, it is true; someone did go with me to Daytona." Then Jordan pauses to think for a minute, but after seeing Sanaa fold her arms across her chest and cocking her head to the side, Jordan knows he needs to come up with something quick because she's tearing a hole in his flesh with her eyes. Jordan quickly fesses up, "Baby, let me explain." Jordan stretches out his hands, reaching for Sanaa to calm her down, but she moves aside, evading his advances. "Jordan don't touch me. I don't need that." Then she shouts aggressively, "All you need to do right now is tell me why you took a girl with you to Daytona Beach? And who is this girl?" Jordan backs up, feeling cornered, and with his testosterone raging, turns slightly as he casts a serious glance at Sanaa's attitude, and with his expression now hardened, Jordan moves in close to Sanaa and explodes, "Sanaa, you got some damn nerve, you know that? Have you forgotten what you said to me before I went to Daytona? Have you forgotten your attitude toward me the day before I went to Daytona? Have you forgotten that you were the one that put a question mark on our relationship before I went to Daytona? Have you forgotten all that, huh!?" Standing with her jaws clenched, Sanaa rolls her eyes vacuously looking into the heavens, trying to avoid listening to Jordan's intensive response. Sanaa eventually sobers in her attitude as the validity in Jordan's words ring true and start to sink in. Jordan pauses Momentarily to take a breath, recognizing his anger, and calmly states, "For your information Sanaa, nothing happened in Daytona; not one thing." As Jordan stands waiting for Sanaa to say something or question him further, holding true to form, with her spoiled persona and explosive temper, she arrogantly declares in a trembling voice, "I think we need a break from each other." And before Sanaa can say another word, she sees Jordan's eyes squeeze shut as hurt contorts his features, and without response or delay, Jordan turns and walks away, leaving Sanaa to drown in a sea of her own words. And now standing alone as she watches Jordan walk away, Sanaa starts crying and regretting her quick and uncompromising reaction to what might have been a very truthful explanation.

CHAPTER 13
(ONE LIE LEADS TO ANOTHER)

LATE IN THE EVENING, CHRYSTAL RECEIVES A phone call from Tyson relaying that his Mother is doing fine. He tells Chrystal that his Mother had a bad case of gas, which made her think it was an eighty-six complete walk toward the light; life was over moment. And Tyson says, "She finally got some relief, and she's ok now. So, I'll be coming back to campus early in the morning. Chrystal says, "That's great, baby. Tell your Mom that she was right to be panicky; gas can be dangerous. My Dad had a problem with gas also and it scared him to death. Tell her it goes away with mild exercise." In the back of Chrystal's mind are the problems between Sanaa and Jordan, which makes her especially glad to hear from her sweetheart. Chrystal thinks to herself she dares not mention the problems that Jordan and Sanaa are having, even though she would give anything to know what Tyson knows, if anything, about this girl Jordan allegedly took to Daytona Beach. She figures that if he knows something, he probably wouldn't tell her anyway, but she contemplates; rather than approaching the subject right now, she'll wait until he comes back, then she'll be able to indirectly pull some juicy tidbits out of him. *I know he knows something, but the real question is if I find out something, do I tell Sanaa?*

On the other side of campus, coming back to her room from spending the night at Courtney's apartment, upon entering the room, Raven sees Daedai sitting on her bed. Daedai is openly unhappy about Raven's lifestyle choices, and intentionally evades eye contact, looking down at the floor and greeting Raven with a dismissive wave of her hand as an acknowledgment of her presence; yet the corner of Daedai's mouth quirks up to ask, "How's your friend? Is she ok?" Raven says, "She's fine, but I seriously need to talk to Toby." Daedai comments, "I've been thinking about what happened to Courtney. I don't believe that Toby had anything to do with what his frat brothers did." In surprise, Raven folds her arms around her body, tilts her head slightly with an expression of curiosity, and inquires, "And what in your infinite wisdom, Ms. Lady, makes you think he doesn't?" Daedai pauses for a minute and states, "There are a few things I do know about men. Toby is not the type to bring other people into his relationship, especially not with the kind of problems you and Courtney present. His ego is already bruised from you leaving him for Courtney. Do you seriously think he wants attention focused on his relationship with you now?" Raven listens with skepticism and interjects, "I just want to make sure he wasn't involved, that's all." Daedai cynically gasps to a fake smile as she comments, "You don't have a clue who your ex-boyfriend, is do you? As a matter of fact, you don't have a clue about men, do you?" Raven comes back, "Well, look who's talking; the fight-girl-put-a-chick-in-the-hospital-over-boy lady brawler. Yeah, you're a real diplomatic guru, Daedai." In disbelief that Raven would even mention that incident, Daedai's face hardens, but she gives a pass with that comment because it's Raven, but replies, "Oh, that's rich, Raven; you had to bring that up. But let me tell you something for your own good, when you talk to Toby, watch your attitude. It's none of my business, but I can see that the man is hurting, and you can find yourself in a bad position if you push him too far." Raven looks at Daedai and arrogantly comments, "If he had anything to do with harassing Courtney, he's the one that's going to find himself in a bad position; and by the way, you are so right, this is none of your business." Daedai answers back with perspective, "True that. True that. But there is one thing I've found out through our conversations. Your mixed emotional bull s**t in an attempt to explain your lifestyle transition is a façade. You've already sold out to the nasty, and you don't even want to admit it. What you need to consider is getting a different jersey, b***h; that might help because right now, you're officially playing for the other team." Both Daedai and Raven engage in a long unfriendly stare, and the tension is so thick you can cut it with a knife. The staredown is only broken when Raven indirectly notices the time on her bedside alarm clock and mutters under her breath, "I'm late for class." Raven then quickly gathers her books without saying another word or even looking in Daedai's direction as she goes through the door, slamming it loudly as she leaves. Daedai continues her stare, watching as Raven slams the door. Still staring vacuously at an inanimate door, Daedai lays back on her bed and reflects on the argument she just had with Raven. However, after a few seconds of contemplative silence, Daedai hears a thunderous and booming voice traveling through the hallways and bouncing off the dormitory walls, echoing the expletives; "F*** you, b****!!!!" But Daedai doesn't react or even pay it any notice; she just lays in her bed, staring at the ceiling silently. Later, when Raven finishes her classes, she goes over to Toby's apartment to confront him. Since the day that she was raped at the frat house, Toby has moved into his own apartment because he didn't want Raven to go to that house again. While lying on the couch watching television, Toby hears a stern knock on the door and hollers out, "Who is it?" Raven answers through the door, "It's me, Raven." Toby jumps up and immediately rushes to open the door. When he sees Raven standing in the doorway wearing the cutoff jeans he likes, his whole face lightens up. He reaches to embrace and kiss her, but she moves aside, evading his advances, and says, "Look, I didn't come over here for that." Bewildered by her attitude, Toby looks at Raven and inquires, "What's wrong, Raven?" Raven presumptuously asserts, "Why did you send your frat brothers to harass Courtney?" Toby's face contorts, "I did what? To whom? Wait, wait a minute; come on in and let's talk." Raven refuses to come in, but just stares at Toby, who is now more confused than ever. Toby leans his shoulders against the entrance part of the doorway, with hands cuffed crosswise his lower region, and calmly inquires, "Can you please tell me what's going on?" Acting purely impulsive, Raven comes at Toby with guns-a-blazing, commenting, "Toby, I told I was going through an emotional phase, and that my friendship with Courtney had nothing to do with my feelings for you. So why did you have your frat brothers harass her?" Shocked by what Raven said, Toby assertively responds, "Raven, I'm surprised that you would accuse me of something like that. I have not talked with my frat brothers since what happened at the frat house." Raven comes back rhetorically, "I guess your frat brothers just decided to harass Courtney under their own volition, right?" Toby replies, "Raven, this is the first time I've heard of this incident. I did not know about or had anything to do with this. The only thing for which I stand accused is for the second time thinking that there could be a future with you. I can see now that it was all a pipedream. You led me to think that Courtney was just the result of an emotional thing you were going through, and I bought that bulls** t." With a look of contempt on his face, Toby stares at Raven and says, "You got real feelings for this girl, huh? Feelings enough that you would come to my apartment, stand in my face, and accuse me of something that I did not do without having the slightest bit of evidence." Raven listens on deaf ears and doesn't believe anything Toby is saying. Toby states further, "Did you ever stop to consider giving me the benefit of doubt, knowing my feelings for you? All this time we spent together being intimately close. I thought you knew me. But, evidently, you don't, do you? That's really sad, Raven, and it hurts; it hurts bad. But that's ok because that makes what I'm about to do much easier." Toby declares without batting an eye, "You and Courtney have a nice life. Now step! I'm closing my door." Surprised and shocked by Toby's resolve, Raven moves sympathetically toward him, but before she can say a word or even think about an apologetic gesture. Toby has stepped back inside his apartment and purposely slammed the door in her face. Raven then gasps in surprise and stands in disbelief the way Toby treated her. Raven now starts to feel a great sense of loss, and gently leans against the door and implores him, "Toby, open the door. Come on; please open the door. I was just a little upset at what happened, that's all. Toby, please talk to me." Toby does not respond, come to the door, open the door, or say one word. Understanding his anger, Raven turns and walks away, knowing she's made a big mistake, and it finally dawns on her the goodness in the man that once loved her. Raven heads to her car and sits brooding and crying, confused with multiple issues torturing her soul; and after about an hour of calling Toby's phone and watching his apartment door for the slightest opportunity to talk to him, she finally decides to leave and head back to campus. The following day, Tyson has made his way back to school and is acting somewhat differently. Chrystal immediately notices a change in his demeanor. He's not acting high-spirited as his name defines. Being concerned that Tyson is still worried about his Mother, Chrystal inquires, "Tyson, is your Mother still doing ok?" Tyson nods his head in the affirmative, "Mom's great. She's doing fine." However, Chrystal still senses that something is wrong, but she does not push him for an answer. Tyson then looks at his girlfriend and grabs and holds her tightly, saying, "I love you, baby," Loving all the romantic attention, Chrystal, however, knows Tyson, and this is not his MO. So, she backs up and maneuvers herself into eye-to-eye contact with him, and with a seriousness, she inquires, "Baby, did something happen at home you want to talk about? You don't have another girl-friend at home, do you?" Tyson quickly responds, "No, baby, everything is cool; that ain't never happening, ok?" After pinning Tyson with an intensive stare, Chrystal relents and pulls back from her questioning, and states, "Tyson, I'm just trying to make sure that you are all right; I'm worried because you're acting differently since coming back." Recognizing that the stress of his troubles at home may be causing him to act differently, Tyson gently takes Chrystal's hand, kisses it, and says, "Chrystal, everything is good. Let's go to my apartment, and I'll show you how much I've missed you." From that suggestion, Chrystal flashes a school-girlish smile from her arousal at the thought of them making love, and quickly says, "I'm with that, baby, but we need to make it a quickie because I have to get back here and study. However, I will give you a rain check on that all-day, all-nighter action; that's a promise." Tyson, visu-alizing her promise, states, "That's a rain check I'm looking forward to cash." Tyson quickly stands up and asks, "Baby, can we meet up at the apartment in about twenty minutes? Me and my boy Jalen have to make a quick stop. I'm doing him a favor, then he'll drop me off at the apartment. If you can wait about five minutes before you leave, by then, I should be back at the crib, ok?" Chrystal says, "Ok, no problem. That will give me a little extra time to get some things together, then I'll be on my way." Tyson kisses Chrystal and urges her, "Don't take too long now. Bye."

Later, in the afternoon, Jordan is still walking around campus; there is not much to do since he and Sanaa are at odds. As he walks through campus for the third time, in the distance, he sees a football player talking to Sanaa, and Sanaa is not trying to discourage his advances. However, Jordan does not know that Sanaa sees him watching out of the corner of her eye. She's intentionally trying to make Jordan jealous with a little flirting, and flirting with someone she absolutely has no interest in. Rather than being confrontational, Jordan takes hold of his emotions and walks straightway to Flagler dorm, and requests Sheila to come down. In Jordan's mind, it's not to make Sanaa jealous but rather to spend time with someone he likes and considers a mature woman that understands his conflict of heart and won't pressure him for a commitment. Sanaa watches as Jordan goes into the dorm and disregards the football player trying hard to keep her attention. Sanaa politely dismisses the jock, then stands up and walks over to where she can get a look at who Jordan has come to see. However, she knows who it is, of course. Toni has given her the 411 on the girl, and Sanaa is now worried about a post-Daytona Beach problem. Feeling a little anxious, Sanaa thinks to herself, *I should go over there and shut that whole thing down right now; everybody on the yard knows it's me and Jordan.* Not wanting Jordan to know she's jealous of his talking with this girl, Sanaa calls Toni and tells her that Jordan is in Flagler dorm, trying to talk to the girl. Sanaa asks, "Can you come help me keep an eye on things. I can't let Jordan see me watching, right?" Knowing that Sanaa is extremely worried about this girl, Toni quickly rushes out of her dorm and down to where Sanaa is standing. Sanaa looks at Toni and asks, "Toni, I need you to watch what's happening with Jordan and this girl. Don't say anything, just let me know what their relationship is all about. I'm going to leave and go to my dorm. Call me and let me know what the deal is. Can you do this for me?" Toni replies, "Yeah, I got you." Sanaa breaks down and confesses, "Toni, you know I hate to ask you to do something like this, but you know how I feel about Jordan." Toni says, "Don't worry I got this. Now go to your dorm before Jordan sees us talking. I'm quite sure by now he knows I'm the one who dropped the tea on him and this girl. So, go on to the dorm. I'm going to blend in out here and keep watch." Sanaa says, "Thank you, Toni. I owe you one." Toni looks at Sanaa, relaying with all seriousness,

"Sisters have to watch each other's backs. I got you." Taking one last look at Jordan inside the dorm, Sanaa says, "Ok, Toni. I'm gone." Comforting her sister, Toni says, "Don't worry, I'll be here. I'll call you if something jumps off." Sanaa then turns and walks toward her dorm, and as she walks away, the football player who was trying to hit on her, yells out her name, trying to get her to come back. Hearing him call, Sanaa walks even faster and tenses up while uttering in a low voice, "Oh, please, shut up." Now almost trotting, Sanaa inconspicuously creeps toward her dorm. Understanding what's going on, Toni turns to the jock and yells, "Yo, man, Sanaa has an emergency she needs to attend to-she'll be back." After advising the ball player of Sanaa's emergency, he stops yelling out her name. Never looking back until she gets inside the dorm, Sanaa takes a look through the dorm windows and breathes a sigh of relief that Jordan did not hear the football player calling out her name. Sanaa then takes a seat on the couch next to the window behind a large potted plant where she can see Flagler dorm. After about ten minutes with no sight of Jordan or the girl, Sanaa hears a familiar voice coming from behind, "Sanaa, what's going on?" Chrystal inquires as she steps out of the elevator, "Sanaa, you're waiting on Jordan?" Always full of pride, Sanaa smartly replies, "No, I wasn't waiting on him. I just came from outside. I was just resting until I got ready to take the stairs up to the room, that's all." Chrystal asks, "Sanaa, why don't you take the elevator?" Acting like she's out of breath, Sanaa gasps, "Oh I'm just trying to be more active and get in some exercise; cardio work, you know." Sanaa takes a deep breath, and looking out the window, stands, looks at Chrystal, saying, "I'm going up now. I'll see you later," Chrystal's facial expression indicates she thinks Sanaa is acting kind of strange, but says, "Oh, ok. Bye." As Chrystal leaves the dorm headed to her car, she thinks to herself, *what is going on with Sanaa?* Then she sees Toni sitting on the quad hanging out with football players, and waves, but Toni gives a half-hearted wave, expressing that she's involved with something or another. At this point, Chrystal can't help but feel that everybody is acting really weird. She thinks to herself, '*it must be that time of the year.* "Oh, well," she says as she shakes her head in wonderment and overlooks all the weirdness because it is a beautiful sunny, cool day, and she's enjoying every bit of it as she smiles, walking to her car. About fifteen minutes of consistently ignoring the sexual innuendos made toward her by the jocks on the quad, Toni sees Jordan walking out of the dorm, talking with Sheila. Her eyes widen to a lifted brow while her jaw drops with a gasp in surprise at seeing Jordan so cozy-friendly with Sheila. Toni immediately stands up and walks toward the couple, and stops close to where they are walking, so Jordan can physically see her watching him. Jordan briefly looks in Toni's direction, and she knows he can see her, but he looks through her like a glass window and continues his playful chit-chat with Sheila. Toni continues watching Jordan and Sheila as they disappear into the student union building. Toni thinks to herself, *Sanaa is going to explode when she hears about this.* Toni then goes straightaway to Sanaa's dorm to drop the tea on Jordan again. Toni runs to the dorm, hoping to tell Sanaa quickly enough for her to catch Jordan in the act. She ignores the elevators and takes the stairs up to Sanaa's room. After knocking several times, Sanaa answers with a sleepy voice, "Who is it?" Toni answers, "It's me, girl, open the door." Sanaa says, "Hold on." Sanaa opens the door appearing to have just woken up. Toni rushes past her and says, "Girl, I waited on the quad just to see what Jordan was up to, and he came out of the dorm with that girl Sheila, all cozy-friendly and stuff. I stood out so he could see me watching, but girl, he really did not seem to care. They walked past me like I wasn't even there and went into the student union building." Now fully awake, Sanaa replies through glassy eyes, "Thanks, Toni, for watching out. I got it from here." Toni excitedly replies, "Sanaa, you not gonna confront Jordan?" Sanaa looks at Toni and says, "I made my bed, so I'm going to lie in it. Right about now, I am sick of all men and their lies. They all just make me crazy. If he wants me, it will be up to him to make the effort. I love Jordan, but I am not running after any man. Life's too short." Toni says, "Ok, I feel you. So, what are you up to tonight?" Sanaa replies, "Nothing, I guess." Toni suggests, "Look, the women from the feminist organization are having another rally tonight. Come go with Daedai, Raven, and I, and if you see Chrystal in time, drag her butt along too, ok?" Sanaa hesitantly says, "Shoot, ok. I'm not doing anything else. I guess I can come and see these ladies you guys are so excited about. What time does the forum start?" Toni says, "Around 8:00. We can all meet on the quad at 7:45 and go in together." Not too pleased with the aggressive nature of Raven, Daedai, and Toni after their last experience from this rally, Sanaa has reservations about going to such a thing, but agrees to come along just to see what all the hype is about. Enjoying herself in the sunny-cool of the day, Chrystal reaches Tyson's apartment and parks her car. She knocks on the door once, and right before the second knock, Tyson quickly opens the door, scaring Chrystal to a surprised gasp. Frightened by Tyson answering the door so quickly, she shouts, "Boy, don't do that. You scared me." Chrystal didn't know that Tyson was watching her through the window as she was parking her car and knew exactly when she was about to knock; and answering the door so quickly he claims he was acting psychic, saying, "I just couldn't wait to let you in, baby." Chrystal sobers from her frightened state and says, "Ok, I like that." As Chrystal comes in and sits down on the couch, Tyson asks, "Do you want something to drink?" Chrystal inquires, "What you got?" Tyson says, "Whatever you want or however you like it, I got it." Dismissing his attempt at being sensual, Chrystal states, "Boy, just get me a Diet Coke, please." Tyson goes and makes her a Diet Coke with ice, and when he hands her the coke, he says, "Chrystal, look, I got to go back home, I got some legal things I need to take care of. After hearing this,

Chrystal's eyebrows lift up, giving him that piercing stare, and exclaims, "Go home again? What are these legal things causing you to miss school?" Tyson quickly responds, "Nothing serious, baby, just some personal things I need to put behind me." Chrystal looks at Tyson with a stare of skepticism, and inquires, "Does this have anything to do with you and Jalen?" Tyson says, "No, that was just a favor I was doing for him." Now with a serious expression on her face, Chrystal further questions, "Tyson, this isn't anything criminal you're dealing with, is it?" Tyson quickly answers, "No, baby, you know me, it ain't nothing like that. It's just something I need to resolve that I rather keep personal right now, ok?" Before Chrystal can fully respond, Tyson makes a passionate move, wetting Chrystal's neck with kisses and playfully fondling to titillate and stimulate her mood. As Tyson continues his arousing foreplay, Chrystal pretentiously struggles to move away from the sensation of his kisses, and whispers softly in his ear, "It's not ok," and while struggling to speak under Tyson's relentless kissing and fondling, she eventually surrenders under his arousing foreplay. But irrespective of his sexual maneuvering, Chrystal still asserts her dissatisfaction about his going home, whispering in a sexy yet stern voice, "I still have a serious problem with you going home." However, for the next hour or two, with Chrystal being preoccupied sexually, Tyson is temporarily off the hook from answering any questions as they go the way of a married couple.

After Tyson and Chrystal finish their lovemaking, Chrystal notices the time, and now totally satisfied, she jumps out of bed, gets dressed, and tells Tyson she needs to get back to campus right away. Chrystal stares at Tyson with all seriousness and states, "We still have things we need to talk about; you call me later." Tyson bends forward to get up, but Chrystal smiles and says, "No, don't get up. I know the way out. Go ahead and relax; you're going to need that energy for later." Tyson lays back down and replies, "Alright, Ms. Independent, see you later." Chrystal slips into her shoes and leaves the room, throwing him a kiss. As Chrystal leaves the apartment, she sees Jordan parking his car and pauses from getting inside her car, waiting to speak. But as Jordan gets out of his car, Chrystal can't speak for noticing a girl in the passenger seat. Chrystal stares at the girl relentlessly, and now dismisses any notion of speaking. Chrystal stares at Jordan straight in his face, searching for an explanation. Jordan looks straight ahead, saying nothing as he continues into his apartment with the girl waiting for him in the car. Chrystal enters her car, still looking at the girl, and as she backs out of her parking space to go forward, she passes Jordan's car, still trying to identify this girl, who is now looking in the opposite direction evading her nosey stare. Chrystal thinks to herself, *I got to hurry back to campus and hip my girl to what this negro is doing.*

CHAPTER 14
(MY SISTER IS GONE)

BACK ON CAMPUS, TONI IS IN RAVEN AND Daedai's room, gossiping girl stuff and bashing all men under the guise of toxic masculinity. Noticing the lateness of the hour, Raven exclaims, "Hey, y'all! It's almost time for the rally; let's go drag Sanaa and Chrystal along with us." Excited about the event, Toni comments, "I've already talked to Sanaa, and she said she's coming with us. Maybe we can get Chrystal to come too. Doubtful that Sanaa and Chrystal will come to the rally, Raven states, "I'll believe it when I see it." Daedai follows with like skepticism, "We shall see." The girls then scatter to get themselves dressed. About twenty minutes later, they meet in the dorm's lobby and head over to Sanaa's room. While on the way there, they see Chrystal headed the same way. Toni waves and yells, "Hey, Chrystal." Chrystal waves back and walks toward the girls, inquiring, "What are you guys up to?" Toni says, "We're headed over to your room to get Sanaa; she's going with us to the feminist rally. We want you to come too." Not believing that Sanaa would ever go to this forum, and not knowing that Sanaa had already agreed to go, Chrystal answers in a pacifying manner, "Well, if Sanaa goes, I'll go." With a big smile, Toni says, "You're going because Sanaa has already committed to go with us," The girls gleefully look at Chrystal as she responds with an appeasing halfhearted smile as they walk toward the dorm. Chrystal thinks to herself, *Oh, Lord, what have I gotten myself in to now. I need to tell Sanaa what's going on with Jordan. But I guess I better wait until I can get her alone before I say anything.* Raven says, "Hey, let's speed up the pace, ladies. It's getting close to time for the rally to start. You and Sanaa got to hurry up and get dressed. Oh, by the way, the affair is very casual." With that information, Chrystal gives another appeasing smile and says, "O—kay." Pressed for time, the girls pick up the pace. As they enter Sanaa and Chrystal's room, Sanaa is already dressed. Toni exclaims, "Guess what, Sanaa? Chrystal is coming with us."

In total surprise, Sanaa immediately looks at Chrystal and comments, "Oh, is that right?" Chrystal flippantly rolls her eyes as she walks past Sanaa to her closet. Chrystal picks out her outfit and rushes to get ready. Looking down at her watch, Raven says, "I'll meet y'all at the place." Daedai interjects, "Yeah, we know, you gotta go feed that little tapeworm, don't you?" Raven smacks her lips at Daedai, rolls her eyes, disregards the comment, and remarks, "To hell with you, Daedai, you're just jealous." Daedai quickly responds, "Nah, chick, I like men." After that statement, there is complete silence in the room; everybody is baffled by the comment, and Raven stares at Daedai intently, saying nothing. Then, she turns to leave on her way to the rally. Daedai watches as Raven leaves, and then she turns to Chrystal and asks, "Hey girl, you aren't ready yet." Chrystal answers sarcastically, "You guys are certainly welcome to go without me." Toni interrupts, declaring "No, you said you were coming, now put on that lame-ass outfit and let's go." Chrystal, brightly insulted, comments, "Oh no, you didn't, and for your information, Ms. Lady, I don't do lame. Neither do I do that trashy, hand-me-down thing you have on." Daedai breaks out laughing, and before Toni can rev up to toss another jaw-dropping insult, Sanaa quickly interrupts, "Ladies, it's late. Let's go." Chrystal and Toni break from their playful rant and gather their stuff to leave. As they go out the door, Daedai jokingly comments, "I hope that girl has fed that little tapeworm before we get there." Knowing what Daedai is referencing, everybody breaks out laughing as they head to the rally. When they arrive at the amphitheater, they can hear the crowd inside going crazy. They enter the lobby door and immediately see Raven feeding her face while talking with Courtney. Courtney sees the girls coming and abruptly leaves, saying, "Raven, I'll talk with you later, ok?" Raven nods her head and walks to meet her girls while supporting a mouth full of hotdog and holding a soda. Raven speaks to the girls through a mouthful of food, "Y'all ready to go in?" Seeing the food and the soda in Raven's hand, Daedai jokingly inquires, "Oh! You didn't get us anything? Or did your little tapeworm friend consume ours?" Toni starts laughing, and Raven warns Daedai, "Girl, don't mess with me this evening. I ain't with your stuff; this rally is too important, and you need to give it your full attention instead of slinging childish jokes." Daedai giggles and laughingly replies, "Oh, what made you think I was joking?" All the girls start giggling, and Raven gives Daedai the mean eye and says, "Later for you, Daedai. Let's go inside." Raven leads the girls into the rally amongst a heard of the most fired-up feminist women to be found on campus, all led by the student sponsors of the event. The girls find an area where they can all sit close to each other. When seated, they watch as the student host of the ceremony takes the podium to give the purpose of the rally and introduce the speaker. Attending the first rally, Raven, Daedai, and Toni are familiar with the speaker, who is an apostle of Simone De Beauvoir and Betty Friedan, the trailblazing members of the feminist movement. When the speaker comes to the podium, she opens up with a message from the philosophies of those trailblazers who have argued that: "…placing women solely in the home limits their possibilities and waste talent and potential. The perfect nuclear family image depicted and strongly marketed… does not reflect happiness and is rather degrading for women," (Friedman

1963). The speaker continues in saying, "The biggest challenge facing women in the United States today is patriarchy. This is especially evident in the realm of politics. Regardless of a woman's experience, education, or abilities, the patriarchal nature of US society fosters the perception that women are less qualified and less competent than men," (Bane 2019). The speaker was giving the same message she had given in the first rally; preaching equal treatment for women, declaring their social and economic rights, encouraging the continued fight against sexual harassment, and declaring how the movement is changing the traditional image of the woman from a victimized stand-behind-your-man housewife to the board room executive. The speaker again brings a message defining women socially equal too, or above men, in all things; and women should never see themselves limited in not possessing all of life's chances, irrespective of their traditional maternal and or conjugal instincts. The message conveyed in this rally was the same as the last rally, but stronger and more resolute, and she commented about the inclusion of other aggrieved groups, such as BLM, LGBTQ, ANTIFA and the Pro-Choice Movement, all existing under the umbrella of intersectionality to strengthen their political and marketing position. Then she strongly criticized the instinct of women to work toward a strong nuclear family in the traditional sense; stating again how that mindset degrades and impedes the progress of all women. A new twist added to the rally this time was having participants break into focus groups for a more intensive small group briefing. As the girls leave the rally and group sessions, they are, once again, pumped up, believing the information to be culturally on point; they start discussing feminist doctrines amongst each other with more enthusiasm than ever. For the first time buying into all the hype and rhetoric is Sanaa, who unexpectedly comes away from the rally convinced, more than ever, that what she heard was the truth; regrettably, her newly found revelation is fostered by her own personal feelings relative to Jordan and her Father. She is now satisfied that these feminist women have the right message and attitude toward men. However, Chrystal remains skeptical about the whole thing. As the girls take a slow walk back to Sanaa and Chrystal's dorm, the girls engage themselves in a full range of debate relative to the feminist rally. When they finally arrive at the room, the girls are still deep into their discussions, so much so that they continue for hours. Sanaa and the girls get so involved with the back-and-forth discussions they forget about any studying, until Chrystal, still not totally convinced by the rhetoric, inserts a crimp into the conversational mood by informing everyone that she and Sanaa need to study. Understanding the pressures of law school, Raven, Toni, and Daedai understand that it's time for them to leave. However, before leaving, still excited about the interaction, Raven says, "I don't know about you guys, but I enjoyed our collaboration. We need to continue the conversation. Toni enthusiastically agrees, "I enjoyed the conversations too. Can we get together tomorrow and talk some more?" Sanaa says, "Sure, why not? I liked the discussion myself; it feels empowering." As Chrystal walks past Sanaa, she rolls her eyes and says in a placating tone as she motions toward the door, "Time to go now, see y'all tomorrow." Taking note of Chrystal's patronizing attitude, Daedai cynically responds, "Ok, Ms. Thang, we get your hint; we'll see you when we see you, and do us a favor, burn that hideous lame-a** outfit, okay. Bye, Felicia." With that insult, the girls giggle as they leave the room. Chrystal quickly closes the door, then turns to look at Sanaa and thinks for a minute on how to tell Sanaa what she saw at Jordan's apartment. Chrystal takes a deep breath and says, "Sanaa, I saw a girl in Jordan's car as I was pulling out to leave the apartment. It could have been innocent. I don't know; however, she did not go into the apartment, she waited for him in the car. What happened after that, I don't know. I left, coming here." Sanaa listened attentively to what Chrystal was telling her but acted unfazed. However,

Chrystal could feel that Sanaa was upset because she kept evading eye contact, turning away to do busy stuff, and hiding her reaction. Chrystal leans forward, maneuvering to see Sanaa's face, and asks, "Sanaa, you ok?" Sanaa turns and arrogantly declares, "That's ok. Hell, if he can do it, so can I. From now on, hear me roar, damn it." Being aware of the sometimes-volcanic eruptions of her roommate, Chrystal immediately gives Sanaa a curious stare and knows that something is about to jump off. A couple of days pass, and the girls continue to have their little pro-feminist debates in each other's rooms. One day after a meeting, leaving Sanaa's room, Toni, Raven, and Daedal see Teri, their dorm-mate, rushing out to meet them. Teri shouts, "Daedai, I've been trying to find you for hours." Daedai says, "Girl, I forgot my phone, it's in the room. What's wrong?" Teri, with a sad expression on her face, says, "Daedai, you need to call home right away, it's an emergency." Daedai becomes visibly upset, thinking that something may be wrong with her Mother. She reaches for and uses Toni's phone to call home. When she hears her Mother answer the phone, Daedai is somewhat relieved, but realizes that her Mother has started crying. Then nervously, her Mother delivers the bad news that her older sister has been shot and killed. Daedai screams and gasps in cramping pain, "No Momma, please, no! Don't tell me that, please! Her Mother continues talking and crying, "Daedai, they killed her; she wasn't doing anything to anybody, just walking down the street, and those fools shooting at each other hit her." Crying steadily, Daedai says, "Momma, I'm on the way home. I'll be there as quickly as I can. Are you going to be alright?" Daedai's Mother says in a trembling voice, "Just hurry home, baby." Daedai says, "I'm coming, Momma. I'm on my way." Daedai hangs up, visibly shaken and crying profusely as she attempts to makes haste, but her legs begin to wobble as she staggers trying to walk, and the girls alongside her reach out and grab her arm to keep her from falling. Woozy from overwhelming grief, Daedai cannot manage well on her own, so Toni and Raven, now crying themselves, help Daedai to the dorm and up to her room. After hearing from Daedai the information leading to her sister's death, Toni and Raven state that they are coming to Chicago to be with Daedai for the funeral. The girls are now crying, hugging, and comforting Daedai. Toni repeatedly says, "Daedai, it's gonna be alright. We got you; it's gonna be alright." Still out of her mind in shock and grief, Daedai just bows, shaking her head in disbelief. Then there's a knock at the door, and without waiting for a response, Chrystal and Sanaa rush in to hug and console Daedai and start crying with their friend. Sanaa says, "Girl, we rushed right over after Raven called us. Daedai we are so sorry to hear about your sister. We know this is tough for you." Sanaa says, "Whatever you need, Daedai, I got you, ok?" Still a little woozy with swollen and teary eyes, Daedai sobers in her demeanor and says to her friends, "Thank you guys so much for caring about me, but right now, I need to get ready to go home and be with my Momma; she's taking it very hard." Understanding the difficulty of this situation, Toni, Sanaa, and Chrystal advise, "We're going to go and let you get some rest and prepare to go home. Whatever you need, we got you, Daedai. We will check back with you and help get you home, ok?" Daedai shakes her head in the affirmative, and Raven walks the girls to the door. Chrystal looks back at Daedai and says, "Let us know when she feels a little better, and we'll come back and help with everything." Raven says, "I'll call you as soon as she gets back to her normal self." In tears, Sanaa says, "Ok, see you in a little bit." Chrystal and Sanaa, walking back to their room, get into a discussion about Daedai's sister's killing. When they get into the room, they go on a tirade about guns, gangs, violence, and toxic masculinity. The discussion transitions into a mild condemnation of all men, and using feminist talking points, Sanaa asserts, "If women were in charge, all this killing and violence would be eliminated or radically reduced. Men seem only to care about their insignificant egos, spawned by too much testosterone, making them not able to think clearly and act like little boys with no control. They do not have the emotional sensibilities to just back off." Chrystal adds, "You know I'm not down with this feminist stuff, but I'm feeling you on this one. I think a woman has to be on guard all the time. Take Tyson, for instance, he thinks I don't trust him, but I've seen too much in dealing with men. I think for any woman it is difficult to trust a man completely; they will always disappoint you in some way or another." Sanaa says, "That's alright, sometimes you have to beat them at their own game. They say women cannot do what men can do and still be a lady. I refute that, and in the words of soul brother number one, James Brown, 'WATCH ME!'" Chrystal then laughs as Sanaa cuts a James Brown dance move with an attitude of defiance, and the girls continue their diatribe on the shortcomings of men late into the evening. Three days later, Daedai has already gone home to be with her Mother. Toni and Raven catch a plane to Chicago to support Daedai at her sister's funeral. Daedai meets Raven and Toni at the airport, and since Daedai's house is full of family members and relatives, Toni and Raven check into a hotel near the house. Later in the evening, Daedai comes to the hotel to be with Toni and Raven, attempting to break away from the pain of everything in her house. The girls get together, have some drinks, and all except Toni, get plastered, trying to forget about what has happened; but for Daedai, the drinking only intensifies the hurt she feels in losing her sister. She cries, but her friends comfort her all night long. At about one o'clock in the morning, after going to the bathroom to freshen up, Daedai wakes up her friends and tells them she's going home. Filled with emotion, Daedai says, "Thank you for coming to be with me. If you had not come, I don't know how I would be handling all of this." Toni says, "Daedai, we are your sisters, we always got you." Hearing Toni and Raven say that means the world to Daedai. Toni says, "Daedai, I'll walk down with you." Daedai says, "No, no. Go back to sleep. I'm ok. I just need to be by myself right now. I'll see you later at the house, ok?" In a sleepy voice, Toni says, "Ok, Daedai, you sure you alright?" Daedai says, "Yes, I'm fine. I'll see you guys later." Toni watches Daedai as she closes the door. As the sun bursts through the curtains and the alarm clock rings, the girls wake up to see its eight o'clock in the morning, and knowing the funeral is at eleven o'clock, Toni and Raven jump up and get ready to go to Daedai's house. After Toni and Raven get dressed in their all-black attire, they catch a taxi over to Daedai's house. When the girls arrive at the house, Daedai has already assigned Toni and Raven to ride to the church in one of the family limousines. When inside the house, they notice that Daedai is very giddy and school girlish, mainly because her Father, now divorced from her Mother, has come back to mourn his daughter and give support to his ex-wife and the other children. Daedai is all over her Dad like a little girl. So, when the procession arrives at the house, Daedai, her Mom, and her Dad walk arm and arm, followed by Toni and Raven, riding with the family to the church. Toni and Raven enter the church with the family and are seated about two rows back from where Daedai and her immediate family are seated. Because Toni, Raven, and even Daedai do not go to church at all, they act like fish out of the water, not knowing much about traditional church services. They feel odd not knowing the hymns and when to stand up or sit down. The church is Daedai's Mother's church, passed down by membership through Daedai's great grandparents. Daedai's Mother does not go to church either; however, she does know some hymns and the church order of service from going to church as a little girl. All through the funeral services, Toni and Raven are reading and sending text messages totally oblivious to the preaching of the Word that is being spoken; until one of the elders in the church walks over and whispers, "Young ladies, you are now in the House of the Lord. Y'all got to put those away." A little embarrassed, Toni and Raven humbly whisper, "Oh, we're so sorry." The girls put away their cell phones, and for the first time, they listen to the funeral services. Then a young girl in the choir steps forward to sing the lead on a song by Andrae Crouch, "The blood will never lose its power," and as this young girl and the choir sing, the delivery is so powerful that something begins to come over Raven that in the past she has felt before; and as she starts crying and wiping her eyes, she tries to evade looking at Toni; however, Toni has already noticed the waterworks and is surprised at an emotional Raven, and she asks, "Raven, you ok?" Still wiping her face with her hankie, Raven responds, "I must have gotten something in my eyes." Toni whispers sarcastically, "Uh-huh, ok. That would explain it." The hardest part of the services for Toni and Raven was seeing Daedai and her family break down when reviewing the body for the last time. Watching the family grieving at the casket was heart-wrenching and difficult for Raven and Toni. After the church services, the internment, and spending some quality time with Daedai at the re-pass, Toni and Raven hug and kiss Daedai and offer final condolences to her family and tell Daedai they are going to leave in the morning and head back to school. Daedai cries at the thought of her friends leaving but understands the need for them to get back school. Daedai can't give them a definite time when she will be returning; she's not rushing to come back to school right now because she's incredibly happy to be able to spend time home with her Mom and Dad. Not wanting Toni and Raven to catch a cab again, Daedai says, "Y'all wait a minute." She looks around the room, sees her cousin Ronny, and calls him over. Daedai says, "Ronny, I need you to do me a favor. I need you to take Toni and Raven back to their hotel." Ronny says, "Ok, whenever they ready." Raven looks at Daedai and says, "Girl, you ok?" Daedai says, "Yes, and I'm so grateful to have sisters like you. Now you guys have a safe trip back, and I'll be back when I come back." The girls hug goodbye and follow Cousin Ronny out to his car. Now, Ronny is this young baller-type personality, with the gold bling around his neck and all up in his mouth. He has the typical baller-type car that the girls think is fly. But when he starts the car, the music is so loud with profane hip-hop, the people outside the re-pass holler at Ronny to be respectful and turn that music down, and being embarrassed, he does so immediately. Riding back to the hotel, the girls start to feel a little uncomfortable in the car because Ronny is acting a little funny. He is looking all around like he's on the lookout for someone or some group of people. So, the girls, they start looking around too, anticipating that they might have to stretch out on the car floor or something, and now their attitude is one of being cautiously apprehensive. When Toni and Raven finally reach the hotel, they fake like everything is ok as they wave goodbye to Cousin Ronny. However, happy to be out of Ronny's car, Raven and Toni look at each other and start breathing a sigh of relief because they knew from the way Ronny was acting, somebody of the not-too-friendly kind was looking for Cousin Ronny, and Lord knows they did not want to get caught up in that mess. So, the girls, thankful to be back at the hotel, rush up to their room to start preparing to leave for school early in the morning. In the early morning, the girls rush out to the airport without eating break-fast, which is extremely difficult for Raven, but they were a little behind schedule and had to rush to the airport. Attempting to rush through checkpoints, the girls depart for their destina-tion about fifteen minutes later. Hours of flight time later, the girls land at the Fort Lauderdale International Airport, where Chrystal and Sanaa are already there to pick them up. Sanaa greets them and says, "Welcome back. How was Daedai and her Mom?" Toni says, "It was so painful to see Daedai and her family hurting so bad, but we got to meet Daedai's Dad, who Daedai treasures, and we got to spend some time with Daedai's Mother and the rest of her family. The service was beautiful with all the flowers, and the mortician did a great job on Daedai's sister." Making sure that there was no doubt that they supported their friend well, Chrystal asks, "Were the flowers and the spray we sent all there?" Raven says, "Yes, they were, and they were so beautiful. Daedai cried when they read the cards, hearing that the flowers and the spray were from us." Sanaa says, "I'm glad she knows how much her friends care for her. By the way, when is she coming back?" Toni shrugging her shoulders with palms raised up, replies, "She didn't specifically say. She just said she'll be back soon." Taking off some of her clothes, Toni says to her friends, "Girl, it was cold as all-out up there. I'm so glad to be back in this sun. I don't know what in the world to do." On that note, Raven and Toni high-five each other in agreement. On the way to campus, Raven's stomach starts making funny noises. Needing food immediately, Raven offers to buy everybody food if they can just stop and let her get something to eat. Sanaa did not plan to stop, but says, "Ok, I'll stop. What do you want to eat?" Raven, not having a par-ticular taste, says, "Shoot, you know me. I ain't particular. I'll take the first thing smoking." Knowing how much Raven likes to eat, the girls start laughing as they look for the next fast-food place, and they don't let Raven forget she's buying. The girls finally stop at a Chick-fil-A, go inside, sit down, and enjoy their food. Fifteen minutes later, Raven has gotten full and sat-isfied, and the reality of her having to pay for everybody's food has set in, and she's feeling like she has gotten the short end of the deal, and now she's impatiently rushing to get back to campus. Raven impatiently asks in a rude tone, "Y'all ready to go?" Sanaa stares at Raven intently, insulted by her lack of respect for her friends, and responds, "If you don't mind, I'd really like to finish chewing my food. Evidently, that function of the mouth is not for people like you who swallow their food whole, but for people like me, who find it particularly important to properly digest what they eat." Toni gasps for air as she bends over laughing while at the same time trying to hold food in her mouth, and says, "Damn, Sanaa, you starting to sound just like Daedai." Everybody breaks out laughing except Raven, who abruptly gives Toni a little open-mouth cocked-head ravenesk stare, and comes back smooth in her response, saying, "Look, I'm not mad at you. I understand how hard it is for you guys to know that I can eat anything and everything and stay this extremely gorgeous, and you can't. But you do need to get over it! Don't you think?" Chrystal, with raised eyebrows, responds quickly, "Ladies, please hurry up so we can leave because Raven and her little tapeworm are starting to wreck my last nerve. The girls get up laughing as they head toward the car, and as they ride, they crack jokes on each other all the way to campus. They even give Raven's alleged tapeworm a new name; they name him Tapeworm Charlie. However, that did not sit well with Raven, but the girls figured it was time to take her down a peg or two.

CHAPTER 15
(AN EXPRESSION OF <u>ANGER?</u> OR <u>SPIRITS</u>?)

AFTER ARRIVING BACK ON CAMPUS, THE GIRLS help Raven and Toni carry their bags to their dorm. On the sidewalk, at a distance, Raven sees Courtney near the student union area sitting with a girl on the steps of the science building. Raven cannot fathom in her mind that she's seeing Courtney intimately holding hands with this girl. Raven stops and stands lifelessly while Momentarily trapped in a state of cognitive dissonance, as she watches Courtney amorously involved with someone else. Not paying attention and walking behind Raven, Toni nearly bumps into her, and Toni says, "Watch out, Raven." As Toni side-steps and passes by, she looks at Raven and says, "What's going on with you, girl?" After hearing Toni's plea for caution, Raven snaps out of her trance, and not wanting Toni to learn of her relationship with Courtney, responds, "Oh nothing, I was just thinking about something; something I need to deal with later." With that comment, Raven and the girls continue heading toward the dorm. However, along the way, Raven is occasionally looking back, keeping an eye on what Courtney is doing. After the girls reach Raven's room, they congregate and talk for a Moment, then Sanaa and Chrystal leave, headed back to their dorm across campus. Toni stays for a few more rounds of gossip. Then after a pause in the conversation, Toni yawns with a stretch and says, "Hey, girl, I'm tired. I'm going down to my room. We did Daedai righteous, didn't we, Raven?" Raven answers, "I was glad to show up for my girl. I think we represented well, Toni." Toni says, "That's good to hear. Girl, I'm out." Toni stands up and walks toward the door, headed to her room. After saying goodbye and seeing Toni out of the door, Raven immediately races to get her phone to call Courtney. The phone is continuously busy after she tries multiple times. Raven eventually hangs up; however, she is in frantic mode, anticipating confronting Courtney about the girl she was with. When Chrystal and Sanaa get back to their room, Chrystal gets a call from Tyson, saying he is going to make another trip home to take care of some business. Suspicious about Tyson's constant need to go home, Chrystal comments, "First, it was that your Mother was sick. Now, what is it?" Tyson, on the defensive, says, "Baby, it's just some stuff I need to take care of." Chrystal comes back, "Well, does this 'stuff' you need to take care of involve a woman?" Tyson quickly responds, "Chrystal, I told you, it's nothing like that. I don't want or need anybody but you. When I get back, I will tell you why I had to keep going home. With an expression of confusion on her face, Chrystal loudly replies, "If it's not a problem to tell me what's going on when you come back, why should it be a problem for you to tell me now? As the person you supposedly love, I think I'm entitled to know why my man has to constantly keep running home." Tyson takes a deep breath, pauses for a minute, and says, "Chrystal, baby, please don't push me in a corner with this. I promise I will explain everything when I come back, and you are right; you are entitled to know what I'm doing at home. But I am asking you to please trust me on this. I'll share everything with you when I come back." Suspicious of Tyson's need to be so guarded, Chrystal asks, "Tyson, are you in trouble with the law?" Tyson looks up at the ceiling, inhales, breathes, and says, "Chrystal, it's nothing like that, trust me." Chrystal, with a no-nonsense type of tone, says, "Tyson, I don't know what's going on with you and this constant going home business, but you need to tell me something when you get back here, or you and I are going to have some serious issues. You feel me?" Feeling the stress and tone of her ultimatum, Tyson says, "I understand, baby." Chrystal pauses, then goes silent, and asks, "When are you leaving?" Overwhelmed by her total lack of trust, Tyson slowly answers, "I'll be leaving tomorrow." Chrystal further asks, "When will you be back?" Tyson says, "Hopefully I'll be back in two or three days; that should be enough time to take care of my business." Not satisfied with any of Tyson's answers, Chrystal hesitantly gives in, saying, "Call me before you leave."

Tyson quickly answers, "I will, baby; love you. I'll call you." Tyson keeps the phone close to his ear, waiting for a reciprocal response from Chrystal, but she says nothing as she holds the phone. He can hear the soft sound of her breathing, but in ghost-like silence, she hangs up. Worriedly thinking about his predicament, Tyson can sense from Chrystal's attitude that she is not happy about all the secrecy; and he understands that he's possibly in deep doo-doo. He realizes that he needs to come clean with her when he comes back, or he may jeopardize his relationship. On the other side of campus, Raven is anxious to talk with Courtney, seeking an explanation to why she was with another girl. Raven paces the room floor back and forth until jealousy takes control of her better thinking and urges her to rush to Courtney's apartment. When Raven gets to Courtney's place, she climbs the stairs to the door and can hear people talking inside. But, after she knocks and calls Courtney's name, the voices inside abruptly go quiet, and no one comes to answer the door. Mad as hell, Raven starts banging on the door, but Courtney or whoever is inside with her, does not make a sound. Raven yells at the door in frustration, "That's ok, b***h. I know you hear me. I know you are in there. Is this the way you act? I leave town for a couple of days, and this is what you do. When I see you, it's gonna be on you, slut." Then Raven angrily kicks the door while spewing expletives, and retreats to her car. When Raven gets inside her car, she is angry and in tears; however, she waits for a minute to calm down before starting her car. After calming down, she heads back to campus. When Raven arrives back on campus, she immediately goes to her room, and while sitting on her bed, she thinks to herself, *did I really just do that? I cannot believe I just did that; what came over me? I am too pretty and definitely too much of a lady to have ever acted like that. I do not understand these feelings I have for Courtney; are they real? Am I really gay? Or are my feelings heightened from the act of being traumatized, betrayed and rejected?* As Raven ponders a host of things running through her mind, she eventually becomes emotionally drained and falls asleep. The next morning, Chrystal's phone rings, and it's Tyson, telling her that Jordan is taking him to the bus station. He says, "Baby, I know you have concerns about what I'm doing, but please know that I am not cheating on you. I'm just handling some personal business. I will explain everything fully when I come back, ok?" Somewhat distraught about having to wait for answers, Chrystal dispassionately says, "Have a safe trip; see you when I see you." Tyson notices her words and the coldness of her interaction toward him, but he doesn't have time to pacify her insecurity, so he just says, "I love you, Chrystal. I'll see you when I get back." With that, he hangs up. After Tyson gets himself together, Jordan takes Tyson to the bus station, and while driving, Jordan notices that Tyson is in serious thought mode. Jordan asks, "Hey, man, everything alright?" Tyson takes a deep breath and says, "Nah, man, I got problems. You know I got this thing at home right, and Chrystal thinks if I'm not cheating on her, why can't I tell her what I'm doing? So, I told her when I come back I'm going to tell her everything. I know when I tell her she's not going to like it and think bad of me." Jordan nods his head in the affirmative. Tyson looks at Jordan and changes the subject from his problems to Jordan's, asking, "Have you and Sanaa talked yet?" Jordan stares back at Tyson and answers, "Nah, man, that girl... I don't know how to deal with her." Sharing what he thinks is the problem, Tyson comments, "You know Sanaa thinks that you and Sheila go together." Jordan replies, "You know that probably wouldn't be a bad idea if I wasn't in love with Sanaa. Sheila would be someone right for me because she's mature, and I can talk to her. Sheila is turning out to be an awfully close friend, but we haven't gone past that point yet." Offering what he thinks to be true, Tyson says, "Jordan, I know for sure Sanaa still loves you; she's just got this ego, man, that's bigger than Mt. Everest, which gets her into relationship problems by not being able to compromise." Jordan looks at Tyson in astonishment and replies, "Damn, Dr. Phil, if you can see all that, you need to diagnose your own situation with Chrystal." Ironically, Tyson looks at Jordan and replies, "Bruh, you know what they say about good mechanics; they can fix everybody else's car, but they don't spend enough time fixing their own." Jordan nods laughingly and says, "I hear you, man." Then, after a Moment of silence, Jordan points ahead, saying, "Hey! There's the station." Jordan pulls into the station and puts his car in park. Tyson exits with his bag, and now bent over and looking through the car window, he says, "Thanks, man. I'll see you when I get back. I'll call you if I need a ride, ok?" Joking with Tyson, Jordan says, "Yo. man, what I look like, an Uber driver?" Tyson, with a look of seriousness and surprise on his face, says, "Don't play, man." Jordan lightheartedly says, "Don't worry man. I got you. Have a safe trip home and say hello to Moms for me." Jordan and Tyson say goodbye by pointing at each other as a way of silently indicating an approval of their close friendship as Tyson goes into the station. Jordan then pulls out into traffic, headed back to his apartment. Three hours later, back on campus, Sanaa and Chrystal are entering their dorm room after studying on the yard, and Sanaa says, "What's wrong, Chrystal? You've been acting preoccupied all day. Are you worried about Tyson?" Chrystal responds quickly, "Nah, I'm not worried about him. I'm worried about what he is doing at home." Sanaa intently looks at Chrystal and says, "You really think Tyson is cheating on you, don't you?" Chrystal tightens her lips with raised brows and answers, "If it were only that simple, I would know how to handle things. I know when Tyson is lying, but with this going home thing he's doing, I'm not sure, and I don't like to be kept in the dark about anything." Sanaa thinks a minute and comments, "I think you need to keep the pressure on, girl. You need to call his butt at home and keep digging for answers. Believe me, he will break." Chrystal looks up at Sanaa, and then with lips clenched and eyes closed, she shakes her head non-confirmatively and answers, "Sanaa, he did say he would explain everything when he gets back."

Intently staring at Chrystal, Sanaa sarcastically replies, "Oh! Ok then, why you worried?" Looking down at the floor and thinking about what Sanaa is asking, Chrystal hesitantly answers, "I think, I just might do what you say. But I'm going to wait a day and see if he calls me." Seeming more like an instigator rather than a problem solver who is helping a friend navigate through a situation, Sanaa states in an opinionated tone, "Alright, but it seems to me, the longer you put it off, the more you are going to agonize over the situation." Drained from assuming the worst, Chrystal looks up at Sanaa with an empty stare, pauses, and says, "I think I'm going to play it by ear. I have to allow time for trust Sanaa, but thanks for the advice." Looking at her roommate through compassionate eyes, Sanaa concedes and says, "Ok, but if you need to talk, I'm here." Sanaa then grabs some of the feminist information she was given at the rally, and while reading, she starts laughing loudly. Thinking that Sanaa is laughing at her, and agitated from her laughing, Chrystal asks, "You want to let me in on what's so funny?" Still chuckling, Sanaa says, "These feminists women have no mercy on men, and this stuff is so funny. Chrystal, check this out: Sheng Wang, the comedian writes, 'Why do people say, 'Grow some balls'? Balls are weak and sensitive. If you wanna be tough, grow a vagina. Those things can take a pounding.' Chrystal and Sanaa both break out laughing and forget all about everything else. Sanaa continues, "Wait a minute, wait a minute; check this out," Still laughing, Sanaa says, Caitlin Moran, the journalist writes, 'Here is the quick way of working [figuring] out if you're a feminist. Put your hand in your pants. a) Do you have a vagina? and b) Do you want to be in charge of it? If you said 'yes' to both, then congratulations! You're a feminist." (NPR.com 2016). Both girls have a good laugh at all the funny material inside the rally packet, and Sanaa says, "I'm starting to feel these women. I feel their anger and frustration." Chrystal and Sanaa, going through all the rally material start to understand the attitude and emotions behind each feminist writer's assertion. Chrystal unexpectedly confesses, "I never thought I could or would understand this movement, but I can sympathize with the frustration behind it." Nodding her head in agreement, looking at Chrystal, Sanaa says, "My feelings exactly; my feelings exactly." Both girls are quiet as Sanaa reads *A Vindication of the Rights of Woman*, by Mary Wallstonecraft, Sanaa quotes, "My own sex, I hope, will excuse me if I treat them like rational creatures instead of flattering their fascinating graces, and viewing them as if they were in a state of perpetual childhood, unable to stand alone," (Mary Wallstonecraft 2004). Internalizing the message, the girls look at each other reflectively silent as they change the activist atmosphere to focus their attention on gathering law books to study for their classes. Two days later, Daedai has arrived back on campus, but she did not call or let her girlfriends know she would be coming back. She figured she would sneak in and surprise her friends. As she enters her dorm room, she sees Raven, as usual, chomping down on a sandwich. When Raven sees it's Daedai, she's so surprised at seeing her friend she almost chokes on the food in her mouth. Raven immediately jumps up and runs to hug

Daedai. After the emotional hugging and crying, Daedai even forgets about making tapeworm jokes. Daedai just throws up praising hands and proclaims loudly, "Free at last, free at last. Thank God Almighty, I'm free at last." Astonished by the comment, Raven jokingly comments, "Come on, Daedai, home life couldn't have been that bad." Daedai quickly answers, "Girl, you don't know. I love my Mom, my Dad and my sisters with everything within me, but Moms would not let me go out of the house. I know she's afraid and does not want me to get caught up in anything and get hurt. I understand her fear; my sister's murder was traumatic for all of us, but damn, Raven, you know me. I'm not a fearful person, and I'm not meant to be closed up in the house. I was climbing the walls wanting to get outside. So maybe now you can see why I feel happy as a runaway slave to be back here." Chuckling at Daedai's comments about being at home, Raven says, "On that note, I feel ya." Attempting to catch up on things happening at school, Daedai inquires, "You guys still getting together in Sanaa and Chrystal's room to talk that rally stuff?" Discouraged by the lack of effort to keep the thing going, Raven says, "Not as much since you left to go home; however, I hope now that you're back, we can get things moving again." Daedai nods her head in the affirmative, saying, "I sure do hope so. I loved the interaction we had with each other, especially when we jump all over these crazy men." Daedai and Raven smile at each other as Daedai begins to unpack and settle in. After Daedai gets her clothes squared away and sits on her bed, she asks, "What's been going on in your life while I was at home?" Feeling duped by Courtney, Raven does not want to give Daedai an "I told you so" Moment, so she holds back information about her situation with Courtney, and looks at Daedai somewhat passively, saying, "Girl, I don't know. I've been busy with classes." Attempting to make conversation, Daedai simply asks, "What's up with you and Courtney?" Surprised by the question and answering somewhat quickly, Ravens responds in a serious tone, "What do you mean what's up with me and Courtney?" Thinking that Daedai has heard something about her situation with Courtney, Raven asks in an unfriendly tone, "What about me and Courtney?" Awestruck by Raven's change in attitude, Daedai replies, "Hold up, wait a minute, I was just asking how you guys were doing, nothing more than that. What you do and who you do it with is your business. I was just trying to make conversation, woman!" Aware now of Daedai's innocent intentions, Raven apologizes and reluctantly confesses, "I'm sorry Daedai. Courtney and I aren't together anymore; things have happened." With a better understanding of Raven's attitude, Daedai asks, "You want to talk about it?" As tears begin to well up in Raven's eyes, displaying all the hurt and stress from holding everything inside, she now figures she can share her situation with somebody she trusts and get things off her chest. Raven says, "When I got back here from your sister's funeral, I saw Courtney engaged intimately with another girl. I was mad as all hell. So I went to her apartment and showed out." Daedai looks at Raven, and holding true to form, asks, "How do you want to handle this b***h?" Quickly responding, Raven says, "Dog, Daedai, you just got back here and you're trying to get it on already?" Daedai looks at Raven intently and unapologetically says, "Girl, you know me. I stay ready for whatever, whenever. So, what you want to do?" Attempting to lower the tension a little bit, Raven says, "I'll let you know when I'm ready to do something, but for right now, leave it alone." Daedai replies, "Let me know when you want to do something." Raven nods her head and says in a placating tone, "I will definitely let you know, Daedai."

CHAPTER 16
(THE PACT)

A DAY OR TWO LATER, WHILE STUDYING IN HER room, Chrystal receives a call, and it's Tyson, letting her know that he's at the apartment. He says, "Baby, I'm back. Can you come over?" Chrystal answers, "It depends. Only if you are going to do what you promised and fill me in on the urgent need for you to go home so many times." Tyson promptly answers, "Baby, that's why I need you to come over, so I can talk with you face to face." Chrystal says, "Ok, I'll be there in a little bit." Chrystal immediately jumps up and tells Sanaa, "I'm going to see Tyson. I'll be back." Sanaa warns, "Chrystal, don't fall for the 'okey-doke,' ok? These guys are professional liars. They lie about everything." Chrystal looks at Sanaa in surprise and counters, "Sanaa, girl, you have really turned into a man-hater." Sanaa bluntly replies, "Could be, or maybe I'm just a little bitter over my situation with Jordan, but what difference does it make? We know how men are, right?" Baffled by the comment and trying to make sense of it, Chrystal just stares at Sanaa in unbelief, and then says, "I'll be back, Sanaa." Chrystal leaves the room, headed to her car, and while on the way to the parking lot, she sees Toni walking in the opposite direction, and asks, "Where are you off to?" Flashing a big smile, Toni says, "Chrystal, Daedai is back." Chrystal asks, "When did she get in?" Toni gleefully says, "She called herself sneaking in; she surprised us yesterday. I was coming to talk to you and Sanaa to see if we could get together." Glad to hear that Daedai is back, Chrystal says, "Hey, we can do that later, but right now, I'm on the way to see Tyson, but I'll be back soon; go ahead and tell Sanaa." Joyfully enthusiastic about the crew getting back together, Toni says, "I will." On a mission to deal with Tyson, Chrystal says, "I'll see you guys in a little bit." Toni says, "Ok," as she makes her way to Sanaa's room. Chrystal continues to her car, then heads to Tyson's apartment. On the way there, Chrystal is visibly nervous, thinking about what Tyson might tell her, but she quickly dismisses any negative thoughts as she focuses on the mounting traffic. When Chrystal finally arrives at the apartment, she does not see Jordan's car in his parking space, so she assumes he is not home. Chrystal thinks to herself, *I'm glad he's not here because it gives me time to be with Tyson uninterrupted.* Chrystal exits her car and walks toward the door, and as she raises her fist to knock, the door opens suddenly. Surprised by the sudden opening, Chrystal gasps in fear, saying, "Boy! Why you keep doing that, scaring me like that?" Tyson calmly replies, "Ain't nobody here to hurt you, baby. Come on in." Chrystal walks in and politely sits on the couch, and Tyson nervously says, "Baby, you want something to drink." Chrystal answers in a serious tone, "No, Tyson. I came over here to hear what you have to tell me." With his eyes closed, Tyson takes a deep breath, and says, "Chrystal, I had to go home on all these times because two girls I was only with maybe once or twice a long time ago, alleged that I was the Father of their babies." Chrystal falls back into the couch with raised eyebrows and mouth wide open in shock, and says, "What!? Nigga, WHAT!?" Chrystal, with a crazy stare is ready to explode, but then suddenly, Tyson stands up to explain, "Baby, I swear I didn't know about any babies or that these girls were even pregnant. My Moms called and told me about this situation. That is why I had to go home the first time. I had to get legal counseling because I never knew anything about anybody being pregnant. Chrystal, I only had a casual affair with these girls." Tyson watches as Chrystal's face contorts, reflecting the hurt she is feeling inside. Then with tears in her eyes, Chrystal loudly goes off on Tyson, saying, "With something like this, you mean, you couldn't just tell me?" Staring at a voiceless Tyson, who has his eyes closed and his head hanging down, Chrystal thinks for a minute, and then surmises, "So, it was a lie about your Momma being sick, huh? Ah man, ah man, what have I gotten myself into with you?" Tyson quickly looks up and responds, "Chrystal, baby, I thought I could straighten everything out without having to bring you into all this mess because I knew you would react just the way you are acting. I needed time to find out if what they were saying was true because I'm not the type of guy that would get a girl pregnant and run away from my responsibilities." Shaking her head negatively, Chrystal thinks for a minute and forcefully asks, "Couldn't you at least have used some protection?" and then in a contemplative panic, she asks, "Boy, do I need to go get tested?" Tyson says, "No, baby, you know we use protection." Chrystal says, "No, no. I use protection. So, I ask you again, do I need to go get tested?" Visibly getting upset, Tyson says, "Baby, you make it sound like I've been with every woman in the world. I haven't been with anyone but you since we started dating." Now seething with her head rotating like crazy, Chrystal answers sharply, "Oh, and that's supposed to make me feel better? You tell me all this and you think that's supposed to make me feel better?" Attempting to calm things done, Tyson says, "Baby, I think you are being very unreasonable; everything that we're talking about happened a long time before I even met you." Still in a rage, Chrystal dispassionately says, "That may be true, but you still should have told me about this when you found out so I could at least have the option to decide how deeply I would allow myself to be in this relationship, if at all." Shocked by what Chrystal said, Tyson stares at Chrystal through eyes expressing a feeling of surprise and hurt, which causes Chrystal to feel a Momentary sense of empathy to forgive. However, Chrystal, feeling she is about to give in emotionally, promptly sobers in her resolve as she imagines the possibility of more women coming forth saying that Tyson is the Father of their child or even children. Caught between her feelings for Tyson and not being convinced that he's telling her the truth, Chrystal says, "Tyson, I love you, but I just don't believe you are telling me everything, and with me, I have to trust the person I'm with. So as it stands right now, this relationship is not going to work." Speechless, Tyson watches tears well up in Chrystal's eyes as she stands up and hastily walks toward the apartment door. Tyson follows closely behind, vigorously trying to explain himself. However, not interested in hearing any further explanation, Chrystal opens the apartment door and goes straightaway to her car. After she gets in, she sees Jordan pulling into his parking space, but does not speak to him or make eye contact with him. Baffled by the goings-on between Tyson and Chrystal, Jordan turns off the car's ignition and sits, silently watching as he sees Tyson unsuccessfully plead his case, only to be silently rebuffed by the love of his life. Emotionally despondent, Chrystal leans her head against the steering wheel, and with her eyes closed, reluctantly listens to Tyson explain through her car window, but then suddenly, with tears streaming down her face, she starts her car and drives away, leaving Tyson standing in the parking lot, alone and dejected. Jordan then gets out of his car, with a look of concern on his face, and asks, "Hey, man, what happened here?" Tyson answers in a troubled voice, "I tell you the truth, man. I don't know. I told this girl the truth about everything, and she went off on me in twenty different directions I had not even thought about. I told her the truth, dog, but she still thinks I'm lying." Jordan thoughtfully looks at his roommate and says, "Welcome to the club, bruh. Now you know what the hell I've been going through. It's like these women hear what they want to hear. They follow a preconceived pattern of who they think we are and how we are supposed to act, irrespective of trying to convince them differently. The truth does not work with them, man. I guess, if they feel they can't trust us it might be time for us to move on, and believe me, I know that would be exceedingly difficult for you and me. But that's the reality we may eventually have to face." After about fifteen minutes of DWC (driving while crying), Chrystal finally reaches campus and sits in her car reflecting on whether she acted unreasonably in dealing with Tyson. After about ten minutes of convincing herself that it is Tyson who is in the wrong and not her, she gets out of the car and heads straight-away to her room. When Chrystal enters the room, Sanaa, sensing that something has happened, can immediately see that she has been crying, and promptly comes to her side, asking, "Girl, what's wrong?" Drying her eyes with her fingers, Chrystal says, "I don't want to talk about it right now." Looking at Chrystal through caring eyes, and assuming to know the reason for her being upset, Sanaa thoughtfully says, "Well, when you ready to talk, I'm here, ok?" Chrystal nods her head in the affirmative and drops face-first onto her bed. Sanaa then gets Raven on the phone and asks, "Are you guys still coming over for our little pow wow?" "Yeah," Raven says excitedly. "Everybody I've talked to misses our little meetings together, so the pow wow is definitely on." Sanaa says, "Great, now get everybody together and we'll meet in my room at about six o'clock. I've got something special for you guys." With curious surprise, Raven asks with anticipation, "Oh, girl, you going to have some food for us?" Sanaa answers quickly, "No, no, nothing like that; you'll see what I'm talking about when you get here." In a lamenting voice, Raven responds, "Dog, girl, I thought you were going to do something special like catering or refreshments or something like that. You know, something other than that doggone cafeteria food. But that's alright; we'll be there at six." Sanaa chuckles at Raven's continuous need to feed, and laughingly says, "Bye, girl." After Sanaa hangs up, resting on her bed, listening to the conversation, Chrystal turns over, sits up, and says, "Sanaa, I'm not feeling like this tonight." Sanaa walks over and sits beside Chrystal and says, "Look, talking with the girls for a short time will take your mind off of Tyson, ok?" Staring at Sanaa for a minute with an expression on her face as if to say, "oh really," then thinking about it a little, Chrystal hesitantly agrees, saying, "Ok, but right now, I'm not in a friendly mood, and I know I'm not ready for idle chit-chat." Sanaa affectionately grabs Chrystal's hand and says, "That's ok. What I'll share with you guys tonight I think will be very therapeutic, and a good exercise for all that ails us." Chrystal gazes at Sanaa and asks, "Girl, what are you up to?" Sanaa, looking down at the floor, thinks for a minute and answers, "Oh, nothing much." Sanaa then gets busy gathering papers that she has been working on and says, "Chrystal, I got to go out for a minute to take care of some things. I'll be back shortly, ok?" "Oh, alright," but Chrystal responds strongly, "Just make sure you're back here before the girls get here." Sanaa looks at Chrystal and answers assuredly, "Don't worry Chrystal. I'll be back long before they come here," Feeling a little more assured about Sanaa's quick return, Chrystal says, "Alright." At about five o'clock, Sanaa gets back to the room and finds that Chrystal has gone off somewhere. So, Sanaa gets busy preparing for the girls, and while she is busy doing her thing, Chrystal calls and says, "Hey, I had to run to the store. I'll be back in a couple of minutes." Sanaa says, "Ok," and asks, "look, while you're at the store, I need you to pick up a couple of those plastic gallons of juice for me; get grape and cherry. I'll pay you back when you get here." Not knowing or caring what the juice is for, Chrystal hurriedly agrees, saying, "Ok, not a problem. See you in a minute." When Chrystal arrives back on campus and is walking to her dorm, she sees Toni, Raven, and Daedai about fifteen yards in front of her, walking in the same direction. Chrystal hollers out, "Hey, you guys, hold up." The girls hear her calling and turn around. Daedai and Toni hastily run to help her with the bags she is carrying, and when they reach her, Chrystal says, "Hey, Daedai, I'm glad to see you back, girl." Smiling from ear to ear, Daedai replies, "You have no idea how glad I am to be back." Looking around at everybody, Chrystal asks, "You guys headed to my room for our little pow wow?" Toni answers excitedly, "Yeah, we're ready to talk about these conniving a** men." Now in total agreement, Chrystal quickly nods her head with a closed-mouth gasp and says, "I heard that. They are conniving, and then some." When the girls arrive at the room, Chrystal opens the door, and to their surprise, Sanaa has set up a feast of doughnuts, finger sandwiches, and coffee, all free for the taking. Raven, as usual presumptively prompted by urging of Tapeworm Charlie, rushes past everyone to get to the food. Surprised by all the fixings, Chrystal says, "Dang, Sanaa, you went all out, huh?" "That's because this is a special meeting," Sana replies. Sanaa then says, "Ladies, indulge yourselves with food, drink, and conversation; after which I want to give a presentation, I think you will all like." Most of the ladies are so busy stuffing their faces and enjoying the refreshments that Sanaa, wanting to do a presentation, eludes their comprehension except for Chrystal and Daedai, who gives Sanaa a very inquisitive stare. Chrystal is aware that Sanaa has been working on something privately for quite some time; she wonders if this has anything to do with her presentation. However, curiosity concerning Sanaa's presentation quickly wanes after watching doughnuts and finger sandwiches slowly begin to vanish before her eyes. So, Chrystal temporarily ignores her curiosity for the time being, and decides to enjoy the refreshments like everyone else. The ladies, while eating and drinking, begin to engage in the gossip of the day.

Meanwhile, Sanaa is silently observing the girl's conversational interests, prequalifying the environment for when she can start her presentation. When the subject matter collectively turns to the girl's dissatisfaction with men, this is

Sanaa's cue to make her introduction. Sanaa then walks into the middle of an ongoing conversation and politely dings a glass with a spoon, intentionally interrupting the conversation to get the girls' attention. Sanaa looks around the room at all her friends, raises her glass, and says, "Ladies, let's make a toast to the most beautiful, intelligent, and self-sufficient creatures that God has ever made-to women; salute!" The girls, in full chorus, holler, "Salute!" Speaking softly to the group, Sanaa says, "Ladies, you know that we have a special bond between us, right? And because of this sisterly bond, I think we should formulate a secret group and give ourselves a name. I propose that we name this gathering of sisters The Diva Pack Sisterhood. How does that sound to you?" Wide-eyed with excitement, Toni says, "Sanaa that's great. I like it. You guys like it?" Raven contemplates over the name for a minute, then supportively says, "That's real inventive, Sanaa. Diva Pack, huh? Like a wolf pack or lionesses pride. Sounds voracious, Sanaa. But, damn, I like it." All the other girls nod their heads in agreement. Seeing that all the women like the name, Sanaa enthusiastically urges, "Guys, for us to establish our special sisterly bond, we need something in writing to say who we are and what we represent. So, I have worked on a pledge that we can all take and sign, pledging our commitment to each other and our cause. Are you willing?" Always the skeptical one, Chrystal says, "Sanaa, before I agree to sign this thing, I need to see the credo and the pledge." Sanaa, with a big smile on her face, anticipating Chrystal's skepticism, says, "I think I can accommodate that request." Unsuspecting that Sanaa has already done everything, Chrystal's eyebrows raise in surprise as a prepared Sanaa begins to distribute a document called The Diva Sisterhood Pact. Sanaa confidently looks at Chrystal and asks, "Everybody has a copy?"

The girls answer, "Yes." Sanaa then begins to read out loud, word for word, from the Pact. She reads: "We are all joined in common this day, as Ladies of the Diva Pack Sisterhood

Pride, to affirm and duly pledge that: 1) We will always defend the sisterhood of the Diva Pack Pride. 2) We will always be respectful, responsible, and assessable to one another. 3) We will always fight for the cause of women's rights. 4) We will always endeavor to seek wisdom and knowledge in our chosen fields and stand out professionally, as the absolute best. 5) We will never interfere negatively in the relationships of our members. 6) We will always financially assist our sister on demand. 7) We will always share information for the betterment of the individual member and the group collectively. 8) We will always be on guard and prepared to defend the wellbeing of each member. 9) We will always fight, and/or offer protection in the cause of each member; and if need be, become the warrior soldier. 10) We will never allow new membership except by two-thirds approval. 11) We promise that after graduation, we will meet every three years in furtherance of our commitment to the Diva Pack Sisterhood. 12) We promise never to believe in anything greater than ourselves. We are the beautiful, intelligent, and independent women of the Diva Pack Pride. After you say your pledge out loud, in the presence of the sisters, you will then affix your signature and date this document, and I have with me a diabetes lancer for us to do a little prick of the finger and seal the signature with a fingerprint in blood. Does everyone agree with the pledge?" The ladies look at each other in absolute silence as the pledge invades their understanding that this is a real in-blood commitment to be made to each other. Sanaa again asks, "Are we together on this?" The ladies slowly nod their heads and take the pen Sanaa has provided and sign their names and then seal their commitment in blood to the pact. After everyone has signed and sealed the pact, Sanaa hollers out in a joyous rage, "Sisters forever; we are the women of the Diva Pack Sisterhood Pride." Sanaa proudly looks at her sisters with a smile and says, "This is our first meeting, and I propose we look at and discuss the materials from the feminist rally." Everybody agrees. For the rest of the evening, the women indulge in refreshments and discuss the materials given at the feminist rally. The conversation between the women start as casual discussions of the feminist ideology and the strength of womanhood, only to crescendo into a fever-pitched dialogue on toxic masculinity as the reason for their mistreatment and disrespect in relationships with men. The interaction between the women become so personal that each woman confesses the problems they have with each of their boyfriends and other casual flings. The men sentenced to this toxic masculinity chopping block include Jordan, Tyson, Carlton, Michael, Jalen, Toby, Walter, Jevon and many football / basketball/ baseball and soccer players, with various-named members from all the fraternities. However, Raven's previous relationship with Courtney remains a secret. The first gathering of the sisterhood goes deep into the evening, generating a bond between these women that none had expected, and everybody leaves the meeting very enthused. A couple of days later, while relaxing in her room, Chrystal hears her phone ringing, and when she answers, she hears Tyson on the line, saying, "Hey, baby, how are you doing?" Chrystal has not talked to Tyson since they're falling out. However, her attitude has sobered, and she answers, "What's going on, Tyson? I thought we agreed to cool it for a while." Tyson is silent for a Moment, then says, "Baby, I didn't agree to that; you wanted to distance yourself from me. I just called to let you know that I miss you and I love you and wanted to tell you again how sorry I am I didn't tell you what I was doing at home. I just needed to have confirmation of things before I said anything. However, I have good news." Trying not to show interest in what Tyson wants to tell her, Chrystal dispassionately asks, "And what might that be, Tyson?" Tyson says, "Chrystal, the paternity results came back negative. I am not the Father of either of those babies. Those girls were lying or made a big mistake. Chrystal, I'm not the type of person that if I knew I had gotten a girl pregnant, would run away from my responsibilities, and I'm certainly not the type of guy who would intentionally hide this information about myself from you." Chrystal is totally silent on her end of the line because tears have welled up in her eyes, and she can't let Tyson know how she feels. Unenthusiastically, Chrystal says, "I'm glad everything turned out ok for you, Tyson." Tyson then takes a deep breath, and in a nervous voice, asks, "Baby, does that mean we're back together? I mean, can we get back together?" Again, Chrystal is silent over the line, and then in a profoundly serious tone, she says, "Tyson, for us to work, you need to always tell me the truth. That's just who I am, and I will not change; can you do that?" Tyson says, "Baby, I'll do whatever I need to do to keep you loving me. So, are we back?" Chrystal then confesses, "Tyson, I've never stopped loving you, but that being said, it's important for us to be truthful with one another. So, yes, baby, we are back. Tyson, I got some studying to do right now, but I will come to the apartment later. You good with that?" Relieved that Chrystal is back, Tyson gladly says, "No problem, baby. You take your time. I'll see you later." Both Tyson and Chrystal are glad they have resolved their issues and pause silently before hanging up.

Later that evening, when Chrystal comes to Tyson's apartment, they again seal their relationship with a night of intense lovemaking in the way of married people. In the morning, with all issues resolved, Chrystal makes her way back to campus. However, she does not tell any of her newly-made sisters about her renewed relationship with Tyson. After multiple meetings of the Diva Pack Pride, the camaraderie within the group has grown, and their condescension toward men has increased. The Diva Pack will add three new members: Jeanine, Robin, and Beth, affectionately nicknamed the geek squad because of their particular skills with computers and social media; there isn't anything they can't do with the internet, computer programming and coding. Also, Toni is able to maneuver two of her homegirls, Carla and Maria, into the sisterhood; they nicknamed them the Two-Live-Crew for their high-spirited persona. Daedai particularly likes these two women because they're kind of like her; ladylike but won't take no mess. These five new girls would be the first sisters inducted into The Diva Pack through a formalized ceremony, but that's another story. As the sisterhood grows in number and solidarity, relationships with men became more complicated because of the foolish feminist attitudes that emerged. However, Sanaa and Chrystal continued to mask their heartfelt feelings for Jordan and Tyson, but woe unto the girl that breaches those affections; she would suffer the wrath and consequences brought to bear by the entire group. It was understood that Tyson and Jordan were spoken for, and no sister or other girl could breach that under-standing. In furtherance of their pledge to protect each other's interests and wellbeing, sometimes the Diva Pact Pride would be reckless and very vindictive. If anyone crossed the sister-hood, there was always a price to be paid. The Diva Pack would, at times, develop hit lists on women or men, targeted for some form of payback, and every action taken by the group would establish their methodology of instilling fear of the unknown (secret sisterhood). All that the campus knew of the Diva Pack Sisterhood was that there was a covert group of girls taking up for each other, which caused everybody to wonder who these women were. No one, fraternities, sororities, or faculty, intimidated the women of the Diva Pack Sisterhood because, as a result of their feminist activism, they garnered powerfully connected allies nationally. When the Diva Pack would do their dirty work, or as they call it, "put in work," their methods were extremely discreet, and only the victims of their reprisal would have suspicion of its origin. People on campus had no idea that the sisterhood had the ability on social media to destroy rep-utations of those who violated the sisterhood, and thanks to the geek squad, the social media footprint could not be traced back to any members.

People on campus did have a suspicion that a lot of the prank-like antics were probably the result of some form of sanctioned payback. However, no one could say, for certain, that any of these women were the perpetrators of the activity. The Diva Pack was so sneaky in their planning and delivery that nothing could ever be traced back to them. However, it was well known on campus that if anybody messed with certain young ladies, something was going to happen. Some of the things that the Diva Pack would do to people was totally off the chain. The Diva Pack was not biased in handing out payback either because the sisterhood took pride in being an equal opportunity punisher. Among some of the many things that the sisterhood did were to tape victims' room doors shut (while they were in the room) with flyers, saying all kinds of nasty and insulting things about the vic. The Diva Pack would also, somehow, slip laxatives into victim's drinks or put bugs into their food for payback. They would often anonymously slip a note to a boy or girl, saying that their girlfriend or boyfriend was cheating on him or her, and would identify the person with whom he or she were cheating. Also, anonymously, they would post and distribute wanted posters of vics, saying, "This b***h is wanted for trespassing on OPP (other people's property)." The Diva Pack Sisterhood would toilet-paper people's cars and place advertisements on certain scandalous websites, listing names and numbers of students soliciting for kinky sex, bondage etc., with screenshots of the advertisements sent to school administrators. They would write letters to the parents of marked students, saying they had violated academic probation and had to be dismissed from the school. They would flood social media with all forms of derogatory comments, and particularly cheating videos. They would sow chaos between fraternities and sororities. Particularly with sororities they would during the night, spray just a little bit of liquid a** under a soro's dorm door, or if the opportunity presented itself, spray it in their cars to create a mild irritating undetectable stench.

They would call in false claims to the campus police to report a boy in a girl's room who was attacking her; when actually, they were involved in the way of married people. Yeah, they really did all that. I remember when pretty boy Rick Flores, aka the Latin lover from New York, who supposedly had all the pretty girls on campus, figured he could Playboy around, use, mistreat, and womanize Daedai. Wrong! One semester later, Rick went missing, and ain't nobody seen him since. Nobody knows what happened, except maybe Rick. The vine has it that The Diva Pack put the slick to Rick. The vine also has it that some of these girls (the Diva Pack Sisterhood) would use and tease guys for money and different things like that. One day on campus, one guy, who shall remain nameless, concluded that Toni was taking advantage of him. So, he decides to confront her out on the quad in front of everybody (he was crazy!). As usual, Toni gets verbally indignant, and this guy, out of the clear blue sky, b***h-slaps Toni to the ground. Oh! but he shouldn't have done that because when he bends over to try and slap her again, Daedai, standing behind him, lands a hard and serious kick to his family jewels, and while he's bent over cringing in pain, Toni pulls him forward to the ground, and the girls (the Diva Pack Sisterhood) burst through the crowd and go into beatdown mode. Daedai, Raven, the Two-Live-Crew, and the geek squad all jump in, kicking and punching the guy everywhere, and because he can't recover to his feet due to Daedai's well-placed kick and Toni holding him down, they beat his a**. They beat the guy without ceasing until campus police arrives and pulls them back. This incident was the first and only time the campus would physically see these girls (the Diva Pack) actually involved in any violent act. However, the campus would never figure out that this guy's a**-whipping was being delivered courtesy of an organized secret group of women. To the people standing by, it just seemed like a group of girls defending another girl from being beaten up, and even if people standing by were suspicious that the girls were working as a group, The Diva Pack Sisterhood has no public, private, or campus affiliation. So their existence could not be connected to an organization on campus. It is only through rumors from the vine that a group called the Diva Pack exists. The Diva Pack's anonymity is the only thing that gives them cover and protection. Rumors on campus, assisted by the creative covert branding by the sisterhood, helped in the creation of the Diva Pack's mystique, which was forged out of uncorroborated hearsay; but the rumors, no doubt, worked in the sisterhood's favor, giving them a kind of urban legend. No one knows the inner workings of the Diva Pack Sisterhood, nor do they realize that the behavior of the sisterhood is only a statement by these women that they were not going to be abused and misused anymore. The Diva Pack's acts of vengeance were motivated by the accumulation of broken relationships, demeaning verbal assaults, and physical abuse, coupled with the pressure of adhering to a misguided social alliance that cultivated they're attitude toward retaliation.

If anyone crossed one of their members, there would be hell to pay. These acts of the sisterhood were only a small sample of the hundreds of retaliatory actions committed by these women.

PART II

CHAPTER 17
(BACK TO THE PRESENT)

BACK TO PRESENT DAY, OVER IN CHRYSTAL AND Sanaa's room, their study group has ended for the evening. When the group leaves the room, remembering the incident that happened earlier on the quad with Jordan; Chrystal looks keenly at Sanaa, and following through on what she had told the girls earlier, she asks, "Sanaa, what are we going to do about Jordan and Sheila?" Sanaa, then looking quickly at Chrystal, says, "Thinking about it, I can't blame Jordan for talking to Sheila. He is only talking to her because I pushed him away from me, and no matter the relationship he has with her, I know he still loves me. I'll get him back. I know I will." So, Sanaa closes her eyes, shakes her head, and says, "Chrystal, tell everybody to leave Sheila alone-no threats, no media attacks, no pranks, no nothing until I can think this situation through." Chrystal replies, "Sanaa, I think that's a smart move if you want to get Jordan back. Also, we've caused enough problems around here as it is. There are a lot of people trying to figure out the sisterhood with regard to all the rumors. I'll tell the girls to back off from harassing anybody for the time being." After hearing from Chrystal later in the day, Daedai backed off, and so did the other girls. However, as the Diva Pack Sisterhood grew larger in size that year, they would soon get right back into their devious ways, targeting people who pissed them off by instigating campus antics and complex pranks as revenge. The five founding members, on the other hand, settled down into planning for graduation (of course, as head of their class) and whatever future endeavors they would pursue. As strange as having an on-and-off again relationship might have been, Jordan and Sanaa would never overcome their love for one another, no matter how they acted uninterested and unfazed in front of their friends; everybody knew better, and they eventually did get back together in the year approaching graduation. Sheila was never harassed as Sanaa had asked; however, Daedai would often give the girl the wicked eye to let her know that she was not pleased with her trying to move in on her sister's man. But Daedai never harassed her or did any physical harm to her. Every one of the founding five members were expecting to graduate in the fall except for Toni, who would graduate during the summer session. One day, knowing that Toni wanted to graduate at the same time as her friends, Raven starts to tease and dig at Toni, saying, "A delay in your graduation is what you get for messing with all that science stuff, Ms. Albert Einstein." Toni replies smartly, "Well, at least I know exactly what I want to do when I graduate." Raven is silent as if to squash the whole thing. It was a touché Moment for Toni in that she struck a sensitive nerve, knowing that Raven does not have a clue as to the direction she's headed after graduation. The Diva Pack Sisterhood in this year became more rambunctious than ever, and the founding five were somewhat losing control to the new members. However, the sisterhood always maintained respect and reverence for the founding five. The founding members would consistently talk to the sisters to keep them grounded in the understanding that they are sophisticated and highly educated women with a purpose, and not the purveyors of actions reflecting ill repute. For their graduation, the new Diva Pack leadership threw a big party for the founding five and promised to meet every three years as the charter had demanded.

However, after the founding five eventually graduated and left school, the Diva Pack sisterhood went buck wild. Graduating in the summer session, Toni would see things happening and give other founding members the 411 on what was going on with the sisterhood. In future tri-annual meetings in Miami, the founding five would admonish the undergrad members to be discreet in the things they do. However, they did not make it clear to the sisterhood to put an end to their vengeful actions. As the Diva Pack sisterhood grows regionally, the more powerful they would become, also expanding to more local campuses. The Diva Pack founding five will honor their tri-annual obligations to meet; however, the founding five would also meet spontaneously amongst themselves privately. In future years, Sanaa will work her way to becoming an assistant DA in Miami-Dade County, and a major player in the political arena. She becomes known as the hammer because of her highly combative attitude and prosecutorial stance toward men alleged to have committed rape or abuse of women. Raven, who graduates with a degree in sociology, goes back home to California, and becomes a real mover and shaker as a regional director in the feminist movement. Chrystal becomes a highly paid corporate attorney for TOMMIE International Corporation, a trans-ocean shipping corporation based in Orlando, Florida.

Toni becomes the lead biochemical engineer in a male-dominated environment at Opus Genetics in Atlanta, GA. Carlton does not finish college immediately, but hooks up with Toni in Atlanta, and goes to school on and off, trying to finish his degree in criminal justice. Daedai becomes a high school teacher, marries a preacher, and has five children. Daedai has some problems along the way, but everything gets straightened out spiritually. Jordan becomes an entertainment and sports lawyer, based in Miami, handling a diverse mix of high-valued national and international clientele. Tyson becomes a dentist, with the help of Chrystal, who supports him while he is in medical school. When Tyson eventually gets his license to practice dentistry, it changes him, mostly settling him down. Even Tyson is surprised at how domesticated he has become, from self-proclaimed playboy to laid-back professional. However, the marriages of the Diva Pack founding sisters are not very glamorous, except for Daedai. Toni will marry Carlton, but she suffers an abusive relationship because of his post-traumatic problems after being shot in college, along with other generational things extending from his Mom and Dad. After many years of verbal abuse, Toni threatens to leave Carlton, but she never does. Toni and Carlton have one child together, but when Toni gets pregnant and loses a baby to SIDS, it affects their marriage so seriously that they become distant in their affections for one another, and in the heat of an argument, Carlton unwittingly slaps Toni. Carlton is tearfully sorry, but it's the straw that broke the camel's back. Toni and her son leave Carlton and move to California. While looking for work, Toni hooks up with Raven and joins the feminist movement, where she takes a well-paid position. Eventually, Carlton seeks and gets the counseling that he needs, and begs Toni to come back home. Toni hesitantly agrees to go home against the advice and wishes of her friend Raven. But for the sake of her family, she gets back together with her ex-husband. Toni and Carlton do their best to keep things together for their son, but in the back of Toni's mind, there's lingering doubt if Carlton has changed; notwithstanding, over time, they do manage to give their son two little sisters. As everybody would predict, Sanaa does marry Jordan. They stay in Miami and work on their professional careers. The fact that Sanaa has tried to have children and cannot carry them to term puts a strain on their marriage. Sanaa knows that Jordan wants children, and blames herself, and wrongly starts to feel her marriage is about to end in divorce. So, Sanaa overcomes her pride and goes to a clinic for help, and after a couple of unsuccessful tries, Sanaa surprises herself and knocks Jordan to the floor by getting pregnant with triplets. She gives birth to two boys and one girl. However, even with the birth of their children, Jordan and Sanaa still have problems in their marriage. Lack of trust is a major factor. This lack of trust stems from Jordan's exposure to the fast-lane lifestyles of his clients, causing Sanaa to be worried about the potential for infidelity, which brings problems into their marriage. However, that is not the only lingering thing that keeps Jordan and Sanaa from having a great marriage. The situation with them also extends to two very strong-willed people having a problem with compromising. Now, with respect to Daedai, while teaching high school in Chicago, Daedai meets a preacher from Virginia at her Mother's church. The preacher is there as a guest speaker for a conference the church is having. After Daedai's sister's funeral, Daedai's Mother made a promise to one of the elders in the church that she would attend church more often. Daedai's Mother, keeping that promise and trying to get Daedai involved with the church, almost had to bend Daedai's arm to get her to come to church with her one Sunday. But as fate would have it, at the church reception that evening, the guest preacher takes one look at Daedai and immediately has himself introduced to her. Knowing that the preacher is attracted to her, Daedai is all too aware of who she is, juxtaposed to what he represents, and was not too keen on talking to a preacher, much less taking up with him. But he was nice and so very persistent until it paid off for him because after going back and forth from Virginia to Chicago many times to visit, Daedai falls in love with him and finally gives into marrying the Rev. Dr. Kyle L. Ewing. At the wedding ceremony, Toni, Sanaa, Chrystal, and Raven cannot believe that they are bridesmaids in a wedding where Daedai marries, of all people, a preacher. The night before the wedding, they laughed and joked, reminiscing over all the times Daedai would beat up people and curse everybody out who pissed her off. The sisters wondered and discussed among themselves how long this marriage to a preacher would last. However, after Daedai gets married, she moves to join her husband in Virginia where his church is located. But adjusting to the change in her lifestyle would be difficult for Daedai. However, eventually Daedai will adjust well enough to give the good reverend doctor five beautiful children to add to his table. Chrystal supports and marries Tyson while he is in medical school. Tyson and Chrystal, after a serious miscarriage, are eventually blessed with two little girls. When Tyson becomes a dentist and has his practice going, this is when more problems start to develop. Chrystal claims that Tyson is so busy with his practice that he does not pay enough attention to his home life. Chrystal, being the strong resolute corporate type, is not having it. She gives Tyson an ultimatum extending from the fact that he is not being responsive to his family. Tyson, in response says he could say the same thing about her. He says she is blaming him for doing the same thing she is doing, and he believes she's the one who's not being responsive to the family. The conflict is augmented greatly by the sudden death of Chrystal's Father, who was the love of her life. This tragedy sends Chrystal's emotions in multiple directions, and as the tension between the couple grows more and more, their two little girls caught in the middle of their mess, suffer. Their problem is similar to Jordan and Sanaa's, which is an inability to compromise on the most basic things. The arguing and lack of marital rhythm gets so out of harmony that Chrystal has thoughts of having an affair at work.

However, coming awfully close to this violation of trust, she cannot go through with it, but their marriage, at this point, is in danger of ending in divorce. Following the feminist playbook to the letter, Raven reigns supreme as the regional director of a feminist organization in California, becoming a heavy player in the movement. She communicates with her friends and associates throughout the United States, and strategizes in conjunction with all Diva Pack campus organizations. However, with all the high-powered connections Raven has established, she is still very unhappy. Raven goes through three marriages, several abortions, and a heartbreaking miscarriage with her fourth husband, the only man she swears that she has ever loved. The miscarriage puts Raven in a state of deep depression and makes her an abusive person so out of control that she forces her fourth husband to divorce her. Then being alone and stressed, Raven gets involved in lesbian relationships, having multiple partners that allow for no commitments. Also, she begins using men for multiple sex ventures, thinking that if men can do it, so can she, but then unexpectedly, she falls in love with her female executive assistant, and after many years of being in the relationship and feeling comfortably in love, her lover betrays her by falling in love with a man, of all people, after her lover swore, she had no feelings for men. On top of that, her assistant eventually marries this man. This betrayal breaks Raven's heart, and it traumatizes her so much that she loses focus at work and is caught on video saying, "To hell with these feminist b***hes," which, of course, causes her to lose her high-paying job. In a state of constant deep depression, Raven ends up doing drugs and alcohol, which eventually leads to her being homeless. Her friends try to help, but she is so far gone she won't listen to anyone. Toni tries to have Raven committed, but after being Baker-Acted numerous times, she continually comes out and starts doing the same thing all over again. At one of the Diva Packs' tri-annual meetings, the sisters try to put together a financial package for Raven, but she refuses to help herself.

A year later, while at home, the girls receive a call from the Diva sisters on campus, saying that Raven has died due to a brain aneurysm. When Toni gets the call, she takes it so hard that she faints, and Carlton has to pick her up off of the kitchen floor. Daedai also takes hearing of Raven's death extremely hard, to the point of temporarily not being able to verbally communicate. Daedai, her husband, along with the girls and their husbands, the Diva Pack Sisterhood, and Raven's feminist associates all attend and pay for the funeral in her hometown of San Francisco, California. The going-home ceremony with all the flowers and spray is so incredibly beautiful. Toni and Daedai take it particularly hard at the funeral services, breaking down in tears and crying at the loss of their long-time friend and schoolmate. As they leave the burial site, there is not a dry eye anywhere; Raven was their girl; one of the five, gone forever. At the re-pass, Daedai breaks down crying when looking at all the food, and with tears in her eyes, says, "Y'all know if Raven was here seeing all this food, she and that little Tapeworm Charlie would be the first ones in line, right!" Everybody chuckles, then Daedai raises a glass of wine and says, "To Raven, our friend and sister; gone, but never forgotten; salute." All of Raven's friends and associates raise their glasses in salute and drink in honor of her memory. Walking around the room, Sanaa discreetly collects Chrystal, Toni, and Daedai, and urges them to come outside away from all the people so they can sit and talk. When outside, the women talk and vent about everything bothering them. Sanaa, Chrystal, and Toni are sad, knowing that they have to go back home to troubled marriages, and added to that, most of their children have turned into little spoiled pawns of the almighty cell phone and internet, lacking any ability to communicate with either of their parents. This was something they talked about at length while outside. They were all hurting from the passing of their friend, but also suffering a home life that was not what they expected. The prospect of going back to a troubled home environment weighed heavily on their minds.

They admit and take partial blame for their problems at home, saying that their lack of focus on their families was a big part of it, but they had no answers on how to change things. During this pity party, Daedai is unusually quiet, but the women are so involved with talking about their own failings, they do not pay attention to Daedai's lack of involvement in the conversation. Daedai sits on the stoop with her head down without saying one word. The next day, the women are feeling somewhat comforted from being able to talk about things. So, the girls and their husbands go and have a nice breakfast together at the airport, and after breakfast, they relax, talk, and then shortly after a few hugs and kisses, they say their goodbyes and leave to go their separate ways home.

CHAPTER 18
(MR. TIMMONS)

ONE YEAR AFTER RAVEN'S PASSING, SANAA, Chrystal, Toni, and Daedai, at one of their spontaneous gatherings, can feel Raven's absence, and they become very depressed because their girl is not with them. Sanaa and Chrystal jokingly recall all the fun that they had in college, and Toni says, "You guys remember how much that girl could eat?" Everybody says, "Oh, yeah." Fighting back tears, Daedai says, "Yeah, and you know that heifer wouldn't even gain one ounce of weight." With tears streaming down her face, Daedai struggles to say, "Y'all remember she thought her body was a gift from God to show us all what we supposed to look like, right?" Toni says, "That girl was something else crazy." Now starting to cry, Toni says, "Yes she was, but she was my friend, and I miss her. I miss her so much." The women, now all in tears, hug and comfort one another. However, Sanaa, who is always full of pride, self-aware, and a critical thinker, takes a step back and says, "Hey, look at us; look at us. Our lives have been a royal mess, and it seems like a never-ending maze at each and every turn. Things always go the wrong way. Our marriages, for the most part, are crumbling, and I can barely remember the last time I was really happy. It does not matter how much money we make or what professional status we attain in life, it seems like we are never fulfilled. What is wrong with us? All we do is get ourselves involved with some sort of political or social movement or another, and then live our lives through the lens of our jobs as if that is all that matters. It appears that we are always trying to be something that we are not for the sake of other people." Frustrated, Sanaa breathes deeply, exhales, and with her eyes closed, tilts her head back and surrenders in hopes of any restorative enlightenment. Then while searching her thoughts, she looks across into the eyes of all her friends, and when her eyes contact Daedai's eyes, she stares purposely, and then intently, and contemplates for a moment, and says, "Wait a minute, now that I think about it Daedai, you're the only one of us that appears to have your life together. You have five beautiful, well-behaved children, a good husband, and a happy life. When I look back on everything in our past, you used to be the craziest one of us all. I mean, you were the first one always ready to jump up and beat a b***h's a** just because, and Daedai, you used to curse more than five sailors. I don't know why I didn't recognize your transformation until now. But I do recognize at this moment, that out of all of us, you are the only one that seems to be happy and at peace. Daedai, why don't you tell us where all that fire and aggressive anger went; because you've changed." Agreeing with Sanaa, Toni says, "Yeah Daedai, that's true. You're nowhere near the same as you used to be. I felt something had changed, but I thought it was just due to aging or life experiences. But there's something about you far greater than that. However, I must admit, I like this new you." Echoing support of what Toni and Sanaa have discerned, Chrystal says, "True that! What's going on with you, girl?" Daedai affectionately looks at her friends and steadily says, "I guess meeting and being in love with my husband calmed me down a lot." Toni interjects, "Yeah, I can understand that." Daedai continues, "Maybe it's because he's a preacher. But to be honest about everything, believe me, there was a time when I gave that man a lot of regret about our marriage. You guys know exactly what I'm saying, I was pretending to be someone I was not. I had a problem with a lack of self-esteem and self-control, and I was insecure as to whether I could maintain a long-lasting relationship with this man. I had to come face-to-face with the realization that I had been deceiving my husband about the person I was inside, and it bothered me whether I should or even could keep hidden that part of me that wasn't first-lady material. Y'all know what I'm talking about. This insecurity constantly weighed heavily on me, and I wouldn't talk about it. My husband, not knowing what was wrong with me, in his own way trying to help, introduced me to his close friend and mentor, Mr. Timmons. Thanks to Mr. Timmons's counseling and teaching, which changed my whole way of thinking, helped me change my aggressive attitude and manage my anger through learning who I am, and whose I am in Christ Jesus, and I was transformed. For the first time in my life, I felt free despite all the bad things that had happened in my life. I finally began to love and appreciate me, which elevated my self-esteem and changed my whole life. I now believe in something bigger than me." Deriding Daedai's newfound understanding, Sanaa smiles and sarcastically says, "That's it? That's all? This is what your secret is? Girl, I thought you had something that nobody knows anything about. I mean, I thought you had some unique technique in meditation you were using to calm yourself down. You mean to tell us and all the other ghosts standing in this room that all this is about religion?" Daedai looks at Sanaa and says forcefully, "No, it is not about religion. It is far more than religion. It is the power in the Word of God and having a relationship with Him."

Toni arrogantly comes back, "The power in the Word of God? Look, Daedai, as a person whose job it is to deal with science every day, this power in the Word of God stuff is a little difficult for me to digest." But Daedai steadily argues, "Ok, but do you want some of what I have or not?" Seeing the unquestionable confidence in Daedai's demeanor, Chrystal comments, "Daedai, we're not clowning you. It's just that we don't understand a thing you're talking about." Daedai patiently replies, "Chrystal, all I can ask of you right now is do you want what I have? You do notice the change in me, right? You do sense my peace and the change in my attitude, right? You can see this, right? So, I ask you again, do you want some of this? I mean, what do you have to lose? You can only go up from where you are." Somewhat skeptical, Sanaa answers, "Ok, what if we do? How do we get it? I mean, you know for yourself that we have never been into faith, God, and all that religious stuff. So how do you know it will work for us?" Daedai compassionately states, "I know what you think, and I know where you are. I know your lives have been full of nothing but the things of this world, and it is hard to transition into what I'm sharing with you, but remember, I was there too; however, I've found something life-changing, and I want to share it with you, if you'll let me." Curious about whether it will work, Chrystal says, "I'm game, alright; now what do we have to do?" Daedai shrugs her shoulders and dispassionately says, "Nothing, I just need you to meet someone, someone who helped me. However, you must be willing to open yourselves up to what he says. Are you willing to do that?" The women look at each other, shrug their shoulders as if to say maybe, then give positive affirmation with a head nod because now they are all kind of excited about the mystery of it all. Not understanding the nature of this commitment, but excited about meeting this new guru, Sanaa boldly says, "Let's do this, then," and all the women agree. Daedai quickly discerns that her friends are inhibiting disbelief, mainly for her benefit, but she takes joy in knowing that this is the beginning of their processing. Seeking to make them real, Daedai says, "Ladies, this will require seven days of your time at my home. Are you still willing?" The women think for a minute, look at each other, then at Daedai; and to Daedai's surprise, all agree to come. Daedai smiles and says, "In two weeks, you will come and stay at my house for seven days, and among the things that you must bring are a

King James Bible and any questions you have ever had concerning religion, God, Jesus, and the Word of God, ok?" They all say ok, then Toni, ready to get her party on, says, "But for right now, let's go have some fun." Daedai smiles, and in amazement takes notice of what they decide to do. Normally when they meet, everybody is so quick to run out to the clubs, but this time, they decide to just go to dinner and take in a show. Intrigued by their actions, Daedai discerns the possibility of imminent change taking place in their hearts. Another unforeseen act by the group comes when, out of a compulsive need to know what Daedai has experienced, the sisters decide to cut part of their reunion time short by 4 days, and agree to meet at Daedai's house in three days. Sanaa, Chrystal, and Toni go back home and let their families know that they will be spending a week at Daedai's house in Virginia. They evade any conversation with their family about the nature of this visit, even over the questioning of their husbands seeking a more concrete explanation. After preparing their family as best they could and taking care of any issues at home before they leave, the women finally make their journey to visit Daedai. When they arrive, Daedai finds a place for everyone to sleep, which is not an easy task, given the size of her house whole, but she makes a way, and after everyone is settled in, she tells them that they will go to meet Mr. Timmons in the morning. Daedai says, "He's expecting all of us, so you guys need to get a good night's sleep; we got a long day ahead of us tomorrow." It is Sunday morning, and as the sun breaks through the window, Daedai wakes up early to feed her husband and her children breakfast and gets them on their way to church. Just about this time, Chrystal has gotten up and walks down the stairs to the kitchen area. She sees Daedai and says, "I'm nervous about this, Daedai." Busy making breakfast, Daedai stops for a minute and turns to Chrystal, smiles, and says, "These few days are going to be the best days of your life; don't be afraid, just open your heart and your mind." Chrystal looks at Daedai in a rather apprehensive way, and replies, "Ok, if you say so." Resolute in her belief, Daedai states, "I know so; now go wake up your sleepyhead girlfriends so I can get some coffee and breakfast in your stomachs." Chrystal goes upstairs and wakes everyone, and when the women come down to the dining room, they have fun as they eat their breakfast together. Acting like a Mother hen, Daedai says, "Ladies, y'all go ahead and finish up now, we leave in about twenty-five minutes, and remember to get your Bibles and have your questions in hand." The women go to their sleeping space upstairs, unpack their Bibles, make sure they have their questions, and then head out to the car. As they walk to the car, Toni says, "Where does he live, Daedai?" Daedai says, "He lives in an area way back in the woods. He likes his privacy from all the noise of the carnal world." The women all pack into Daedai's car, and along the way, looking at all the colorful trees, Sanaa says, "It's so beautiful out here, but Daedai you are starting to trip me out with this Mr. Timmons thing. I mean, living out here in the middle of nowhere? Is he mentally ok? We are gonna be alright back in these woods, right?" Daedai laughs and says, "I'll let you judge for yourselves." Daedai then makes a sharp turn off the main highway, and the girls look at each other, expressing concern now more than ever, as their jaws drop and eyes stretch wide when Daedai takes another non-public dirt road and drives about two or three miles further into the woods. The ladies become worried and panic for a minute, but start to feel a little better when they come upon what looks to be an old, aban-doned church. Daedai turns onto the cracked pavement and drives up to the church, then honks the horn, and after about a minute or two, this tall, thin, pepper grey-headed man comes out to the car, smiling. In a kind of country accent, he says, "How y'all doing?" The girls say their pleasant good mornings, and Chrystal inquires, "Are you, Mr. Timmons?" Mr. Timmons says, "Well, as far back as I can remember, after they dropped my first name, that's what they've been calling me. Y'all come on in, we'll talk and get acquainted with each other out in the back." Toni says, "Mr. Timmons," "Yes ma'am," he replies. Toni inquires, "Was this once a Holy church?" Mr. Timmons smiles, looks at Toni, and responds, "No, as far as I can remember, this has always been just a plain old building that was used to house people that believed in or acted like they believed in God." Toni stops dead in her tracks and looks at Mr. Timmons in a state of total confusion as he walks away. Toni gives a befuddled look at Daedai, and Daedai, knowing what Mr. Timmons means, laughingly smiles, shrugs her shoulders, and keeps walking straight ahead. Still with an expression of confusion on her face, Toni can't shake off what Mr. Timmons just said, but she continues to follow the girls to the back. When they arrive at the back of the church, they take note of the scenic but quiet courtyard centered with a little unused raised cement pond. They also notice seven chairs placed in a circle. Mr. Timmons says, "Have a seat ladies." Out of curiosity and respect, Sanaa asks, "Reverend Timmons, is it ok to sit in any one of the chairs?" Mr. Timmons replies, "Yes, sit where you please. Also, I am just Mr. Timmons; there isn't anything reverend about me, so do not call me 'Reverend.' There's only one who is Reverend, and His name is Jesus the Christ. So please, refer to me as Mr. Timmons." Sanaa then sarcastically responds, "Ok, not a problem, Sir." Mr. Timmons says, "My girl Daedai has shared with me that you ladies want and need what it is that she has; is that correct?" All eager with anticipation, the women, answer, "Yes." Mr. Timmons smiles and then asks, "Well then, tell me what it is you think she has." Expressing a state of fogginess, Sanaa looks at Daedai, then back at Mr. Timmons, and states, "Daedai said that she had found something greater than herself." Mr. Timmons says, "Oh, I see. You want to get on the path to enlightenment, right?" The girl's faces light up and eagerly answer, "Yes, that's what we want." While the girls are captured in the prospect of what Mr. Timmons will be sharing, Daedai inconspicuously gets up out of her chair and slowly walks away from the circle. Mr. Timmons says, "Ok, now pay close attention. To put you on the path that you seek, there are several things that you need to do. Write this down because it all has to be done in successive order." As the girls begin to write, Mr. Timmons says, "First, what I need you to do is to run or walk briskly around the church eleven times. Then, I need you to come and kneel in front of this Jewish menorah that I have set up, and then raise your hands, palms upward, in a begging-like position, meditate for twenty minutes, exactly twenty minutes now, then turn your heads slowly, from the right to the center, then to the left, and back to the center. Then, I need you to dip your face in the cement pond six times and shout out loudly exactly four times, 'I receive the blessing, I receive the blessing, I receive the blessing, I receive the blessing,' and lastly, which is most important of all; you are to go into your pocketbooks and write me a check for an offering of one thousand dollars each, and at that time, I'll pray for you and give you the anointed oil to rub on your forehead; you got it?" Looking around for Daedai with a heedful expression, Sanaa says, "Mr. Timmons, that water is dirty, and nobody said anything about any money." Outside of the girls' view, Daedai is silently laughing so hard she's about to pass out as Mr. Timmons somehow manages to maintain a serious composure. The women look at each other in shock, and Sanaa thinks out loud, saying, "This man has got to be crazy if he thinks I'm going to put my face in that pond, and on top of that, give him a thousand dollars. I don't think so." However, knowing full well she is not going to comply with any of those things, Sanaa passively plays along with Mr. Timmons and says, "Ok, alright, and Mr. Timmons what do we get after we do all these things?" Mr. Timmons stares at the women intently, and answers, "Absolutely nothing. No wait a minute, on second thought, I take that back. I could get a good laugh watching you guys do all those things, but that's about it." Kind of relieved, with a slight smile on her face, Sanaa asks,

"Mr. Timmons, why did you tell us this was the key to gaining enlightenment then?" With a smile and a little grin, Mr. Timmons says, "Ladies, I was just toying with your minds, trying to teach you a lesson. Did what I ask you to do make any sense at all?" The ladies answer, "No sir, it didn't." Mr. Timmons says, "Believe me, nothing that I asked you to do is in Bible Scriptures. Ladies, on your journey to know the Father, sometimes He may ask you to do something that might not make much sense but learning the Scriptures will help you discern His voice and His will. In God, there are no tricks, gimmicks, magic, potions, voodoo, witchcraft, or anything like that attached to the Father; you cannot purchase the blessings of God. If it is not scriptural, do not believe it or follow it. Even if I say something that is not in the Scriptures, do not believe me. Understanding and wisdom comes with your obedience and your decision to follow God's Word. The Word asks a question, 'If the foundations are destroyed, what can the righteous do?' (Ps. 11:3 KJV). The answer is, 'But through knowledge, the righteous will be delivered' (Prov. 11:9b ASV). That knowledge which the Scriptures reference, is the Word of God. So, to get what Daedai has is only going to cost you a decision." Appearing perplexed more than ever, Chrystal responds, "A decision?" Mr. Timmons says, "Yes, that's it. All you have to do is decide to have what Daedai has. I will be here to make sure you get the proper foundation, and then you will make your decision. Now, I want everybody to clear your minds of all that carnal crap they taught you in high school and college. Know first, that everything that you have been conditioned to know through your senses is a great deception. Understand that there is only one truth, and that is in the irrefutable Word of God. To receive a revelation of His Word, you must have faith (the Word of God) in Him, for without faith (the Word of God), it is impossible to please Him. 'For he that cometh to God must believe that He is-and that He is a rewarder of those who diligently seek Him' (Heb. 11:6 KLV)." Mr. Timmons continues, "So, first, ladies, let us debunk and dismiss this ludicrous theory of evo-lution. I hope you don't really believe that you evolved from a monkey or that your existence is the result of a cosmic burp, do you?" Toni sits up and says, "But Mr. Timmons, we were taught that humans as a species evolved over billions of years ago. I'm a scientist, and I have studied this all of my life. Are you saying that evolution is incorrect?" Mr. Timmons answers unequivocally, "I am not only saying it's incorrect, I'm saying it is a bold-faced lie. Ladies, we live on a young earth, the radio-carbon dating methodologies they use to claim that the earth is billions of years old is scientifically inaccurate and fallible in most cases. Carbon (14) is a weak substance, and has a life span of fewer than l00,000 years; also, its atoms have unstable particles in the nuclei, which are so unstable it inevitably leads to false readings. Plus, scientists cannot account for the con-tamination in the data; not being there at the beginning, they do not know the condition or developmental stages of the item or items being dated (Ham 2017). Also, the heavily-re-lied-upon fossil record has been debunked, so, it is impossible to declare something's age as millions or billions of years old. Moreover, as it relates to the evolutionary origin of the species, there are no accounts of evolution in the biochemical system. There has never been found a transitional leap from one kind of species to another. However, there has been transitional alterations within the same species, but no verifiable leap from one species to a new species. All that scientists can pos-tulate, for the most part, is purely theoretical, unproven assumptions (beliefs) concerning evolution. Moreover, Charles Darwin, the Father of the evolution theory, stated emphatically that: 'If it could be demonstrated that any complex organ existed which could have possibly been formed by numerous, successive, slight modifications, my [his] theory would abso-lutely break down. But I can find no such case,' (IDEA 2020). Well, it did break down, Charlie; it broke down horribly, but we might give old Charlie a pass on this one because the scientific technology to research Thomas H. Frazzetta or Michael Behe's irreducible complexities discovered in molecular machines, like the bacterial flagellum or the cell itself, hadn't been invented. 'Irreducible complexity (IC) means that certain biological systems cannot evolve by successive small modifications to pre-existing functional systems through natural selection. Irreducible complexity has become central to the creationist concept of intelligent design...' (Encyclopedia 2020). With a slight grin, Chrystal says, "Charlie, huh, that's what you call Darwin, Mr. Timmons?" Mr. Timmons replies, "Calling him Charlie is better than the other name I would like to call him, but my Christian better half won't let me. Ladies, I joke about his name, but this man's theory and the believers in this theory have played a major role in Satan's deception of a non-existent God. The bad part in this is the refusal of scientists to make corrections to errors in textbooks about Darwin's theories, which have been proven incorrect. As taxpayers, we are paying money for this false information to be taught to our children, and our children have religiously bought into the deception as infallible. The falsehoods in Darwin's theories were the foundation for which his cousin Francis Galton became the Father of the eugenics movement, which later spawned another movement by racist / eugenicist Margret Sanger's Planned Parenthood (abortion on demand); all at taxpayers' expense. Doesn't anyone think it is time to tell the truth? At the least, an opposing view such as creationism should also be taught in our classrooms. Furthermore, we must also dismiss this crazy false premise of man as the cause of climate change. The beauty in climate change is only further evidence of the Creator's awesome design. Understand that God created carbon as a material of life; the ground, the sea, the trees, the water in the clouds, the moon, and all things in nature are all actively engaged in a symbiotic cycle of carbon, activated by solar flares from the sun to produce a change in the weather and seasons. To any extent, global warming is not the major threat of humans; however, global cooling to an ice age would be the ultimate killer. So, no matter what so-called scientists say, they have not figured out the many vicissitudes generated by this cycle, but if you're a believer in the Word of God, there's no need to be a scientist; you can see the intelligent design. Believe me, God got us. He is always in control, for His light of Glory holds everything together, and there is no need to panic. '...And the Lord smelled a sweet savor; and the Lord said in his heart, I will not again curse the ground any more for man's sake; for the imagination of man's heart is evil from his youth; neither will I again smite any more everything living, as I have done' (Gen. 8:21-22 KJV). 'As long as the earth endures, seed-time and harvest, cold and heat, summer and winter, day and night will never cease' (Gen. 22 NIV). You see, ladies, we have been deceived concerning many things, and the fact that we dare to distinguish or stereotype ourselves as being superior or inferior, based on the color of the skin, is also a false con-struction propagated by the enemy. Hear this: what I will be sharing with you while we are together is the irrefutable Word of God, which is the absolute truth."

CHAPTER 19
(THE REVELATION OF TRUTH)

"LADIES, WE ARE GOING TO TAKE SEVEN DAYS and try to get you acquainted with that truth, to help you with your decision." Somewhat cynical, Toni asks, "Mr. Timmons, is the reward we get from God what Daedai has?" Mr. Timmons says, "All I can tell you right now is that God gives good gifts." Chrystal says, "Ok, I like the idea of getting gifts, but what is this decision we have to make?" Mr. Timmons says, "You must decide if you will accept Jesus Christ as your Lord and Savior." Toni quickly replies, "Mr. Timmons, I'm a scientist, and this is unfamiliar territory for me, and I'm trying to figure out what does this have to do with what Daedai has?" With a smile on his face, Mr. Timmons looks at Toni, and without answering her question, replies, "Daedai has told me that none of you have been exposed to the Word of God; is that right?" As the women reflect inwardly in silence, Mr. Timmons inquires, "You mean to tell me that none of you have ever had explained to you the joy of having an intimate relationship with Jesus Christ?" Sanaa says, "Mr. Timmons, none of our families were ever into religion and that kind of stuff, and life as a professional doesn't provide any time for religion. As a child, the only time I ever went to church was for a funeral, wedding, or with a friend. I don't know much about the church or the Word of God. I always thought it to be kind of mythological." Mr.

Timmons looks around the room in utter astonishment as he notices that all the women agree with Sanaa about the extent of their religious experience. Mr. Timmons then looks at Daedai, through searching but empathetic eyes, and accepts this sad state of affairs, and asks, "Have you guys ever contemplated and questioned, 'Who am I? What am I? Why am I here?' and is there a God behind every one of those questions?" Toni answers enthusiastically, "Yes, I wonder about this all the time, but all of us, especially Raven, was led to believe from feminists groups that God was an invention to promote male dominance, and that we as women aren't here to be a help meet for men or be held back by the idea of the traditional family trapped in a role of wife, because if we succumb to that type of thinking, it inevitably leads to men seeing us as second-class citizens, primed to be slaves or held back by a man-made, mythological, religious ideology." Mr. Timmons closes his eyes and slowly shakes his head in sorrowful discord. Toni continues saying, "One of the founding members of the feminist movement, Gloria Steinem, says, 'Patriarchy requires violence or the subliminal threat of violence to maintain itself... The most dangerous situation for a woman is not an unknown man in the street or even the enemy in wartime, but a husband or lover in the isolation of their home,' (Steinem 1993). So, you see, Mr. Timmons, our understanding of truth and things in life has resided in lessons learned by reading books from such feminist authors, like Betty Friedan, Gloria Steinem, Catherine MacKinnon, Robin Morgan, Sheila Jeffreys, and Andrea Dworkin, all liberated women. Mr. Timmons, this has been our perspective on everything, and I personally feel that is why we have had challenges in our marriages. Mr. Timmons looks at these women through confrontational eyes and says, "Ladies, it's time for you to learn the truth. All that you have learned from the feminist movement, throw it out of your minds because it is antithetical to God's original intent for men and women. I do not want to waste a lot of time on this subject, but since you were indoctrinated in this way of thinking, I need to shine a light of truth on this misguided ideology. First of all, Gloria Steinem was a covert operative in the CIA, tasked to sow chaos relative to heterosexual relationships during the 1960s. The operation centered around the female ascension to power by branding and maneuvering political power, utilizing a false dialectic of tolerance to camouflage a movement toward establishing a new-world order. Ms. Steinem was a closet Marxist and Eugenicist. Part of her effort was also to deescalate the power inherent in the fast-progressing civil rights movement of the sixties, and covertly change its mandate to fit into an organized multicultural progressive agenda. Read articles by Henry Makow, Ph.D., March 18, 2002, at henrymakov.com: 'Gloria Steinem: How the CIA Used Feminism to Destabilize Society.' It gives revelations on feminism promoted by disingenuous elite and morally deprived persons in diverse capacities such as government, education, and media, all involved with attempting to manipulate societal ethos. That being said, ladies, you will learn as you grow in the Word that God does not see you as a lesser being. You are an equal part of a whole, separated to have a different function. In God's order, however, He has designated the man as the head of the family. It is about His order and not about servitude or second-class status. Men and women are separate parts of a whole, having different distinct functions with gender-exclusive idiosyncrasies specifically designed for that function. The man has been designated the captain, and the woman his lieutenant. God has organized it that way for the sustainability of the family. When a man or woman pursues a lifestyle or gender role that goes against God's original order, that man or that woman will run into trouble. One example of being out of order is found in the reason for Adam and Eve's fall. Eve exceeded the chain of command to go past Adam, and Adam exceeded the chain of command to go past God. The resulting penalty was their fall. We will revisit this subject later and make it much clearer for your understanding." Mr. Timmons then says, "Listen, ladies, 'In the beginning was the Word, and the Word was with God, and the Word was God.[2] The same was in the beginning with God.[3] All things were made by him, and without him was not anything made that was made.[4] In him was life, and the life was the light of men'" (John 1:1, 2, 3, 4 KJV). Mr. Timmons continues, "Ladies, at this stage of your spiritual development, you are considered babes in Christ. What I am saying is that you do not know much right now, and you need to be fed the Word of God in amounts you can easily digest. So, I will feed you the Word just like a baby being fed its Mother's milk, fed according to your ability to digest until you mature in knowledge of God." Mr. Timmons says, "'Wherefore, laying aside all malice, and all guile, and hypocrisies, and envies and all evil speaking, As newborn babes desire the sincere milk of the word, that ye may grow thereby...' (1 Pet. 2 KJV). 'Being born again, not of corruptible seed, but of incorruptible, by the word of God, which lives and abides forever'" (1 Pet. 1:23 KJV). Mr. Timmons continues saying, "Your nurturing through Christ Jesus will be a brand new process of growth; for example, when you consider your own triune physical makeup (mind, soul, spirit), your flesh (mind) is stronger than your soul or spirit within this physical plane, and with all things, new birth always takes place in the spiritual (spirit), rebirth manifests in the form of a seed (the consciousness of God) located in your spirit, which has to be developed. When your seed (the consciousness of God) grows in your spirit, likewise it changes your soul. However, the soil that will cultivate your seed must have a righteous and virtuous environment. The knowledge and glory of God is the catalyst for the expansion and growth of your seed. With this expansion in your seed empowering the spirit, it will empower your triune alignment (pathway) of spirit, soul, and mind, raising your level of faith to manifest in your physical existence more and more of what God has provided for you before the foundation of the world. It's a process you will go through, but I tell you the truth, you are now on the correct path, and with more foundational learning and revelation, you will hopefully receive all the things God has planned for you. I know you don't fully understand what I'm talking about right now, and comprehending things of the Spirit is sometimes difficult, but the simplicity in everything will be made clear; all I ask is that you keep an open mind, ok?" The women answer, "Ok, we got it." "Let me ask you this," Mr. Timmons inquires, "Do any of you have young children or have been involved with trying to teach young children?" Chrystal answers, "Yes, and it's not that easy, especially when they become teenagers; oh my Lord!" Mr. Timmons asks, "Why do you think that is?" Toni quickly blurts out, "Because they think they know every doggone thing, and they don't because they haven't experienced life yet. They aren't aware of all the pitfalls that can give them pain or cause them to lose their lives." Mr. Timmons responds, "Absolutely, and without the proper guidance, the problems in life can change destinies, right? Now, let us role play. I want you to think of God as your parent who loves and cares for you, and you are that innocent young child who cannot or will not listen to His instruction. Thus, we know that children can really try our patience, can't they? However, our God, as a patient and good parent, will never give up on you. He is always trying to teach you something to save your life because the deceiver of the world, Satan, who acts like a roaring lion, is seeking to devour you. Understand that God is love; love will not force Himself on you. You must decide to want love. I know you can't see God or feel His love right now, but believe me, He's right here, right now, this very second, and He even knows the number of hairs on top of your head, and it is because of Him that you are able to take your next breath. Ladies, I will lead you to discover, feel, and come to know His love through His written Word. Jesus Christ is the demonstration of God's love, the illustration and manifestation in the flesh of who the Father is. For when you study Jesus, you become intimate with the Father because they are one. Thus, you will see that God is a parent committed to caring for us, and as a good parent, He is always trying to instruct us. The question is, do you have a desire to hear His voice? And after hearing, will you obey? If the answer is yes, this is an indication that you have faith in Him. Understand that it is impossible to please God without having faith [The Word of God]." Looking at the faces of his neophytes, Mr. Timmons reasons, "So, I guess you would need to know what faith is, right?" Mr. Timmons pauses for a second, and looks into the eyes of each woman, then proceeds to say with a serious tone, "'Now [This instant], faith [The Word of God] is confidence in what we hope for and assurance about what we do not see' (Heb. 11:1 NIV). So, ladies, we fix our eyes not on what is seen, but on what is unseen. For what is seen is temporary [fades away], but what is unseen is eternal; this is the most important lesson you will need to learn. What I am saying is, believe God, even when you do not or cannot understand, how, when, where, why, or what He is doing. Thus, act according to His Word, over all objections, persuasions, persecutions and even over your own will, and never be afraid to question, but persistently seek answers. Then, ladies, this is what I call, the audacity of faith; bold, strong faith." Sanaa comments, "Mr. Timmons, not to speak for everybody here, but I'm pretty sure none of us understand this seen and unseen business." Mr. Timmons thinks for a minute and then says, "Ladies, there's a world all around you in another dimensional space that you cannot see with the human eye. In this world, time no longer exists. This is called the spiritual realm." Being the consummate scientist, Toni has a frown on her face as she makes fun of the term, "Woo, the spiritual realm; sounds creepy to me." Mr. Timmons interdicts and corrects her, saying, "Toni, there's nothing spooky or allegorical about this realm; it exists. It is a real place. I tell you truly, the spiritual realm is more real than this physical realm we are in right now. The

spiritual realm is where everything seen, invented, or conceived in this physical realm has come from. Our spirit resides
in this realm. The flesh that you see in the mirror is only a
reflection of the house (shell) that the spirit lives in. If by some
means, your spirit leaves your body, the flesh house that you
think of as the real you, would immediately fall dead to the
ground. Moreover, the flesh that we live in seeks to maintain
dominion over our spirit while we live in this physical dimension. The carnal (sinful) flesh mitigates the urging of the spirit
within us, which is our connection to the will of God. Your mission, if you chose to accept it, is to align your flesh to be subservient to the spirit within so that your spirit can effectively
implement through the flesh, God's will. Toni, there is nothing
seen or made that did not come from the spiritual realm. This
is so important that it bears repeating. There is nothing, absolutely nothing, that is seen or made that did not come from
the spiritual realm. The key to everything that you will learn
with me is in understanding the spiritual realm. So, the eventual alignment of your spirit to control your flesh is key to
receiving the things that God has ordained for you before the
foundation of the world. Through faith (the Word of God), you
have access to this realm. In this realm, a person can manifest
things into this physical dimension, preferably the spiritual
things that God has prepared for you. The spiritual realm is a
place where God and His angels reside because they are spirit
beings. The evil one, Satan is also a spirit-being, and he exists
in the spiritual realm also, but he and his cohorts are restrained
by the constitution of God, which governs the spiritual realm.
So whatever dirty work Satan is going to do, has to be done
within and under certain laws of restraint. But don't get it
twisted, God is sovereign over everything, and everything that
happens in the spirit and physical realm goes through God's
fingers. Satan and demonic entities are restrained under God's
laws from spiritually touching His children; however, demonic
and satanic forces can have an effect on the physical life of a

person through the spiritual realm when given permission by an agreement with a human person. To be clear, if given permission, Satan or demonic forces can possess or oppress the flesh, causing human beings to do ungodly things to other human beings and themselves; but again, the demonic entity under God's law cannot touch you unless there is a cause (sin). When a person prays (or dreams), he or she can wittingly or unwittingly give permission to spiritual beings (good or bad) to have an effect on physical life. Hopefully, you will stay away from all forms of witchcraft, and those persons who participate in the supernatural because when opening ungodly portals, you allow evil entities to affect your physical existence. Therefore, your prayers should always be in alignment with the Father's will for your destiny. But know this first, that Satan and his demonic forces have been defeated at the cross of Jesus Christ. Listen to this." Mr. Timmons picks up his tablet and reads a story from the Bible, He says, "'There was a certain rich man, which was clothed in purple and fine linen, and fared sumptuously every day: And there was a certain beggar named Lazarus, which was laid at his gate, full of sores, And desiring to be fed with the crumbs which fell from the rich man's table: moreover, the dogs came and licked his sores. And it came to pass, that the beggar died, and was carried by the angels into Abraham's bosom: the rich man also died and was buried; And in hell he (The rich man) lifts up his eyes, being in torments, and seeth Abraham afar off, and Lazarus in his bosom. And he cried and said, Father Abraham, have mercy on me, and send Lazarus, that he may dip the tip of his finger in water, and cool my tongue; for I am tormented in this flame. But Abraham said, Son, remember that thou in thy lifetime receivedst thy good things, and likewise Lazarus evil things: but now he (Lazarus) is comforted, and thou art tormented. And beside all this, between us and you there is a great gulf fixed: so that they which would pass from hence to you cannot; neither can they pass to us, that would come from thence. Then he (The rich man) said, I pray thee therefore, Father, that thou wouldest send him to my Father's house: For I have five brethren; that he may testify unto them, lest they also come into this place of torment. Abraham saith unto him, they have Moses and the prophets; let them hear them. And he said, Nay, Father Abraham: but if one went unto them from the dead, they will repent. And he said unto him, if they hear not Moses and the prophets, neither will they be persuaded, though one rose from the dead'" (Luke 16:19-31 KJV). Mr. Timmons explains, "Recognize what is happening here. God is revealing two deceased men in an eternal state (spirit realm), talking to one another. You notice that in the spiritual realm they can communicate with one another, see each other, feel and have feelings, recognize each other, have a sense of right and wrong, have memories, and regrets; human consciousness in a spiritual existence. This conversation underscores where the rubber meets the road. We will discuss the significance of this later on. Understanding the spiritual realm is especially important to your daily warfare, but for now, know this: God is love, and love will always allow you to have a choice. So, He sets before us death and life, and asks us to choose life in Him. For He commands us today to love the Lord your God, walk in obedience to Him, and keep His commands, decrees, and laws; then you will live and increase, and the Lord your God will bless you. On the other hand, the evil one, Satan, brings with him death, and seeks to infiltrate, defile, undermine, and dominate all that God has made, and spiritual death is the other choice. So, you see, we must take the spiritual realm very seriously; it is a place where spiritual warfare is waged, and it is not to be taken lightly; it is the key to everything; Remember, everything which is seen came from that which is not seen. Toni, therefore, we must all seek to develop an audacious faith, for now, and for what is to come." Mr. Timmons, sensing that the information given is overwhelming and seemingly too unreal for persons lacking knowledge of the Word, says,

"Ladies, things will be made clearer as we continue to study the Bible." So, he pauses and asks the ladies if they have their questions ready. Sanaa eagerly responds, "Yes. I have a lot of questions for you, Mr. Timmons." Mr. Timmons says, "Sanaa, you won't understand the answers to those questions until you get a proper foundation in the Word. So, for right now, I'll tell you what I'm going to do. I need to give you an assignment. I want Daedai to have you guys read and study the Book of Genesis up to chapter six, and she is going to discuss those chapters with you before you come back tomorrow, ok? So, I want you to hold onto your questions until then. Remember, everything flows from God's original intent for man. Now, think over that statement: 'everything flows from God's original intent for man,' and I'll see you guys tomorrow."

The ladies leave and take a different scenic route back home. They arrive back at Daedai's house early evening. They all exit the car, and Chrystal says, "Girl, I am so tired. Do we have to read this Book of Genesis?" Daedai answers, "You want what I have, right? At least that's what I thought you said." Chrystal quickly says, "Ok, you made your point, but first, we need to go freshen up and get something to eat, then we can start a Bible study." Daedai enthusiastically affirms, saying, "I wouldn't have it any other way. Do you want me to cook something, or do you want to order out?" Toni quickly responds, "I bet I know what my girl Raven would say with her greedy butt: 'Chinese food, please.'" Sanaa replies, "Hey, that will work; we can eat and study at the same time." Daedai agrees and comments, "That sounds like a plan. Write down the Chinese food you like, and we can order a variety for everybody." In full agreement with the plan, Toni replies, "Go ahead girl, make that call." When the women are finished freshening up, they come downstairs to the living room. Daedai stares at her friends and is beside herself when seeing that they have come downstairs empty-handed. She immediately scolds them, "Hey, go back upstairs and get your Bibles." Chrystal frowns and says, "Do we need a Bible? We can listen to you read, Daedai." Daedai aggressively responds, "No, it's very important that you have your Bibles, so you can visibly see the written Word of God." Attempting to settle Daedai down, Sanaa says, "Ok, give us a minute. We'll get our Bibles, jeez." Before the women can get back downstairs, the food comes, and Daedai sets out the plates on the dining room table. When the women finally get downstairs, Daedai says, "Let's pray." Daedai grabs Toni's hand, and the other women follow suit, grabbing the hand of the woman next to her. After Daedai finishes praying, they all get their food, and the lesson begins. While everybody is eating, Daedai asks her friends to turn to the Book of Genesis. Then they read, discuss, study, and read, discuss, study some more, while Daedai answers all the questions to which her friends have many.

At the end of the session, Daedai prepares a list of challenging questions for the group to answer. She asks, "What was God's original intent for man and creation? Did God make a woman from the ground, and why did He make her anyway? Did God create Satan? And what was found in Satan's heart? Did God make Adam twice? And what did Adam describe the woman as? Did the Fall take place right after the woman ate of the forbidden fruit? Did the Fall take place when Adam ate of the forbidden fruit? Why did God ask Adam and Eve where they were? Why did God remove Adam and Eve from the tree of life? Why did Satan go after Adam and Eve? Why did Satan approach Eve first, and what is God's divine order? Where was Adam when Eve was being deceived, and was he deceived also? What happened to the creation because of the Fall; what did man lose, and who gained? Why did God allow Eve to be deceived? And what would be her punishment? Why do you think God allowed Satan to approach His creation? Did Adam and Eve know they were naked before the Fall? Who was with God in the beginning? And when did God create time? With what did God clothe Adam and Eve when they discovered they were naked? Was Satan the anointed cherub made beautiful and manifests as an angel of light? What was God's punishment for Satan? And who would administer Satan's punishment? Did God put a curse on man?" Daedai would not quit challenging everyone, even though her friends persistently claimed to be tired and sleepy. She was persistent until everyone could answer and expound on all the questions she posed. When she finally felt comfortable with everybody's response and understanding, out of nowhere, Daedai stares at her friends, and they all notice her face giving birth to a smile, which was a welcomed relief after the torturous work she had put them through. Seeing this calm expression, Chrystal sarcastically inquires, "Daedai, what in the hell are you smiling about?" Trying to keep from tearing up, Daedai says, "I just feel good that my friends are on their way to finding truth through the Word of God, which is the enlightenment all of you need."

Sanaa then states, "I'm getting a little nervous about all of this." Daedai looks at Sanaa and asks, "Why?" Searching for words to express her feelings, Sanaa confesses, "I'm starting to feel that all this is too in-your-face-real, and it's scary to me. I feel overwhelmed at times by all this religious indoctrination. I have never been exposed to anything like this." Chrystal and Toni echo in agreement with Sanaa that they feel the same way too. Understanding that her friends feel overwhelmed with what they have learned and experienced, Daedai replies with all seriousness, "Remember this day, this time, this hour, and this very moment because your journey in truth has begun."

CHAPTER 20
(WHAT ABOUT MRS. TIMMONS?)

AFTER THE WOMEN SHARE A MOMENT OF SILENT introspection, Toni, the ever inquisitive one, looks at Daedai, contemplating something she's thought about all day, and blurts out, "Daedai, about Mr. Timmons, what does he think about women? Where is Mrs. Timmons? Is she still alive? And if there is a Mrs. Timmons, where is his better half?" At hearing this question, Daedai gives Toni a confused look and thinks to herself, *What?* She asks, "Why do you need to know this?" Then Daedai looks closely at all her friends and can see by their silence and body language that they are also interested in knowing about Mrs. Timmons. Sanaa smiles, and then speaking very softly, says, "Well, Mr. Timmons is so very impressive, we wanted to get acquainted with the woman behind the man." Knowing the feminist perspective from which their probe is generated, Daedai takes a deep breath as she rolls her eyes to the ceiling, then reluctantly, but purposefully, responds, "Firstly, ladies, there is a Mrs. Timmons. Secondly, in terms of what Mr. Timmons thinks about women; my husband says that he is quite the gentleman, and one of his favorite songs he loves is "Treat Her Like a Lady," by the Temptations, and when in con-versation about women, he often quotes from the author W.T. Barlow, saying, 'Women are wondrously made; intrinsically beautiful, copiously tolerant, inherently powerful, and addictively alluring; yet deliciously complicated, wildly posses-sive, and pretentiously vain. Consequently, since time imme-morial, have driven men completely insane, and life would be meaningless without you.'" After hearing these words, the ladies are quietly disarmed, and Daedai suggests further, "Mr. Timmons also believes that the woman is the totality of the man. The woman was made from the one man, both designed to live together as separate entities, functionally assigned to different roles in the order of God. The man and the woman are purposed by instructions from God in the furtherance of human sustainability. He says that the Father, who is the archi-tect of our human design, confounds the wise, and chose the weaker vessel to manifest His strength. Understand, ladies, that we wield a lot of power; seen and unseen, but most importantly, women are precious to God; we are a part of that oneness mystery, necessary for the help, health, and protec-tion of the man and the family." Daedai boldly looks at her friends, knowing that she has essentially crushed their feminist inquisition, then she asks, "Now, how does that work for you? I think the real question here is, what do you think of men?" Daedai smiles as her friends look on in astonishment, won-dering when, where, and how did Daedai develop such under-standing? Daedai evades eye contact and continues saying, "Ladies, there's a whole lot to Mr. Timmons's story, but I'm only going to share a small part of it with you because I think his story serves as an example of how the spirit of darkness present in this world can beat a person down to the ground unmercifully, leaving a residue of what appears to be a life in irreversible turmoil. But know that Satan is a liar; he was a liar from the beginning, but you will learn that there is a promise, a covenant signed in blood, which is sufficient for all circum-stances. As our world groans the labor pains of Jesus' return, Satan is working harder to deceive and oppress humanity because he knows his destruction draws near. So, the time has come, and is now, that people learn to be fully suited in the armor of God and have what Mr. Timmons calls the audacity of faith to stand against the power of demonic forces. Hopefully, you will develop that kind of faith here, and come to see that sometimes all is required is simply the ability to be still and just know that He is God." And feeling the power of Daedai's confident assurance, Toni excitedly yells, "Oh, preach, Daedai." Staring down at the ground, Daedai, intently thinking about how to share something so personal about Mr. Timmons, says, "My husband reluctantly told me that Mr. Timmons was once struggling to hold on to life, trying to keep from being swallowed up by depression and paralyzing heartache. What happened to him is now commonplace everywhere in America. Mr. Timmons's first wife was unfaithful to him for a long time, and he didn't have a clue as to her betrayal." Sanaa interjects, saying, "I've seen this type of betrayal before, and it's hurtful and so shameful." Daedai nods her head in agreement, and goes on to say, "Mr. Timmons invested everything into his marriage; time, money, love, everything. There was nothing he would not do for his wife and children. During this time in his life, Mr. Timmons, like yourselves, did not have revelatory knowledge in the Word of God. However, he would often unsuccessfully try to bring the Word of God into his home, attempting to make sure that his wife and children learned at least as much as he did about the Word. However, irrespective of his reading and searching the Word and praying, he was not able to be fruitful in his business and investments as the Word of God says. He was aware that his wife didn't do things right in her previous marriage, but he justified her leaving the ex-husband to be with him from the perspective of a woman under stress trying to escape an abusive relationship. He never considers that both of their infidelities could be the causal connection to his lack of business success. For a long time, Mr. Timmons could not figure out why there was always an uneasy feeling about his marriage; even though he knew he loved his wife, everything just didn't feel right. Initially, Mr. Timmons's wife was very patient, kind, and did everything for the family, which was proof enough for Mr. Timmons that he married a virtuous woman as he had been reading in Proverbs 31:10-31. However, things never seemed to go as planned, and he could not put his finger on what was wrong. One day while at home, Mr. Timmons became extremely sick, and his wife made him go to the hospital. While in the hospital, they found a mass in his brain. Fortunately for Mr. Timmons, the tumor would eventually prove to be nonmalignant. Mr. Timmons was told that the tumor had gotten so large that it burst inside his head, which was affecting his eyesight. The doctors told Mr. Timmons that they needed to operate right away. It just so happens that at this hospital, they had in residence the top surgeon in the country for this type of surgery. Fortunately for Mr. Timmons, the tumor was situated in the frontal area of his brain; a place inside his head where doctors could go through the nose to operate and remove the tumor without having to go through his skull. Time was sensitive, and the doctors needed to get Mr. Timmons into surgery as soon as possible. After finishing a week of surgical prep, Mr. Timmons went under a four-hour surgery. When the surgery was finished, Mr. Timmons opened his eyes to find a lady standing over him, holding his hand, and praying. He looked up at her, and immediately, without thought or question, Mr. Timmons starts praying in tongues. He had never remembered speaking in tongues before, and when the lady finished praying, she looked at him and smiled because she heard him praying in a spiritual language. She comforted him by saying, "You are going to be fine." Mr. Timmons assumed that since he was a patient in a religious hospital, the praying lady was one of the nuns making her rounds. However, later reflecting on his encounter with this praying lady and her comforting impact, he soon believed that what he had experienced was an angelic visitation because nobody knew this lady, and he never saw her again. Mr. Timmons's wife was at the hospital, off and on, to help take care of his needs and supposedly comfort him. He also received multiple visits from all his children, who were happy to see their Daddy doing well. When Mr. Timmons was finally released from the hospital and went home to recuperate, with inactivity due to painful arthritis, he found himself putting on an excessive amount of weight, but he was insistent on going back to work and continuing his study in theology. However, he found himself becoming worse from the paralyzing arthritis, and he knew this was due in large part from the great amount of weight he had gained. Mr. Timmons thought that his wife loved him and would always be there for him, but he started growing insecure because he was not the same vigorous man that he once was. He couldn't help but think that his physical condition and being much older than his wife would eventually lead to problems in their relationship." Daedai looks up at her friends with a sad expression on her face and says, "To make a long story short, Mr. Timmons's worst fears would eventually come upon him. After Mr. Timmons had somewhat recuperated, his wife started acting very distant and indifferent toward him, and while at his weakest point, she told him that she fell in love with someone else and was leaving him. Mr. Timmons was so terribly upset he wanted to strangle and beat the snot out of his wife but calmed himself down because he had already discerned in his spirit that she could leave. Being lost and mixed up in his feelings, Mr. Timmons blamed himself for his wife leaving. He summed it up to not taking proper care of himself." With a sad expression on her face, Daedai pauses and says to her friends, "There's more. Mr. Timmons and his wife had four children; two children were from Mrs. Timmons's previous marriage, and she had two children with Mr. Timmons."

Daedai comments, "Now check this out. Remember when Mr. Timmons came home from the hospital? Well, after about two weeks of trying to recuperate, his wife told him something surprising. She told him she was pregnant. Although Mr. Timmons knew that their sexual activity was not on the same level as it once was, he still said without question, "Hey! That's great, babe." However, in the back of his mind, this pregnancy was very surprising given his condition. Contemplating, Mr. Timmons starts to recall the times that he had sex with his wife pre and post-hospital. Mr. Timmons figures that he did have sexual relations with her before going to the hospital and was sure that he had sex after coming home. However, after a time, Mr. Timmons would not give thought to it anymore because Mrs. Timmons had never done anything to make him suspicious that she had something going on outside of their marriage. So, Mr. Timmons settled into the fact that he was going to have a new baby son. Mrs. Timmons would give birth to a baby boy, but for some reason, Mr. Timmons could not get it out of his head the possibility that the child may not be his, especially knowing how deceptive his wife had been in her previous marriage." Daedai says, "To make a long story short, later when Mr. Timmons's eighteen-year-old daughter found out that her Mother was leaving to go and live with some other family, she decided it was time to come clean about what she had been keeping secret from her Father for years. With tears in her eyes, Mr. Timmons's daughter told him that her Mother did not just fall in love and decide to leave. His daughter told him that her Mother had left their marriage long ago. The daughter said that her Mother had been in an adulterous relationship with another man for over twelve years. She told Mr. Timmons that even during the time that he was in the hospital, this man was in the house. She said this man was also spending time in his bed with her Mom. She knew this because she had caught them in bed having sex when she unexpectedly came home from school one day. She said the guy jumped up and tried to hide behind the bedroom door, but she saw the guy through the corner of the door trying to be unnoticed while her Mother was doing all she could to cover up the situation. She told her Dad that on many occasions, her Mom would often bring food to this man and his son, and even buy them clothes, and sometimes sneak and meet with him in the malls. During that period of time when reviewing his bank statements, Mr. Timmons could see that money was being drawn from his account, sometimes in large quantities, but his wife always had believable excuses for the withdrawals. Mr. Timmons's daughter also told him that when her Mother was supposed to be going out of town on company business, she was rendezvousing with this man at hotels. She said her Mother would get terribly angry with her because she would aggressively tell her Mom that what she was doing was wrong and that she hated this man. She told Mr. Timmons that she asked her Mother not to bring this man around anymore, arguing that this man was not her Father and that what she was doing to her Father was upsetting her. Mr. Timmons's daughter hated this man, and this guy did not hide the fact that he did not like her either. Mr. Timmons had absolutely no idea that this was taking place, and in learning this information, was very hurt by such a betrayal. Also, being such a conniving woman, Mrs. Timmons, before leaving, tries to manipulate Mr. Timmons into believing that her affair was recent and that her leaving was his fault. She would say to Mr. Timmons that he was the reason that she started up with another man because of his lack of attention. Of course, this was the lie she told before the daughter would later come clean with the truth about her Mother's long-time affair. When Mrs. Timmons eventually did leave the house, she left all the children except for the baby boy, who at this point, was now in the third grade. Although the other children were grown or in their high teens, Mr. Timmons was not physically capable of taking care of the house and the other children. Moreover, adding salt to the wound, his daughter confirmed his deepest fear, telling him that from what she had overheard, his youngest child most likely was not his. Having this information confirmed, devastated Mr. Timmons, putting him in a mild state of depression. The daughter also told Mr. Timmons that to keep everything secret, her Mom would often buy her brothers clothes and electronic things to keep them quiet. Moreover, the daughter stated that as a result of all the drama taking place in her life, she was constantly getting into fights at school and talking back to her teachers. Suffering so much from what her Mother was doing, she had to eventually talk to a school counselor. She said that when the school counselor contacted her Mother about what she had shared, her Mom lit into her and her brothers about talking her business. From that point on, the children feared to go against their Mother. However, when Mr. Timmons's children would find out that their Mother was not only abandoning their Dad, but also abandoning them, they took it extremely hard and saw it as a major betrayal that she wanted to be with some other family rather than with her own. Mr. Timmons's children admitted that they were afraid to tell what was going on for fear of what he might do to their Mother, or even that he might run off and leave them. However, through all the many lies and deceptions, the children still loved and wanted to be with their Mother." As Daedai continues adding meat to this salty bone, she says, "I would be remiss if I didn't share that Mr. Timmons was not an innocent victim in this adulterous drama. As stated earlier, the two children of Mr. Timmons's were the product of an adulterous relationship he had with Mrs. Timmons during the time that she was still married. The way it all happened was a chance encounter at a party where Mr. Timmons would meet the woman that would be his first wife. She came on to Mr. Timmons very aggressively during the party. However, Mr. Timmons did not know at the time that she was a married woman, until her husband, who was supposed to be somewhere else, showed up at the party. Mr. Timmons surmised from watching the husband interact with people at the party that he was her husband. But as fate would have it, phone numbers had already been exchanged. However, Mr. Timmons, at this point, was relieved, assuming that there was not a snowball chance in hell that she would call now, especially after her husband made this appearance at the party. Mr. Timmons really did not want to get involved with this type of relationship because he knew in his heart that it was wrong. You must understand that during this period of time in Mr. Timmons's life, he was a baby Christian, and knowing what he should not do, he would do. So, when the woman (the future Mrs. Timmons) unexpectedly did call and come over to his house explaining not to worry because her relationship with her husband was over, and that her husband did not love her anymore, and that he was caught cheating on her with multiple women, Mr. Timmons then stupidly bought into this secular reasoning and gave in to lust, reasoning in his mind that having intercourse with her would not be an adulterous affair because her marriage was already broken and could not be repaired." Shaking her head negatively, Daedai says, "Boy, Mr. Timmons was so gullible." Then Daedai strongly encourages her friends to recognize the lesson in this story, saying, "Like a watchful parent, God's Word exists not only for your salvation but also for your instruction. He loves you, and His plans for you are only for good and not for disaster. He wants to provide for you a good future, with the hope of glory in Christ Jesus. 'For I know the thoughts that I think toward you, saith the LORD, thoughts of peace, and not of evil, to give you an expected end,' (Jer. 29:11 ASV). You see, ladies, Mr. Timmons, not being spiritually mature in the word, made a bad decision by taking an adulterous path." Continuing on with the story, Daedai says, "Ladies, after about a year or so of cheating with Mr. Timmons, the woman would eventually leave her then-husband. However, when she left the marriage, the two children she had with Mr. Timmons were believed to be her husband's. Their birth certificates would have the husband's name as the Father. Being a stranger to this type of situation, Mr. Timmons found himself not being sure about the relationship with this woman while being trapped by a strong paternal instinct to do the right thing by his children. So, against that small voice screaming in his head that this woman could do the same thing to him as she had done to her husband, Mr. Timmons married her anyway. However, while married and feeling convicted in his spirit, Mr. Timmons started having regrets about the wrong done to his wife's ex-husband. He confessed to God that his role in the situation was wrong, and he took ownership of an offense against a covenant relationship that he had no right to breach. He accepted that he was an adulterer, no matter how much in his mind he would reason that he was manipulated by his wife. Mr. Timmons knew in his heart that he was more than an unequal co-conspirator. So, Mr. Timmons repented for all that he had done and asked God for forgiveness, and God forgave and blessed him.

CHAPTER 21
(HE PRAYED)

"REFLECTING ON HIS BAD DECISIONS, MR. Timmons totally believes that all the unseemly things that he had experienced during his marriage was the result of a relationship forged outside of the will of God for his life." With a gleam in her eyes, Daedai says, "But guys, check this out. Because of Mr. Timmons's growing relationship in Jesus Christ, he learned that he had to forgive his ex-wife. He knew that as Jesus forgave, so he would have to do the same thing in forgiving her. We are all God's children and have breached the laws of God. However, through Christ Jesus, all our sin, our faults, our failures, and our disobedience are all forgiven. Mr. Timmons came to understand through obtaining knowledge in God's Word that he is not qualified to be the judge of any person, and that vengeance does not belong to him; it belongs to God. He is judgment. Mr. Timmons decides to put his faith in God and believe that God would give him greater and better in all facets of his life, and God delivered on His faithfulness. After a season, while in a short but intense prayer session, Mr. Timmons audibly hears the voice of God. What God would say and reveal to him would change his life forever. God simply said, "YOU ARE NOT ALONE," and revealed to him the source of his troubles. God revealed first that his fight was not with his ex-wife but with the spirit behind her, guiding her to commit adulterous affairs. It was revealed that Mr. Timmons's troubles manifested because of sin, particularly the breaking of a marital covenant. Then God revealed to him a host of Scriptures and principles of order and law that Mr. Timmons had read multiple times but had not discerned their meaning. Mr. Timmons became somewhat perplexed at what God was trying to tell him, so God laid in his spirit a particular Scripture, 'My people are destroyed from a lack of knowledge. Because you have rejected knowledge, I also reject you as my priests; because you have ignored the law of your God, I also will ignore your children' (Hosea 4:6 KJV). Mr. Timmons, after getting this message, felt that God could not have been talking about him. So he began to question himself inwardly, 'I read, and I study the Word of God.' Mr. Timmons, now pressed by the Holy Spirit, realizes in his heart that it cannot be that God made a mistake or does not communicate well; so there had to be a whole lot of stuff in the Scriptures that was hidden from him or that he just did not understand. Mr. Timmons asked for wisdom from God concerning these Scriptures, and was dumbfounded when God, in response, laid on his heart three more Scriptures, 'By faith (the Word of God) we understand that the universe was formed by God's command so that what is seen was not made out of what was visible' (Heb. 11:3 HCSB). 'So we fix our eyes not on what is seen, but on what is unseen. For what is seen is temporary, but what is unseen is eternal' (2 Cor. 4:18 NIV). And finally, 'For we do not wrestle against flesh and blood, but against the rulers, against the authorities, against the cosmic powers over this present darkness, against the spiritual forces of evil in the heavenly places' (Eph. 6:12 ESV). Searching for understanding, Mr. Timmons meditated on these Scriptures day and night until one day, he gets it; he reasons that it had nothing to do with how he felt or how he perceived the Word; it was just that he wasn't taking every single word in the Bible literally. This revelation helped him to eventually understand that the spiritual realm is a seed-sowing realm, a realm of transfer, exchange, and substitution; a realm in which diverse deities have their dwelling, both good and bad. So, when he began to digest everything in the Bible, word for word, like a lawyer reading a transcript, analyzing everything that the main characters in the Bible did, and how they were blessed or cursed as a result of their actions, everything became clear. He came to understand that prayers and dreams open up avenues for spiritual engagement or portals; they offer the ability to give permission or make covenant with spiritual beings. He figured out that when a human being agrees or covenants with a spiritual being, a manifestation in the physical realm can take place because the laws of God policing the realm of the spirit has been satisfied. It was made clear from his reading and learning in Genesis about man's dominion in the earth that spiritual beings, whether good or evil, must have permission (agreement) from a man on earth, to sow anything into the spiritual realm to go forth into the physical realm. This revelation profoundly illuminates everything for Mr. Timmons, in that everything seen in the physical realm came from the spiritual realm. The light then suddenly comes on as Mr. Timmons looks at everything in his environment, and being so much more enlightened, staggered and shouted, 'My God,' as he realizes, looking down and around the room, that even the shoes on his feet, the house he was sitting in, his bed, his clothes, his Bible, and even the very underwear he was wearing-all came by way of the spirit realm. But most importantly, Mr. Timmons realizes that someone, at some point, in the physical plane, had to agree in the spirit to manifest these things into physical existence. This revelation was so overwhelming that Mr. Timmons fell to his knees, shouting, 'I see Father! I see!' Thinking introspectively, he figures that his actions, good or bad, are also seeds sown in the spiritual realm, and that his actions, good or bad, in agreement with spiritual beings in the spiritual realm, are the seeds sown that can manifest things into physical existence. Mr. Timmons would never read Scriptures the same way again. He would now see spiritual sowing, spiritual transfer, substitution, and exchange in the Scriptures he would read. This was made clearer when reading, 'Why do you complain to Him that He responds to no one's words? For God does speak-now one way, now another though no one perceives it. In a dream, in a vision of the night, when deep sleep falls on people as they slumber in their beds. Then he openeth the ears of men, and sealeth their instruction. That he may withdraw man from his purpose, And hide pride from man; he keepeth back his soul from the pit, and his life from perishing by the sword' (Job 33:13-18 ASV). Mr. Timmons surmises correctly that God, most times, communicates with men through their sleep and visions to influence their lives. Mr. Timmons sees many examples throughout the Bible where God gave instructions and warnings to men in a deep sleep. As a matter of fact, Mr. Timmons remembered, in reading Genesis, that Eve was made from Adam's rib while Adam was in a deep sleep. Mr. Timmons surmises that Adam must have agreed with God or had given permission to manifest Eve into the physical realm. Moreover, Adam and Eve themselves were first conceived in the spiritual. This sealed the deal in Mr. Timmons's understanding, especially when reading with full comprehension the following, 'But while everyone was sleeping, his enemy came and sowed weeds among the wheat, and went away' (Matt. 13:25 NIV). He understands now that the spiritual realm is the parent to the physical realm, and that Satan and other demonic forces can transform themselves into a pleasing light to infiltrate our dreams and influence our physical lives. Satan and his cohorts deceive us in the spirit realm (dream state or consciousness), disguised as something familiar, such as the dead, a wife, people from our past, or present relationships presented as a movie trailer with familiar or unfamiliar characters and action plots; when in deep sleep, we unwittingly or wittingly engage with these demonic characters to form an agreement (covenant) through our actions, words, or deeds. Then that evil spirit(s) under God's order or laws (divine constitution) for that realm now has permission to attempt to manifest evil into our physical lives unless the dream is rebuked. Mr. Timmons learns that Satan and his ministers have a right to attempt to deceive us in this manner because God has set in order certain laws governing the spiritual realm, and knowing that God won't go back on His Word, Satan and demonic forces have figured out legal loopholes in the court room of God to deceive us while we sleep. So, Mr. Timmons surmises correctly again that Christians just saying, 'I'm redeemed from the curse of the Law,' even though true, must be accompanied with obedience to God's commandments; not from a legalistic perspective, but through faith (the Word of God) in Christ Jesus our Redeemer. Portals to allow the accuser (Satan) to legally have access to oppress us comes through sin, transgression, and iniquity. Jesus's sacrifice provided the spiritual framework for resistance to the powers of darkness; now it's up to each Christian to repent and invoke God's Word in Jesus's name, obey His commandments to rebuke demonic spirits, and receive deliverance from the possibility of or the actual physical manifestation by way of our sin, transgressions, and iniquities. The same holds true to manifest the things that God has already prepared for us before the foundation of the world. Mr. Timmons surmises that this is the way to engage spiritual warfare; blocking the enemy by closing portals of sin, transgression, and iniquity from propagating evil into our physical lives and from stealing the good things that God has prepared for us. Mr. Timmons now comprehends that our warfare is a daily battle; if the deceiver can't trap us or open portals through sin, transgression, or iniquity on our physical plane, there is the spiritual realm through dreams where Satan and his ministers can disguise themselves as anything familiar: family members, close friends, someone deceased, sexy persons of imagination, any animal, insect or object in the air or under the sea, creating in deep sleep an action plot appearing mostly as a real-life episode of a story taken from our daily lives as an entrapment to get us to agree (covenant) with a demonic figure, and once that agreement is obtained, the demon now has permission and the right through our spirit to manifest evil into our physical existence. Mr. Timmons then positions himself to take the attitude to 'Be sober, be vigilant; because your (our) adversary the devil, as a roaring lion, walks about seeking whom he may devour' (1 Pet. 5:8 KJV). 'Wherefore gird up the loins of your mind, be sober, and hope to the end for the grace that is to be brought unto you at the revelation of Jesus Christ' (1 Pet. 1:13 KJB). Mr. Timmons, filled with understanding, now reads the Scriptures with greater revelation, discovering the seed-sowing and reaping properties of the spiritual realm. 'Praise be to the God and Father of our Lord Jesus Christ, who has blessed us in the heavenly realms with every spiritual blessing in Christ. For he chose us in him before the creation of the world to be holy and blameless in his sight' (Eph. 1:3-4 NIV). 'For as the rain cometh down, and the snow from heaven, and returneth not thither, but watereth the earth, and maketh it bring forth and bud, that it may give seed to the sower, and bread to the eater: So shall my word be that goeth forth out of my mouth: it shall not return unto me void, but it shall accomplish that which I please, and it shall prosper in the thing whereto I sent it' (Isa. 55:10-11 KJV). Mr. Timmons now realizes that the Word of God is the constitution for all creation in both the seen and unseen world, and now knowing his rights, he sets out to get back everything that was stolen from him. He did this by living righteously and rebuking every negative dream or sinful thought that demonic figures would use to influence a covenant. In discerning his rights, Mr. Timmons learned that there was a law for restitution that says, 'Yet if the enemy (thief) is caught, he must pay sevenfold, though it costs him all the wealth of his house' (Prov. 6:31 NIV). Mr. Timmons, knowing that Satan had robbed him of everything he had and was still actively engaged in trying to steal his future prosperity, began to fight in the spirit realm with his newly found revelation in the Word. Mr. Timmons formulates a special prayer he would pray while fasting or non-fasting, reciting whenever he had a dream or even if he couldn't recall the dream after sleeping, he prayed this daily: 'Father God, I confess all of my sins, and I repent. I ask for Your forgiveness and that You cleanse me from all unrighteousness. My Lord and my God, I cover myself in the blood of Your son Jesus Christ, and I confess that the blood of Jesus has rendered powerless all satanic or demonic blood sacrifices or dreams speaking against my destiny. Heavenly Father, I apply the blood of Jesus to bind satanic and or demonic spirits assigned against me and my family members. Father, every evil voice or covenant speaking against my destiny, my children, my property, my prosperity, my home, my health, and my job opportunities, I reverse that curse or denounce that dream in the name of Jesus. I command it according to Your Scripture in Psalms 7:15 KJV, which says, 'those who have dug ditches for me-be consumed by those very ditches they have made for me.' In Luke 10:19 KJV, it says, 'You have given me the authority to trample on snakes and scorpions and to overcome all the powers of the enemy,' and nothing will harm me because your Word says in Isaiah 54:17 KJV, 'No weapon formed against me shall prosper; and every tongue that shall rise against me in judgment thou shalt condemn.' Heavenly Father, I remind You of this Your Word. I come against all generational curses brought by me or my foreFathers, and I bind these generational curses by the blood of Jesus. So, in Jesus's name, I command the fires of the Holy Spirit to rain down and consume tormenting spirits, monitoring spirits, adulterous spirits, delaying spirits, blocking spirits, confusing spirits, lying spirits, crippling spirits of infirmity, spirits of being offended, spirits of poverty, spirits of fear, spirits of addiction, spirits of lust, spirits of low self-esteem, and spirits of anxiety that are coming against me and my family.

I bind these spirits powerless, and I send them back to the abyss, in the name of Jesus Christ. Father, Your Word says in Psalms 119:89 NIV, 'Your word, LORD, is eternal; it stands firm in the heavens.' In Joel 2:25 KJV, 'You said you will restore to me the years that the locust hath eaten, the cankerworm, and the caterpillar, and the palmerworm, your great army which you sent among me.' Father, right now at this very moment, I denounce and disconnect with any dreams or ancestral covenants made on altars through my lineage or through ignorance out of my own mouth that is against Your will for my destiny, and I command these generational curses be broken and consumed by fires sent from the Holy spirit. Father, whatever is in my house beyond my knowledge or with my knowledge that is against me and my family, Father, send fires from heaven to sever and consume it away, in Jesus's name. Father, Your Word says in Deuteronomy 28:3 NJKV, 'I will be blessed in the city and blessed in the country.' In verse twelve, You said You will open the heavens, the storehouse of Your bounty, to send rain on my land in season and to bless all the work of my hands. I will lend to many nations but will borrow from none. In verse thirteen, You said You will make me the head, not the tail. You said also in Your Word that I will be blessed going in and blessed coming out; above always, and not beneath. I remind You, Father, of this Your Word. Father, I now release and open myself to the blessings that have been delayed or denied or held back from me, to now come forth into my life, and because the enemy has been identified and caught, he must now release my blessings and return unto me sevenfold as Your Word says in Proverbs 6:31 NIV, that, 'Yet if the thief is caught, he must pay sevenfold, though it costs him all the wealth of his house.' Therefore, I command you evil spirit of darkness, in the name of Jesus, recompense to me more than you took from me. Father, I open myself for total restoration. I am now free from the curse of the enemy, and the blessings which have been stolen from me, and the blessings which You have ordained for me, before the foundations of the world, must flow to me right now. Father, I receive these blessings in accordance with Your Word. That the Father may be glorified in the Son; all these and other blessings I ask in the mighty name and in the blood of Your Son and my Lord and Savior Jesus Christ. Amen. Thank You, Father. I receive.' Mr. Timmons, having become wise in the laws of God and in obedience to those laws, started a campaign of giving to the poor and the needy, and now he is a multi-millionaire at the age of sixty-six, adding, also, two younger children to his table, and a beautiful wife that loves him; he has truly been blessed. Mr. Timmons is at long last, as it says in the Bible, equally yoked. The ex-Mrs. Timmons faked her Christian belief and had everyone fooled. But his new wife is a born-again, spirit-filled Christian woman, who helps him in his business and ministry, and has added much to his life. Ladies, believe me, I also pray Mr. Timmons's prayer daily, I fast, and I give joyfully to the poor and needy. I beseech you to do as I have done; receive Mr. Timmons's story as a good lesson in the audacity of faith, that when all around you is falling apart, hold on, never give up, hold on, even in the face of everything and everyone coming against you; hold on, just stand; pray, search, and seek the knowledge of His kingdom, and know that God can change and completely turn around any situation. With God, all things are possible. Know that you plus God is always a majority, and that no weapon formed against you will be able to succeed. Mr. Timmons's older children, for a season, suffered through some of the effects of a broken home (generational curse), and would experience trying times in their lives. So, Mr. Timmons fasted and prayed with deeper specificity, saying, 'Father I repent of every negative thing I have spoken about my children in anger and or disappointment. I intercede and repent for my children, and by faith, I believe that you have removed all the clutter in my life and in my children's lives, and have enabled spiritual help to unshackle our momentum to prosper and be successful in our business, investments, job opportunities, and our daily walk with You. We seek first, Heavenly Father, Your kingdom and Your righteousness, and we know all these things will be added unto us. Father, Your Word says in Psalms 115:13-15 KJV, 'He will bless them that fear the Lord, both small and great. The Lord shall increase me more and more, me and my children. We are blessed of the Lord which made heaven and earth.' Father, we remind you of this Your Word, and thank You for releasing unto us great financial blessings and the best wife and or husband a man or women can have. Thank You, Father, that You have silenced our enemies against us and have severed and removed those evil spirits of addition, lust, low self-esteem, slow learning, infirmity, and uncleanliness that have distorted our minds and our destinies opposite of Your will for our lives. God, right now, this very moment, we speak Your Word and believe You have given Your angels charge over us to manifest spiritual blessings into our lives, putting us back in alignment to Your will for our destiny. That the Father be glorified in the Son; we receive all these blessings in the name and by the blood of our Lord and Savior Jesus Christ. Amen.' Eventually, all Mr. Timmons's older children would change their worldly lifestyles and become extraordinarily successful, God-fearing professional people. Nowadays, Mr. Timmons helps others who are in distress through his firsthand experience with making bad decisions and the consequences that follow. So, he shares the Word of God with people, assisting them to renew their minds so they can have a different perspective on life; make better decisions and live in peace by having a relationship with Jesus Christ." Attempting to get a handle on Mr. Timmons's motivation, Toni asks, "Is that's why he's so motivated to help us?" Daedai says, "Well, yeah, that's part of it. Mostly, he is just committed to sharing the good news of Jesus Christ."

"God commands us to give, and by this we know we will receive; it's God's principle of exchange." Daedai tells the ladies that they will be given a copy of Mr. Timmons's prayer; then she stares at Toni, and testing her understanding, asks, "Toni, where did those nice shoes you're wearing come from?" With a weird and surprised expression on her face, Toni is perplexed by Daedai's question. She looks down at her shoes, and with all seriousness, she says, "Girl I got these at Macy's, why?" Without answering her back, Daedai looks around the room and sees that none of her friends discerned that she was speaking spiritually in questioning where Toni's shoes came from, relative to Mr. Timmons's story." But understanding that her friends do not yet have revelatory knowledge, Daedai just smiles and says, "Ladies, listen up. I've shared this information about Mr. Timmons with his permission because he knows his story is a lesson on how not to lean to your own under-standing about anything. Mr. Timmons wants you to always seek the Word of God and follow it to the letter. I feel satisfied that when we meet with Mr. Timmons tomorrow, the ques-tions you have prepared for discussion will be more on point, considering your newfound understanding. So, now with all this information crowding your brain, I think it's time to take a break from studying and go have some fun for the rest of the evening."

CHAPTER 22
(THE FOUNDATION)

DAY TWO: MR. TIMMONS GREETS THE LADIES, and after praying, he says, "Hear the truth. In the beginning, the earth was without form and void, and darkness was upon the face of the deep. And the Spirit of God moved upon the face of the waters. And God said, let there be LIGHT: and there was LIGHT. And God saw the light, that it was good: and God divided the light from the darkness." Mr. Timmons, with a smiling face, asks, "Did you ladies read and discuss the Book of Genesis as assigned?" And the ladies all answer, "Yes." Mr. Timmons says, "Ok, then, what are your questions?" Chrystal angrily speaks up and comments, "I understand about Adam and his fall and all that, but where was God when my Father and Raven died; where was He then, Mr. Timmons?" Not expecting that type of question, Mr. Timmons stares at Chrystal intently, and with a fierceness, he answers with likewise forceful energy, saying loudly, "You don't have a clue what the fall of Adam entailed. But to answer your question, God is at the same place, as He was during Raven and your Father's tragedy, as He was when He was pouring out His wrath upon His only begotten Son; when He witnessed His innocent Son in obedience to His will, step down out of divinity to be beaten, whipped, tortured, shamed, and crucified on a piece of wood for the world's redemption, allowing mere mortals made from the very same ground that He created to shed His blood and then forgive them in strict obedience to His Father's will. Oh, I tell you, the price was steep and could only be paid by God Himself in the flesh. Chrystal, dear lady, when you eventually come into the revelation of what Adam lost by his disobedience, and the price in blood that had to be paid so that eternity in the bowels of hell you would not have to stay, you will fall quickly on your knees and scream loudly, 'Thank You, Lord Jesus. Thank You for Your grace and mercy. Thank You, Father God.' Ladies, I tell you truly, the price paid for Adam's betrayal took an act of love that only our God Himself could manifest, and because of that love, mankind is redeemed from all sin and death. So, rest assured, Chrystal, because of Jesus's sacrifice, you will see your Father and Raven again, for Jesus has overcome the world and has defeated hell, death, and the grave." Sober in her attitude from hearing the forceful polemic from Mr. Timmons, Sanaa politely inquires, "But Mr. Timmons, if God loves us as His children, why then does he still let bad things happen to us?" Mr. Timmons again aggressively replies, saying, "Sanaa, dear heart, you ask the wrong question. The question you should ask is why doesn't a holy, perfect, and sovereign God, knowing what you did yesterday and last night, does not completely obliterate you out of existence? There is a reason He does not because love forgave and had a plan. God will never go against His Word. He holds His Word even above His Name. When you read about the fall of Adam and Eve, you must understand that Adam's disobedience opened a portal for sin to enter a perfect world, and that sin brought with it the spirit of death; so Adam and Eve and their generation, in fulfillment of God's Word, would have to die. God, who loves us beyond our comprehension, gave Adam and Eve a choice because they were made perfect in his image, and God does not make anything that is not perfect, and perfect love is always an expression of choice (will). God gave Adam and Eve dominion over the earth and everything in it, and as a result of Adam's bad decision, breaching a covenant (agreement), transferred, seeded, exchanged, and substituted dominion to the evil one, resulting in his generation suffering the consequences (generational curse) for his actions. It is especially important for you and me to understand that our Father changes not, and we can always trust His Word as the ultimate truth that never changes as it relates to you, me, and everything else. God, before the foundation of the world, had already set a plan in motion to deliver His children from the evil one and his deceptions. God, before the foundation of the world, poured out His wrath on Himself as the Lamb in spirit for our redemption; to reconcile our sin erased, and to bring us back to Himself. Remember, everything has to first take place in the unseen (spirit) to eventually manifest in the seen. Whatever evil manifests in the world does not come from God, but from the evil one, Satan; but everything that happens, good or evil, goes through God's fingers, or to be more illustrative, comes across God's desk, and is sanctioned by Him. God created good and evil, light and darkness, and Satan was made perfect. It was Satan's choice to turn evil, as iniquity was found in his heart. God took advantage of Satan's defiance in developing His plan for mankind, whose plan is a mystery still unsolved. I do not know why God did it that way, but who are we to second-guess the infinite, all-knowing, all-seeing, omniscient, omnipresent, omnipotent God and His wisdom, for He knows humanity far beyond our comprehension. He's the designer, knowing the ending from the beginning, and has given you and me the light of His goodness and mercy. So, whatever Satan means for evil, God uses in developing something divinely greater, something much bigger, which often comes in a mystery hidden inside a riddle and wrapped in an enigma, far beyond the understanding or comprehension of Satan and his ministers. Remember, God is always in control. He knows the ending from the beginning, and if you are in Him and He is in you, you will never die." Sanaa perks up in her seat, expressing in her body language that she is enthused as to what Mr. Timmons is teaching. Then, Toni abruptly interrupts, asking a question about religion the ladies had discussed in many private debates but had never gotten a clear explanation. Toni, the inquisitive science professional asks, "How do we know that Christianity is the right way over all other religions?" Mr. Timmons smiles and reads confidently, in a preacher-like tone, 'For we (apostles) did not follow cleverly devised stories when we told you about the coming of our Lord Jesus Christ in power, but we (apostles) were EYEWITNESSES of his majesty. He received honor and glory from God the Father when the voice came to him from the Majestic of Glory, saying, this is my Son, whom I love; with him, I am well pleased. We (apostles) ourselves HEARD this voice that came from heaven when we (apostles) were with him on the sacred mountain. We also have the prophetic message as something completely reliable, and you will do well to pay attention to it, as to a light shining in a dark place, until the day dawns and the morning star rises in your hearts. Above all, you must understand that no prophecy of Scripture came about by the prophet's own interpretation of things. For prophecy never had its origin in the human will, but prophets, though human, spoke from God as they were carried along by the Holy Spirit' (2 Pet. 1:16-21 NIV). Now, 2 Peter should be enough for you, but I shall continue. First, young ladies, Christianity is the only truth because it is a compilation of reliable documents, written by eyewitnesses during the life and time of other eyewitnesses that could testify of miraculous events of a divine nature. The Bible was written by forty authors, writing sixty-six books, all harmonizing, coherently-inspired through the Holy Spirit, spanning over 1,500 years. Know that Christianity is the universal authority because when the Bible is spoken anywhere in the world, power is seen and demonstrated through Christ, the living Word. It is the only book that promises eternal life, and it's the only book that works, and when a relationship is established with the Holy Spirit, it distributes nine usable gifts (word of wisdom, word of knowledge, faith, gifts of healing, miracles, prophecy, distinguishing between spirits, and tongues) manifesting for the believer, as the Spirit wills. Secondly, you know that Christianity is the only truth by the universal authority that is in the name of Jesus. You can say the name of Jesus worldwide, and demons, principalities, and all forms of evil beings on earth and under the sea tremble at the name, for they know who He is. Thirdly, you can know Christianity is truth by the power of the Holy Spirit, that when He manifests, people all over the world act the same way. When people even in remote corners of the world who never heard of the Word of God, receive the Word, and are baptized in the Holy Spirit, they always act the same. Furthermore, the Bible lays it out, day by day, how God created the heavens and the earth. So, it is simple; all people need to do is look up at the sky; the heavens declare and reveal God's fingerprints all over His wonderful creation. Today, with our technological advancements and space travel, we know that outside of the earth's atmosphere, there is nothing compatible to earth in sustaining life. Earth was set in a place where it should not or could not be able to sustain life unless all the elements and forces surrounding it were perfectly aligned. Think about it. If the earth were just a little bit closer to the sun, we would burn. If the earth was a little bit further from the sun, we would freeze; think about that. We have the exact mixture of all elements, forces, and movable parts in the earth's atmosphere to sustain life. According to Frank Turek (Turek 2008), an American Christian author, public speaker, and radio host quoting Steven Hawking, states that: 'The universe would not exist if there was a decrease in the expansion rate one second after the (alleged) big bang by only one part in one hundred thousand, million millionth; leading Hawking to conclude that it would be exceedingly difficult for the universe to have begun this way except as an act of God designed for beings like us.'

God is making a statement. He's trying to show us that earth was supernaturally designed as a place for the habitation of His children." Mr. Timmons pauses and then continues, "I tell you the truth; God hung earth out on nothing, and arranged elements, atmospheres, forces, the firmament, and the things that are in it specifically for His creation here on earth. So, when one who has wisdom looks up into the heavens, he knows that it could only exist by the handy work of God, our creator. He is the substance of your very next breath. He is omniscient, omnipotent, and omnipresent, and in Him are all things that be. Now, back to your question, 'But you are not in the flesh, but in the Spirit if so be that the Spirit of God dwells in you' (Rom. 8:9 KJV). Therefore, any place in the world that people receive the Holy Spirit-we share a common bond. Lastly, understand that the Word of God is the only message that can profoundly change the heart of a man. It is the elephant in the room that our society refuses to recognize. It is simply the panacea for all our social ills; simply being obedient to the Word of God. However, this understanding only comes through the revelation of the truth. Pastor Ravi Zacharias (Zacharias 2016) says, and I agree with him that there is a test to prove that Judeo Christianity is the only truth. He says, 'For any religion to be the absolute truth, four questions must be answered, defined, and aligned. They are ORIGIN (where do we come from?), MEANING (what is our purpose?), MORALITY (how are we to treat each other?), and DESTINY (where are we going?). The Judeo-Christian religion is the only religion that is coherent on all four questions with corresponding answers to each that stand the test of time, with the promise of hope in Christ Jesus.' Moreover, it is undeniable that God's fingerprints are all over the Bible, evidencing that He is the one and only Author, Creator, and Designer. For that reason, the Bible will always be the bestselling book of all time. Other religious books read like a novel, and are devoid of a promise of salvation, without power or gifts of the Spirit, and no accurate prophetic revelations. In an article by Wayne Jackson (Jackson 2020), he references J. Barton Payne's Ensighclopedia of Biblical Prophecy, which lists 1,239 prophecies in the Old Testament, and 578 prophecies in the New Testament, for a total of 1,817. These prophecies encompass 8,352 verses. Multiple prophecies have already been fulfilled, and all others will be completely fulfilled in the future. Whereas the Bible is historically consistent, other religions are not. You have already noticed the transforming power of the Holy Spirit in Daedai's life, haven't you? So Toni, did I answer your question?" Toni concedes in a small, yet satisfied tone, answering, "Yes, sir, I understand." Mr. Timmons says, "Ladies, hear me well, when God created Adam, He created a duplicate image of Himself. When the angels looked upon Adam, they saw the image of God. From the beginning, God's desire has been to commune with His children. We are a part of him; He breathed Himself into us. Adam was perfect, with full one hundred percent usage of his brain; but as a result of the Fall, we presently only use about ten to fifteen percent of our brainpower. Understand that Adam would have never known pain or sickness; he could control all the elements. He would have control over time and space, and his only job would have been to subdue and fill the earth, for God gave him dominion over the earth and everything in it; this is the magnitude of what Adam lost. I am not sure most people understand the full extent of the power that Adam possessed. Everything we read that Jesus could do, Adam could do also. Jesus is the second Adam who came in the flesh, and being sinless and obedient even unto death, conquered death, hell, and the grave, becoming the firstborn of the fruit of the Spirit. I tell you a truth, the flesh will profit you nothing. I repeat, the flesh profits nothing. Jesus (God in the flesh) crucified the flesh for us. Overcoming the flesh means not your will be done, but rather the Father's will be done. 'God chose the foolish things of the world to shame the wise; God chose the weak things of the world to shame the strong; He chose the lowly and despised things of the world and things that are not, to nullify the things that are, so that no flesh can boast in his presences...' (1 Cor. 1:27-29 NIV). It is only through the shed blood of Jesus Christ, the spotless (sinless) Lamb that we have salvation; the life is in the blood of Jesus. I pray you will receive revelation as it relates to this lesson, and with that, I will see you tomorrow." The ladies are overwhelmed and convicted by truth as they silently look at each other and prepare to go home."

DAY THREE: In the morning, when the ladies finally arrive at the church, Mr. Timmons is waiting and greets them good morning. They greet Mr. Timmons, and then they pray. Mr. Timmons says, "Today, we will learn the consequences of the Fall, which necessitated the blood of Jesus to make atonement for our sin / disobedience. Listen and hear with a spiritual ear, for Jesus has sent the Holy Spirit to lead us into all truth; He is already in you, and as we make progress in the Word, hidden things will be revealed in your understanding. To truly know Jesus, He must be revealed to you through the Holy Spirit. I will explain later, but for right now, do you remember when the serpent permitted Satan to use his body to deceive the woman (spiritual exchange)? God says, 'Because you (serpent) have done this, cursed are you above all livestock (farm animals regarded as an asset), and every beast of the field; on your belly will you go, and dust you will eat all the days of your life. I will put enmity (hatred) between you and the woman and between your seed and her seed. He will crush your head and you will strike his heel' (Gen. 13:14-15 ESV). For your punishment, God says to the woman, 'I will sharply increase your pain in childbirth; in pain, you will bring forth children. Your desire will be for your husband, and he will rule over you' (Gen. 3:16 BSB). The punishment for Adam as spoken by God states that, 'Because you have listened to the voice of your wife and have eaten of the tree from which I commanded you not to eat, cursed is the ground because of you; through toil, you will eat of it all the days of your life...'" (Gen. 13:17 ESV). Mr.

Timmons continues, saying, "As you can see, Adam and Eve, through their disobedience, caused the eventual death of us all (Generational Curse), and that disobedience sent shock-waves through the spiritual realm, and gave rise to everything changing here on earth. Thus, disorder was set in motion on all things; the earth is now in entropy, slowly winding down." Mr. Timmons sees a raised hand and asks, "Sanaa, you have a question?" Sanaa asks, "Mr. Timmons, why if only Adam and Eve were disobedient, does all mankind have to suffer and die for what they did? That is not fair." Mr. Timmons responds, "Mankind came out of the loins of Adam, and through his dis-obedience, the generations of Adam are born into sin (gener-ational curse). You see, sin separated Adam from God because no sin-filled flesh can glory in the presence of God. God loves us very much, and His original intent is to commune with us, His family, but because of Adam, we lost that intimacy with Him when Adam and Eve's eyes were opened to the knowl-edge of good and evil. At that point, they were separated from God by the flesh and could not live in His presence. So, God had to make a blood sacrifice of animals (law of substitution) to temporarily cover their sin, and the sacrifice of animals were also clothes for their naked bodies. Understand that the life of the flesh is in the blood; it is so important to remember that phrase. Jesus Christ would come and shed His own blood in the flesh, as a perfect sacrifice, to bridge that gap between us and God (law of exchange or substitution). His sacrifice was perfect because He came in the flesh through a virgin birth, and was not born into sin. Jesus Christ would be the sacrifice to end all sacrifices, for the Bible says, 'For since death came through a man, the resurrection of the dead, comes also through a man. For as in Adam all die, so in Christ, all will be made alive...'" (1 Cor. 15:21-22 NIV). Mr. Timmons continues, "The Bible also states, 'Nevertheless, death reigned from Adam until Moses, even over those who did not sin in the way that Adam transgressed. He is a pattern of the One to come. But the gift is not like the trespass. For if the many died by the trespass of the one man, how much more did God's grace and the gift that came by the grace of the one man, Jesus Christ, abound to the many! Again, the gift is not like the result of the one man's sin: the judgment that followed one sin brought condemnation, but the gift that followed many trespasses brought justification. For if by the trespass of the one man, death reigned through that one man, how much more will those who receive an abundance of grace and of the gift of righteousness reign in life through the one man, Jesus Christ! So then, just as one trespass brought condemnation for all men, so also one act of righteousness brought justification and life for all men...' (Rom. 5:14-18 NIV). Listen, Adam's fall brought upon us spiritual and physical death, but through Christ's perfect sacrifice, which defeated spiritual death, we will rise again, cleansed sinless, washed in the blood of Jesus, and have immortal bodies, like Jesus had when He rose from the dead." Sanaa replies, "Ok, I got that, but I don't understand why we have to die in the first place just to be raised again?" Mr. Timmons responds, "Remember in the story where Adam and Eve were banished from the garden, and God set cherubim with a whirling sword to guard the tree of life?" Sanaa answers, "Yeah, I remember that part; they didn't want them (generations) to be as them (Father, Son, Holy Spirit), knowing good and evil and live forever." Mr. Timmons answers, "You are right, and here is why. If we were allowed to eat from the tree of life, we would never physically die, and be doomed to live eternally in a sinful state, limited in the ability to commune with God as He originally intended because no imperfect sinful flesh can live in the presence of an all-perfect God. So, through God's planned gift, we die physically once, and rise in immortality, cleansed from sin and death through the blood of Jesus." Sanaa replies, "Oh, ok, I see. That makes sense. I got it. We all must physically die in the flesh, and because of what Jesus did, we will rise spiritually clean and have new bodies, free from sin, and not have to die again." Mr. Timmons smiles, and says, "You got it." The women nod their heads in the affirmative. Mr. Timmons continues, "However, now as we live in the flesh, understand that we are not alone until our physical death because God has sent us through Jesus Christ a Comforter, an Advocate, the Holy Spirit, who will teach us all things." Always very inquisitive, and presently finding it hard to get something out of her head; Toni asks her thoughts with prejudice, "Mr. Timmons, where was Adam when Eve was about to eat that doggone forbidden fruit?" Mr. Timmons says, "He was right there with her." Toni aggressively blurts out, "What!? Say What!? So why in the hell did he not stop her? Excuse my language, Mr. Timmons, but he should have stopped her." Mr. Timmons says, "I don't know. The Bible is silent on that, but I do know that Adam was not deceived; maybe like the Father, the love in Adam for Eve was allowing her to express her choice; or maybe he could not stop her since at that point, he had not been made to rule over her. I surmise from what Eve told Satan that Adam, in his effort to control the situation, added a little extra warning, telling her that God said don't even touch the fruit. God did not say that. I believe Adam added that part, attempting to seal the deal in Eve's mind that the fruit was very dangerous. There are many theories out there on why he ate the forbidden fruit. I think it might have been something to do with Adam's love for Eve and or her influence over him. It might have been that he loved the gift (Eve) more than the giver (God), and chose to endure the promise of death with her, or there is another possibility that I would hate to believe. Adam took on the same mindset as Satan and Eve, to be like the Most High God. This would be insane since Adam was already made in the image of God. This further illustrates the great deceptive powers of Satan. Alice Von Hildebrand, a Catholic philosopher, theologian, lecturer, author, and former professor, has commented, 'The serpent chose to beguile Eve because of her influence over Adam,' to which theory I am compelled to agree; that may have been the situation. Furthermore, I believe that's why, as part of Eve's punishment, God assigns man to rule over the wife, and anything to the contrary is against God's commandment, and extremely dangerous, recognizing the highly influential power that women can wield over men, especially their husbands. However, there is a larger question afoot. Were Adam and Eve equal in authority before the Fall? Huh, maybe? But whereas Adam was given the direct command not to eat the forbidden fruit, this means that Eve was not Satan's primary objective. The primary target was Adam by way of getting him to break an agreement (covenant) with God by way of beguiling Eve. However, no matter the woman's influence, the test for Adam in this situation was not to recognize his (Adam's) will, or to give ear to anything outside or over the voice of God, but rather to be obedient to God's Word. Being obedient to the Father, who loved him, walked with him, talked with him, and greeted his coming (making) as a proud parent. Adam was to lean not to his own understanding or ambition. Understand that the Fall did not happen when Eve ate of the fruit; it was only when Adam broke covenant and ate of the forbidden fruit was the condition met for death to manifest into the world. In God's order of things and His original intent, the man is the head, and God gave Adam in the physical realm dominion over the earth and everything in it, and Satan, being aware of this fact, knew he couldn't come to Adam straightaway, so he used the power in Eve's position to influence Adam. Understand that Eve had no power of spiritual transference. Adam was responsible for everything God had given, not the woman. If Adam remained obedient, I believe he would have been able to save (cover) Eve because before Adam ate of the forbidden fruit, death had no legal claim over him; the LORD God commanded the man, not the woman. Adam would have had power through his relationship with the Father, as Jesus did, to redeem Eve. But like I said before, this only proves how cunning and deceptive the adversary can be; he is the Father of all lies. Remember, Satan's power of deception was enough to convince one-third of the angels in heaven to follow him, and as a result, God threw them all out. Satan's deceptive tools or method of operations are basically always the same as you see him working to beguile Eve through injecting unbelief, disrespecting God's divine commandment through the lust of the eye, that the fruit (carnally adorned) was pleasant to the eye. Through the lust of the flesh, she had to see that the tree (carnally adorned) was good for food; through the pride of life, she was convinced that the tree was not to be dreaded, but to be desired to make her wise reference (James 1:14-15). I think Satan's plan was to divest the glory of God from man, and to keep us from being able to commune with the Father by creating a veil or a spiritual gulf between us and God; it gives him (Satan) time to work his opposition to the throne of God. Satan's ambition is to transfer worship from God to a worship of himself. However, God had hidden from Satan a mystery, a mystery in the blood for our redemption, and Satan, existing only as an anointed cherub, could not comprehend that mystery." Focusing deeply on the lesson, Chrystal inquisitively asks, "Mr. Timmons, what do you mean 'mystery in the blood'?" Mr. Timmons smiles and says, "Here is the end of the lesson. I will explain this mystery tomorrow." Intrigued by the subject matter and wanting more information, Sanaa aggressively demands an explanation. She says, "Mr. Timmons, Mr. Timmons, come on now, don't do us like this. You can't stop just when it's getting good." Mr. Timmons responds, saying, "That's enough for today, ladies. We'll explore everything in full tomorrow." The ladies give a collective sigh with an expression of total disappointment, then Chrystal says sarcastically, "Ok, I guess we will find out tomorrow then, huh?" Mr. Timmons, recognizing their enthusiasm, says, "Tell you what, I'll give you a clue, but I know you won't be able to figure it out." The women, now relying on their current level of understanding and sleuth-like enthusiasm, excitedly say, "That's alright, just give us the clue." Mr. Timmons says, "In the Book of Genesis, God spells out the punishment for Eve and the serpent, in that He, God, will put enmity between the serpent and the woman, and between his seed and her seed. The woman's seed will crush the serpent seed's head, and the serpent will strike the woman's seed's heel. That's the clue, ladies." Chrystal says, "What? That's it? Come on, Mr. Timmons. That's it?" Mr. Timmons says, "Yes, I told you it would be difficult, but you must do research on this clue and ask questions." The ladies look at each other curiously perplexed, and Toni sarcastically replies, "That's really all you going to give us? Ok then, we'll see you tomorrow; you have nice evening Mr. Micaiah Christopher Timmons." Mr. Timmons turns, smiling, as he walks away, taking note of being verbally chastised by the tone of Toni's voice addressing him by his full name. However, he leaves with a smile on his face because he hears Chrystal telling the group, "Don't worry, we got this. We are highly-trained professional women; we can figure this out." Mr. Timmons steadily walks on, recognizing the pride in these women to never give up. He knows that they will be up all night researching this clue but discerns in his heart that God would release a word of wisdom into their spirit.

CHAPTER 23
(UNRAVELING THE MYSTERY)

DAY FOUR: MR. TIMMONS GREETS THE WOMEN as they come in, and he immediately leads them in prayer; when he finishes, he feels so good after praying. Mr. Timmons remarks, "I feel better now, how about you guys? Oh, I'm sorry, you look rather sleepy, are you ok?" The women give Mr. Timmons the evil eye with unflattering expressions on their faces as if to say, 'you are the reason we look like this.' With a little frustration in her voice, Chrystal says, "Mr. Timmons, we couldn't find an answer to that clue you gave us anywhere, mainly because we didn't understand what we're supposed to be looking for." Then Chrystal playfully comments, "And you know what, your girl Daedai wouldn't even help us out." Mr. Timmons smiles and says, "Let him who has an ear to hear, listen. The plan of Satan is always to chase you, overtake you, then snatch from your life the spoils of what he thinks is his victory. For the Christian in God's kingdom, to use the game of chess as a metaphor, there is never a way in God that Satan can ever put you in checkmate; there's no victory for him because in a strategic chess match between God and Satan, God will always have another move. Of course, He will. He created the game. Now, check out this mystery wrapped in an enigma. Your Bible says the life of the flesh is in the blood, right? Do you believe that the blood speaks?" Sanaa keenly looks at Mr. Timmons as though she might have misheard what he said, and asks, "What? Did you say, blood can talk?" and jokingly she remarks, "I've seen blood up close and personal, and it has never spoken to me." Mr. Timmons responds, "I've never heard blood speak either. But I believe it speaks." Chrystal quickly chiming in, says, "Hold on, wait a minute, Mr. Timmons. How can you ask us to believe that blood can speak when you say you never heard it yourself?" Mr. Timmons then makes his case, stating, "You remember the story of Adam's two sons, Cain and Abel, where Cain killed Abel out of jealousy because God accepted Abel's offering and not his, right? Well, remember when God asked Cain what he had done; because God said, 'The voice of your brother's blood cries out to Me from the ground' (Gen. 4:10 BSB). Ladies, in the spiritual realm, God can hear your blood, and it is not a singular voice, it is multiple voices. What God heard from Abel's blood crying out from the ground was the generations of Abel not yet born." Mr. Timmons says to the women, "It's important to hear what I'm saying; the blood in a man's loins is generational. God heard generations in Abel's blood because the life of the flesh is in the blood. I have never heard blood speak. But I believe it speaks. Satan was created a spiritual being without revelation; he could never comprehend the mystery in the blood. It is the glory of God to conceal a matter and the glory of kings to search it out." Sanaa says, "Ok, alright. I feel like we're getting close to something here. I think you are about to help us decipher this clue about the blood, right?" Sanaa now pauses, considers her thoughts, then continues anxiously, saying, "Hey, but Mr. Timmons, if it's the glory of kings to search out a thing; then tell me, how can we know the mystery?" Mr. Timmons smiles and replies, "The Bible says that Jesus is the King of kings and the Lord of lords. Now, who do you think these kings and lords that Jesus reigns over are?" Confused by Mr. Timmons words, the women look at each other and say, "We don't know." Looking at the women intently and surprised they didn't get it, Mr. Timmons yells out, "We are!" The ladies look at each other, now more perplexed than ever; they think about it for a minute, and Sanaa, now with a big smile on her face, says, "Oh, so that means that we are kings, and it's for us only to know the mystery, but we have to search it out. Is that right?" Mr. Timmons quickly says to Sanaa, "You're correct, but before we approach this further, I have a question for all of you." The ladies are now enthused and paying close attention when Mr. Timmons continues and surprisingly asks, "Does a woman have a seed?" Again, their enthusiastic smiles and expressions turns to blank stares as the women ponder the question, and Toni, with a confident look, quickly responds, "No, the man has the seed, and the woman has the egg." Mr. Timmons says, "Ok, but did not God say 'I will put enmity between you and the woman, and between your seed and her seed. He will crush your head and you will strike his heel?'" Sanaa says, "Ok, I remember that; so what am I not seeing here?" Mr. Timmons says, "Read what God said again, Sanaa." Sanaa says, "Alright," and then she begins reading slowly out loud, "I will put enmity between you and the woman, and between your seed and her seed." Sanaa then pauses and questions, "Her seed?" She says, "Wait a minute, women don't have a seed; it comes from the man. Mr. Timmons, I'm lost. I don't understand." Mr. Timmons says, "That's alright. Don't worry about it. Satan couldn't figure it out either. Satan only knew that a woman would give birth to a boy who would end his existence, but he could not figure out all the minutiae. You'll learn from studying the Bible that Satan, in his attempt to disrupt prophesy, went about influencing rulers to kill male children because he was worried about the promised one to crush his head, and he knew that it had something to do with the generation of Adam; that's why he influenced Cain to commit the first murder. You'll see throughout the Bible how Satan influenced kings and rulers to kill male babies, hoping to murder the one who would eventually crush his head. Even though the prophets foretold of His coming, Satan still could not divert, influence, or stop prophesy." Chrystal says, "Mr. Timmons, but Satan surely knew that women don't have a seed." Mr. Timmons replies, "Yeah, but there's another way of looking at this. If you can imagine, for a Moment, a young man plants the image of himself as a seed into the woman. That which comes forth as fruit is from his blood. The woman, as good ground, nurtures the seed to bring forth its fruit. The man and the woman in a relationship can now both lay claim to the seed. That's why Satan couldn't figure out the mystery of the blood, let alone anything relating to a perfect sacrifice, or the mystery of a baby born of a virgin girl. It is the nature of God to hide a thing." Mr. Timmons pauses a minute and says, "Check this out. Satan was defeated before he got started. I even believe the murder of Abel was a strategic setup. Satan is a tool, not only a fool. Let him who has an ear to listen, hear and gain knowledge of this mystery." The ladies, at this point, are clinging to every word coming out of Mr. Timmons's mouth when he says, "Gabriel, the archangel, the messenger of God, says to the virgin Mary, 'You are honored very much. You are a favored woman. The Lord is with you. You are chosen from among many women. You will become a Mother and have a Son. You are to give Him the name Jesus.' Then Mary gives her permission. Ladies, we said that women do not have a seed, right? So how does Mary have a child? I mean, it is a fact that the blood had to come from the male, but she has not known a male. Satan, not having revelatory knowledge and not being privileged to the secrets and dimensions of the Holy Father, could never understand the mystery tied to the blood and how God could step out of Himself in the form of the Holy Spirit-God head-and come upon Mary in the power of YAHWEH, supplying the (His) blood for this baby to be conceived; the personification of the God head in the flesh would be God's only begotten Son. You see, ladies, God is the one and only master strategist. He knows the ending from the beginning. 'But we speak the wisdom of God in a mystery, even the hidden wisdom, which God ordained before the world unto our glory: Which none of the princes of this age (Satan and his crew) knew, for had they known, they would not have crucified the Lord of glory' (1 Cor. 2:7-8 NKJV)."

Mr. Timmons continues, "So, you see, as cunning and deceitful as Satan thinks he is, even in the face of written prophesy, he still does not have a clue about the mysteries of God. It is written that eye hath not seen, nor ear heard, neither have entered the heart of man, the things which God hath prepared for them that love him. But God hath revealed things unto us (Kings and Lords) by His Spirit; for the Spirit searches all things, yes, the deep things of God. Ladies, Satan can never have revelation, nor can he ever know the future. Satan is not omnipotent, omniscient, or omnipresent; he is just a powerful fallen angel with restricted powers, trying to decipher the Bible like you and me. You were made in the image of God, and Satan has tried to strip you of your relationship and position that you have in Him, even to the point of corrupting some of our DNA. But as spirit beings, when you love God your Father, you can have access to the knowledge of the things, which Father God hath prepared for you because you love Him. Now, let us focus in on the blood as the life and the mystery in the blood. The blood is a substance in both the physical and the spiritual realm, and as a result of the Fall, the two realms of the seen and the unseen are out of alignment with each other. The blood is our anchor or umbilical cord that connects the spiritual realm and the physical realm nourishing (man's) life. In both the spiritual and the physical realm, God is sovereign, and He mandates a constitution of His divine order in both realms. In the physical realm, however, God has given man the authority, and as a result of the Fall, man is now subject to his own ethos of right and wrong. So, as you can see, the two realms have dueling authorities that rarely agree. Something great had to be accomplished in both the spiritual and the physical to redeem man back in alignment with the main source of life (God). Remember in the Bible when Adam and Eve fell, and God had to kill animals to use their skin as a covering for Adam and Eve's nakedness. Well, as a result of the shed blood of these animals, the first blood covenant (agreement) between God and man was established. The blood sacrifice in the skin of animals would serve as clothing in the physical. In the spiritual and the physical, the blood would serve as a temporary substitute (activating the law of substitution), a covering for the sin that Adam and Eve had committed. However, the blood of animals would not be enough equity to completely wipe out the sin that Adam and Eve had allowed into the world. So, for the blood to accomplish the great task needed, the sacrifice in blood would have to be of equal or of greater value than Adam and Eve's transgressions. 'For if the blood of bulls and goats, and the ashes of a heifer sprinkling the unclean, sanctifies to the purifying of the flesh: how much more shall the blood of Christ, who through the eternal Spirit offered himself without spot to God, purge your conscience from dead works to serve the living God? And for this cause He is the mediator of the new testament, that by means of death, for the redemption of the transgressions that were under the first testament, they which are called might receive the promise of eternal inheritance. The sacrificed blood of Jesus would be the price to be paid as our link to salvation, and even after Jesus paid such a heavy price, love (Jesus) still gives us a choice; praise His Holy name.' (Heb. 9:13-15 ESV). Jesus, the perfect sacrifice, as a man (God) in the flesh, had to use His sinless blood to repair the breach, redeeming us through that blood from sin and the curse of the Law. Know, therefore, that our ability to live forever with God is in the life of the perfect blood of Jesus (life of the flesh is in the blood)." Toni quickly responds, "But Jesus was a man like us, Mr. Timmons; born into sin just like us. I don't understand." Mr. Timmons explains to the ladies, "Yes, He was a man in the flesh, but remember, His blood comes from the Father as seed given to Mary to be with child, right?" Sanaa, discerning, gets all excited to the point of having trouble catching her breath in trying to speak, "Oh! Oh! Wait a minute! The blood of Jesus came from God Himself, and is not tainted by sinful flesh; that's why it is sinless, right?" Mr. Timmons looks at Sanaa, almost in tears, and says with a trembling voice, "You got it." Sanaa continues, "Hold on, wait a minute. If God can hear the blood and knows people before they are in the womb, then abortion is murder, no matter what the stage of development." The women, now having a revelation adverse to their previous beliefs and actions, bow their heads in deep sorrowful thought, feeling convicted concerning past transgressions. Mr. Timmons, seeing their sorrow, says, "Rest your hearts, ladies. Through Jesus Christ, God has forgiven all ignorance. He is our Redeemer; just repent and believe in Him. Those babies lost to abortion are in heaven right now. Mothers and Fathers will see them again and come to know them. Mr. Timmons thinks introspectively for a Moment, and then suggests a crazy comic relief question to teach another lesson. He asks, "When a man and a woman, hopefully in marriage, have intercourse, and the man finishes his business, does the man then depart with his penis? Or can the woman legally demand that he leave it there?" The ladies giggle and look at each other red-faced with their jaws dropped and eyes wide open in shock at what Mr. Timmons has asked. But being forward as ever, allowing the question to survive possible absurdity, Toni replies, "Mr. Timmons, the man leaves with his manhood, right?" Mr. Timmons asks, "Why is that? And why can't the woman legally make the man leave it there?" Toni gasps air while looking around all confused, laughs and shouts out, "Because it's his! It's his body. Duh!" Mr. Timmons smiles and says, "You are right. It belongs to him; even though it was in the body of the woman, it belongs to the man. It's a part of his body; it has served its purpose and cannot stay. Listen, ladies, the instant before engaging in intercourse is the woman's only right of choice. If she decides to become one with a man in intercourse with the possibility of the sperm (blood) from the man connecting to make another human being, then the woman, at that point of conception, has no right to choose anymore because the developing body of a baby does not belong to the woman; it's not her body. It's now an equally protected human being, made in the image of God. The woman, by having intercourse, made a conscious or unconscious decision as to the possibility of creation, which means that the woman, by her actions, gives permission that another human being can be nurtured and born through her body. It is an agreement, both in the physical and in the spiritual. That's why God's original intent is for sex (a covenant) to be between married couples, bonding as one in covenant, between a man and a woman. The great pleasure derived from the sexual experience is an incentive to become one flesh, to procreate joyfully and lovingly, intended to benefit the sustainability of the family. The idea of sexual orientation beyond God's original intent is only the behavior of lust, which is a satanic construct, deceptively spawned through pornography, rape, molestation, experimentation, or moreover, through a society that has allowed itself to be completely and unabashedly normalized by the homosexual practice or other deviant sexual orientations. It is of great benefit for a society or nation to promote heterosexual relationships, mainly for the benefit and sustainability of humanity and the family. It is also good for males to be married to one woman. It settles the male down or tempers the testosterone. The bigger problem God's children face, however, is that churches are not teaching spiritual warfare or are not aware of the serious nature of spiritual warfare behind the deception in the movement of sexual immorality. In the majority of churches, the deliverance ministry has been relegated to a file in the back drawer as something old testament and mythical in nature. Remember, ladies, everything that is seen, came from that which is unseen; it can be for good or for bad, depending on the human interaction to give permission. Spiritual warfare is real, and it is being waged daily for the purpose of deceiving the world away from the worship of God. Dr. Pat Holliday in *The Witchdoctor and the Man: City under the Sea* says, '...behind the problems of the world and behind every evil, which manifests itself in mankind, there is a hierarchy of evil spirits, namely the devil and his angels in an organized kingdom influencing this present world.' Ladies, in terms of the nature of spiritual warfare, I will save for another more advanced lesson. But back to my point, people in the homosexual lifestyle might say that people in America discriminate against homosexual people, but America does not discriminate against any person; it discriminates or should discriminate against certain types of behaviors-behaviors that might be detrimental to the well-being of society or humanity. Since there are no biological or genetic reasons for diverse sexual orientations, it all boils down to a behavior environmentally learned, stimulated, propagandized and (or) allowed by a society or a culture, which ignores or thinks itself to be beyond the boundaries or limitations of God's original intent for mankind. So, when looking at America, you have to ask the question: does that shoe fit?" Mr. Timmons continues, "Ladies, did you know that before 1973, homosexuality was listed in *The Diagnostic and Statistical Manual of Mental Disorders* as a mental disease? However, in 1972, after the Rockefeller World Population Council, with influence and political pressure from organizations like Planned Parenthood, it would mandate that homosexuality no longer be treated as a mental abnormality. So, in 1973, at the Annual Psychiatric Association Convention, deception would come by way of that organization, voting homosexuality out of *The Diagnostic and Statistical Manual of Mental Disorders* as a mental disease. Deception further crept in by special interest groups striving to normalize this behavior by using the Black civil rights movement in a covert tactic of intersectionality to equate Black civil rights with that of gay (homosexual) rights. This was absurd, but the masses of people not understanding the spiritual warfare that was being waged bought the deception, hook, line, and sinker; the right to engage in homosexual behavior was somehow equal to the inalienable rights of human beings. I don't think God was too pleased with that, and there's always a consequence for being disobedient to God's Word; check out what happened at Sodom and Gomorrah." Captivated by hearing this information, Sanaa states, "Mr. Timmons, no one has ever taught me what you're teaching, but in listening, I think, from what I under-stand, I can expand on God's original intent." Sanaa goes on to say, "Through the blood in a man's loins, God personally knows the seed (blood) given to the woman, and He can see the many generations to be born of that seed. Any deviation in sexual orientation away from His original intent will have an effect on generations. It's about the sustainability of the family and the ability to pass along the wisdom of the Word of God. In His original intent, God created sex such that when a man and a woman comes together in marriage as one, the merging of the two produces a human being created in His image, thereby producing a trinity incased in a man; body, soul, and spirit." Overwhelmed with understanding, Chrystal also speaks the wisdom of her thoughts, saying, "Mr. Timmons, then the debate over when a fetus is physically alive is a moot conver-sation because the joining of a man to a woman is the multi-plying of life, and the life is in the blood." Immediately thinking about what she and Chrystal have discerned, Sanaa suddenly interjects, "But wait a minute, Mr. Timmons, doesn't what you are teaching qualify as being homophobic?" Mr. Timmons smiles at Sanaa and calmly says, "I don't fear homosexuals, or neither do I hate homosexuals. Do you? I think not, so how can that be a phobia? I can separate the person that I love from the abominable behavior that God and I detest. Sanaa, do you understand?" Sanaa respectively nods her head in the affirmative, and Mr. Timmons continues, "Ladies, truth has been laid in your spirit, and sometimes the truth can be so surprising and overwhelming that when revealed, the very power of it can knock you down to the floor when coming to the realization that certain beliefs, customs, and traditions once held as sacred were all barefaced lies. Understand, ladies, the world has been deceived and has done wrong things because of a lack of knowledge, and that knowledge is the knowledge of God's Word. You see, Satan had a cunning strategy, but he was defeated out of the gate because God is the ultimate chess master. Satan thought that by deceiving a third of the angels, devising the fall of Adam, the infiltration of our blood line, and the crucifixion of Jesus Christ, he had the all-powerful God in checkmate, and that victory was his. However, all his efforts were pointless; what a pathetic plan. Ladies, understand that God is sovereign, and He is the only grand master strategist. God can never, ever, ever be in checkmate because He always has multiple moves. Everything is always what He says it is. For example, if you are living presently in the moment, Monday, 2017, at 9:00 am, and for some unknown reason, God says, it's now Saturday, 1820, at 9:00 pm, you are now living in the moment on Saturday, 1820, at 9:00 pm because everything is what God says it is. However, rarely does love (God) interfere with choice. He just gives. It's always our decision, our will. Yet in all things and all situations, be cautious, for the Word says, 'When tempted, no one should say, God is tempting me. For God cannot be tempted by evil, nor does He tempt anyone; but each person is tempted when they are dragged away by their own evil desire and enticed. Then, after desire has conceived, it gives birth to sin; and sin, when it is full-grown, gives birth to death'" (James 1:13-15 NIV). Mr. Timmons continues, "I tell you the truth, one of the greatest deceptions that Satan has ever devised is having people believe he does not exist. In not believing he exists, it allows Satan to maneuver without ever being detected. People will always lose to an enemy they do not know or believe exists. For those of us who knows he exists, Satan's ultimate aim is to make us feel that we are not worthy to be used by God. He tries to make us think that we have not lived up to the standards demonstrated by Jesus. Listen, all have sinned and come short of the glory of God. Day by day, all we can do is strive to emulate that perfect standard that Jesus set. The great British writer and lay theologian, C. S. Lewis (Lewis, AZQUotes 202) states: 'There is someone that I love even though I don't approve of what he [she] does. There is someone I accept though some of his [her] thoughts and actions revolt me. There is someone I forgive though he [she] hurts the people I love the most. That person is...me.' Ladies, learn to forgive yourself. God does not condemn you; we all have our faults, our failures, and our disobedience. God knows we can't live up to that perfect standard set in the Law; that's why Jesus (God in the flesh) had to be the perfect sacrifice for us. Satan will try to deceive you into not recognizing your worth to God. He will say, 'forget that Bible stuff. God cannot do anything with you; you have done too many wrong things.' When Satan tries to assert his influence against what you believe, fight as Jesus did; quickly cancel Satan's evil rhetoric and oppression by declaring the Word of God. Satan is a liar; he is the Father of all lies. Understand that no one is out of the reach of God; know that God can use anyone; '...His arm is not too short to save, nor His ears too dull to hear' (Isa. 59:1 NIV). All you must do is confess your sins, repent, and God will give you rebirth, a clean bill of health, which has been made available through the blood of Jesus. Remember, God loves us; we mean everything to Him. He is our Father, and we are His beloved children. You got it?" The ladies answer, "We got it." Mr. Timmons says, "Well, then, this is the end of the lesson. I'll see you tomorrow, guys." The ladies prepare to leave, but are hungry for more information, but grudgingly concede, "Ok, see you tomorrow, Mr. Timmons." When the ladies arrive back at Daedai's house,

Daedai notices a calming difference in her friends' attitudes. These women, who would normally be excited to rush right out to have fun, now seem reserved; more interested in reading the Bible and communicating with their families. In witnessing what is going on, Daedai thinks to herself, *I don't think they realize how much they've changed. God is so good.* For the rest of the evening, the women settle into their own space and prepare for the next day.

CHAPTER 24
(TRUTH OR CONSEQUENCES)

DAY FIVE: THE MORNING OF THE FIFTH DAY HAS come. Mr. Timmons greets the ladies, and this time, they follow him inside the old church, and he immediately leads them in prayer. The women, looking around, note that the church looks far more beautiful inside than the obscurities outside. Mr. Timmons then quotes, "'And God said, let the water teem with living creatures, and let birds fly above the earth across the vault of the sky. God created the great creatures of the sea and every living thing with which the water teems and that moves about in it, according to their kinds, and every winged bird according to its kind. And God saw that it was good. God blessed them and said, be fruitful and increase in number and fill the water in the seas, and let the birds increase on the earth. And there was evening, and there was morning—the fifth day.'" Mr. Timmons says, "Who will you believe, Darwin or God? I know clearly from Scripture that the chicken came first and not the egg. God, therefore, gives me the ability to know the truth in all things through knowledge in His Word. I have a question for you. Were you told in college that the Bible consistently contradicts itself?" Chrystal and Sanaa answer, "Yes. All the time." Mr. Timmons emphatically says, "Nothing could be further from the truth. Their summation is only the testimony of seemingly powerful men attempting to imprison your mind in the hope of making you believe that God is not the author of absolute truth because they believe there is no absolute truth. Know and understand that the earth is not billions of years old, and there is no man-made global warming; this is a deception of the enemy. Carbon is a substance of all living things in God's creation, and the lack of revelation as it relates to the carbon cycle has made them fools, which is the genesis of their fears because God is presently allowing strong delusion. People without revelation will not give credit to God for this organized system (the universe) created to sustain life here on earth. However, those in God know that climate change, as reported in the media, is a hoax. Furthermore, the carnal man's lack of knowledge in the Word of God blinds him from seeing the truth. Truth helps you discern that the spirit of the antichrist is dividing our country through a satanic deception about evolution, climate change, feminism, pigmentation in the skin, ideological differences, polices in immigration, socialism, abortion, homosexuality, the deception of fluidity in gender identity, and the aggressive covert tactics of the illuminati, all satanic constructs warring against God's original intent. Everybody wants to be God, putting forth their own self-righteous agenda, devoid of the restrictions in moral discipline. Their position is if it feels good, why can't I do it? This attitude will ultimately lead people, as the Bible says, to be given over to a reprobate mind. Can they not see that there must exist a constitution forged in absolute truth, and there must be discipline in obedience to that truth? The wisdom of God is that absolute truth. It is the only unifying force that can save us from ourselves. Ladies, this is the only time in my life that I can honestly say that a generation could be born that may not know the Word of God. I never thought that it could or would be possible in America. The thought of this looming possibility is so very scary to me. The idea that America, with its once unshakable Judeo-Christian foundation, could fall away from its belief system, is presently a looming possibility. The founding Fathers of this country were brilliant in understanding the rudiments of power and politics. They knew the power of prayer and having God at the center of their being, even though a small politically-active minority were very dubious in asserting their faith. These men had firsthand experience with tyranny, and some were more knowledgeable biblically and politically than we give them credit. Do you think it is by luck that America is the most successful and powerful country in the world? No, it was only through a foundational belief in a Judeo-Christian God that our American constitution was formulated, which, other than the Bible, is the only orga-nizing principle that closely emulates the wisdom and char-acter of God.

I understand that the founding Fathers were steeped into paganism, freemasonry, idolatry and rosicrucianism. But according to (Horn 2013) 'The rise of the Christian church broke up the intellectual pattern of the classical pagan world.' So what they (freemasons) did was to clothe themselves in Christian phraseology, but in secret, kept the symbols of their pagan allegiances. But be that as it may, these men, whether White, Red, or Black, were not perfect, but what man or man-made system is? We have all sinned and come short of the glory of God, in need of a Savior. To borrow a phrase: 'The saint is only the sinner who fell down, but then got up.' So, no matter how imperfect the founding Fathers may have been, God had a purpose for America, and His blessings on this country resulted in a more prosperous united nation (America) than any other in history. When people talk about the founding Fathers as racist, I say, who can know the heart of a man except God? I must advise also that even though slavery was morally wrong during this period of time, the law allowed men to own other men as property. The act of slavery was totally against everything the founding Fathers were supposed to represent. However, in the coming years, the religious moral consciousness of the American people would soon force a repentant nation to spend that measure of blood and treasure in a great civil war, to correct the scourge that was placed on Christian humanity through the ungodly act of slavery. Over 350,000 lives would be lost in a war to put an end to the social nightmare of slavery. People only need review the past in order to go forward, united in a common understanding that America, at one time, did fall, but then got up, and even though some of our ancestors were brutally mistreated, we are commanded by God to forgive. It will make us greater and more prosperous than ever. However, presently, there are still more problems in America than meets the eye. Some who have been hurt by the idea and indignity of slavery find that they will not forgive and will not forget. People must understand that no matter what America's past failings, in the final momentum towards things to come, we must realize to a certainty, that united we will stand, but divided, we will surely fall. Americans have been spoiled with having too much in my opinion. We drive up into our two-car garages and our air-conditioned homes; flip the switch and we have light; we turn a nob and immediately there's fresh running water; we go to the grocery store, and there are aisles of food to choose from. People all over the world wish they had half of what we have, and some in our nation lacking any semblance of gratitude act like the spoiled children of parentally dysfunctional billionaires. I also hear people saying that there are persons in America that can't pull themselves up by the bootstrap because they do not have the boots; well, that's the biggest lie I ever heard because if you live in America, you got a variety of boots the world wishes they had. We have it so good in this country that we forget the genesis of our prosperity; we take our God and the flag of our unity under Him for granted, not being cognizant that it can easily all be taken away. Understand that whoever the president of our country may be at any given time, it is not by accident. Nothing just happens. Remember, God raises up kings and puts down kings for His purpose. Goodness, mercy, and prosperity always follow the good king. Tyranny, lawlessness, and poverty always follow the bad king. But all things work according to God's plan. No matter what our political disposition in any given season may turn out to be; there will come a judgment, and every Christian needs to be ready and watchful. So when the naysayers, politicians, and anarchists / professors try to put into your spirit the doom and gloom of systemic racism, Black Lives Matter, social justice, cultural Marxism, global warming, and other alleged victimization accusations to protest, know that their fear is demonic, and it comes from a strong spiritual delusion allowed by God. The great British author and lay theologian C. S. Lewis (Lewis, AZQuotes 2020) says, and I agree, 'The greatest evils in the world will not be carried out by men with guns but by men in suits sitting behind desks.' Irrespective of the evil in the world, remember God is now and is always in control. His Word will always sustain His people, no matter what the world throws at them, and that judgment, when it comes, as it says in the Book of Revelation, is going to renew everything in this world. But for right now, remember that God promises to never destroy earth again, nor interfere with seed time and harvest, or the seasons (Gen. 8:21 NIV). So, I ask the question again: who will you believe? Man as a cause of something like climate change, or can you see God's perfect symbiotic cycle of carbon, rhythmically and harmoniously functioning in a system of exchange, propelled by solar flares from the sun to engage the moon, ocean, trees, and all living things mandated by the Creator to manage the sustainability of man's existence here on earth? The truth is that man cannot change or control one thing as it relates to the weather or anything else that God has set in motion. I hope you are starting to realize by now that every negative thing your professors or other naysayers have told you concerning the inaccuracy of the Bible was only a précis of their limited appraisal of a movement of God far beyond their mental or sensorial comprehension. No matter how much they try, their arms are too short to fight with God, and their minds too simple to think on His level. Malcolm Muggeridge (Muggeridge 1985), one of the world's greatest writers, observes what seems to be the prophetic. He writes '... the final conclusion would surely be that whereas other civilizations have been brought down by attacks of barbarians from without, ours had the unique distinction of training its own destroyers at its own educational institutions and then providing them with facilities for propagating their destructive ideology far and wide, all at the public expense...' Muggeridge makes a great point about the propaganda that is originating and emanating from our educational institutions, which could lead to the dismantling and or destruction of Western society. It is unfortunate that our American educational institutions are filled with carnally-minded educators who cannot receive the Spirit of God.

Thus, they cannot see what you and I see; they cannot comprehend the four-dimensional length, width, breath, and depth of our Creator. America has made an awesome mistake in taking prayer out of the school system. It has bred a form of humanistic atheism to a belief that people's morals evolved from nothing, and that we exist only as automatons with an ability to propagate DNA. On the contrary, we are made in God's image, and it has been etched in our consciousness to instinctively perceive and know morality because it is the personification of who He is, which is love. He did not create love; He is love. That is, His being, and we are made exactly in His image. So, to a degree, we recognize a sense of morality was fashioned in our consciousness. The more society moves away from an understanding of God's Word (truth), the more society collectively limits the degree to which its moral foundation can exist. The Supreme Court, flexing its judicial wisdom in 1962, wrongly decided that school-sponsored Bible reading was unconstitutional. This decision dealt a serious blow to the moral foundation of our society (Wagner 2012). Education expert William Jeynes comments: '... there is a correlation between the decline of U.S. public schools and the U.S. Supreme Court's 1962 and 1963 decision' (Caucas 2013). The Congressional Prayer Caucus Foundation further giving statistics on that decline sited:

> Criminal arrest of teens is up 150% according to the US Bureau of Census; teen suicides in ages 15-19 years up 450% according to the National Center of Health Services; illegal drug activity up 6000% according to the National Institute of Drug Abuse; child abuse cases up 2300% according to the US Department of Health and Human Services; divorce up 350% according to the US Department of Commerce, and SAT scores fell 10% even though the SAT questions have been revamped to be easier to answer. Violent crime has risen 350%, national morality figures have plummeted, and teen pregnancy escalated dramatically after prayer and the Bible were removed from the schools. One of the most damning statistics follows sex education in the schools. As the school's involvement in sex education increased from grade level to grade level, promiscuity followed, and the increase of premarital sex increased.

God, forgive us for what we have done; the evidence in the statistics listed above reflects a society in chaos. As a result, our society has incrementally transformed itself into a pretentiously 'woke' post-truth culture, susceptible to all forms of deception. We now have a society in which men are autonomously relying on their own understanding, feelings, and preferences, believing themselves to be recipients of an evolved morality rather than relying on the inerrant Word of God. Their progressive philosophical migration has devolved into a crippling blindness. Presently, the blind (industrialist, financers, and bankers) are seriously trying to lead the blind, creating, and propagating images of themselves, thinking quite mistakenly the Word of God to be foolish, satirical, and even unworthy of this present age. The interplay between reason and faith in the pursuit of truth has always been a tug of will. But consider this as I tug on your will. The Word states, 'We speak, not in words taught us by human wisdom, but in words taught by the Spirit, expressing SPIRITUAL truths in SPIRITUAL words. The natural man does not accept the things that come from the Spirit of God. For they are foolishness to him, and he cannot understand them, because these things are spiritually discerned' (1 Cor. 2:13, 14 BSB). Many people will be deceived by an inability to discern things that are not from God. Satan will target and seek to deceive our leaders first, and them not being able to discern truth, will play a pivotal role in Satan's deception. Dr. Pat Holliday (Holliday 2005), in her book, states: 'The Bible shows that the devil always seeks to pollute and destroy the head, the leader, the king, and the priest. It was not the misfits and the confirmed defeatist, but the emperor on his throne that were given over to all forms of demon manifestations and worship that were inspired by Satan.' The blindness of our leaders will cause lesser-informed people to wander into darkness, unaware of the spirit of the enemy causing our county to become less effective in the world. Jim Nelson Black, in his book, <u>When Nations Die</u> (Nelson 1994), states: 'The entire nation must pay the price for the arrogant defiance of Divine Authority.' He further lists ten reasons for the decline and fall of nations in the past, and potentially for the future (Nelson 1994): '<u>crisis of lawlessness, loss of economic discipline, rising bureaucracy, decline of education, weakening of cultural foundations, loss of respect for tradition, increase in materialism, rise in immorality, decay of religious belief, and devaluing of human life.</u>' He further points out that there is a (Nelson 1994) 'Life cycle of nations' that incrementally signals that a fall could be imminent; it comes in stages:

'abundance, liberty, courage, spiritual faith, complacency, apathy, dependency, and then a return to state of bondage.' Bondage (socialism) is the stage of no return for that nation. Those of us who have eyes to see discern that America is now at the far end of the complacency stage, headed straightaway toward the apathy stage of the cycle. In (Tsarfati 2015), citing Albert Einstein, who at the turn of the twentieth century, saw a problem within a German system for which he was living and observed, which may be recognizable in our system that: 'The minority, the ruling class at present, has the schools and press, usually the church as well under its thumb. This enables it to organize and sway the emotions of the masses and make its tool of them.' I agree with his assertions wholeheartedly, and see the parallel to our American situation. I believe likewise that it is in Satan's plan to weaken America from the inside, thereby leaving nations, such as Israel and others vulnerable to military aggression without the assistance of a once-powerful God-conscious America to stand alone against an imminent one-world government whenever the antichrist raises his demonic head in power. But take heart, God is always in control; all things work toward His will." Listening closely to the lecture, Chrystal raises her hand and asks, "What is this thing, this spiritual discernment you keep talking about, Mr. Timmons? I think I have an idea what it is, but I'm not sure." Mr. Timmons responds, "Ladies, the best way to explain it is to give you an example from the Bible of spiritual discernment or revelation. In the Bible, Jesus inquires of His disciples, 'Who do the people say that I AM?' The question arises from people seeing the miracles Jesus had performed, and them trying to label Him as a reincarnated John the Baptist, Elijah, Jeremiah, or one of the prophets. Based on these rumors, Jesus then inquires of His disciples, 'Well, who do you say that I am?' Simon Peter responds confidently, 'You are the Messiah, the Son of the living God.' To that, Jesus replies, 'Blessed are you, Simon son of Jonah, for this was not revealed to you by flesh and blood, but by my Father in heaven.' Mr. Timmons instructs, saying, "Peter got the answer from the Holy Spirit, which sur- passed all of Peter's natural senses to reveal to him the truth." Being a little skeptical and perplexed, Toni inquires, "Mr. Timmons, what do you mean 'surpassed all the natural senses'?" Mr. Timmons explains, "You know, hearing, seeing, smelling, feeling, and tasting; our material senses. The Holy Spirit, in communication with us, bypasses all physical senses. He communicates like that when our spirit aligns with His Spirit. The Spirit of God aligned with Peter's spirit and revealed to him the truth. Just like yesterday, when God connected with your spirit to give you revelation concerning life in the blood. That is how the Bible was written, inspired by the Holy Spirit, manifesting the Word of God in its authors; what we call rev- elation. You see, the Holy Spirit, with permission of a human being, can manifest all things into our physical existence by way of the spiritual realm, which has no connection with our material senses other than when a person speaks or senses what the Holy Spirit has conveyed, or something physically materializes. When your spirit (light) connects with God's Spirit (light), then God can speak to you through His Spirit (light). In some cases, the Spirit (light) can be heard audibly. But, to any extent, you must be in harmony (alignment) with God's Spirit (light) to receive. However, on some occasions, God uses things common or uncommon to spiritually interject His will. Remember, He is sovereign, and cannot be limited or placed in a familiar box. The mystery of God is to hide a thing, so trying to predict how or when He will interact or interdict, in most cases, is not for us to know. For example, I don't think at the time of the Bible's writing, the Jewish people, apostles, Romans, Sanhedrin, or early Christians would have ever imag- ined that the Old and New Testament would combine as one Bible (His-story), and would turn out to be the greatest-selling book of all times. Thus, to dispel any lies as to the authenticity of the Bible, know that God spiritually told the writers of the

Bible exactly what to write." Sanaa then blurts out in excitement, "I be dog. I had always been told that the Bible was subject to the bias of the men who wrote it, making it full of mistakes and add-ons." Mr. Timmons says, "Believe me, the truth makes everything clear, so when people tell you that the Bible is inaccurate, you must understand that they misinterpreted what they read, gave up, and stopped searching for the truth. The audacity of faith, which I will be talking about in these lessons, always resides in your belief that the Bible is the inherent Word of God, above all arguments to the contrary. Keep learning and searching, and the truth of what you do not or cannot understand will be revealed to you. Believe me, there are no contradictions in the Bible. Jesus said, "I tell you the truth, until heaven and earth disappear, not even the smallest detail of God's law will disappear until its purpose is achieved." Mr. Timmons pauses and says, "So, ladies, you can rely on the Word of God to live by, for it is true; it is God-breathed, and it lives. In God's Word, it reveals to us that we have been redeemed by grace. Therefore, we believe, without condemnation, being boldly confident in the Word of God. 'For by grace are you saved, through faith, and that not of yourselves' (Eph. 2:8 KJV). Mr. Timmons continues, "The only way any of us are eligible to enter into a relationship with God is because of His grace toward us.

Grace began in the Garden of Eden when God sacrificed animals; the first sacrifice in blood to temporarily cover the sin and nakedness of Adam and Eve. Grace is the expression of God's love for us.

He's always giving to us. He sacrificed Himself for us, for it is written, 'No greater expression of love has no man than this, that a man lay down his life for his friends.' You find that love reflected in the sacrifice of Jesus Christ (God in the flesh). The expression of this love is so powerful it is hard for the carnal mind to fathom the level of love given because the depths of this type of love is spiritually discerned and far above the reach of carnal flesh. However, for those of us who love Him, we understand and can feel the magnitude of this love as we weep at the thought of the excruciating pain and torment that Jesus had to suffer so that we might live in His kingdom forever." With tears streaming down his face, Mr. Timmons tries to continue speaking, but immediately falls under the power of the Holy Spirit from hearing his own words. Mr. Timmons bends over and starts trembling, with his arms clutching his stomach. The ladies, not knowing what is going on with Mr. Timmons, thinks he's trying to cough up something, and they look on, frozen in shock. When Mr. Timmons starts jumping up and down, then staggering around the room drunkenly, the ladies' eyes expand to a wrinkled brow, with their mouths gaped wide open, startled by the unfamiliarity of what is happening to Mr. Timmons. The ladies now have become very afraid and are not sure whether to run or just shelter in place. They freeze and watch, feeling the awesome power of the Moment, and not uttering a word until they hear some kind of noise coming from behind them, and when they turn around, they see Daedai, who has just totally lost it and gone wild, arms flailing everywhere, jumping up and down around the room, crying, worshiping, and falling all over the place. Sill trying to make heads or tails of what is going on, the ladies can feel something move in the atmosphere around them, and they start experiencing a warm electrical tingling sensation moving through their bodies; it was the greatest unexplainable sensation they had ever experienced as they looked at each other through questioning eyes. Then after about ten minutes of Mr. Timmons and Daedai doing their thing, worshiping and speaking in tongues, Mr. Timmons preaches loudly, "I am crucified with Christ; nevertheless, I live; yet not I, but Christ lives within me, and this life I now live in the flesh. I live by the faith of the Son of God who gave Himself for me. Jesus be praised." Then Mr. Timmons walks over and helps a spiritually drunk Daedai back to her feet, and takes a couple of minutes to calm himself down, then he continues teaching, saying, "Understand, ladies, God's grace is not an unconditional license to sin, heaven forbid, but a net to catch you when you fall, allowing for your repentance and the ability to renew your mind. The apostle Paul says, 'Not to copy the behavior and customs of this world, but let God transform you into a new person by changing the way you think. Then you will learn to know God's will for your life, which is good and pleasing and perfect'" (Rom. 12:2 NLT). Mr. Timmons instructs, saying, "Ladies, this is what Daedai has: a renewed mind transformed by the Word of God. Do you still want it? The ladies answer enthusiastically, "Yes, yes we do." Mr. Timmons replies, "Then you certainly can have it. I apologize for getting caught up as I did. I know this experience is new for you, and I probably scared you, but sometimes the Spirit is so strong you have to move with it. When you are in His presence, you lose all consciousness of things around you, and you must humbly surrender to the experience. As a matter of fact, I'm feeling the remnant of that experience now, so I think this is a good place to end the lesson for today. I'll see you guys tomorrow." Feeling highly unusual, trembling, and experiencing something she's never known, Toni says, "Mr. Timmons, I felt it too, and I didn't want it to leave. Was that the Holy Spirit?" Mr. Timmons says, "I'm quite sure it was, Toni, because what I felt was spiritually strong, and I've come to recognize His presence. Toni, I believe you got a taste of His goodness, and I hope that you will always remember this experience. Now, you guys go home and study your Bibles. I'll see you all tomorrow."

CHAPTER 25
(THE HOLY SPIRIT)

DAY SIX: AFTER MR. TIMMONS GREETS EVERYONE good morning, they see that he has set up chairs outside the church again. They get seated, and he leads them in prayer. After which, Mr. Timmons starts teaching, saying, "God said, let us make man in our image, after our (Father, Son, Holy Spirit) likeness, and let them have dominion over the fish of the sea, and over the fowl of the air, and over the cattle, and over all the earth, and over every creeping thing that creeps upon the earth. So, God created man in his image, in the image of God created He him; male and female created He them. And God blessed them, and said unto them, Be fruitful, and multiply, and replenish (fill) the earth, and subdue it, and have dominion over the fish of the sea, and over the fowl of the air, and over every living thing that moves upon the earth." Mr. Timmons says, "Ladies, understand that we are spiritual beings, having a human experience. We are fashioned like God in that we are also three in one. God is Father, Son, and Holy Spirit. We are body, soul, and spirit. When you grow in the Word, you will start to see how the Trinity is expressed throughout the Bible. For example, when you begin learning about the Holy tabernacle of God, you will see that there is the outer court, inner court, and Holy of Holies. Similarly, in our flesh, there is the body, the mind (soul), and the spirit; likewise in divinity, there is Father, Son, and Holy Spirit. Ladies, do you see the triune relationships?" Toni says, "I see it, but I never understood the Trinity or thought of it that way." Mr. Timmons replies, "As you grow in the Word, you'll see how God centers everything around Jesus, bringing salvation to man after being exiled from God's glory, reunited totally by Jesus's shed blood to now enjoy new life again in God's kingdom. After the Fall, our condition in the flesh made it impossible to stand in the presence of God. His perfection is like trying to stand in the presence of our sun; it could not be done. At one time in our physical plane, for men to enter His presence, they had to pass through different stages of purification. For example, think of sinful flesh separation as the outer court, the first level of closeness, which there is one and only one entryway (Jesus) to that level. Then to move and get closer to the Father, one would prepare himself by performing certain rituals (sacrifices and purification); think of this level as the inner court. Next, is the final step in the process for standing in God's presence under the law of substitution. You see, God is Spirit in total perfection, and the only way that our flesh can exist in His presence and live is that the flesh must be purified and covered by the blood (animals), and nourished by communion, wine, and bread (Jesus, the true vine and bread of life). The life of the flesh is in the blood, right? So, when a blood sacrifice has been made, and the flesh has been purified and nourished along with other prescribed rituals, then only the priest of the people could go past the veil and enter that third stage, which was the Holy of Holies, the presence of God. However, God wanted to commune with us all individually without these steps, but with the fall of Adam, we lost our perfected bodies. Nothing imperfect can survive in the presence of a perfect God. So, Jesus was that perfect unblemished blood sacrifice in the flesh for us all. His sacrifice would not just cover our sin but would wipe it away completely lifting the veil of separation between mankind and God forever. Now we can come boldly to the throne of God. Jesus would be the bridge to reunite us with the Father in His state of perfection; through grace and mercy, the Holy Spirit, in witness of the Son within our spirit, perfectly aligns to God's glory, allowing us to commune with the Father forever. Jesus accomplished all these things at the Cross, and as such, we are bought with a price, and that price was paid in blood. Without Jesus, we would die in sinful flesh, the heirs of nothing. Jesus said, 'Abide in me (Jesus), and I in you. As the branch cannot bear fruit of itself, except it abide in the vine; no more can ye, except ye abide in me (Jesus). I am the vine, ye are the branches: He that abideth in me (Jesus), and I in him, the same bringeth forth much fruit: for without me ye can do nothing' (John 15:4-5 EVS). Blessed be the name of Jesus. However, while we are still in imperfection, until we make that final journey home, Jesus has provided for us a Comforter, who will guide us in all things." Trembling, with tears streaming down her face and trying to contain herself, Sanaa declares, "Mr. Timmons, I got it. My God, I think I understand it now. For the first time, I believe this is real. The reality of Jesus is so large in my understanding right now. I am overwhelmed. I used to think of Jesus as just a symbol of religion, intangible and without life. But He's real. I know He lives, with everything within me, I know it." Mr. Timmons smiles with an expression of surprise on his face as a teacher witnessing his student's light come on for the first time, and he says, "Sanaa, likewise with Toni, I know by your words and by what you are saying, you are having a supernatural revelation of Jesus Christ. To truly know Him, He must be revealed to you. Ladies, you finally know the truth, and when you see the Son in the Bible, you see the Father because the Son can do nothing apart from the Father because they are one. In your Bible, when you read about Jesus and the things He said and did, He is showing you the Father. God made it such that you could see Him in written form plus experience Him in human form through Jesus Christ. God gave us an image (personification) of Himself that looked like us. You get to know God's character, His deeds, and His love through the biblical accounts of Jesus's life. How about that? Isn't God wonderful? Young ladies, believe me, the power of God is still in the world today, and it is real. I have friends who have physically seen people raised from the dead by people praying with the gift of healing, and the dead came back to life. I have preacher friends who have seen people who had one leg shorter than the other, corrected to the right length by the laying on of hands. I have testimonies of pastors who have seen empty sockets in a person's face, after prayer, and the laying on of hands, miraculously grow eyeballs in those sockets. I have preacher friends who have witnessed the hand of God draw limbs where there were none. I know preachers and friends who have seen all sizes of tumors just fall off people. I know people who have witnessed an obese person sitting right next to them in a church service miraculously shed so much weight until his clothes fell off. I have also heard of teeth growing back in the mouth of people who only had gums. I know pastors who have witnessed gold dust appear in congregations where the Holy Spirit's presence manifested. I have heard of cancerous tumors being vomited up by people while in healing conferences. I have witnessed the evidence of the gifts of the Spirit, when people speaking in languages they did not know have it confirmed by people who knew the language that was spoken. All these miracles had one thing in common, and that is God manifesting in the form of the Holy Spirit, revealing evidence of His power. Feeling emotionally charged, Toni says, "Mr. Timmons, have you ever seen any of these miracles personally?" Mr. Timmons smiles, looks at the ladies, and says, "Yes, you are my miracles." The ladies smile as they look up at Mr. Timmons, who continues, saying, "The feelings and things you have experienced in these teaching sessions are but a small taste of the wonders of His power; we've only scratched the surface, ladies. Keep searching and growing in His Word, and I know you will receive the fruits of the Spirit. All of a sudden, Toni starts crying profusely, shouting loudly, "I knew it! I knew it!" Placing both hands over her face, Toni bends to her knees as if in pain. Concerned about her health, Mr. Timmons walks over to her side and asks, "What's wrong, Toni? What's wrong?" Toni takes a brief minute to pull herself together, takes a deep breath, and says, "Mr. Timmons, I have witnessed this type of miracle before, but I didn't believe it or knew what it was until now. In college, I witnessed my husband, my boyfriend at the time, get shot at a party by a jealous ex-boyfriend, and while riding with him to the hospital and seeing the emergency techs feverishly work to save his life, I felt in my heart that he was not going to pull through, and everything in that noment seemed so surreal. I was thinking, 'This cannot be happening; this cannot be happening.' It didn't dawn on me the gravity of the situation until the techs gave me that look as if to say my boyfriend was slowly slipping away. Later at the hospital, after he was pronounced dead, these same ladies right here were hugging me and consoling me in the hospital lobby. Then a couple of minutes later, my boy-friend's grandmother showed up at the place where we were standing crying. She sat down and began moaning and speaking in an indiscernible language, and afterward she said to me, 'He's waiting to see you.' I remember just staring and looking at this woman like she was crazy or something. But when the nurse came running down the hallway saying that my boy-friend had started breathing, I was stunned to the point that I could not move because I saw him take his last breath. Mr. Timmons, I saw him take his last breath, and I have been con-fused about that night ever since. Mr. Timmons, I knew with the type of wound my boyfriend had he could not have just come back like that, but listening to you, I know. Lord, I know now that I was a witness to a miracle. I believe my boyfriend's grandmother had that gift of healing that you are talking about, or maybe she had some kind of strong praying power. I don't know, but I do know this, that after his grandmother got to the hospital, sat down, and prayed, it was like she had gotten something in her spirit because I could feel the fiery confidence in her voice when she told me that my boyfriend was up and waiting to see me. She spoke this before the nurse came running down the hall to tell us about the change in his condition. Because of the very impossibility of what the grandmother was saying, I figured the woman was in shock from the loss of her grandson. She was not in shock. I know this now. She was just focused in a trans-like state, not recognizing anything other than what she had declared to me. Mr. Timmons, I think I understand what was going on with the grandmother because, through your teaching, I have gained some insight into the supernatural. I do believe that the power and virtue of God was released through the grandmother that night. I can understand and come to grips with the healing part, but it's been exceedingly difficult for me to conceive of someone being brought back from the dead." Sanaa then confirms everything Toni said concerning the incident that night. Emotionally exhausted, Toni says, "Mr. Timmons, please help me understand how this works." Mr. Timmons explains, "Now, concerning the power of the Holy Spirit relative to the raising of people from the dead, in the Bible, Jesus poses a question. He asks, 'Which is easier, to heal the lame or to raise from the dead? Both require the power of the Holy Spirit.' Mr. Timmons pauses for a moment so the women can think, then he asks, "Toni, do you understand?" She gasps air and says, "Yes, I get it," and without thinking or being cognitive of her words, she further says, "The power of the Holy Spirit is not constrained by anything." Then Toni shouts out loud, "Oh! My God!" Immediately knowing that what she just said came from somewhere else and not of her own reasoning. Toni says, "Mr. Timmons! Mr. Timmons, I think I just had one of those Peter-type revelations, because what I just said came out beyond my thinking about it. I just knew what to say. I mean, I just opened my mouth, and it came out." Mr. Timmons says, "Revelation comes with understanding truth." With her eyes wide open, full of excitement from hearing and seeing these things, Sanaa says, "Mr. Timmons, tell us about the gifts of the Spirit. Sanaa says, "Mr. Timmons, I got to know, we all got to know, everything you can teach us about these gifts of the Spirit." Mr. Timmons says, "Ok, but first things first, you need to know the person of the Holy Spirit." Chrystal interrupts, and in astonishment, states, "Person?" Mr. Timmons answers, "Yes, person; the Holy Spirit is the third part of the Godhead, and HE is a person. He is the administrator of the estate of Jesus Christ. He testifies and witnesses to the truth. The Holy Spirit revealed that Jesus could do nothing apart from the consent of the Father, likewise, the Holy Spirit can do nothing apart from the consent of the Son. The Godhead operates as three in one, the Holy Trinity, separate but equal, Father, Son, and Holy Spirit. In John chapter fourteen, Jesus is explaining to His disciples that He must go away, and it is hard for them to understand what He is talking about. Jesus says 'Do not let your hearts be troubled. You believe in God; believe also in me. My Father's house has many rooms; if that were not so, would I have told you that I am going there to prepare a place for you? And if I go and prepare a place for you, I will come back and take you to be with me that you also may be where I am. You know the way to the place where I am going.' The disciples are having a problem understanding what Jesus told them, so Thomas says to Jesus, 'Lord, we don't know where you are going, so how can we know the way?' Jesus answered, 'I am the way and the truth and the life. No one comes to the Father except through me. If you really know me, you will know my Father as well. From now on, you do know him and have seen him.' Philip said, 'Lord, show us the Father and that will be enough for us.' Jesus answers, saying '… Don't you believe that I am in the Father and that the Father is in me? The words I say to you I do not speak on my own authority. Rather, it is the Father, living in me, who is doing his work. Believe me when I say that I am in the Father and the Father is in me, or at least believe on the evidence of the works themselves. Very truly I tell you, whoever believes in me will do the works I have been doing, and they will do even greater things than these because I am going to the Father. And I will do whatever you ask in my name, so that the Father may be glorified in the Son. You may ask me for anything in my name, and I will do it. Jesus then promises his disciples the Holy Spirit to come. Jesus says, If you love me, keep my commands. And I will ask the Father, and he will give you another advocate to help you and be with you forever— the Spirit of truth. The world cannot accept him because it neither sees him nor knows him. But you know him, for he lives with you and will be in you. I will not leave you as orphans; I will come to you. Before long, the world will not see me anymore, but you will see me. Because I live, you also will live. On that day you will realize that I am in my Father, and you are in me, and I am in you. Whoever has my commands and keeps them is the one who loves me. The one who loves me will be loved by my Father, and I too will love them and show myself to them.'" Mr. Timmons says, "The only way to truly know and have intimacy with Jesus is that He must be revealed by the Holy Spirit; the person who testifies of Him. Jesus declared to His disciples, saying, 'All this I have spoken while still with you. But the Advocate, the Holy Spirit, whom the Father will send in my name, will teach you all things and will remind you of everything I have said to you.'" Mr. Timmons continues, "As you now see, the Holy Spirit is a He, and not an it. He is an exceptional person, not just a power or an inspiration. The Holy Spirit may be grieved, quenched, in terms of the exercise of His will, and the Holy Spirit can be resisted. Being one with the Father and Son, the Holy Spirit was the agent of creation in Christ. All Scripture is God-breathed, thus, the Holy Spirit as the breath of God is the author of the Scriptures. The inspiration to write the Bible was by way of the Holy Spirit. He revealed the Word of God to men because the Word of God could not possibly come by way of the five senses. The men of God wrote the Bible inspirationally through the Holy Spirit." Mr. Timmons says, "Now that you know the person of the Holy Spirit, let's talk about what happened at Pentecost. After the crucifixion of Jesus, when He, the Holy Spirit, manifested His presence to the disciples, coming in like the sound of a mighty wind, the disciples were filled with Him (the Holy Spirit), our Advocate and Comforter, our conduit, revealing the mysteries of God. The Holy Spirit brought evidence of His presence as it is written. They (the disciples) began to speak in other tongues as the Spirit enabled them. After that, the disciples, who were once hiding and fearing persecution, became bold as lions and went out into the world spreading the Holy Word, with confidence and boldness. The disciples had been transformed, not fearing anymore for their own life because having the evidence of the gifts of the Spirit, <u>they knew that our Lord Jesus Christ was in them</u>. The apostle Paul, in his letter to the Corinthians, explains to the followers of Christ the nature of the Holy Spirit. He explains that he wants them to know about the gifts of the Holy Spirit. He said, 'You know that at one time you were unbelievers. You were somehow drawn away to worship statues of gods that couldn't even speak. So I want you to know that no one who is speaking with the help of God's Spirit says, May Jesus be cursed; And without the help of the Holy Spirit, no one can say, Jesus is Lord.' Paul continues to explain, 'There are different kinds of gifts. But they are all given to believers by the same Spirit. There are different ways to serve. But they all come from the same Lord. There are different ways the Spirit works. But the same God is working in all these ways and in all people. The Holy Spirit is especially given to each of us. That is for the good of all. To some people, the Spirit gives a message of wisdom. To others, the same Spirit gives a message of knowledge. To others the same Spirit gives faith. To others, the Spirit gives gifts of healing. To others, He gives the power to do miracles. To others, He gives the ability to prophesy. To others, He gives the ability to tell the spirits apart. To others, He gives the ability to speak in different kinds of languages they had not known before. And to still others, He gives the ability to explain what was said in those languages. All the gifts are produced by the same Spirit. He gives gifts to each person, just as He decides' (1Corin. 12:2-11 NIV). Toni, I think your boyfriend's grandmother was a prayer warrior, with the gift of healing, and at the time, you were not spiritually knowledgeable to know that she was praying in the spirit for her grandson's healing. The grandmother had to be a woman of tremendous faith, intimate with God. The Holy Spirit in us makes possible these gifts, and perhaps one day, you may find yourselves a vessel to manifest these spiritual gifts. Keep learning and growing in the Word. When you give thanks, pray, or intercede, you must do it in the Spirit or in the presence of God, this brings a fast result, most times, but mind you, God is not predictable; you can't put a formula on His ways. Your job is to pray according to His will, speaking what you desire; believe that you have received what you asked for, and you shall have it. If God says it, no matter what you feel, see, taste, or hear, the only truth is in God's Word. Have confidence in the fact that you have a right to come boldly to His throne and ask for what you will because, through the blood of Jesus Christ, it is finished. Again, I say IT IS FINISHED. Now, ladies, say it again with me, believing that the final work of the Son is complete. Say it again now, with conviction, knowing in your heart that grace and mercy were sealed in a perfect act of love that transcends our carnal understanding. Say it! 'IT, IS FINISHED.' Ladies, from now on, when praying for healing, interceding, or for whatever reason you pray, you now have confidence that through the shed blood of Jesus, Satan, hell, and the grave are defeated. Jesus has overcome this world, and we are victorious through and in Him, our Lord, Savior, and King. IT IS FINISHED! Scream it out loud, ladies; let the world know, 'IT IS FINISHED!'

CHAPTER 26
(LEARN & GROW)

DAY SEVEN: EARLY IN THE MORNING, THE LADIES arrive at the old church, ready for their lesson. Mr. Timmons brings the ladies back inside the church, where he has set up a big-screen television, multiple videos, and various books. As they walk, Sanaa leans over to Daedai and says, "I hope he doesn't think we gonna read all that today." Daedai answers, "Just watch, look, and listen; you might learn something." With that statement, Sanaa jerks her neck and stares at Daedai with an insulted expression on her face, and then replies, "Excuse me?" Daedai doesn't respond but rolls her eyes as she and the other ladies walk to their seats. After morning prayer, Mr. Timmons opens up, saying "'...and on the seventh day God ended his work which he had made, and he rested on the seventh day from all His work which He had made; God blessed the seventh day and sanctified it'" (Genesis 2 KJV). Mr. Timmons continues saying, "Now, ladies, don't get it twisted. God was not tired. God is a spirit, and He does not need physical rest; what this means is that God just stopped from His labor because what He had created was perfect, and there was nothing else to add. Remember, everything that comes from God is perfect. Know also that the number seven is a significant number with God; it is the number representing completion. As part of your study, you should research Bible numerology (gematria). It is important, and as a foundational starter to your development, learn the Hebrew alphabet and then some of the language; some surprises await your understanding. Let your wisdom be grounded in learning God's feasts; they will lead you to a deeper understanding and will increase your faith. I have given you a very brief rundown of these assignments because I want to make sure you keep searching for His knowledge. Now, back to the lesson, I hope you have discovered how intricately complex this thing called creation is. I hope the lessons learned have unveiled in your understanding the evidence of God's fingerprints all over His design. I would suggest that when talking to people about creation, please try to debunk the idea of evolution, for it is one of the biggest lies Satan has used to deceive mankind. Check this out, Toni. Noted American author, borderline agnostic, philosopher, postdoctoral mathematician, and molecular biologist Dave Berlinski, observed in his book, _The Devil's Delusion: Atheism and its Scientific Pretensions_ (Berlinski 2008), asking and answering the following questions:

> Has anyone provided proof of God's inexistence? Not even close. Has quantum cosmology explained the emergence of the universe or why it is here? Not even close. Have our sciences explained why our universe seems to be fine-tuned to allow for the existence of life? Not even close. Are physicists and biologists willing to believe in anything so long as it is not religious thought? Close enough. Has rationalism and moral thought provided us with an understanding of what is good, what is right, and what is moral? Not close enough. Has secularism in the terrible 20th century been a force for good? Not even close to being close. Is there a narrow and oppressive orthodoxy in the sciences? Close enough. Does anything in the sciences or

their philosophy justify the claim that religious belief is irrational? Not even in the ballpark. Is scientific atheism a frivolous exercise in intellectual contempt? Dead on.

Scientists and believers in evolution will not concede to a supernatural God because they are blinded by their lack of revelation in the Word of God. So, they regrettably hold on to a materialistic / atheistic faith argument, and this unwavering faith in evolutionary theory taught to many generations of students has been the foundation to subvert truth in God's Word. The religiously-minded instruction in the lie of evolution has been more destructive to our society than any other ideo-theology. Yes, evolution is more of a religion than a science; most things that evolutionist scientists postulate can't even be proven, requiring them to formulate an assumptive belief, and when the scientific evidence is not apparent, they run to the tranquilizer of theoretical gradualism, arguing that proof needs time to become realized, and if that doesn't work to convince their peers, they flat-out lie. How can anyone believe that they have scientifically solved the origins of life's mystery when they cannot even define energy, gravity, consciousness, or even light? Oh, they can describe what it does, but its definition has not been revealed to anyone yet." Surprised by the scientific acumen of Mr. Timmons, Toni listens closely to Mr. Timmons's lecture and becomes intriguingly engaged with the lesson. Mr. Timmons continues, "My purpose here is to debunk the deceptive lie in the religion of evolution, and to fight against this deceptive tool of Satan that brings confusion to man's belief in God. Think very seriously about the following premise offered by Dr. Kent Hovind:

If evolution turns out to be true, then there is no Creator. If creation turns out to be true, then there is a Creator. If evolution turns out to be true, then there are no rules. If creation turns out to be true, then there are a set of rules. If evolution turns out to be true, then there is no purpose for life. If creation turns out to be true, then there is a purpose and a meaning for life. If evolution turns out to be true, then man is evolving with no need of a savior. If creation turns out to be true, then man is a fallen being, in need of a savior. If evolution turns out to be true, then death brought man into the world. If creation turns out to be true, then man brought death into the world. If evolution turns out to be true, then there is no afterlife. If creation turns out to be true, then there is an afterlife, or life after death; and finally, if evolution turns out to be true, then we have no comfort in our future because we only have death to look forward to. However, if creation turns out to be true, then there is comfort in knowing the magnificence of our future.

The truth is that the evolutionist / atheist will not believe in God because he is guided by his lust and does not want for himself the discipline or restriction in God's rules that restrict his lifestyle. The scientist / evolutionist /atheist, not being subject to God's morals, follows his own set of values or rules, living under the misguided impression that good morals somehow evolved into man's awareness rather than through divine proscriptions of God. Some scientists / evolutionists / atheists just flat-out refuses to believe in a God they cannot quantify. To any extent, for your continued learning and apologetic prowess, evaluate the science of creation in God's Word by becoming knowledgeable in such areas like quantum physics (mechanics); it will increase your faith as it relates to the glory of God and His creation. Check out a scientific experiment called the double-slit experiment. What was discovered during this experiment will open your eyes to the light of God relative to our reality or consciousness. The information you will learn should guide you in answering some of the questions concerning: do we live in a digital simulation, hologram, or virtual reality? Is our existence purely informational? Is our dimension the only dimension, or are there many? If we are not observing a thing, does it still exist? Is space, time, matter, and dimensions all derived from consciousness? Is consciousness informational or informationally integrated (entangled)? Does consciousness determine existence? Who is the creator outside of our informational consciousness? Has science really proved the existence of God? Speaking of science proving the Bible, new scientific discoveries explain how a man under divine power of the Holy Spirit (light) could walk on water, heal the sick, walk through walls, levitate in the air, dematerialize, command nature, raise the dead, and even rise up from the dead. Ladies, God is light; not every aspect of God is light, but the greater part of His glory in His identified presence is light. Discoveries in quantum physics in the last five to twenty years reflects that scientists have found that there is an abundance of evidence that prove the Scriptures to be correct in repeatedly saying that God is light. This substantiates that the light of God is at the instance of creation. To substantiate that the light of God created the world, scientists, using a particle accelerator at C.E.R.N (we'll discuss the occult behind this later), have been able to trace earth's beginning back to the instance of creation at the point scientist call singularity, which has no time, matter, or space, condensed back to pure energy when the explosion (creation / big bang?) takes place. Scientists say that the light (light of God) was at the instance of the big bang / creation. Dennis Zetting (Zetting 2016) postulates that, 'Light is the major factor for life to originate on earth and be sustained.' All the particles and forces that exist in the universe are held together by light (God). So, the Christian can easily surmise how God in His glory of light is omniscient, omnipresent, and omnipotent. Scientifically, it has been proven through quantum physics that light is everywhere throughout the entire universe. Light is *omnipresent*; light (God) is everywhere with substance. Light is *omniscient*; in the revelations of wave particle duality, quantum physics shows how light is used in the transition, from an invisible wave particle to a physical manifestation, as a particle of matter in our reality. The human consciousness is a participant in the energy of light. The light somehow has knowledge entangled with our consciousness to produce information and physical manifestation. Without consciousness to perceive, the wave particle to produce physical manifestation (matter) does not occur. Matter does not exist as a wave of energy prior to observation, but as a wave of potentialities. God is the ultimate observer (designer), collapsing the wave particle potentiality after each succession of observers are not observing. Light (God) is the transactional wisdom of everything interacting in the universe. Quantum physics proves that light is always the same yesterday, today, and tomorrow, no matter the distance or perceived time horizon. Light (God) is eternal. Light (God) is always the same yesterday, today, and forever; *omnipotent*. Need I say more? But I will. I believe, like most Christians, that we live on a young earth. I believe the Bible quite literally, in terms of the six days of creation. In the study of polonium halos, particularly 218 Po (primordial polonium), found in Precambrian granite rock (called the Genesis rocks because they contain polonium halos; they are the foundation rocks of the continents, and they are empty of the fossils seen in sedimentary rocks) as determinative of the age of the earth. It was shown (Gentry, Polonium Halos 1973) through scientific research that these polonium halos 218 Po, formulating in granite rock, indicated a rapid crystallization of the Precambrian granites, and it could only have taken form within a three-minute time elapsed from nucleosynthesis to the formation of a solid earth. The conclusion is that the earth was created instantaneously. A creation event lasting longer than three minutes after the initial moment of creation energy would not produce the alpha particle distribution construct of polonium halos 218 Po found in Precambrian granite rock research." Toni then interjects after being curiously aroused, saying, "Mr. Timmons, I knew of and studied polonium, but I did not have chance to study information about the radioactive decay ratios of polonium halos relative to creation." Mr. Timmons continues, "Toni, the scientist who was credited with this finding was Robert Gentry (Gentry, Creations Tiny Mystery 1988), who also in his book, *Creations Tiny Mystery*, postulates that, '...Whatever data can be fitted into a one-singularity model must also fit into a model with three singularities...' Gentry continues that based on the Genesis account, '...three special periods, or singularities... cannot be explained on the basis of known law. These singularities are the creation, the fall of man, and the flood-events marked in a major way by the intervention of the creator.' Ladies, this stuff is just a little too heavy for me to explain, and I'm getting a headache just from trying to talk about this, but the main point here is that the earth is young, and God is the creator, unquestionably. Now, continuing on, you need to beware of artificial intelligence (transhumanism) and genetic crossbreeding. I have a bad feeling about the future of a new science intentionally opening portals to demonic or dimensional manifestation. Beware of the experiments and demonic practices that are taking place at CERN (acronym for the French Conseil Européen pour la Recherche Nucléaire) and their particle accelerator (Large Hadron Collider); their motives are not purely scientific. Jesus proclaimed that in the last days leading up to His return would be 'as the days of Noah' (Matthew 24:37 NIV). Back in the days of Noah, Nimrod, a king, Noah's great, great, great grandson attempted to open a door into the spiritual realm, utilizing the tower of Babel as stated in Genesis 11. Today, CERN is involved in attempting to do the same thing as the people in Nimrod's kingdom. These people at CERN are experimenting with something that can easily be destructive to mankind, either by opening black holes in our universe, experimenting with antimatter, developing particle beam weapons, distortion and star gates, DNA sequencing and artificial synthesis, and finally, strangelets. Their overall intention is to break into new dimensions, which have the possibility of spawning demonic creatures that are not of this world, or the unleashing of elements that can wipe out populations of people. One of the research directors at CERN, Mr. Bertolucci (Register 2009), has stated, 'The Large Hadron Collider could open a doorway to another dimension, and out this door might come something, or we might send something through it.' So, keep your eyes on the developments at CERN, and watch the following videos for more information: "The Truth About CERN's Large Hadron Collider" https://www.youtube.com/watch?v=49dGknES0, "SYMMETRY–CERN dance-opera film (official trailer)." https://www.youtube.com/watch?time_continue=9&v=Cllqr1nmdYk&feature=emb_logo, and "Full Bizarre, Demonic Gotthard Tunnel Opening Ceremony, Satanic, New World Order, Illuminati Ritual" https://www.youtube.com/watch?time_continue=3&v=zW5gkllKcDg&feature=emb_logo. Lastly, involving the satanic symbolism at CERN, the logo at CERN has three intertwined sixes (as in 666). CERN (Register 2009) is the birthplace of the World Wide Web (WWW). Interestingly, the Hebrew equivalent of our 'w' is the letter 'vav' or 'waw,' which has the numerical value of six. So, the English 'www' transliterated into Hebrew is 'vav vav vav,' or '666.' This place is loaded with satanic symbolism, inside and outside of its facility. Again, watch all developments at CERN. Finally, reject the idea of globalism and hold fast to America's right of sovereignty. Reject open borders at all costs, and pay close attention to the religious, political, and historical ascension of the European Union through Germany, Rome, Sweden, and Turkey; they are all players in the rise of the antichrist. Reject the false science establishing a crisis in global warming. The ultimate aim of satanic deception is to facilitate a one-world government, and the alleged crisis in global warming is a way to accomplish that task; the antichrist needs the one-world government to put into motion what he thinks is his ascension to godhead in the flesh. President Obama's Chief of Staff used to say, 'Let no good crisis go to waste,' meaning, most politicians take advantage of a crisis to increase budgets and bureaucracies. Chuck Missler (Missler, Twiligh's Last Gleaming 2000) asserts, and I agree: 'Some people say that immorality causes social crisis, maybe governments have an incentive to promote immorality. As the crisis grows, the public's liberty gets smaller. It is within the nature of those who are enslaved by their own desires and fears to yearn to enslave others.' In asserting a coming one-world government, and without sounding the conspiracy bell, I must sound the conspiracy bell because I believe there is a grand conspiracy in the making that has been in the planning for quite some time to facilitate a one-world global family. I predicate this idea based on the fact that nations are forcibly implementing and promoting a crisis in population control. The emergence of an allure towards a one-world religion and the emergence of a fake crisis in global climate control, they all purpose an incentive toward a one-world government. From the things I've seen and read, I do believe that Georgia's seventh congressional district Democrat, the late Larry P. McDonald 1976 (McDonald 2020) had it right when he said, 'The drive of the Rockefellers and their allies is to create a one world government combining super capitalism and communism under the same tent, all under their control... Do I mean conspiracy? Yes, I do. I am convinced that there is such a plot, international in scope, generations old in planning, and incredibly evil in intent.' Shortly after these assertions were made, the Korean Flight 007 that the congressman was flying on, along with all the other passengers, was said to have been shot down by Soviet interceptors. However, there have been confirmed reported sightings of the airplane, the congressman, and other passengers being held captive in Russia."

Chrystal raises her hand with a satirical frown on her face, interrupts Mr. Timmons's rant, and asks, "Mr. Timmons, you actually mean to tell me you buy into all this conspiracy stuff?" Mr. Timmons stares at Chrystal with a slight smile and confesses, "Personally, I would normally pass on these conspiratorial assertions, but I see what's happening. I see the divisive turmoil in our society, pitting the poor against the rich, capitalist against communist, and Christian against atheist. I see the inclusive attitude toward an engagement of a one-world religion. I see the effort of invisible hands (university professors) to foster cultural Marxist regimes to divide this country. I see the deceptive creation of a crisis in climate change to panic nations toward global resolutions. I see the emergence of the illuminati / witchcraft and its demonic foundations, images, symbols, and possessions to enslave the young and the innocent, and it all fits into the one-world order playbook. Ladies, the plan is too extensive to try and explain in our short time here, but my goal in mentioning this imminent dilemma is to make you aware that there does presently exists an evil plot to give rise to the antichrist. I would ask that you preview Major Amir Tsarfati's YouTube videos, "The Illuminati & the One World Government" and also "The Rise of the One World Religion." It will expose this plot and give you an in-depth look at the major players and their agenda. I purposely remain vague on all these topics so that curiosity will motivate your research and continued learning. However, most importantly, the only thing that the Christian needs is the inherent Word of God. Learn and digest all the Scriptures over everything else." Toni looks around the room and wonders, "But Mr. Timmons, what are all these reading materials for?" Mr. Timmons explains, "I have assembled them only as supplements for your review, a special collection of my books and videos that will give you a greater perspective into the awesomeness of our God. First, you must understand the supernatural, so the first book we will explore together is Pastor Renny Mclean's book,

Eternity Invading Time. Then from the Lion of Judah on YouTube, "Most People Don't Even Realize What's around Them." And for everything in defeating or deliverance from evil spirits, we will view all of Minister Kevin L.A. Ewing's YouTube videos, and books by Zit Grant, especially, *Be Free From Spiritual Spouses*; also, books by Pastor Uzor Ndekwu, especially, *The Blood of Jesus as a Weapon*, and Dr. Pat Holliday's powerful book, *The Witchdoctor and the Man: City under the Sea*. For training in marriage and the family, we will view on YouTube, Voddie Baucham, "Centrality of the Home" and "Love & Marriage Pt. 1, 2, 3" (full series). Then for the rest of the day, or when you go home at your leisure, visit YouTube to watch the following Christian apologetic videos and read these reference books: try to view everything you can find by Chuck Missler, especially "Hidden Messages: Torah Code." To understand how to refute evolution, study "The Genesis Theory Part 1." Study everything of Dr. Kent Hovind; his videos are also on YouTube. Start with "Creation Seminars 1-7." Then watch videos on YouTube like, "5 Quantum Phenomena Supporting God's Existence" by Dennis Zetting. Watch "Evolution vs. God – The Skeptic's Journey Part 6," then view videos of Dr. Michael Behe, "Darwin's Black Box," and Dr. Stephen C. Meyer; especially his appearances on "Socrates in the City." His books include: *Return of the God Hypothesis*, *Signature in the Cell*, *Explore Evolution, and Darwin's Doubt*, and *The Explosive Origin of Animal Life and the Case for Intelligent Design*. Also, especially important, to debunk evolution in astronomy, see on YouTube: "What Aren't You Being Told about Astronomy, Volume II." For the origins and myths debunking the alleged manmade climate change theory, see on YouTube: "Luke Warming: A discussion with Climate Scientist Patrick Michaels of the Cato" and Mark Levin's "Life, Liberty & Levin: The Truth about Global Warming." Finally, digest and learn completely everything Ravi Zacharias, Abdu Murry, and Amir Tsarfati. For scientific revelations, view Charles Nestor II's YouTube video:

"A Proof for God's Existence from Quantum Physics," and others: "Digital Physics Meets Idealism: The Mental Universe," "Quantum Physics Debunks Materialism," "Connecting with Universal Consciousness," and "Amazing Evidence for God: Scientific Evidence for God." In terms of debunking same-sex marriage, look at Frank Turek's video: "Same-Sex Marriage: Legal Marriage Has NOTHING to Do with Love." For proof of a young earth, see on YouTube Dr. Andrew Snelling's "Science Confirms a Young Earth" or Ken Ham's "Science Confirms the Bible Language in the DNA." For information on the coming one-world religion, see on YouTube Amir Tsarfati's "The Rise Of the One World Religion" Use all these YouTube videos and books as reference materials. All of the authors listed above believe in God; however, a few of them believe in an old earth, billions of years in the making. However, I believe that the earth is young, between 6000 to 10,000 years old. In my opinion, God is not limited to waiting billions of years for the completion of His creation. God has no limits. As He speaks, so it is done. I believe as the Bible says; everything came into existence finished and good, which resolves for me the question: which came first, the chicken or the egg? Or more scientifically, was space, time, and matter all created at once? Human beings cannot comprehend beyond four dimensions, or even define strong force, weak force, light, time, or gravity. So, why would anyone with a belief that God is God believe that He is limited? His thoughts and actions are far beyond our ability to even come close to comprehending. Also, remember, everything that is seen came from that which is unseen; everything we can see in this physical plane came from the spiritual realm. Ladies, you cannot trust the secular news media or scientists / Atheists that have ulterior motives because most of them have been swayed by political correctness and follow misguided special interest and or their personal opinion / preferences. I remain weary and always afraid of an alliance between the media (big tech,) and special interest groups or politically affiliated regimes that assist in generating a desired political outcome or change in ethos rather than reporting but attempting to suppress the truth. Ladies, understand that everybody is talking about or coining the phrase: 'what the science says.' Know that science has never said anything; it is always the scientist that interprets or postulates, and since most of them do not believe in God or have little understanding of His Word, they lean unto their personal understanding, lusts, and preferences, which keep them from visualizing the unifying force that is in God's commandments. They cannot see the Father of glory, who is trying to save us from ourselves. Learn and digest these materials I'm giving you; be ready to take a position, and converse with others on how the Bible not only proves science, but everything as well; their argument will not prevail against the truth." After Mr. Timmons and the group take most of the day reviewing some of the videos and books, Chrystal, gazing at Toni, who is now uncharacteristically quiet and expressing a somewhat skeptical attitude about everything, is urged through Chrystal's stare and body language to ask, "Mr. Timmons, how in the world do you know that all this information is accurate? Are you a scientist?" The ladies immediately perk up, waiting to hear his response. Mr. Timmons thinks for a second, and then replies, "No, Toni. I'm not a scientist." She then inquires, "Well, then, how do you know that this scientific stuff is the real deal? How do you know that this is accurate?" Mr. Timmons looks to Chrystal, then turns back to Toni, and without hesitation, he says, "I know, that I know, that I know. It fits in harmony with the Word of God. I have tried the information by the Spirit and the knowledge of God within me. I have comfort in knowing that nothing is equal to the Most High God. I know that those who lack understanding or refuse it altogether are destroyed for the lack of knowledge. I know that there will come a day that the wise, the not-so-wise, the genius, the-not-so genius, the naysayers, and the scoffers will all bow and confess that He is

Lord, our Creator, our Savior, our King, and our God. Moreover, I have read the end of the book. I know the ending from the beginning. Ladies, there's a quote by Robert Jastrow (Jastrow 2000) in *God and the Astronomers*, in which he states: 'For the scientist who has lived by his faith in the power of reason, the story ends like a bad dream. He has scaled the mountains of ignorance, he is about to conquer the highest peak; as he pulls himself over the final rock, he is greeted by a band of theologians who have been sitting there for centuries.'" Mr. Timmons says, "I guess the 'woke' aren't so awake at all, huh? So, you see, I do not have to be a scientist to know that what I've shared with you is spot-on. I have the inherent Word of God as my guide. So, then, my scientific acumen does not matter that much at all now, does it? Before science or scientists existed, God is!" Before Mr. Timmons can say another word, Sanaa interrupts, asking Mr. Timmons a question totally unrelated to all the Christian apologetic information presented, "Mr. Timmons, what political party do you belong too? Republican, Democrat, or Independent?" Mr. Timmons looks at the ladies with a perplexed look on his face relative to Sanaa's question, and considers that the information presented might have been a little too much, and maybe she needs to change the subject matter. However, Mr. Timmons probingly responds, "Sanaa, that's a strange question you're asking; where did that come from?" Sanaa surmises, "Well, from what I've heard and understood, most Christians belong to the Republican party. So, should I belong to that party?" Mr. Timmons, now understanding the genesis of her question, and incredibly happy that she now considers herself to be a new Christian, replies, "I don't know, Sanaa; that's your choice. I guess it depends on what you believe. I belong to the Jesus party, for which there is only one. However, right now in this physical dimension, I vote Republican. I find it difficult to vote with any party that promotes homosexuality, communism, abortion / infanticide (sixty million murdered), identity politics, a propensity to remove God from its platform, and a belief in evolution and climate change as anthropogenic. I tell you the truth, though, I experienced a lot of backlash for my switch from Democrat to Republican. I remember telling my folks I was switching, and they acted like I had cursed God or something. To them, that was taboo; you just didn't do something like that, even though they couldn't give me a good explanation why I shouldn't. It was just one of those unquestionable things as Black people you just didn't do. But I'm an independent thinker, ladies. I think for myself and don't move with the herd. I make my decisions based on God's Word. Ladies, understand that in the Republican party, as with any other organization, there are good people, and there are bad people. Sanaa, never take any person or organization's word on anything, that includes mine; do your homework. Look at each party historically up until present date, measure the platform by God's Word, then you decide. You must learn to try the spirit in everything, and learn not to lean unto your own understanding. Try the thing by every word that precedes out of the mouth of God. If your decision is in harmony with His Word, then and only then will your decision be on the right track; again, I say, try the spirit of a thing by the Word of God. As for me, if God says it, I believe it, and I act on it. I believe that God has opened my eyes to see certain truths in this world; that is why I vote the way I do. Do you understand?" Sanaa concedes yes, and Mr. Timmons turns to the other ladies and asks, "Do you understand?" They also acknowledge yes. He continues saying, "When you know the Word of God, I mean, really know the Word of God through revelation, then you should be able to discern if a thing is right." I mean, right as within God's Word, and you know in your knower that you know. Within that small voice, therein lies wisdom. Ladies, for the sake of my inquiry, I would like to know how you plan to integrate into your daily home life what you have learned during your time here. If you do not know right now, that is ok, just keep growing in the

Word of God, and wisdom will enter in like a cool breeze on a hot day. But right now, I'd just like to hear what you think." Chrystal nervously stands and says, "Mr. Timmons, I think I speak for all of us that our lives started changing from the first day of these meetings, and we have been so enlightened by the Word of God, but in a larger context, how do we continue in this makeover and translate it to our home life? This is an issue our group has been discussing every night. Mr. Timmons, this is a serious problem; we are going back to a mostly secular environment. Our friends, families, and organizations we belong to do not have a clue of the things we have learned here. We face an awesome challenge with everyone we know. So, you see, the problem is complicated; where do we go from here?" Mr. Timmons reflects for a moment and does not give a direct answer, but gives an indirect answer, saying, "Be aware; a lot of people in this world have been given over to strong delusions, and the spirit of the antichrist has stolen truth from their understanding and reasoning. You can see and feel it in our society. Everybody is now trying to be self-righteous, and even judgmental, wanting to have a personal sense of truth; in effect, trying to be God, which eventually leads nations to chaos and destruction. 'For the time will come when they will not endure (tolerate) sound doctrine; but after their own lusts (desires) shall they heap to themselves teachers (will multiply teachers for themselves), having itching ears (because they have an itch to hear what they want to hear); and they shall turn away their ears from truth, and shall be turned unto fables (myths)' (2 Tim. 4:3-4 NKJV). For us, it's not hard to see that the adversary's goal is to break up the family, confuse gender identity, lead people into unimaginable types of fornication, kill babies in the womb, corrupt the human bloodline, segregate people into special interest groups with unthinkable ideologies, such as feminism, Black Lives Matter, LGBTQ, communism, Nazism, ANTIFA, and pro-choice movements, all under the disguise of intersectionality for the purposes of facilitating a transference of power, and to have us fight amongst ourselves with the ultimate goal of a one-world government. Satan knows that a people divided against themselves cannot long endure. One of the greatest deceptive tools Satan has ever devised was to hide behind the idea of the differences in people by race. Out of all the colorful differences we see in the world, I do not believe God originally intended this distinction between human beings. I think as a result of the Fall, mutation in human DNA and proteins influenced by differing environmental signals led to the transformation in the amount of melanin different groups of people would have in terms of their pigmentation (skin color); thus, in truth, we are all the same color, just in different shades of brown; but people with iniquity in their hearts supporting bigotry, whether learned or otherwise, who have ulterior motives or agendas to malign or marginalize those they consider the opposition, help Satan's direct or indirect strategy to corrupt, divide, and promote conflict between nations. The spirit of the antichrist continually seeks to distort everything that God originally intended for mankind, and the world has not yet realized that Jesus Christ, by the wisdom of God, has revealed Himself as the only unifying force that can overcome Satan's strategy. Sometimes the sick do not realize the genesis of their sickness, or maybe do not realize that they are sick at all. If you have eyes to see, you are a witness to a nation (America), which is slowly losing its knowledge of God, led by forces of darkness attempting to wipe away everything that is of God, leaving generations bankrupt of truth and understanding. The question is, how do you hurt a perfect God? God is perfect, but He has a weakness. His weakness is us; His children. We have God's heart, and Satan aims and strategizes his attacks on what he perceives as God's vulnerability, which is His very own image trapped in the corrupted mortal flesh of mankind. So, what does a good Shepherd (God) do? He protects His flock, at all costs, even to the point of sacrificing His own life, for He .

understands the innocence and naïveté of the lamb running aimlessly, easily deceived, and not recognizing the danger posed by a cunning predator. The good Shepherd tries to restrain his flock, but still, some go astray and are devoured. Man is representative of that flock of lambs, leaning unto a personal understanding. Some men will be easily deceived and lead astray, and as a result, will be devoured. 'For since the creation of the world God's invisible qualities—his eternal power and divine nature—have been clearly seen, being understood from what has been made, so that people are without excuse. For although they knew God, they neither glorified him as God nor gave thanks to him, but their thinking became futile and their foolish hearts were darkened. Although they claimed to be wise, they became fools[3] and exchanged the glory of the immortal God for images made to look like a mortal human being and birds and animals and reptiles. Therefore, God gave them over in the sinful desires of their hearts to sexual impurity for the degrading of their bodies with one another. They exchanged the truth about God for a lie and worshiped and served created things rather than the Creator—who is forever praised. Because of this, God gave them over to shameful lusts. Even their women exchanged natural sexual relations for unnatural ones. In the same way the men also abandoned natural relations with women and were inflamed with lust for one another. Men committed shameful acts with other men and received in themselves the due penalty for their error. Furthermore, just as they did not think it worthwhile to retain the knowledge of God, so God gave them over to a depraved mind, so that they do what ought not to be done. They have become filled with every kind of wickedness, evil, greed and depravity. They are full of envy, murder, strife, deceit and malice. They are gossips, slanderers, God-haters, insolent, arrogant, and boastful; they invent ways of doing evil; they disobey their parents; they have no understanding, no fidelity, no love, no mercy. Although they know God's righteous decree that those who do such things deserve death, they not only continue to do these very things, but also approve of those who practice them' (Rom. 1:20-32 NIV). Chuck Missler (Missler, Twiligh's Last Gleaming 2000), quoting the ancient words of a centuries-old poem carved into a gothic, medieval alphabet on a towering, ornate cathedral door right in the heart of Lubeck, Germany. Translated into modern English, quotes a frightening poem:

> *You call me eternal, then do not seek me; You call me fair, then do not love me; You call me gracious, then do not trust me; You call me just, then do not fear me; You call me life, then do not choose me; You call me light, then do not see me; You call me Lord, then do not respect me; You call me master, then do not obey me; You call me merciful, then do not thank me; You call me mighty, then do not honor me; You call me noble, then do not serve me; You call me rich, then do not ask me; You call me Savior, then do not praise me; You call me shepherd, then do not follow me; You call me the Way, then do not walk with me; You call me wise, then do not heed me; You call me Son of God, then do not worship me; When I condemn you, then do not blame me.*

I'll just let that marinate in your mind and spirit a little bit.

CHAPTER 27
(AUDACIOUS FAITH)

"LADIES, WHEN YOU LEAVE HERE TO GO BACK TO your families and face the things of this world, understand that you are in this world, but you don't have to be of it; in all things, follow His commandments, and remember, you are a spiritual being having a human experience. In this physical dimension, things are not always as they seem, but know that God is always in control and has made you an active participant to have a choice in His creation, whereupon He has given you dominion over it. Never forget that through prayerful meditation, God hears you and will guide your path. Understand that this earthly vessel in which the Spirit is housed must be in tune with God's frequency, either through His written Word or spiritual revelation. But in all things, I repeat, lean not to personal understanding, but be guided by every word that proceeds out of the mouth of God. Jesus's life in the flesh will serve to be your example. Recognize also that knowing the Word does not insulate you from trouble; there will still come a time in this human experience that you will be attacked, tried, and tempted, even more so now that you know the truth. Satan knows his time is short, and he is afraid, jealous, and angry, and seeks to devour you and people like you; particularly because he does not want you to communicate that truth with others, so he will try to move against you through people under his influence. Understand that you can live in the peace of God, even when you face severe trouble because your peace does not have anything to do with your circumstances. When you live in that kind of peace, your circumstances will automatically get in line. So, put on the full armor of God and you will be equipped to protect yourself. Know that no weapon formed against you will be able to prosper. Speak what you have learned with ultimate confidence, knowing that you are a child of the King; you are worthy, entitled, and able to partake in the full inheritance of Jesus Christ; whereupon your steps are ordered by God and your pathway made clear by the light of His Word. Ladies, we already have God's heart. He seeks ours because He cannot have us completely until He has our heart. Choose God. Give Him your heart; die to self and make His will your will. Now, listen as I read this poem, "The Audacity of Faith," as written by my favorite author and composer, W.T. Barlow, as an example of a certain type of faith; a surrender of will, even unto death:

Not so long ago, or far away; a young man stands in the shadow of death, where a crowd of nonbelievers will judge this sinless man to be guilty, though in the heavens above His Father has already declared His victory. What happened is that after affirming himself to be the promised Son of God, came forth echoes of blasphemy to sway and subvert men's heart. Notwithstanding, he performed diverse miracles that many people had seen, those witnesses were deemed as liars; Sanhedrin with their blinded eyes and hardened hearts would never dub him the Messiah. They spread lies of heresy to scandalize his name and sought death by crucifixion to defame his claim. Then by conspiracy, politics, and ignorance of men, they petitioned a reluctant government to crucify

Him. So, death by this method the verdict would bring, yet they beat Him, whipped Him, and mocked Him a King. Cat o' nine tails, the whip they did wield, though with His stripes, all men are healed. Under the weight of His passion, a battered Jesus cried, forgive them Father, for this reason, I abide, and during the hours of His torture, men were heard to boast, where is your kingdom now? Or was it just a hoax? Yet in fulfillment of His assignment, the Son declared it finished, but men could not comprehend, the accomplishment in it; and as they witnessed His blood-stained cross; Gambling men the lots they did toss; Sanhedrin cheered with raised fist stirred and thought death to be, His just deserve. But from the blood of Jesus, in heaven could be heard, an advocate for mercy, though it was undeserved; and God ever faithful, forgave for Jesus's sake, redeemed men from bondage, and death their looming fate; as sin, love, judgment, and justification are nailed to the Cross; His blood cries for mercy, the Holy Spirit indwells by grace; for the atoning lamb has paid the price, to reconcile men's sin erased. To the risen King be the glory, for His sacrifice so great; to the risen King be the glory, our author and finisher of faith; to the risen King be the glory, the truth, the life, and the way; for He is the Resurrection of men in God's kingdom, no flesh can replicate. Jesus proves all men; the audacity of faith."

Mr. Timmons continues, "Yod Hey Vav Hey (הוהי) I AM that I AM; YAHWEH, the truth, the way, and the life, the author, and finisher of our faith, hallelujah. Understand, ladies, the Crucifixion was not a tragedy, it was an achievement. Jesus was fighting a supernatural battle for our redemption. 'For just as through the disobedience of the one man the many were made sinners, so also through the obedience of the one man the many will be made righteous' (Rom. 5:19 NIV). 'But if the Spirit of Him that raised up Jesus from the dead dwell in you, He that raised up Christ from the dead shall also quicken (make alive) your mortal bodies by His Spirit that dwelleth in you'" (Rom. 8:11 NIV). Mr. Timmons further states, "Ladies, to spotlight the magnitude of Jesus's audacity of faith in obedience to God, there was also something that was especially important that took place." Sanaa inquires, "What was that Mr. Timmons?" Mr. Timmons gives a slight smile and explains, "Remember when Jesus was in the Garden of Gethsemane with some of His disciples, and He told them that He was overwhelmed with sorrow to the point of death?" Toni says, "Yeah, we remember that part." Mr. Timmons continues, "Well, what actually happened was that Jesus was expressing the natural fleshly human desire to avoid the pain and suffering that He must endure. Jesus asked three times in different ways the possibility that the cup (the crucifixion) he was about to partake be passed (taken) from him. What is significant is that Jesus, even though knowing the will of God, did not know the full picture of His sacrifice. God even hid things from Jesus (Himself in the flesh). In my opinion, this magnified a greater audacity of faith, expressed when Jesus declares in total obedience to the Father (though I can't see it, feel it, or comprehend it). Yet not as I will, but as you will. As a result of His obedience contra to that of the first Adam, we have victory in Christ Jesus, who is the example and author of audacious faith. Ladies, understand that irrespective of our fallen nature, we have never been forsaken; we are His children, and we have God's heart, and He so loved the world that he gave His only Son that we might live. So, believe in God audaciously; give Him your heart. He will deliver us as He did Christ Jesus. Listen. I declare and decree that I am crucified with Christ; nevertheless I live, yet not I, but Christ lives within me, and the life that I now live in the flesh,

I live by the faith of the Son of God who loved me first, loved me best, and who gave Himself for me, and as such, has forgiven all my faults, failures, and disobedience. Ladies, greater is Jesus within you than he (Satan) who is in the world. All that Jesus is, is in His Name. All that Jesus did is in His Name. Therefore, you can do all things through God who strengthens you. Ladies, you ask where do you go from here? May I offer a suggestion? With an understanding of the signs of the times prophesied in the Bible pertaining to the last days. Christians with an eye can see with revelation, understand, and take joy in the signs of His coming. Yes, the good news is that Jesus is coming back again very soon. He is going to rule and reign forever. Think of it. There will be no more crying, dying, hate, pain, or sin. It is going to be a never-ending party with the King. However, before that day, people will believe in a great lie and fall away from the truth of God, facilitated through satanic deceptions. A strong delusion will be allowed by God that they would believe this lie. I suggest you take your newfound knowledge and share the love of Jesus Christ with the world; there are still a lot of uninformed souls that need this message. Therefore, likewise as Jesus, we do battle to win souls to God; but first, win your own families to Him. Ensure that your lineage knows and becomes intimate with someone greater than themselves, someone who gave Himself for them, who loves them unconditionally, and who wants the best for their lives. This will give you the practice of patience you will need when speaking to others. Also, remember to guard your tongue with all due diligence. Know that life and death are in the power of your tongue; what comes out of your mouth can go into your future or someone else's future, so be careful what you speak, especially to your children; say what God says. Your words are powerful; they have authority, so when you speak in His will, speak with confidence that what you speak will come to pass, and then SHUT YOUR MOUTH! Never retreat from nor dilute that which was spoken according to God's will. Nurturing your families in the Word is your initial starting place and foundation to build upon, then spread the word to others." Mr. Timmons concludes, saying, "Can you not see that's what I did for you?" Then with a staggering recognition of how Mr. Timmons has changed and transformed their lives, Chrystal starts to tremble, and with tears in her eyes, stands and says, "Thank you, Mr. Timmons. Thank you for teaching me the Word of God and for opening my eyes to understand things I absolutely knew nothing about. Words cannot express how much I appreciate you because, for the first time in my life, I know the truth of where I come from, my sense of morality, the meaning and purpose in my life, and my destiny to live eternally with Christ Jesus. Y'all look at me; there is something deep inside my soul right now that makes me feel whole. I cannot describe it. I just feel complete, and it feels great. Mr. Timmons, I've finally found my glory hallelujah." Toni and Sanaa, now crying, confess to feeling the same way and say they will follow Mr. Timmons's suggestion and start first with guiding their families in the light of what they have learned. Mr. Timmons then cautions the ladies to keep themselves refreshed. He teaches, "It's important that you stay in the Word and continually learn. It will strengthen you in times of trials." Mr. Timmons then pauses and looks at Daedai in reverence and says, "Daedai, blessed woman of God, thank you for bringing in the lost and the needy." Mr. Timmons then embraces Daedai's face with his hands, and gently kisses her on the forehead and says, "You are truly a fisher of men; job well done." Mr. Timmons proudly looks at all his new young Christians and says, "When I look forward, ladies, I need to believe that you have the audacity of faith to break through the predominant philosophy of intersectionality (the delusion of victimization) in this post-truth culture, to help people turn away from the arresting satanic deception in feminism, evolution, homosexuality, fluidity in gender identification, abortion, socialism, deceptiveness in social justice, and the allure of the illuminati. Let me put in your hearing something about this post-truth culture: Abdu Murry (Murray 2018), in his book, *Saving Truth Study Guide: Finding Meaning and Clarity in a Post Truth World,* states, 'Truth is no longer the standard... our preferences in society matter more than truth,' meaning that without a revelation of God's Word, people will only recognize their own 'preferences.' Take, for example, the misguided lie in White privilege, social justice, Black Lives Matter, gender identity, and feminism, all giving rise to a strategy in intersectionality (the fractionalization of society), which is a deceptive strategy for obtaining equality / power through the redistribution of wealth. Understand that in America, most groups that are considered minorities have been swayed to allege systemic racism as a mechanism to redistribute wealth or create division. Institutional racism is best defined as racism perpetrated by government entities. In America, there are multiple governmental acts, executive orders, amendments, and laws that debunk the idea of any institutional racism. So, where are the oppressive chains and shackles? There are none. Don't buy into the lie. The truth is that the genesis of racist allegations is born out of jealousy, class envy, and pride. Racism or social bias in America is only, at best, episodic, not systemic. There is more than enough evidence to substantiate that with hard work and effort, people can have a piece of the American dream. However, the size of that piece is measurable by life's chances in pursuit of happiness. Regrettably, the realization of the American dream for some people has been subverted and swayed by a propagandized delusion of victimization made intersectional by way of certain preferences, which they do not understand is a political strategy used to divide and control the opinion of the masses. So, the question is, what happens when the propaganda leads to a convergence of multiple dueling preferences, and believe me, they will converge. The resulting outcome will ultimately lead to some form of conflict, potentially fostering an unhealthy change in the cultural hegemony, facilitated by him who has the most power, guns, and (or) control of the media. The politics and practice of these dueling preferences will keep people and nations continually at odds with one another, quite possibly leading to societal destruction because truth is subverted by the immense power of the agency supporting its dogma, and that agency will not be revealed, but corruptly manipulate covertly as a hidden puppet master. Milton Freidman (Freidman 2020), noted economist, author, and winner of the Nobel Memorial Prize in Economic Sciences for his research on consumption analysis, monetary history and theory, and the complexity of stabilization policy, recognized: 'A society that puts equality before freedom will get neither. A society that puts freedom before equality will get a high degree of both.' To quote two other great authors, Shelby Steele (Steele 2020), columnist, documentary filmmaker, and a Robert J. and Marion E. Oster Senior Fellow at Stanford University's Hoover Institution writes: 'Since the (alleged) social victim has been oppressed by society; he comes to feel that his individual life will be improved more by changes in society than by his initiative. Without realizing it, he makes society rather than himself the agent of change. The power he finds in his (alleged) victimization may lead him to collective action against society, but it also encourages passivity within the sphere of his personal life.' Moreover, economist Thomas Sowell (Sowell 2020) states succinctly, and I paraphrase [with some people]: 'It takes considerable knowledge [just for them] to realize the extent of [their] own ignorance.' I believe these men are on point with their assessments founded in truth. Chrystal speaks her thoughts, saying, "Wow! Mr. Timmons, that's some great insight." Mr. Timmons continues, "Many people in our society have become slaves to their preferences or predicaments, irrespective of hearing and seeing the truth; they have been conditioned by their feelings and swayed by public opinion, instead of being bound by foundational truths. They do not understand that equality alone does not substantiate freedom; true freedom cannot be realized without established boundaries. There must be a correlative observance of freedom in relationship to established boundaries. Those boundaries are established in God's cherished and invaluable truths, which are often camouflaged and obscured from view by a pack of lies (intersectionality).

For example, when you see politicians or special interest groups change the name of something to euphemize or cover up the political / social impact of the previous name, such as from global warming to climate change; a movement toward financial control and power by way of globalization in pursuit of a one-world government; or illegal aliens to undocumented person: the chipping away and subverting of the rule of law; liberal fascism to Antifa or Black Lives Matter (devil worship): the enforcers of a covert anarchistic movement that is divisive in its agenda, financed through an immense financially powerful cabal that is international in scope, generational in planning, and incredibly evil in intent. Ladies, God's Word is the only panacea for everything that ails nations; it annihilates all deception. It is the unifying force for all men, and it is sufficient for all instruction. Knowing that we are all sinners in need of a savior, the Creator, our loving Father, who designed the blueprint of our human condition, totally knows the full range of our vulnerabilities, and has provided for us His only Son to be our light in the darkness, within the hope and promise that is in Christ Jesus. So, be audacious when spreading God's truth, knowing that this post-truth culture can be redirected. The truth will serve as a strong cleansing agent of change, causing a boomerang effect against those evil spirits that are propagating deceptions. Just spread God's Word and pray and fast for His intervening guidance. Help people understand that the greatest innocuous freedom they can possess is in the loving parameters established in God's Word. It is not for Him; it is for them. God investigates the future and knows the direction they are headed, and like a good parent, He imparts wisdom to His children so that they will not be deceived and corrupted. People need to learn that clinging to every word that proceeds out of the mouth of God is the only truth and path that they must seek because the deceptions proliferating in our toxic post-truth culture by way of atheistic organizations, leading people to believe that they are the manifestation of an evolved enlightened consciousness, puts them unwittingly in a position of acting as or trying to be as God. They will need to learn that there is someone greater than themselves. He is the one who created all things, the one who gave of Himself to die in their place, proving His love for them. When they take hold of this understanding, they will develop confidence in the hope of a life eternal by putting their trust in God and leaning not unto their own understanding (feelings). However, ladies, breaking through with this kind of message will require unrelenting diligence, persistence, patience, and perseverance." The ladies, recognizing this truth, breathe deeply and nod their heads in agreement. Mr. Timmons further offers, "'You will experience trouble on every side, but you will not be crushed; you will be perplexed, but not driven to despair; you will be persecuted, but not abandoned; you will be knocked down, but not destroyed, always carrying around in your body the death of Jesus, so that the life of Jesus may also be made visible in your body. For we who are alive are constantly being handed over to death for Jesus' sake, so that the life of Jesus may also be made visible in our mortal body...' (2 Cor. 4:8-12 NIV) Ladies, I believe you can do this. I believe you can make a difference, so like my Father, I'm declaring the ending from the beginning. I declare and pray that you will have, the audacity of faith, to break through and help save the lost and the needy; the audacity of faith to always put God first; the audacity of faith to continue sharing with others His inherent Word; the audacity of faith to persistently pursue wisdom and understanding in the word; the audacity of faith to never let go of God's Word, no matter what your eyes will see, your ears will hear, or your feelings might be; the audacity of faith, to always speak truth to power; the audacity of faith to speak the truth, even when those you love act against you, threaten you, or desert you; the audacity of faith to keep doing what is right, even when you believe His voice has gone silent and the way forward is not readily apparent; the audacity of faith to know that whatever your circumstances, God loves you and will never leave you, nor forsake you; the audacity of faith, not fearing to stand alone, even in the face of hostile opposition to what you believe; the audacity of faith, even when eclipsed by rejection, you keep love in your heart, loving people as Christ loves you; the audacity of faith-if standing in the shadow of death, you fear no evil, knowing that you reside under the shadow of the Almighty, and that you are not alone, for you know He is with you. Ladies, I see it, and I declare it. It is finished. With this understanding, let us pray to our God. I pray that God bless you and keep you; make His face to shine upon you; be gracious unto you; lift up His countenance upon you and give you peace. Now, go forth with a renewed mind and confidence in your purpose. Amen. If you need me, just call; class is dismissed, but your journey has just begun; remember, your success resides within your boldness of faith." The women say their goodbyes to Mr. Timmons and head back to Daedai's house. On the way, the women briefly share their experiences from the seven days. Smiling and feeling good all over, Toni says, "Daedai, I think we found what you have; and now we have it." Flashing a big smile and nodding her head in the affirmative, Daedai, under her breath, praisingly says, "Thank you, Jesus." The next morning, before the ladies are ready to return home, they conversate for a while, and then overcome with emotion from seeing her friend's Christian conversion, Daedai begins to teach and encourage them through God's Word, saying:

... teach what is appropriate to sound doctrine. Teach the older men to be temperate, worthy of respect, self-controlled, and sound in faith, in love and in endurance. Likewise, teach the older women to be reverent in the way they live, not to be slanderers or addicted to much wine, but to teach what is good. Then they can urge the younger women to love their husbands and children, to be self-controlled and pure, to be busy at home, to be kind, and to be subject to their husbands, so that no one will malign the word of God. Similarly, encourage the young men to be self-controlled. In everything set them an example by doing what is good. In your teaching show integrity, seriousness and soundness of speech that cannot be condemned, so that those who oppose you may be ashamed because they have nothing bad to say about us... For the grace of God has appeared that suggests salvation to all people. It teaches us to say "No" to ungodliness and worldly passions, and to live self-controlled, upright and godly lives in this present age, while we wait for the blessed hope—the appearing of the glory of our great God and Savior, Jesus Christ, who gave himself for us to redeem us from all wickedness and to purify for himself a people that are his very own, eager to do what is good. These, then, are the things you should teach. Encourage and rebuke with all authority. Do not let anyone despise you" (Titus 2 NIV).

The women are moved to tears by Daedai's teaching. They hug and thank Daedai for everything she has done for them. They recall the memory of their friend Raven, wishing she could have been with them as they pray together. After they finish praying, Daedai can sense the apprehension they feel in going home with their renewed mindset. In order to rebuke the spirit of apprehension, Daedai shouts loudly, "You plus God is a majority. If God is for you, who in the world can stand against you? Now go home and show your stuff." The ladies, hearing a confident Daedai, receive her confidence, and feeling the love, they manage a smile and are now more relaxed. They say their goodbyes and Daedai drives them to the airport for their trip home. Daedai pulls into the airport departure lane, and before they leave the car, Daedai tells them that if they need her, call. They say they will, and they leave the car, headed to their individual destinations.

CHAPTER 28
(THE TRANSFORMATION)

WHEN THE GIRLS REACH HOME, THEIR HUSBANDS notice an immediate and significant difference, starting with Sanaa. Jordan is surprised when she walks through the door, and she has this glow on her being. He does not say anything; he just looks at her speechless, and notices that she is extremely different. She comes in the house, saying, "Hey baby, I love you." Jordan's eyelids immediately flip up to a raised brow, surprised with this humbling show of affection. He immediately thinks to himself, *damn, she said I love you the way she did when we were in college.* Jordan then stares at Sanaa playing with the kids with a perplexed and skeptical look on his face. He searches his thoughts, trying to figure out what the hell is going on. Jordan thinks in his mind, *something has got to be up because she's submitting to me, and that ain't Sanaa.* It seems as though something in Sanaa's attitude has magically changed the atmosphere in his house, and not understanding how this is taking place, Jordan goes into the bedroom and calls Tyson. Tyson picks up and says, "Yo, what's up, bruh?" Quick and precisely to the point, Jordan asks, "Hey, man, Chrystal made it back yet?" Tyson says, "Yeah, why?" Jordan says, "I don't actually know how to ask you this, but does Chrystal seem different to you?" Acting anxiously excited and captivated by what Jordan is asking, Tyson replies, "Whoa!

Whoa! Jordan, I wasn't going to say anything about this man, but since you asked, Chrystal has been acting a lot differently, bruh. Since she got back, I don't know what's going on with her; I didn't say anything, but it's like the woman who left is not the same woman who came back. When she walked in the house a couple of days ago, the girls and I were at the dining room table horsing around, and Jordan, when I looked at her, you going to think I'm crazy, but she had some kind of a glow on her. Now, the first thing running through my mind was that she was having an affair or something; you know what I'm talking about; that look of calm right before the storm; that big sign that Jodi got your girl and gone, right? However, her attitude toward me and the children after she settled in didn't comport with someone having an affair, so I paid it no mind until you called. Do you know something I need to know, bruh?" Jordan is quiet over the phone, astonished that Tyson is describing the same changes in Chrystal that he has witnessed in Sanaa. Jordan slowly says, "Nah, man, I don't know nothing, but all I can say is that the very same changes you are seeing happening with Chrystal I'm seeing happening with Sanaa, and I don't understand it either. Sanaa came in the house pleasantly different. I mean, totally opposite of the Mrs. Wonder woman DA prosecutor of all crazy-lazy low-life chauvinistic men; you know what I'm talking about, man." Tyson understandingly replies, "I hear you, man." Jordan then inquires, "I wonder what happened to them at Daedai's house?" With a mystified expression on his face, Tyson says, "I don't know man, but to tell you the truth, I like this new attitude." Jordan quickly asserts, "Me too, man; me too, but I'm still a little worried about this all-of-a-sudden new change in attitude." Jordan ponders about it for a minute and then says, "Hey, Tyson, let's get Carlton on the phone and see what he knows." Tyson nods his head in the affirmative and says, "Alright, I'm up with that." In the process of engaging the call, Jordan says, "Hold on a minute; let me get this three-way line working. Jordan then punches in some digits on his phone, and after the connection is made, Jordan hears the phone ringing, and Carlton picks up, saying, "Hey, what's up, man?" Jordan answers, "Nothing, man, just work; how about with you?" Carlton, in his usual suave manner, says, "Just chill'n, baby." Jordan then calmly asks, "Carlton, is Toni back home from Daedai's house?" Carlton answers curiously, "Yeah, why? Your people not home?" Then Tyson anxiously comes online and says, "Carlton, this is Tyson. We're on a three-way line, man. Hey, look, is Toni acting funny, or is there something about her that has changed since she's come back home?" Carlton says, "Oh, yeah, man. I see something; y'all know about something going on? Because she's acting...I don't know how to put this, man, but it's like she's acting overly wifely, if that's a word. Right now, she acts like when we first got married, and I'm liking it!" Tyson comes back, "Carlton, we called because Sanaa and Chrystal are acting the same way. Look, man, something had to have happened to them at Daedai's house. That was the last place they were before this dramatic change. Check this, guys, whatever happened with our wives took place at Daedai's house." Jordan says, "Carlton, don't get me wrong; I like this change too, man. I can truthfully say that it's a saving grace for me and Sanaa's relationship. However, I still think I need to find out what's going on with her. But for right now, I'm staying cool. I'm holding my peace, trying to let this thing play out, but I'm hoping she'll eventually share with me what's going on with her. Now If I find out anything, I'll let you guys know, ok, and if you find out anything, you contact me, alright?" All the guys happily agree and then they hang up. Jordan pauses after putting away his phone and thinks introspectively for a minute as he listens to Sanaa in the next room playing with the kids. Jordan shrugs his shoulders in submission to not knowing, and walks slowly to the bedroom door where he can see Sanaa and the kids just absolutely going crazy. Jordan smiles lovingly, and then joins in the fun with his family. In the coming days, weeks, and months, as suggested by Mr. Timmons, Sanaa, Chrystal, and Toni, commit themselves to slowly bringing their families into the knowledge of God by having family meetings and one-on-one sessions, teaching, preaching, and pouring into their spirits what had been revealed to them through Mr. Timmons. The big hurdle, however, was getting their husbands to agree to participate in their newly-found revelation. But, after Jordan, Tyson, and Carlton, get an explanation about the genesis of their wives' sudden lifestyle change, they all buy into what their wives are trying to do, and everything else just falls into place. After a time seeing and enjoying the reforming differ-ence they had made in their homes, the women knew in their spirit that they would eventually have to take care of some unfinished business with the sisterhood. After contemplating over the situation with full understanding of the major chal-lenges that would be involved, Chrystal, succumbing to a bur-dened heart over the matter, decides to take the lead initiative and call the founding members to discuss reforming the sister-hood. Chrystal manages to get everyone on Zoom for a meeting and asks, "How's everybody doing?" Everybody says their col-lective hellos, and for ten minutes, the women vigorously engage in chit-chat with the usual small talk until Chrystal forcefully interrupts the conversation, shouting, "Ladies! Listen to me for a minute. For some time now, I've been thinking about the Diva Pack Sisterhood, and I think now is the time that we revisit and reform this monster we've created. What do you think?" With a big smile on her face, Sanaa says, "Chrystal, you must have been reading my mind because I've constantly thought about trying to do something with the sis-terhood ever since we left Mr. Timmons. So yeah, I'm all aboard with trying to reach them." Sanaa and Chrystal advise Daedai and Toni that they would take on the responsibility to talk with the graduate sisters and college campus members to feel them out. Sanaa and Chrystal's efforts to get a sense of how amenable the sisterhood would be to changing a few things soon became a rumor / alert throughout the organization that the founding members were attempting to change the mandate of the Diva Pack Sisterhood. Steeply allied with feminist organizations, the graduate members of the Sisterhood decided amongst themselves that what was being proposed by the founding members was not in keeping with how they viewed the organization. With that attitude, the founder member's initial attempt to bring about change was met with serious opposition. These resolute graduate chapter women were conditioned to the status quo and argued vigorously against any changes. Not liking what the founding members were doing, the officers of the graduate chapters decided to initially mail letters to the founding members, advising them to cease and desist from trying to influence graduate and campus organizations with crazy religious messages. When that didn't work, the graduate members went so far as to collude and conspire against the founding members by making personal visits to all campuses to encourage the sisters not to listen to them. Moreover, to subvert the founding members' message, the graduate members secretly started telling the campus sisters that the founding members went to an occult resort, and the people at the resort brainwashed them with some kind of mystic / religious stuff, and now they've come back to the sisterhood, trying to change things to fit that occult message. The graduate members impressed upon the campus sisters to always treat the founding members with respect; however, take what they have to say with a grain of salt because they've been influenced by an occultist movement. They would advise the campus sisters that if the founding members approached them-remember they are brainwashed with some crazy religious stuff, so just pacify the founding members with a smile, act like you're listening to what they have to say and move on. The graduate sisters convinced the campus sisters that what the founding members are trying to present will eventually dwindle down to nothing but foolishness, so there is no need to worry or argue; the sister-hood is tightly knit. They advised also that they would be fiercely fighting against them at the graduate level. However, irrespective of all the graduate sisters' planning and strategic propaganda, they underestimated the fierce and relentless effort by the founding sisters to implement their message of change. The founding members would not give up or give in; they were determined. The founding members persistently pushed forward with their agenda of change and asked that the campus sisters be allowed to hear what they had to say and make their own decisions. The graduate members reluc-tantly agreed to their terms because they felt confident that they had secretly sabotaged the founding members' momentum. However, Sanaa, Chrystal, Toni, and Daedai, having many ears to the ground on campus, were informed how the graduate chapters were trying to undermine their message. A few of the campus sisters were telling the founding members what the graduate sisters were up to. So, Sanaa, Chrystal, Toni, and Daedai, in receiving the particulars of this devious plot, confronted the graduate sisters with an ulti-matum, declaring that under the current mandate in use by the sisterhood, they could no longer serve as the founding members of record, and would disavow publicly any relation-ship with the organization unless there is a change in the man-date. The graduate members, totally aware of the founding members' clout, quickly realized the potential for the loss of membership, and as a result of this ultimatum, conceded to allowing them to present their proposed changes. However, the graduate sisters felt confident in the belief that the mes-sage of the founding members could not possibly survive under intense scrutiny. Also, reluctantly, the graduate mem-bers agreed that the founding members could participate in campus meetings to present their message. With this conces-sion, the founding members went to work strategizing on how to make a presentation to people who do not understand the wisdom of God. Sanaa contemplates for a minute and then suggests, "The best way to start, I think, is to share our life stories and the roadblocks we faced in pursuit of what we thought would lead to a happy life." In a heartfelt tone, Toni says, "I can share Raven's story in wrongly trying to follow the Diva Pack playbook." Chrystal nods her head in the affirmative and comments, "That will be good, Toni, and to show how we have been transformed, we can all share the story of how Daedai introduced us to Mr. Timmons, who gave us the word of truth that changed our lives. Within the wisdom of her spirit, Daedai decrees, "With the four of us agreeing and sharing the same wisdom in our message, we will put forth a powerful message to bring about change." We can use the same indoctrination process as Mr. Timmons used for us; however, we will have to make our presentations in a much shorter timeframe, taking into consideration the members' school and personal schedules. I think this is a good and righteous thing that we do, but it has to be done effectively. We still need to come up with a way to get all the sisters together in the same place and at the same time." Toni excitedly interjects, "Hey, ladies, we got the Diva Pack tri-annual meeting coming up in a couple of months, and everybody should be in attendance then. So whatever we are going do, we need to plan to do it at that meeting." Chrystal suggests, "Let's set up a pre-tri-annual meeting of select Diva Pack graduates and campus officers, to prime them for what we are going to present at the meeting." Everybody agrees, so in preparation for the meeting, the ladies Zoom meet with Mr. Timmons and ask how he thinks they should go about making their presentation. Calmly, but in a serene tone, as usual, Mr. Timmons indirectly answers their question, saying, "Those who have an ear to hear, will; those who don't, won't." Toni anxiously comes back, "Mr. Timmons, that's it, that's all you have to say?" Then Sanaa jumps in with a sarcastic tone, "Oh gee, well thank you very much, Mr. Timmons, you've been a great help. Do you have any idea what we're up against here?" Mr. Timmons politely answers, "I shall repeat what I said again for those of you who have slow comprehension. Those who have an ear to hear, will; those who do not, will not. Preach the Word, women of God, and leave everything else to the Father." Mr. Timmons pauses for a minute, "Ladies, you have not been given a spirit of fear, but of power, love and a sound mind." And then he says, "'I charge you in the presence of God and of Christ Jesus, who will judge the living and the dead, and because of His appearing and His kingdom: Preach the word; be prepared in season and out of season; reprove, rebuke, and encourage with every form of patient instruction' (2 Tim. 4:1, 2 ESV). Again, I say, preach the Word, women of God, and leave everything else to the Father." Daedai quickly interjects and says, "Mr. Timmons, I get what you are saying. I will explain it to my girlfriends later. You have a great day, and we will talk to you very soon." After Mr. Timmons signs off, Daedai breathes in and exhales in disappointment with her sisters, and says, "What Mr. Timmons was saying is that God's Word is sufficient; notwithstanding, everybody will not come aboard with us. I know we think that we are these high-powered super-anointed women of God on a mission, but some will not believe, no matter what we say or do. So, we will do as Mr. Timmons says, "Preach the Word of God, and leave everything else to the Father; that is our mission. The ladies, being reproved, nod their heads in silent affirmation, and now in a more relaxed tone, Toni asks, "Alright, now what chronological framework are we going to present our message?" Chrystal suggests, "Within the timeframe we've been allotted, we speak about our transformation relative to learning the Word of God and the treasures of His wisdom. We speak on how we had been miseducated to believe in things of this world that were untrue. Finally, and most importantly, we speak about the awesome change that took place within us personally, and how our lives and our marriages were changed for the better as a result of learning, believing, and obeying the Word of God." The ladies all agree that that would be the best way to proceed. They say their goodbyes, and they all start working on their individual pre-sentations. After weeks of preparation, the ladies are now ready to give their message, and have included Mr. Timmons as their special guest speaker. No doubt, they are all nervous with anticipation of the meeting because it doesn't take a rocket scientist to surmise that there exists cognitive disso-nance on behalf of the sisterhood to what they propose. Enthused and encouraged by the seriousness in preparation his wife Chrystal and the ladies are putting into their project, Tyson is motivated with an idea. He decides to call Jordan and Carlton on a three-way line, and when they pick up, he asks, "What's going on, fellas?" Jordan and Carlton answer, "Nothing much, man, how about yourself?" Tyson says, "The same old, man, you know." Then Tyson pauses for a minute and forcibly says, "Look, you guys know from school all about the Diva Pack Sisterhood, right, and I know damn well y'all know the crazy things they were doing to people at the school. Now, our wives started this organization, and now because of their religious convictions, they are seriously trying to do the right thing in helping their sisters understand the flaws in the Diva Pack play-book. They don't want these girls to make the same mistakes they made trying to live up to the sisterhood's ugly, misguided philosophy. So, in recognition of this good thing my wife is trying to do, I'm just calling to let you guys know that I will be going to this meeting with her for moral support, so how about you guys?" Carlton says, "Hum, I did think about it for a minute, but I hadn't planned on going, well, at least not until now. No doubt, I think I need to be there too, man." Jordan then breaks in and responds, "Look, with the changes I've seen in my wife, I mean, loving on me and the children like she's doing, nothing in this world could stop me from going and standing with my wife. So, I guess we'll all get together at this meeting, right?" The husbands all agree and hang up.

About three days later, my wife Chrystal, in preparing for the meeting, makes one last phone call to her sisters to organize inflight pick-ups and confirm room reservations at the Knight Center in Miami. It's the hotel site where the organization will be having its tri-annual meeting. Chrystal and I arrive early from Orlando and get together with Jordan and Sanaa to make sure that everything is set up at the hotel a day before the meeting. After Chrystal and I pick up Toni and Carlton from the airport, coming in from Atlanta, and later going back to pick up Daedai, Dr. Ewing, and Mr. Timmons, coming in from Virginia, we take them straight to the hotel and get everybody settled in. Chrystal asks everyone to come down to the foyer at about 3:00 pm to go over the entire presentation. After everyone in our group comes down to the foyer, we immediately indulge ourselves in conversation. Mr. Timmons is the last part of the group to come down, and all of us greet him with much-deserved respect. Carlton, Jordan, the sisters, and I make sure that Mr. Timmons and Dr. Ewing know that they will not have to pay for anything at the hotel. After allowing for brief catch-up conversations amongst old friends, Chrystal huddles everyone together and asks that the group of presenters engage in a dry run. She advises that the lineup for tomorrow's meeting will be Sanaa, Toni, Daedai, and Mr. Timmons going mid-program, then ending with her. After my wife's group is feeling comfortable with their presentation, knowing in their hearts they have put forth the Word of God, we disburse and agree to meet in the morning for breakfast and then come back together one hour before the presentation. The next morning, Chrystal and I go down to the dining area and have breakfast with our group, and Mr. Timmons notices that the wives are a little nervous, and he calls for their attention and says, "Ladies, be bold in your delivery; remember the audacity of faith we talked about, especially in numbers ten through eleven: 'I will have the audacity of faith, not fearing to stand alone, even in the face of hostile opposition to what I believe' and 'the audacity of faith: even when eclipsed by rejection, I will keep love in my heart, loving people, as Christ loves me.' So, ladies, preach with boldness the inherent Word of God, and leave everything else to the Father. His thoughts are not our thoughts, neither are our ways His ways." With that word of wisdom, Chrystal says, "Thank you, Mr. Timmons, I think we got it. Now, everybody, get yourself a little rest, and we will meet back in front of the conference room an hour before the start of the conference." As Chrystal and I enter the elevator to go up to our room, she turns to me and says, "I love you." As I confirm to my wife that I love her too, I think to myself, *Wow, just nine months ago, we didn't even know where we were headed in our marriage, much less confessing our love for one another, and look at us now; we're in great harmony, hugging and kissing all the time; what a change God has made in our lives. Like most women attorneys, my wife is extremely competitive and comes off hard to the core, and I know as part of her legal training and personality, she doesn't back down from anything, which was a major part of our problem; talk about 'women, submit yourselves to your husband.' At times, it was hard to even get a good compromise out of her. But, my God, what a change You have made in my wife. Chrystal has always been brilliant, witty, and a serious thinker, but now, added to that, she has again become my best friend and that precious jewel, which they talk about in the Bible. I have anchored myself with a godly woman. God, I thank You because she's the best thing that has ever happened to me.* As we get off the elevator and walk to our room, I can't hide this euphoric smile on my face as I look at my wife in awe and amazement. Later, after a short rest period which was so relaxing we didn't want to get up, but after thinking about our mission, Chrystal and I put on our game faces and walk to the elevator, headed down to the conference room. As we walk and get closer to the conference room area, we can see the registration table and all the Diva Pack sisters gathered around, engaged in a meet and greet. Looking through the crowd of people, Chrystal points to Jordan and Sanaa, standing near the wall opposite the registration table; with them are the other members of the presenter group. When Chrystal and I finally reach our people, Sanaa suggests that we walk around and find a little private area where we can discuss the presentation and say a word of prayer. We find our little space about twenty yards away from the conference room entrance. We take about ten minutes to do some thinking over our topics, and about eight minutes later, the Diva Pack sisters hanging outside in front of the lobby area now start entering the conference room. Mr. Timmons then puts forth one of the most intense motivational statements I've ever heard. Mr. Timmons solidifies the mission as he reads from an anonymous African pastor who was going to be killed if he did not deny Jesus Christ, and as he went to his death, this statement was nailed to his wall. Mr. Timmons quotes with heartfelt passion, saying,

> *I'm part of the fellowship of the unashamed. I have Holy Spirit power. The die has been cast. I have stepped over the line. The decision has been made. I'm a disciple of His. I won't look back, let up, slow down, back away, or be still. My past is redeemed, my present makes sense, and my future is secure... I will not flinch in the face of sacrifice, hesitate in the presence of the adversary, negotiate at the table of the enemy, ponder at the pool of popularity, or meander in the maze of mediocracy. I won't give up, shut up, or let up until I have stayed up, stored up, prayed up, paid up, and preached up for the cause of Christ...* (Missler, Anti-Christ Session 6 2020)

After making this impassioned decree, Mr. Timmons continues, "We are like a tree planted by streams of water that yields its fruit in its season, and its leaf does not wither. In all that we do, we prosper." And he further states, "'Trust in the Lord and do good; dwell in the land and befriend faithfulness. Delight yourself in the Lord, and he will give you the desires of your heart. Commit your way to the Lord; trust in him, and he will act'" (Ps. 37:3–5 ESV).

"Ladies, I believe that you have that audacity of faith, not fearing to stand alone, even in the face of hostile opposition to what you believe. You have that audacity of faith; even when eclipsed by rejection, you keep love in your heart, loving people as Christ loves you. Women of God, go and change this organization for the better." With this encouragement, our wives and Mr. Timmons enter that conference room, and as for Jordan, Carlton, Dr. Ewing, and I, we sit outside and try to listen in on what is going on inside. I could not help but be intrusive and pull one of the chairs from the registration table and sit right next to the conference room door. After listening intensely for about twenty-five minutes of Diva Pack Sisterhood programming, I hear that it's time for our wives and Mr. Timmons to make their presentations. With the host announcing that the founding four members come forward, there is a hush from the crowd, followed by a lackluster applause given to our wives and Mr. Timmons. Nonetheless, Sanaa steps to the podium and comes out the gate fearless and strong, blasting the Word of God, and then forcefully giving an intense talk about her horrible experiences trying to live up to the principles within the Diva Pack Sisterhood that she herself created. She also railed against the feminist movement and their toxic agenda as she tries to convince her listeners that what they stand for is antithetical to God's original intent for mankind. From then on, as the founding members step to the podium, it was like the old folks used to say, "It was on like a pot of neck bones." With tears in her eyes, Toni commenced to tell Raven's story with boldness and so much love in her heart for her fallen sister; and then she strongly urges the women not to follow in Raven's footsteps, and she tries her best to make them understand that the knowledge and revelation of Jesus Christ is what they need to pursue. Toni shares with her sisters that working as a biochemical scientist, she had problems believing in a God that she could not see or quantify until after watching her husband, her then college boyfriend, get shot, die, and then be miraculously brought back to life by a praying grandmother. Toni then says in trembling voice, "When I saw all of this happen, I was confused for years. But after being taught the awesome power in the Word of God, you can't tell me that my God isn't real; moreover, I can also testify that I have visibly seen the power of His Word work within my marriage, transforming from what was a volatile relationship into a refuge of love and harmony. So, I urge you to follow the Word of God. He will bring peace into your life; this is the truth, ladies." Up next, Daedai spoke very scholarly in delivering the truth of her not too amiable life's story. She reminded her sisters that she was not always filled with the Spirit and seeking to be the wife of a preacher. Daedai confides, stating, "I know you've all heard stories of how I used to behave in college; full of pride, mouth like a sailor, and ready to fight at the drop of the slightest insult. But look at me now; thank You, Lord. Look at me now, a totally transformed person. I tell you the truth, it happens only by having a revelation of who you are and whose you are in Christ Jesus." Then Daedai shared Mr. Timmons's story of repentance and redemption as she introduced him as their special guest speaker. Mr. Timmons's delivery and presentation definitely did not disappoint. He astounded the conference attendees with his Christian apologetics and scientific acumen as he spoke on the spiritual things of God and the empirical evidence of things related to science within the Bible, advising these women that before science or scientists existed, God is. The audience was so intrigued and focused on Mr. Timmons's presentation that you could hear a pin drop as he taught the wisdom of truth in the Word of God. Then my wife Chrystal, bringing up the rear, put forth a powerful message with a plea for the transformation of the Diva Pack Sisterhood. She called for the members to denounce the written Sisterhood Pact and that agreement sealed in blood they had made. She shared with the conferees information that Mr. Timmons taught her about covenants, altars, generational curses, and demonic spirits, particularly a marine spirit, an evil deity called "Mami Wata." Chrystal shared, saying, "Mr. Timmons became aware of the influence of this evil spirit after examining the generational nature of his ex-wife's family, and some in his own family, seeing that mostly all of the women and men in his and her family had multiple adulterous affairs, and with the women in her family having multiple children out of wedlock from different men. He also discovered that a majority of the women in both families would always try to be the dominant vessel in the relationship, and both men and women had a propensity toward never completing anything. Chrystal looks out into the audience and asks, "Does this sound familiar to anyone in your family?" Chrystal continues saying, "Through Mr. Timmons's research of demonic spirits, he learned that both his and his ex-wife's problems were generational, due to having what he learned was a curse coming from having a spiritual wife or spiritual husband; these are powerful evil marine spirits called Incubus: a male demon believed to have sexual intercourse with sleeping women, and Succubus: a female demon believed to have sexual intercourse with sleeping men. As it relates to a covenant with these demonic spirits, Zita Grant (Grant 2017) offers information about this powerful evil deity, saying, '...She or he (Incubus or Succubus) can bring good fortune in the form of money for those in agreement (covenant) with her or him.' However, Chrystal warns that with any demonic or satanic covenant, agreeing with or receiving anything from them wittingly or unwittingly will inevitably lead to a tortured or destructive end. Chrystal passionately asserts that the blood covenant and philosophy in the Diva Pack Sisterhood Pact emulates the philosophy behind the feminist movement; it resembles or mirrors that of being motivated by a Mami Wata spirit, having the evil intent of fostering and perpetuating the transference of power and wealth from men to the dominance of women, changing the gender hegemony in direct contradiction to God's intent for men and women." Again, citing Zita Grant (Grant 2017), Chrystal says, "These type of patterns in dreams like getting married, wet dreams, being pregnant, giving birth, swimming, or seeing bodies of water in a dream, or even if you reflect on your life and note that there has been at least one of the following: miscarriage, impotence, financial failures, hardship (no matter how much you work, you cannot get ahead) ..." Chrystal pauses as she looks around the audience and says, "These are probable signs of a marine spirit oppressing your life. I know this is difficult for you to believe, but these spirits are real, and those dreams and or generational patterns should not be overlooked, but you can be delivered form these evil deities." As Chrystal looks at the crowd, she sees fear in the eyes of some of those who can relate to the patterns of generational curses or the dreams she has mentioned. Chrystal continues saying, "God commands that the head of the woman is the man, and the head of the man is Jesus Christ, and the head of Jesus Christ is the Father." Chrystal further offers that this demonic spirit, particularly for women, is a spirit of manipulation, and its approach is very subtle, making entry by way of human vulnerabilities; it beguiles women into thinking they don't need a man, and women lacking in understanding, who live and work fostering this misguided attitude, never find the balance in their lives that men bring to a woman and the family. The result is a breach in the sustainability of the nuclear family and (or) an unfulfilled relationship in marriage, by disrespecting the distinctive characteristics that God has created in men and women. Believe me, I've seen it. I've lived it; survived the crisis, and got a t-short to prove it." Chrystal then hammers and slams these women with the truth for about another twenty minutes, declaring the need for an attitude adjustment. She asserts a need for an alignment to the wisdom of God, and when she finishes, there's an eerie silence, demonstrating great cognitive dissonance to her message.

When the conference host comes to the podium to acknowledge and thank our wives (the founding four members) for their inspirational message, the applause is lackluster, and after that reception, our wives and Mr. Timmons immediately exit through the conference room doors, and as we stand up to receive them, I can see the look of disappointment on our wives' faces. I could tell they thought they had failed to convince the sisterhood that the Diva Pack way of life is a means to a destructive end. Mr. Timmons, sensing their disappointment, says, "Ladies, ladies, never frown on small beginnings; the acorn is an exceedingly small seed, but, 'Oh my!' can be heard when one marvel's at the oak tree that the seed produces at maturity. Ladies, our job was to plant seeds and then watch God the Father do His thing. Jesus told a parable to His disciples-the parable of the sower. 'A farmer went out to sow his seed. As he was scattering the seed, some fell along the path, and the birds came and ate it up. Some fell on rocky places, where it did not have much soil. It sprang up quickly because the soil was shallow. But when the sun came up, the plants were scorched, and they withered because they had no root. Other seed fell among thorns, which grew up and choked the plants so that they did not bear grain. Still, other seed fell on good soil. It came up, grew and produced a crop, some multiplying thirty, some sixty, some a hundred times'" (Mark 4:3-8 NIV). Mr. Timmons stares intently at his friends and says, "It's like I told you earlier: those who have an ear (heart) to hear, will; those who do not, will not. Ladies (farmers), you did exceptionally well; you added works to your faith; now use faith to affect your works; let God be true and all men a liar." At first, I did not understand what Mr. Timmons was talking about because it was clear to me and the guys that my wife Chrystal and her sisters were facing an uphill battle. All I could see was that the graduate sisters were resolute in not allowing the changes that our wives were demanding. However, understanding exactly what Mr. Timmons was saying, Chrystal, Daedai, Sanaa, and Toni became noticeably confident and unwavering in their demands. After multiple engagements with the organization, and a couple of years gone by with our wives still meeting with campus Diva Pack groups, preaching their message, and sharing their stories, eventually, to my surprise, Mr. Timmons would be proven right about the parable he had shared with us at the conference. Some really did hear the Word, and I know from the way the Diva Pack Sisterhood has changed, some did produce as he spoke of in the parable. At first, the guys and I were cautious to believe it. But the evidence was clear to me when seeing the once infamous Diva Pack shorten their name to just the Sisterhood, and then dismiss that twelve-step pact and the agreement in blood they used to make. All of the rituals were pulled out of the initiation; gone forever. Then I knew for certain our wives had done it; against all kinds of adversity and rejection, they stood bold in their faith, kept love in their hearts, and transformed the Diva Pack Sisterhood. How about that! These days, the Sisterhood aligns themselves with the wisdom and knowledge of God, believing in the promise that is in Christ Jesus. The Sisterhood, at present, behaves totally different from the way they used to; they have become noticeably visible on campus, engaged in all forms of charitable projects, letting their good light shine. Believe me, I have witnessed it. What they are doing is for real; it's from the heart, and not some calculated outreach projects to collect quality points for notoriety. Their passion for doing the many things they are doing is real, and people appreciate them. Some of the old heads from the graduate chapters, after seeing the progress of the new Sisterhood, finally surrender to the transformation epidemic and decided to participate with a surprisingly new attitude. So, at the end of the day, there it is: proof that you can teach an old dog new tricks. Chrystal, Daedai, Sanaa, and Toni are always on Zoom, talking about what God has done with the Diva Pack Sisterhood, and they give Him all the glory before they all start bragging about the work they did or are going to do with the campus sisters. I enjoy seeing my wife happy like this. It makes me feel good. So, with assistance from my wife Chrystal and Pastor Ewing, I pushed myself to start digging deeper into the Word of God. One year later, after getting off the phone with Chrystal driving home from the office, I started mumbling, rambling on, praying, and thinking out loud to myself, and then I just started praising right out of nowhere, saying, "I thank You, Lord, for changing me, my wife, my children, and my whole life. Then all of a sudden, I had a thought: if my wife and her sisters can change an organization like the Diva Pack Sisterhood, then I think my guys and I can do something even bigger than that. So, I started thinking to myself, *why not?* For greater is He in me than he who us in the world, right? Man, If God can change my wife, her friends, and the Diva Pack Sisterhood, God can change anything and anybody. I know this because I have seen His work up close and personal. God is the only person who can reform the hearts of men and women. Anybody who needs it or wants it can bank on it because the transaction has already taken place in heaven. It's like Jesus says: He is the truth, the way, and the life, and I reflect on all the things my wife and I have been through, and reflecting back on my college years with all the fornication and sinful things I used to do. I remember back at the conference, when Mr. Timmons was talking to me and the guys about soul hunters, and how our lives can be fragmented through people and evil spirits attempting to steal our destinies and even take our lives. What really scared me was when he said that when you sleep with someone in a dream or in real life, or you have sex with multiple partners in dreams or even in real life, your soul has now become fragmented by everyone or every evil spirit (in dreams) with whom you have had a sexual encounter. Your soul is fragmented with you possessing a part of them and them possessing a part of you. It is in the mystery of becoming one flesh reserved only for married couples; it's a covenant which has to be honored. While Mr. Timmons is talking, I see my boy Jordan swallow deeply in his throat hearing what is being taught, and I can read his thoughts without him saying a word. We look at each other with fear in our eyes, and we were both convicted by the words coming out of Mr. Timmons's mouth. However, to show us that there is an escape from this stronghold, Mr. Timmons, staring straight at us, says, "'If the Lord had not been on our side when people attacked us, they would have swallowed us alive when their anger flared against us; the flood would have engulfed us, the torrent would have swept over us, the raging waters would have swept us away. Praise be to the Lord, who has not let us be torn by their teeth. We have escaped like a bird from the fowler's snare; the snare has been broken, and we have escaped. Our help is in the name of the Lord, the Maker of heaven and earth'" (Ps. 124 NIV). Mr. Timmons repeats again for our sake, "You have escaped like a bird from the fowler's snare; the snare has been broken, and you have escaped. Your help is in the name of the Lord, the Maker of heaven and earth; learn His commandments and follow them to the letter, with praying and fasting, always." I was relieved and enjoyed being taught the Word. I now had to sit back and surrender in humbleness, praying, "Thank You, Lord, for not taking Your hand away from me, for I would have surely been lost in the confusion and craziness of this world." While at the conference, Mr. Timmons also said it was time for repentance, and now, more than ever before, people need to hear the truth that is in Christ Jesus. So, eventually, I got together with the fellas to set aside seven days so we could get taught by Mr. Timmons. The guys and I, we figured we can't let the wives do it by themselves. Hey, we are the head of the family, and God expects us to lead. That being said, my guys and I visited Mr. Timmons, and the things we had learned from our wives were enhanced by what we learned from his sessions with us. After discovering the truth about who we are, who it is that we belong to, where we come from, and where we are going, for us, a lot of things started to make sense. I remember during one of our sessions, Jordan had a big smile on his face. He told me that he had finally figured out and understood why his pops was no longer active in his fraternity, and without asking him to explain any further, I kind of had my own revelations on the matter. The time we spent with Mr. Timmons was really great, and boy did we ever get our minds and hearts right, and I dare say we also have the audacity of faith. So, after our time with Mr. Timmons comes to an end, the guys and I head back to our homes. On the plane ride home, man, I'm all jacked up with confidence and ready for some serious spiritual warfare. I'm thinking about the mess that Satan has created in the world and the consequences of what will happen to people if we don't spread the Word of God. Then, in that very same Moment after being all hyped up, the realization and enormity of the situation starts to confront me, and that big imaginary superman "S" painted across my chest begins to fade. I was challenged by all the negative things in America that was difficult to change, and in contemplation, I find myself to have surrendered to meander in the maze of mediocrity. Now, back at home, as I'm driving into my garage, I start to visualize an idea. I mean, it just pops into my head, and I can visualize the particulars as clear as day. Being skeptical at first, I ask God if what I was thinking came from Him. I really wanted to know because I figured that from the ideas in my head, my guys and I can get started on doing something really meaningful; I mean, with issues like protecting the unborn, promoting school choice, assisting in pushing legislation that offers young boys positive role models, putting together a movement to maintain an aggressive voice to fight against the miseducation of our children, gathering petitions to fight against curricula and professors antithetical to the knowledge of the Word of God, and then, most importantly, establishing youth-friendly platforms for our young children to be taught, heard, and be led in the Word of God. As believers, we know unequivocally that the Word of God is the only way to change the hearts of men and facilitate a positive self-esteem. This is something that this young generation and likewise their parents need desperately. Then another revelation burst forward in my spirit on how to get started and what to do. I can't explain it, but I know this plan came not by my senses because I heard it in my spirit with clarity, saying, "You must engage in transforming the nerve centers of influence in American (government, education, politics, media, arts, entertainment, sports, and religion). So, now as I sit in my garage, still overwhelmed and skeptical, I'm thinking, *boy, this is going to be an impossible task.* But as I further meditate on this undertaking, surprisingly out of nowhere, a big smile starts flashing across my face, and as wisdom manifests in my spirit, I jerk so hard with enthusiasm that I hit my head on the ceiling of my car because then I knew. I understood, at this point what was happening, and I immediately started thinking about the parable of the sower Mr. Timmons taught us, particularly ..."As he (the farmer) was scattering the seed, some fell along the path, and the birds came and ate it up." I then knew that Satan was trying to steal what God was putting into my spirit. I remembered God's words and I thought, "... *Resist the devil, and he will flee from you,*" (James 4:7 NIV). So I reared up like a conqueror and boldly shouted out loudly, "IT-IS-WRITTEN, and thinking, 'With man, my ideas are-impossible; but with God, all things are possible'" (Matt. 19:26). In confessing these Scriptures, I realized my strength in the God who is, who was, and who is to come, and while planning my strategy for tackling the issues me and my guys would pursue; I gave pause remembering something that my wife would often shout and proclaim around our house when she was steep in the middle of the Diva Pack controversy; So in reverent affirmation of the greater one within me, I shouted it myself: "IT-IS- FINISHED." Believe that! (The beginning).

BIBLIOGRAPHY

Bane, Keisha. 2019. *Politic Magazine.* March 8. https://www.
politico.com/magazine/story/2019/03/08/women-big-
gest-problems-international-womens-day-225698.

Berlinski, Dave. 2008. *The Devil's Delusion: Atheism and its
Scientific Pretensions.* Crown Forum Publication.

boazolaosebikan. 2016. *boazolaosebikan.* February 14.
https://boazolaosebikan.wordpress.com/2016/02/14/
get-delivered-from-the-word-or-spirit-of-diva/.

Caucas, Prayer Congressional. 2013. *Congressional
Prayer Caucus.* https://cpcfoundation.com/religious/
religious-freedom/.

Encyclopedia, Wikipedia The Free. 2020. *Irreducible
complexity.* June 12. https://en.wikipedia.org/wiki/
Irreducible_complexity.

Freidman, Milton. 2020. *Milton Friedman Quote Citation.* June
16. https://www.azquotes.com/quote/351906.

Friedman, Betty. 1963. *The Feminine Mystique.* W W Norton
Company.

Gentry, Robert. 1973. In *Polonium Halos*, by Robert Gentry, 356.

Gentry, Robert. 1988. "Creations Tiny Mystery." In *Creations Tiny Mystery*, by Robert Gentry. Earth Science Associates.

Grant, Zita. 2017. *Be free from spiritual Spouses (MARINE SPIRITS)*. 2 Tigers LLC.

Ham, Ken. 2017. *Answers In Genesis*. 7 12. https://www.youtube.com/watch?v=CFYswvGoaPU.

Holliday, Pat P.hd. 2005. "The Witchdoctor and the Man: City under the Sea." In *The Witchdoctor and the Man: City under the Sea*, by Pat Holliday and Bishop Vagalas Kanco, 180. Agapepublishers.

Horn, Thomas. 2013. "Zenith 2016: Did Something Begin In The Year 2012 That Will Reach Its Apex In 2016?" In *Zenith 2016: Did Something Begin In The Year 2012 That Will Reach Its Apex In 2016?*, by Thomas Horn, 451. Defender Publishing.

IDEA. 2020. *Intelligent design and Evolution Awareness Center.* http://www.ideacenter.org/contentmgr/showdetails.php/id/840.

Jackson, Wayne. 2020. *How Many Prophecies Are in the Bible.* June 13. https://www.christiancourier.com/articles/318-how-many-prophecies-are-in-the-bible .

Jastrow, Robert. 2000. "God and the Astronomers." In *God and the Astronomers*, by Robert Jastrow. New York: W.W. Norton & Company.

Lewis, C.S. 2020. *AZQuotes*. June 13. www.azquotes.com/quote/964418.

—. 202. *AZQUotes*. June 13. Accessed January 20, 2020. https://www.azquotes.com/quote/876705.

Mary Wallstonecraft, Miriam Brody (Contributor). 2004. "A vindication of the rights of women." In *A vindication of the rights of women*, by Mary Wallstonecraft, 269. Penguin Classics.

McDonald, Larry. 2020. *bing.com*. 7 17. https://www.bing.com/images/search?view=detailV2&ccid=Hd2ehI4U&id=4477CD6FE-8447240656B61104383A8C862BF122C&thid=OIP.Hd2ehI4UUvDGn3dLezoa_wHaDf&mediaurl=http%3a%2f%2fwww.azquotes.com%2fpicture-quotes%2fquote-the-drive-of-the-rockefellers-and-their-allies-i.

Missler, Chuck. 2020. *Anti-Christ Session 6*. August 6. https://www.youtube.com/watch?v=pvgf1NngCv8.

—. 2000. *Twiligh's Last Gleaming*. October 1. https://khouse.org/articles/2000/293/ .

Muggeridge, Malcolm. 1985. " Vintage Muggeridge: Religion and Society." In *Vintage Muggeridge: Religion and Society*, by Malcolm Muggeridge and Geoffrey Barlow, 192. y William B. Eerdmans Publishing Company .

Murray, Abdu J.D. 2018. "Saving Truth Study Guide: Finding Meaning and Clarity in a Post-Truth World." In *Saving Truth Study Guide: Finding Meaning and Clarity in a Post-Truth World*, by Abdu Murray, 160. Zondervan .

Nelson, Jim. 1994. *WHen Nations DIe*. Wheaton, Illinois,: Tyndale House Publishers.

NPR.com. 2016. *Terry Gross inviews Caitlin Moran*. July 29. Accessed January 20, 2020. https://www.npr.org/2016/07/29/486145139/not-a-feminist-caitlin-moran-asks-why-not.

Register, THe. 2009. *Attack of the Hyperdimensional Juggernaut-Men* . November 6. https://www.theregister.com/2009/11/06/lhc_dimensional_portals/.

Sowell, Thomas. 2020. *AZQuotes.* June 13. https://www.azquotes.com/quote/278457.

Steele, Shelby. 2020. *AZQuotes.* June 13. https://www.azquotes.com/author/25829-Shelby_Steele.

Steinem, Gloria. 1993. "Revolution from Within: A Book of Self-Esteem." In *Revolution from Within: A Book of Self-Esteem*, by Gloria Steinem, 259-261. Little, Brown and Company.

Store, Oxford Dictionary & Translator on the App. 2019. *Powered by Oxford Dictionaries · Bing Translator.* https://www.bing.com/search?q=diva+meaning&form=EDGSPH&mkt=en-us&httpsmsn=1&msnews=1&rec_search=1&plvar=0&refig=fa8f201a9f1446bfb2e62b8f12fdd12a&PC=MSERT1&sp=1&qs=LS&pq=diva+mea&sk=PRES1&sc=8-8&cvid=fa8f201a9f1446bfb2e62b8f12fdd12a&cc=US&setlang=en-US.

Tsarfati, Amir. 2015. *The Illuminati and the One World Government.* August 6. https://www.youtube.com/watch?v=ir2yVa0A9q4.

Turek, Frank. 2008. *Frank Turek Does God Exit? (Frank Turek vs. Christopher Hitchens).* December 9. https://www.youtube.com/watch?v=S7WBEJJIYWU.

Wagner, Micheal. 2012. *When the Court Took on Prayer and the Bible in Public Schools.* June 25. https://religionandpolitics.org/2012/06/25/when-the-court-took-on-prayer-the-bible-and-public-schools/.

Zacharias, Ravi. 2016. *WHy Is Christianity Right / Ravi Internationl Zacharias Ministeries.* March 12. https://www.youtube.com/watch?v=nWY-6xBAOPk.

Zetting, Dennis. 2016. *A Quatum Case for God.* June 26. https://www.youtube.com/watch?v=p1OjX5APDn4.